I0646886

the Dream Merchant Saga

BOOK THREE
the Crack'd Shield

Written by
L.T. Suzuki
in collaboration with
Nia Suzuki-White

Book Cover, graphic design and layout:
Scott White
Shinobi Creative Productions
www.shinobicreativeproductions.com

Note for Librarians:
A cataloguing record for this book is available from the Library and Archives Canada at: www.collectionscanada.ca/amicus/index-e.html

ISBN 978-0-9867240-8-4

Dedication

This book is dedicated to Scott!
Thank you for helping make this book
a reality and for laughing at all the right places!

With love and gratitude,
Nia & Lorna

Contents

1

A Dead End

I AM SO DEAD...

These four small words loomed large in Rose's mind. They squeezed her heart with fear as the floor and walls of this great chamber rattled beneath her feet. Dropping to her knees, she shrieked in fright. It felt like the earth was preparing to swallow her up whole. And then just as quickly, the tremors stopped.

By the loud rumble and cloud of dust spewing from the mouth of the tunnel leading from the dragon's keep into the Sorcerer's lair, she knew this was no ordinary earthquake. The passage Tag and the three Elves in his company had worked so hard to clear to access the chamber had collapsed.

"No! Oh, no!" cried Rose, as she scrambled onto her feet.

Terrifying thoughts darted in and out of her mind, but the one that gnawed at her conscience the most was the fear of dying alone in this God-forsaken hole in the ground.

She was beginning to think it would have been better had she helped Tag and the Elves in removing the debris, than to stand idly by while they toiled to clear the way. Had she been with them in the lair, it would have been far better to die quickly, and in the company of friends trying to rescue a friend than to die alone, wasting away from thirst and hunger, while going stark, raving mad trapped inside this cave.

Fanning away the swirling dust, by the glow of the molten lava, all she could see were more fallen rocks and debris clogging half the tunnel. There was no getting in or out.

"Tag! Where are you?" Rose called in desperation.

She prayed the entire chamber had not collapsed on him, that he was merely trapped with the Elves on the other side. With hands cupped to her ears, she waited, listening anxiously for a familiar voice to answer back.

Instead, her words were met by a numbing silence. Panic gripped her heart as her terrified mind absorbed this profound hush. Gradually, the ambient sounds of the churning lava and the pounding of her heart sounded in her ears.

Rose balled her hands into trembling fists, fighting to remain calm as she struggled to hold back the flood of tears waiting to gush forth.

"Tagius Oliver Yairet! Where are you?" She called out once more, her voice reduced to a pathetic whimper. "Answer me…"

Again, there was no reply, only deathly silence.

Rose drew a deep breath; staring at the mountain of rubble before her that destroyed the small opening Tag and the Elves had worked so hard to clear.

"Why did you have to do this?" Rose moaned aloud, as she despaired over Tag's demise. "I should have stopped you. I should have just ordered you and the others to stop this rescue."

She waited, hoping for Tag to agree with her.

This was the one time she wished the young knight-in-training was here to tell her off. In all her life, she never felt this alone… and this lonely.

Her eyes travelled from this sloping pile of rocks, across the chamber to the narrow passage that brought them here.

She was at a dead end, but the daunting task of attempting to retrace her steps on her own to escape this place held about as much promise. Even if she were able to remain on course, even with all the traps and obstacles that had been rendered harmless on their passing, how was she to accomplish this now? She had no torch; no way to light the pitch black tunnels to return to the mouth of the cave hidden by the curtain of water falling at the Devil's Tears.

Even if she made it, she had no way to escape from behind this waterfall, no way to climb back onto the cliff.

"Either way, I'll go absolutely crazy!"

"Am I going insane?"

"I *am* going insane… The first sign is to speak to one's self."

Scrutinizing her subterranean prison, she muttered beneath her breath, "And the second sign of madness is to answer back."

Her teary eyes opened wide in surprise as an idea formed in her wobbly mind.

"That's it! If I go insane, it won't matter what happens or how I meet my end! I'll be too loopy to care."

With the kind of gay abandon only possible for one on the brink of madness, Rose proceeded to run in circles; whooping, hollering and spouting a litany of swear words appropriate for this dismal occasion.

When she depleted the supply from her personal and limited lexicon of profanities, she proceeded to invent all new swear words, babbling gibberish as she galloped about like a deranged pony trapped in an underground corral.

Her energy dissipated as quickly as her list of newly invented curse words. Reduced to a plodding stagger like she was now a lame, crazed pony, the tears of dread and frustration began to well as her lower lip quivered in a sad pout of defeat.

As the sting of salty tears rolled down her burning cheeks, an over-whelming sense of helplessness squeezed her heart. In a gasping sob, she struggled against a tidal wave of emotions waiting to swallow her up. In a senseless display of despair and disappointment, Rose hurled a rock at the pile of rubble sealing the tunnel to the Sorcerer's lair.

It landed with a loud clatter. As though to mock her, it tumbled down in a mini avalanche. Rolling to the cave floor, this fist-sized stone came to rest at her feet.

In exhaustion and utter defeat, the Princess plopped down where she stood, staring dismally at the rock she had thrown.

Just as she was about to break down in tears, reduced to what Cankles liked to refer to as the *'ugly cry'*, she heard it.

Tap! Tap! Tap!

This faint sound echoed from somewhere in this mountain of debris choking the tunnel.

She gasped in disbelief as she listened.

Again, there it was, a faint, but rhythmic: *Tap! Tap! Tap!*

Rose hastily wiped away the useless tears from her dirt-smudged face. She listened, attempting to determine if she had finally and truly lost her mind. Perhaps she was only wishing to hear sounds of life, or maybe these sounds were not imagined at all.

Tap! Tap! Tap!

"There it is again!" gasped Rose, crawling on her hands and knees to the base of the rubble pile. Picking up the rock she had thrown, she banged it against a boulder, striking it three times. For the longest moment, she waited for a response.

Silence…

Rose's heart sank to an all-new level of despair as her last glimmer of hope faded.

Tap! Tap! Tap!

"Alive!" gasped Rose. "You're alive!"

In a mad scramble, she began excavating; tossing the rocks aside, but as quickly as she removed them, more would tumble down to fill the hole she had created. It was quickly becoming an exercise in futility and a dangerous move on her part.

Tap! Tap! Tap!

Rose glanced up, noticing this noise was coming from on high.

"That's it!" exclaimed the Princess, clambering to the peak of the sloping heap. "I'll dig from the top! Hold on, Tag! I am coming to your rescue!"

Rose set to work. Tossing the rocks aside one by one, soon, the work was too much for her. She began feebly pushing and clawing at the heavier ones, letting them tumble down the pile to land in a scattered heap.

Driven by the fear of dying alone and motivated by renewed hope of survivors on the other side, as weary as she was, Rose was determined to remove this debris, at least enough to free her friend. As the top of the pile thinned, seams of golden light from a burning torch seeped through from the other side.

Removing another rock wedged between the roof of the tunnel and this barrier of rubble, Rose broke through. She squinted as the bright glow of the torch's light burst forth from the small opening, followed by a filthy hand that was scraped and stained by drying blood.

Rose recognized this hand. Squeezing it in hers, she pressed it to her tear-stained cheek. For the first time in her life, she was never so grateful to hold Tag's sweaty, dirty paw to her face as she sobbed, "You're alive! Thank goodness, you're alive!"

"Thankfully, yes," agreed Tag, his muffled words sounding through this opening as he sighed in relief to feel the warmth of her trembling hands engulfing his.

The combination of the tight squeeze she had on his scraped knuckles and her fresh, salty tears spilling onto these abrasions caused him pain.

"Owww!" yelped Tag.

"Are you hurt?" asked Rose, holding on tight as she tugged on his hand as though she would somehow miraculously pull his body through the small hole that was only big enough for his arm to fit through.

"I am now."

"I am serious!" scolded the Princess.

"Just take it easy. My hands are a bit battered after that last cave-in."

"Sorry!" responded Rose, as she released her grip.

"Worry not, Princess, it looks worse than it feels, but feels all the better now that you've stopped mangling it." Tag withdrew his hand from the hole.

"I am just so grateful to know you are still alive."

"Me, too! And I'm so glad that you weren't hurt or killed in this collapse."

"Is that all you can say?" grunted Rose, relieved, but oh-so frustrated by their dire circumstance.

"I suppose a 'thank-you' is order, but you were squeezing the blood from my hand and it's already lost enough from all the scrapes and cuts I've been getting from trying to dig us out of here."

"*Us?*" repeated Rose, peeking through the hole. "Please tell me Cankles is with you. Were you able to save him?"

"No, it's just the Elves in my company."

"Where did Cankles go? Where is the Sorcerer? Is Dragonite dead?"

"One thing at a time, Princess," ordered Tag. "Let's get out of here first, before the rest of the cave collapses on us. There will be time for questions later."

Rose's heart fell upon hearing this news, but for now, she was just grateful Tag and the Elves had survived this calamity. She held her tongue, concentrating on the task at hand while Tag and the Elves worked from the other side to widen the escape hole.

"Stand back, Princess!" Denatheen's voice sounded through the small opening. "If you carelessly remove the rocks and boulders supporting what is left of the roof of this tunnel, it shall crash down on you."

"I am not about to sit idle, Master Elf," argued Rose. "The last time I did, I wished I had been there with you four, rather than trapped here all alone."

"If you insist on helping, then feel free to remove the smaller, loose debris," suggested Denatheen.

"Yes, do not dislodge these larger, weight-bearing ones or you'll only get us crushed," warned Tag.

"Very well," responded the Princess. "I will be careful."

"Be *very* careful," urged Tag, as he struggled to budge a large rock. "We only need to make it big enough for us to squeeze through."

Together, they worked, meticulously picking away at the opening to remove only the loose rocks and those that were not supporting the brunt of the ceiling's weight.

"One more should do," determined Rose, her hand wrapping around a rock packed into place by loose dirt and pebbles. Giving it a hard yank, the rock broke free, tumbling down as she yelped in pain. "*Owweee!*"

Tag thrust his head through the opening, his eyes wide with fear as he glanced down at the Princess wincing in pain.

"What happened? Are you hurt?"

"Yes," whimpered Rose, squeezing her hand cradled against her body. "I just broke my fingernail on that stupid rock!"

"That's it?" groaned Tag, wiggling his shoulders into the opening as he wormed his way through. "A broken fingernail?"

"That is more than enough if you are a princess like me!" Rose shook off this pain.

"Just stand back," ordered Tag. "We're going to try and get through now."

Rose did as she was told, scooting down the mound of rocks to the cave floor to await her comrades.

One by one, they wriggled their way to freedom. Tag was followed by Roen-Aldus, and then another Elf, while Denatheen squeezed through the narrow opening last, but only after passing their swords, longbows and quivers through first.

"How do you fare?" asked Rose, watching as Tag brushed the thick layer of dust off his raiment.

"Other than rattled nerves and abrasions from using our hands to excavate an opening, we're fine." Tag wiped the sweat from his brows, only to smear across his face the dirt and drying blood from his cut cheek.

Rose threw her arms around Tag, embracing him in a grateful hug, and for once, there was no hesitation on his part as he hugged her back.

"You look a mess," commented the Princess, fanning away the cloud of dust rising from Tag's shoulders when she hugged him. "Quite filthy, indeed!"

"Yes, aren't we a lovely pair!" snorted Tag, dismissing her words. "You're just as dirty as I am."

Rose glanced at the Elves as they refastened the quivers of arrows back onto their belts. Her eyes narrowed in suspicion as she scrutinized them. Tag's hair was matted with perspiration and dirt; his clothes, liberally smothered in earth and dust from the cave-in. The Elves, on the other hand, looked fresh. It was as though they had just stepped out of the Woodland Glade. Not a strand of hair was out of place; their skin and clothes still in pristine condition.

"Hey... Tag is all filthy and sweaty," noted Rose, as she inspected Denatheen and his men. "Why are you not dirty?"

"We are Elves," explained Denatheen, his words matter-of-fact as he tossed his golden tresses over his shoulders. "We do not do dirty."

"Is that so?" responded Rose, staring with raised eyebrows at the

Elves for they did not even break a sweat with all the hard work. "It still does not explain how you three remained so clean, while Tag managed to get so filthy."

"It is an *Elf* thing, like a natural shield that repels all that seem to cling onto the human race," responded Denatheen. "You would not understand, being a mortal."

"The important thing is, we are all safe," reminded Tag, his fingertip gingerly pressing the slash on his cheek delivered by the Sorcerer.

Rose jumped with a start as the Elves suddenly armed their bows, turning their weapons to the narrow, claustrophobic tunnel that delivered them into the dragon's keep.

"What is it?" asked Tag, reaching over for the hilt of his sword that was no longer there.

"Something or someone comes this way," whispered Denatheen, motioning for the Princess to get behind him as a faint glow of light grew stronger.

"Aha! There they are!" A familiar voice sounded from the tunnel to echo across the keep.

The Dream Merchant's face appeared at the entrance of the passageway.

"Silas Agincor!" announced Denatheen. He motioned his men to stand down and lower their weapons.

"Indeed!" greeted Silas. As he ducked into the great chamber, Lord Rainus Silverthorn and his battalion of Elves followed him.

"Hold on! How do we know we're not being duped? This could actually be the Sorcerer playing a trick on our minds," warned Tag.

Rose peered out from behind Denatheen. "What do all of you see?"

"I see the Dream Merchant," answered Tag, as the Elves nodded in agreement.

"Right down to his gaudy, stars and moon robe?" questioned the Princess, staring suspiciously at this being.

"Yes! Why? What do you see?" asked Tag, arming himself with a hefty rock, just in case.

"I see a..." Rose's voice trailed off. "Never mind, he is the real Dream Merchant."

"What do you see?" probed Tag, staring suspiciously at the Princess. "I demand to know."

"She sees *me*, as *you!*" confided Silas, as he gave Tag a shrewd wink of his eye. "Remember? She asked that I appear as an exquisite specimen of a young man; what she most desires!"

"Oh, for pity's sake! Not again!" Tag scolded the Princess, as he shook his head in disgust. "You better not be gawking at a naked him pretending to look like me again!"

"Who said I was gawking," gasped Rose, her cheeks burning bright with embarrassment as she peeled her eyes off of Tag's shirtless doppelganger with the scrub-board abs and nicely toned biceps and triceps. "There is nothing to gawk at. Maybe prod with a stick, but there is nothing to see!"

Silas deliberately flexed his new, muscular arms that only the Princess could see, causing Rose's eyes to bulge in amazement from her head.

"Contrary to what she just said, there is *plenty* to see," teased Silas, giving Tag an affable poke of the elbow to his ribs. "The Princess is mightily distracted."

"Well, for the sake of our safety and this quest, please do away with this distraction," urged Tag.

"The young sir is quite right," agreed Denatheen. "Our mission has been fraught with peril and misfortune from the start. The fewer distractions, the better, if we are to survive this quest."

"Very well then," sighed Silas. "And here, I was quite enjoying my youthful, manly-man appearance."

"You're welcome to do so," offered Tag. "Just conjure up another body, for I refuse to have my likeness used in such a trivial manner. Better yet, why not be yourself?"

"Fair enough," conceded Silas, "as long as I do not have to listen to the Princess complaining about my apparel."

"You won't complain, right, Princess?" ordered Tag. Waving a hand before her eyes, he broke her trance as she stared in wonder at the shirtless version of him.

"Oh – ah… what?" asked Rose, shaking her head as though momentarily confused.

"You won't complain about the Dream Merchant's robe?"

"Right…" Rose agreed with a nod. "No complaining."

"Very well," said Silas. Snapping his fingers before Rose's eyes, he transformed, assuming his usual, fashion-challenged form she so detested.

By the smile on her face that abruptly eroded into a frown of disgust, Tag knew Rose now saw the Dream Merchant in his real form rather than in his likeness.

"Now, where were we?" asked Silas.

"The dreamstone, Princess," prompted Rainus Silverthorn, as he turned to her for an answer. "Did you manage to steal it back from Dragonite?"

"No, I did not," admitted the Princess, her eyes downcast in shame. "I failed."

"And now, the Sorcerer has the magic crystal *and* our friend," explained Tag, heaving a disheartened sigh. "Things went horribly wrong. Dragonite has taken Cankles as his prisoner."

"For what reason?" asked Silas, stroking his grizzled beard as he pondered this mystery.

"The Sorcerer wanted me," revealed Rose.

"*You?* No offence, Princess, but why would he have need of you if he has already laid claim to the dreamstone?" asked Rainus.

"I am not sure. All I know is that he demanded I go with him, if I wanted my friends to remain unharmed. Just as I was about to do so, Denturcleen –"

"*Denatheen*," corrected the Elf, as Rainus and the others stared in confusion.

"Yes. Denatheen, Ron and –"

"And that would be me," interjected Roen-Aldus, so his comrades would know of whom she was referring to.

"Yes," said Rose, as she continued on, pointing to Ayden the third Elf in Denatheen's company, "and unnamed-Elf-Number-Three barged into the dragon's keep. That was when Dragonite fled for his life, taking Cankles with him."

"Hmph!" grunted Rainus. "It is obvious to me that scoundrel has yet to figure out how to work the dreamstone."

"Either that, or he believes it is broken or faulty, not realizing that I had pre-set the crystal to grant the Princess only three wishes in a twenty-four hour cycle," said Silas.

"There is a chance Dragonite believes the Princess knows how to unlock the magic within," determined Rainus, giving the Dream Merchant a thoughtful nod. "Perhaps that is the reason why he wanted to trade Cankles for her."

"Even if this is true, what are we to do now?" questioned Tag. "We've come to a dead-end. The Sorcerer made good his escape, taking Cankles with him. We managed to clear a path into his lair in the hopes of capturing him, but instead, Dragonite was gone. His escape route was sealed by a massive boulder. Not a dozen men would have the strength to move it."

"If we cannot remove it, then we shall go around it," answered Silas. "I know Dragonite enough that he would never seek refuge in a cave if it did not afford him at least one other escape route to exit, should a tunnel collapse or his enemies close in on him."

"So we must find our way out of here and search for another

opening?" determined Tag.

"Exactly!" responded Silas.

"Hey… how did you even find us to begin with?" questioned Rose, scratching her head in thought as she stared at the Wizard.

"You did beckon us, did you not?" asked Silas, motioning as though he was firing an arrow high into the sky.

"Yes," admitted Denatheen, nodding in confirmation.

"Denturcleen was the one to unleash the burning arrow but still, the lands are vast… how did you find us?" asked Rose.

"We saw *Denatheen's* flaming arrow that lit up the sky in the wee hours of the morning," explained the Elf Lord. "We regrouped and headed right over."

"But how did you manage to find us *here*, inside this old volcano, of all the places to look?" queried Tag.

"Simple deduction, my young friend," responded Silas. "Once we established the fiery arrow was launched from the top of a high vantage point, namely from the heights of the Devil's Tears, we journeyed eastward to find our first clue as to your whereabouts."

"Our footprints at the base of the cliff?" guessed Rose.

"That… and a half dozen dragons of the likes I have never seen before, feasting on one of my men," answered Rainus. "We managed to drive the creatures off. They scattered, climbing up the sheer face of the cliff before pitching themselves off to glide away into the night."

"Sadly, Toren Briarwood met his end fighting off those dragons when they attacked us," said Denatheen, bowing his head in respect and sorrow. "We have yet to grieve his passing."

"As tragic as his demise was, it was obvious by the condition of his body, or what was left of it, Toren either fell or was pushed from a great height," continued Rainus. "Logic dictated that we climb up, so it was only a matter of time before we came across a rope dangling over the cliff alongside the waterfall."

"The one we used to lower ourselves to the tunnel leading to the Sorcerer's Lair," concluded Denatheen.

"You mean the rope we used to *hurl* ourselves over the cliff to avoid being eaten by the monster-sized dragon," corrected Ayden, as the troubling memory of their terrifying encounter replayed in his mind.

"You actually met up with the resident dragon? The one you had warned us about?" gasped Rose, looking to Denatheen for an answer. "This gargantuan reptile truly does exist?"

"Fear not, Princess! The creature Denatheen spoke of did not linger," assured Rainus. "The beast was long gone, no doubt on the hunt while the midday sun burns bright and warm. When we came by this way, all that remained were huge footprints, and those left by Denatheen and Ayden as they fled. And, as my men are not the suicidal type, it was clear to me they had used this rope in a bid to escape the dragon."

"By the crumbling earth along the ledge, it was easy enough to deduce that the rope was used to lower mortals and Elves over this cliff," added Silas. "All evidence pointed to your search for a concealed opening to Dragonite's lair, and what better place to conceal it than to hide the entrance behind a waterfall?"

"Still, it was brilliant how you managed to figure out your way to this very spot, knowing how the tunnel branches off numerous times," reminded Tag.

"Brilliant, indeed!" dismissed Silas. "We merely followed the tunnels that were lit until we came across a mime whose foot was skewered by an arrow, well and good, to the cave floor."

"Ayden and I came across that very mime, too," said Denatheen, "but that fellow was useless to us on our first encounter. He was out cold, growing a formidable goose egg on his noggin when we saw him. It was only because we found Roen-Aldus trapped on a narrow ledge, precariously balanced over a river of lava, did we know where to go once we removed him from danger."

"Well, by the time we encountered that very mime, he was wide awake and frantic to be free of the arrow that had his foot securely pinned to the ground," said Rainus.

"That was my handiwork, and then Cankles knocked him out with a club," boasted Rose, holding up the longbow Rainus had gifted to her to prove it did not go to waste. "I deliberately chose to maim, than to kill that menacing mime."

"Good for you, Princess," praised Rainus. "If you had killed him instead, he would not have confessed."

"*Confessed?* Mimes do not speak," reminded Tag. "Not unless they're tortured."

"And I took great pleasure in doing just that," confided Silas, giving the young man a knowing smile. "Had him blubbering like a colicky baby, spilling all he knew in no time at all! We were privy to a great many secrets when I was through with him."

"*No!*" exclaimed Rose; her eyes wide in disbelief. "Pray tell, what did you do to him? Threaten to gouge his eyes out with a burning stick? Cut off his fingers, one by one?"

"Who has time for that? Besides, there are other methods more effective and less barbaric," grunted the Dream Merchant.

"Like what?" asked Tag.

"Nothing is more tortuous to a mime than being subjected to bad miming," revealed Silas.

"You did what?" gasped the Princess.

"I mimed and I did so badly!" revealed the Dream Merchant. "The bugger put up a fight, but not a very valiant one with his foot speared as it was."

"Yes, it was a rather pathetic display, especially all his silent ranting!" sighed Rainus, shaking his head in disgust.

"Ah, but he did have quite the impressive and colourful vocabulary when it came to those expletives!" noted Silas, with a thoughtful nod.

"But how did you know what he was saying, if he was only mouthing those words?" questioned Tag.

"It is easy when you are a great a lip-reader as I am," explained the Dream Merchant.

"But how did you get him to stop swearing and start talking?" wondered Rose.

"A brisk slap to the face stopped his ranting long enough to begin my performance," answered Silas.

"So you did mime?" said Tag, his brows arching up in surprise.

"Absolutely!" confirmed Silas.

"Oh, my! I am afraid to ask what you did," groaned Rose, as she stared at the Wizard.

Thinking this was an invitation for a repeat performance, the Dream Merchant prepared to dazzle his comrades with an impromptu show. He stood before them, looking confused while sliding his hands against the air, as if trapped in an invisible box.

Before they could plea for him to stop, Silas continued his charade. With exaggerated facial expressions, he tugged on an imaginary rope being pulled by an invisible foe.

"Stop!" demanded Rose. "We've seen enough!"

"It is no wonder you got him talking! That was bloody painful!" groaned Tag.

"It worked like a charm!" said Silas, giving him a knowing smile.

"I suppose if mocking the mime with a dose of his own medicine does the trick, why not?" said Rose, her shoulders rolling with an unsympathetic shrug. "Served him right!"

"That fool of a mime pointed us in the proper direction in no time. We merely followed the trail of destruction left in your wake," responded Silas.

"Fortunately for us, by destroying those traps and obstacles, not only did you set us in the right direction, you also made it safe for us to journey on, unhampered," added Rainus.

"So we must retrace our steps to leave this place?" determined Rose, dreading the long journey back to the surface.

"We can," answered Silas, "or we can take the shortcut."

"*Shortcut?*" repeated Rose, frowning in confusion. "What shortcut?"

The Dream Merchant pointed above to where golden seams of light from the world outside seeped through cracks in the ceiling. "Freedom is much closer than you think."

"Close? Yes," agreed Tag, staring up to the roof of the chamber, "but unattainable from where we stand. That is solid rock overhead."

"Not quite. There are fractures; numerous, fine cracks riddling the formation overhead," noted Rainus, as he scrutinized the domed ceiling. "It is nothing some well placed arrows cannot take good advantage of."

"You think so?" responded Tag.

"I am positive," replied the Elf Lord. "Strategically placed, the steel bodkins of our arrows will weaken and compromise the rock formation enough that the sheer weight alone will bring the ceiling crumbling down."

"Once we create a hole large enough to allow our escape, all it will require are nothing more than a length of rope and a grappling hook," explained Silas.

"So we climb out of here?" asked Rose.

"*You* will climb. *I* will magically disappear, only to reappear, up there," answered the Dream Merchant, pointing up to the outside world.

"And where will we find a grappling hook?" asked Tag. "I certainly don't have one."

"Captain Ironwood," called Rainus, waving his personal bodyguard to come forward. "If you please."

Halen Ironwood reached into the shadows of his cloak to produce a three-pronged steel hook attached to a coil of rope.

"Handy," commented Tag, nodding in approval.

"I never leave home without it," said Halen. "No telling when one might need to storm a castle or climb out of an old volcano."

Rainus removed an arrow from his quiver as he gave his order. "Gentlemen, ready your bows."

"What about me?" asked Rose, holding up her Elven longbow.

"By all means, Princess, you are welcome to join us in making an escape route," encouraged the Elf Lord.

Standing in a circle, Rose and the Elves nocked their arrows as they took aim, seeking to target the existing cracks to further damage the structure.

"Fire!" ordered Rainus.

On his command, the arrows were unleashed. Each hit their mark with a sharp *'thud'*.

"Stand back!" shouted Rainus, motioning all to retreat from the falling debris.

For a lingering moment, they waited and watched. Other than small clouds of dust and chunks of rock and dirt coming free on initial impact, the ceiling remained intact.

"Hmph!" grunted Rainus, rubbing his chin in thought. "I expected more."

"Try again," suggested Silas. "Another round of arrows should do the trick."

Once more, Rose and the Elves stood in a circle as they aimed directly overhead.

"Fire!" Rainus ordered again.

Once more, the arrows were launched, and again, each projectile hit its mark with unerring precision.

The only things to rain down on them were dust and crumbs of stone where bodkin bit into the ceiling.

Just as Rainus was about to instruct Rose and the Elves to take aim for a third time, a sharp crackling sound filled the air. The hairline cracks spread rapidly, radiating from the point of impact like the strands of a spider's web. With an ominous *'crrreak'* the ceiling came crashing down.

The Elves scattered to avoid the crush of debris, but Rose froze in terror.

Rainus seized Tag, yanking him back as he rushed to Rose's side to pull her to safety. His warning cry broke her trance, but it was too late. She tripped as she leapt back.

A thick, elongated boulder came crashing down amongst the rain of rocks and ash. Rose's terrified scream echoed through the air, only to be abruptly stifled. She disappeared beneath the monolithic slab of stone.

2

A Little Elven Magic

"NOOO!" cried Tag. His eyes bulged in disbelief and horror, his heart jumping to the back of his throat.

He dare not peek beneath the slab to look upon the Princess; her body pinned and smeared into the ground, squashed well beyond recognition, he was sure.

"She's been flattened!" wailed Tag. "Crushed to death!"

His mind reeled and his stomach churned as he struggled to comprehend what had just happened, and then he jumped with a start. He stumbled, falling over debris as the dead princess rose before him.

"You fool!" snapped Rose, in an absolute snit. She stood up, pushing the massive sheet of rock off her back. "I am not dead, not even slightly mashed!"

"But – but how?" stammered Tag, staring in bewilderment and awe. "By some miracle, you've become immensely strong!"

"Or these rocks are incredibly light," offered Denatheen. With one hand he easily picked up a rock larger than his head, tossing it over his shoulder as though it was as light as air.

"How can it be?" gasped Tag, picking up a stone to sample its weight. The side that formed the ceiling of the chamber was blackened over time by the soot rising from the molten lava. Beneath this residue, the stone was a light ash-grey in colour.

"This is called pumice. In its molten state, tiny air bubbles became trapped inside," explained Silas. "When it cooled and hardened, the air bubbles were so numerous, these rocks can float on water. As light as a cork, they are!"

"Rocks that can float on water? Incredible!" gasped Tag, testing the weight of a brick-sized chunk of pumice.

"Thank goodness for that," Rose sighed with relief as she noted the rock's chalky, gritty feel and the porous appearance where these tiny bubbles now lay exposed.

"It is the strangest thing!" commented Tag, easily moving a boulder with one hand as though it had no weight to it at all.

"Strange, indeed," agreed Silas, as he tucked a couple of palm-sized stones of pumice into his pouch for safekeeping, "but I had discovered the rough surface makes for a great exfoliant, if one suffers from an excessive amount of dead, dry skin on the feet. Wonderful for scraping away those calluses, you know?"

"Now there's a lovely thought," grunted Rose, shaking her head in disgust.

"Well, even though this pumice is a naturally occurring phenomenon, it could just as easily been a slab of granite coming down to crush you." noted Tag. He was just grateful Rose had survived this frightening mishap. "I still consider it a miracle."

"Yes, and even more so when you consider I took a great risk, an educated guess really, that the ceiling was indeed made of the light-weight pumice," admitted Silas.

"I did not need to know that," grumbled Rose, frowning in resentment at the Wizard.

She brushed away the dust from her frock. Tearing off the remaining sleeve, it now matched the other side she had removed to blot the blood from the palm of her hand she had lanced to entice the dragon away from Tag. Rose proceeded to wrap this scrap of cloth around the wound, protecting it for the climb, as the rope was sure to bite into her hands.

"We should leave this place immediately," suggested Rainus.

"Are you sure we should not wait for nightfall when the majority of dragons have taken refuge until the coming of morning?" asked Tag.

"Under normal circumstances, yes, but on this occasion, I would not recommend it," answered the Elf Lord.

"Why?" questioned Rose.

"The ceiling of the chamber actually formed the bottom of the volcano's crater," replied Rainus.

"So?" responded Tag, frowning in confusion.

"The monster dragon Denatheen and Ayden encountered last night was using it as a *nest*, taking advantage of the warmth rising up from this subterranean chamber to keep warm at night."

"Then we should leave immediately," decided Rose. "I hardly think that dragon will be pleased when it discovers what you Elves have done to its nest."

"My thoughts exactly," agreed Rainus, motioning for the captain of his army to step forward.

Halen Ironwood mounted the grappling hook onto an arrow. Taking careful aim, he let the projectile fly, the rope trailing like a streamer behind it. When the modified arrow landed with a clatter, the Elf took up the slack line. Pulling it in, hand-over-fist, he could hear it being dragged, scraping along the rocky surface until, *'thunk'*, a prong or two of the grappling hook latched onto something solid. Giving it a hard yank, Halen made sure it was securely anchored. Dangling from the rope, he tested its strength to make sure it would support his weight.

"I will go first," offered Halen. "Make sure the way is safe."

"Yes, you do that," urged Rose, nodding in agreement as she stared through the opening.

Never had blue sky looked so inviting, but she prayed the great dragon would not suddenly reappear to rampage about upon finding its nest had been destroyed.

"Once I know it is safe, the rest of you can follow," instructed Halen. "My men will climb first, that way, we can lift you to safety, Princess."

"An excellent plan, but I do not think it will require all of you to lift tiny, little me. I am much lighter than I look," stated Rose. She was relieved she would not be made to test her upper body strength to extract herself from this hole in the ground, but put-off by this insult.

"Fret not, Princess. It is not a comment on your weight," responded Halen. "I merely need my men up there to repel a dragon attack, if the beast should appear."

"Of course!" said Rose, blushing as she nodded in understanding.

Donning a pair of gloves, Halen looped the rope loosely around his left foot. Now, should he tire during the climb, he could quite literally stand on the rope to take some pressure off his arms as he pulled himself to the top.

With relative ease, the Elf made his way to freedom. He disappeared momentarily to make doubly sure the grappling hook was safely secured onto a solid anchor and the ground he stepped on was stronger than the pumice floor that formed the very centre of the crater.

Once he was satisfied and there was no sign the dragon was in the general vicinity, Halen waved the others on to follow.

"I shall meet the rest of you up top," said Silas. In a flash of golden light, the Dream Merchant vanished.

"This way," whispered Halen, motioning the others to follow. "We shall hide in the thick of these trees until darkness comes."

"Are you positive we will be safe?" questioned Rose.

"We are in the heart of dragon country, Princess," replied Halen. "I cannot guarantee anything. At least, we will be concealed by the canopy of leaves and branches. It will be much safer than being caught out in the open during the light of day."

"Then into the stand of trees we shall hide!" agreed Rose, creeping along close on the captain's heels as he led the way to cover.

In the shade of the trees, shielded from the eyes of any dragon flying overhead, the mortals, Elves and Wizard bided their time, waiting for the sun to set and the lands to be chilled by a cloudless spring night.

"No fire?" asked Rose, hoping for the warmth and the perceived safety of a campfire.

"Not unless you wish to attract dragons or warn the Sorcerer and his minions that we are here," answered Rainus, passing her a flask of water to drink from.

"Right… No need for a fire," decided Rose, sitting next to Tag as he rested on a log. She took a sip of water before handing the flask to her comrade.

"Here," offered Rainus. Reaching into the folds of his great cloak, he produced fresh, clean apparel, passing them on to the two young mortals.

"Thank you," said Tag, grateful for the warmth provided by this special Elven cloak.

"Yes, thank you," added Rose, nodding her head in gratitude as Tag draped the warm, light fabric over her shoulders.

"Roen-Aldus told me you had graciously sacrificed your cloak so he could make a rope of it to climb up from the ledge he had fallen onto," said Rainus.

"It was a small sacrifice to make." Rose smiled as she drew the cloak up around her neck for added warmth.

"A small sacrifice, but a grand gesture, nonetheless," stated the Elf, as he nodded in approval. "The nights in the north are still cold, but these Elven cloaks will stave off the chill, plus, it shall help shield you from the eyes of the enemy."

"I wish we could freshen up first," said Rose, her nose wrinkling in disgust.

Fishing about the folds of his cloak, Rainus produced a small disk of fragrant soap and a soft, clean cloth.

"Use this." Rainus tossed her the square of fabric and the soap scented with the essence of lavender. "With a little water, you'll smell as fresh as a flower. Much better than…"

The Elf sniffed at the young mortals as their faces grew red with embarrassment. "If I did not know better, I'd say it is the pungent stench of dragon dung! That is the first thing that comes to mind."

"It *is* dragon dung," disclosed Rose. "Your man, Denturcleen, told us to wallow in it to go undetected as we ventured across the lands."

"*Denatheen* is very clever," praised Rainus. "However, the fragrance of lavender would have been just as effective, as dragons are not vegetarians and would have shown no interest in flowers."

"I will bring my own decanter of lavender essence should I ever be made to come this way again," vowed the Princess, holding forth the cloth as Tag poured some clean water on it.

After Rose finished washing away all traces of dirt, grime and dragon feces from her skin, she rinsed out the cloth before handing it to Tag. He winced in pain as the damp cloth rubbed against the gash inflicted by the obsidian crystal that crowned the Sorcerer's staff.

"I wish I had a looking glass about now," groaned Tag.

"Allow me," offered Rose, taking the cloth from his hand.

With tender strokes, she wiped away the grime and dried blood caking his cheek. She carefully cleaned the wound, taking care not to set it bleeding a-fresh.

"That was quite the heroic feat back there," praised Tag, grimacing as Rose cleaned the gash. "I never thought you had it in you to confront the dragon as you did."

"Neither did I, mind you, I was not even thinking. I just did what I had to," admitted Rose.

"But that's just it. You didn't have to."

"I know," said Rose.

"Whether your actions were pre-meditated, or not, it was quite the heroic feat nonetheless."

"Who would have ever dreamed this damsel would come to the rescue of a knight in distress?" teased the Princess.

"Yes, yes!" Tag smiled sheepishly. "But just remember this, a true hero does not brag about his exploits, no matter how grand."

"True enough. This is no time to gloat."

"Yes, I must fix this disaster of a misadventure I have led us on," said Tag, heaving a distraught sigh.

"Misadventure *you* led us on?" Rose's brows furrowed in confusion. She stopped dabbing this wound to search his eyes. "Are you saying what happened was all your fault?"

"I steered us directly into danger."

"You led us to where we should have been safe, at least for that moment," countered Rose. "It was fate that conspired against us, allowing danger to follow."

"But this wouldn't have happened if I had not insisted on it. We should have waited until the Wizard came to our aid."

"Given our dire situation, our options were very limited. You know that."

"Yes, and obviously, I chose the wrong option," muttered Tag.

"A lesser man would have chosen to do nothing. You have the makings of a great knight because you had the courage to take a chance," argued Rose.

"This shouldn't have happened…"

"But it did, and now you feel guilty," determined Rose.

"How can I not? I kept you safe, but Cankles was my responsibility, too. He trusted me to keep you both safe."

"I say you feel guilty more because he is your friend and you feel like you have let him down."

"Let him down?" groaned Tag, his hand dragging down his woeful face. "He can die because of me."

"You mean to say *me*," corrected Rose, unleashing a dreary sigh. "If you need to blame someone, then it should be me. This is all my fault."

"Trust her, young sir," interjected Silas, as he nodded at Tag. "This whole miserable situation could have been avoided completely from the start."

Rose's chin drooped in shame.

"It's not as though the Princess planned for all this to happen," countered Tag, coming to her defense.

"Thank you," whispered the Princess, as she resumed gently dabbing the cut.

"Just saying what needed to be said."

"Oooh! I see a face under all this grime," teased Rose, watching as Tag winced under her touch.

"Ha, ha!" Snorting in mock laughter, he took the cloth from her hand. "I think I can take it from here."

"If I may?" asked Rainus, motioning for the Princess to make some room on the log where they sat.

"May you what?" asked Tag, staring up in confusion at the Elf as he bumped Rose along on the log when she was too slow to move over.

"I can vanquish that nasty gash with a little Elven healing magic," offered the Elf Lord.

"I've heard of the magic of the Elfkind, but I've never been witness to it," admitted Tag. "Will it work on a mortal?"

"Of course, perhaps not as perfectly as had you been an Elf, but that wound can be healed quite easily, leaving only a slight scar, if that," explained Rainus.

"What is involved? Potions? Salves?" questioned Tag. "A chant or a charm, perhaps?"

"As I said, Elven magic and a little healing incantation," responded Rainus.

"Is it painless?" asked Rose.

"It will be far less painful than what he had experienced getting that gash in the first place," answered the Elf.

"I can deal with a little pain if it heals this wound so infection doesn't set in," said Tag. "What do I need to do?"

"Not a thing, my young friend. Just relax and let me do my work." Rainus pushed up the sleeves of his tunic.

Having never experienced this healing magic before, Tag fidgeted about, nervous of what was to come.

"Please, my friend, it will be easier for the both of us if you can stop squirming so. It makes my work harder and the chances of a near invisible scar all the more impossible with all this unnecessary movement," stated Rainus. He rested his hands on Tag's shoulders to steady this bundle of nervous energy.

"Very well," conceded Tag, drawing in a deep, calming breath.

"Let the healing begin!" exclaimed Rainus, clapping his hands and rubbing them together to generate warmth and his Elven magic. With his eyes closed, he placed his hand over Tag's cheek. Just a hair's-breadth away from the wound, the close proximity would ensure better results.

While Rainus mumbled words of Elvish under his breath, Tag's cheek started to tingle and warm. He felt his skin tighten, as if it was being pulled back together again as torn fibres of muscle and skin began to mend.

All through this healing session, Rose held her breath, anxious to see the results. She thought of the cut on her hand that Rainus would most likely want to heal, if he had his way. Not wanting to have Elven magic performed upon her in case it hurt and the results were less than miraculous for the amount of pain she'd have to endure, the Princess discreetly shifted away, sitting on her hands so she would not draw attention to them.

Rose watched intently as Rainus removed his hand from Tag's cheek.

"There you go! Much better now," said the Elf, as he scrutinized his handiwork.

"Oh my! How very magical!" gasped Rose. She marvelled at the results while she teased Tag. "Now, can you use some of that magic to fix his entire face so he can look handsome, Lord Silverthorn?"

"Cankles was right, you're the one who should have been the court jester," grunted Tag. His tone was smug as he gave his head a dismal shake in her direction.

Using his fingertip, Tag gingerly traced the newly healed wound. To his surprise and pleasure, he discovered not only did the sting fade away, as the tingling sensation subsided, the gaping flesh and skin had fused, sealing the once nasty gash.

"Had you been an Elf, that wound would have healed completely, but being that you are human, you shall be left with a slight blemish of a scar," said Rainus.

"I can live with that. As far as I'm concerned, a scar or two only serves to add to a knight's character." Tag nodded in appreciation. "At least there is no risk of infection setting in now."

"Very true," agreed the Elf, as he turned to face Rose. "What say you, Princess? Perhaps I should take this opportunity to mend your hand while I am in the mood to heal."

She squirmed uneasily. "It is not that bad. I believe this cut can heal on its own in time."

"Yes, as long as infection does not impede the healing process," cautioned Rainus. "But you are free to decide for yourself."

"Go on, Princess," urged Tag. "It didn't hurt at all, if that's what you're so concerned about."

"I am not afraid it will hurt, I just do not wish to impose on Lord Silverthorn," argued Rose.

"What are you talking about? You've imposed on everyone here because of that cursed dreamstone, take no offence Master Agincor," rebuked Tag. "If anything, allow Lord Silverthorn to heal that wound so the blood does not draw the attention of dragons that may be lurking near to us."

"Oh, I never thought of that," said Rose, hastily removing the scrap of cloth she used to dress the cut on the palm of her hand.

Presenting her injury to Rainus, the Elf murmured the same Elvish healing incantation as his left hand hovered over the wound, barely even touching it.

Rose bit her lower lip, hoping to stifle her scream in case Tag had lied about the lack of pain.

A warm, tingling sensation, much like the feeling of pins and needles when one's foot falls asleep, dulled the sting as flesh and skin mended together.

"There you go!" announced Rainus, removing his hand from hers. "Good as new! Just remember, you are not an Elf, so there is a chance you will be left with a faint scar after the healing process is complete."

"I would be more concerned if the scar was on my face, but it is not." Rose balled her hand into a fist, testing to see if the newly healed wound would somehow come undone with pressure.

"I suppose your race is used to such flaws, having imperfections that remind them of their mortality and the frailty of the human condition," decided Rainus, watching the Princess as she examined her palm. "Being that we Elves are as close to perfection as God deemed willing to make us, I would be more than a little put off if my features were to be somehow marred in this matter."

"Don't get the Princess started," warned Tag. "She thought *she* was as perfect as they come!"

"Contrary to what you say, I have discovered perfection does have its privileges, but it is just an illusion," stated Rose. "Where I once believed I was perfect, I now know perfection is truly all-encompassing, and next to impossible to achieve. Though I look perfect, I still have much work to do to better the person inside."

Tag's eyes narrowed in suspicion as he stared at her. "Alright... what have you done with the real Princess Rose-alyn?"

"Oh, shut it!" snapped Rose, jabbing him with her elbow.

"I'm serious," said Tag. "The real Princess would never admit such a thing."

"Look here, outside of Pepperton Palace, it is not as though I am distracted by issues like what to wear, or when and what to eat," grunted Rose. "I have decided that having too many choices can be a burden unto itself."

"I believe that is called 'being spoiled', Princess," said the Dream Merchant, giving her a thoughtful nod.

"Call it what you will, Master Agincor, however, out here in the middle of nowhere, my mind is forced to consider other matters that are far more pressing."

"Like?" asked Tag, prompting her for an answer.

"Like matters that pertain to my survival, rather than figuring out what gown I will wear and how often I should change my wardrobe in the course of a day."

"Oddly enough, you sound rather sincere," noted Tag, as he rubbed his chin in pensive thought.

"That is because I am speaking the truth. I am no longer in a position to even *wish* for a fine meal, and yet, I find I am now grateful to share even a simple meal amongst trusted friends."

"I find this hard to believe," marvelled Tag.

"Me, too," admitted the Princess. "As much as I detest embarking on a quest such as this, it has forced me to reassess my values and take stock of my life. In doing so, I have developed a new sense of... "

Her eyes rolled skyward, as though searching for the correct word. "Gratitude?" offered Tag.

"I suppose you can call it that. What I do know for sure is that I have a newfound appreciation for all the things I once took for granted."

"Finally!" announced Silas, slapping his thigh in delight. "Had you felt this way from the start, you would have never summoned me for the dreamstone."

"In hindsight, I suppose you are correct," admitted Rose, smiling sheepishly at the Wizard.

"Better late than never, I always say," responded the Dream Merchant.

"Hey… are you saying you had granted me that magic crystal in the first place to teach me a lesson?" gasped Rose, staring with suspicious eyes at Silas.

The Wizard rolled his shoulders in a shrug as he answered, "Life is one big lesson. What an individual derives from it is in direct correlation to how they perceive and respond to the hardships of life."

"Obviously, your life wasn't hard enough, Princess," teased Tag, as he shook his head in dismay.

"Aha! So you do like to see me suffer!"

"I never said that. What I do like is knowing that you shall one day be a better ruler because you now understand the common man and can finally appreciate what truly matters in life."

"So, you do not frown on me that I have somewhat adapted to this commoner's way of life; living like a vagabond on the run and eating what there is to get by on, when there is something to eat?"

"It speaks of your resilience and resourcefulness, if nothing else," commended Tag.

"And that is a good thing?"

"In my mind, it is far better than being regarded as petty, spoiled and thoughtless," answered Tag.

Rose blushed, her back straightened as she sat a little taller.

"Well, it is just a pity that you had not found your true potential early on," sighed Silas. "It would have spared us the grief of trying to reclaim the dreamstone, not to mention save the life of your friend, Cankles Mayron."

"Poor Cankles," lamented Tag. He heaved a disheartened sigh as he thought on their missing comrade.

"Despair not, young master," said Rainus. "We are here to help you in this quest."

"I am grateful for that, Lord Silverthorn. However, what good is a knight without a sword on such missions?" responded Tag, removing the empty scabbard hanging at his left hip. "I've lost my father's sword, of all things, this time forever."

"You are right, Tag. A knight is rather useless without his weapons and a quest is no quest without a trusty sword to do battle with," agreed Rose. Reaching inside her pack, she removed a long object wrapped in a sheath of ragged cloth. "You will be needing this."

Tag peeled back the fabric.

"My father's sword!"

"Your father's sword, indeed!" Rose nodded as she smiled at him.

"But – but how?" stammered Tag, his eyes wide in surprise. "I dropped it into the river of lava when I was trying to rescue you."

"You did drop it, but your father's sword has a will of its own. It had the good fortune of landing on a narrow ledge below, the tip of the blade biting into the earth to prevent it from toppling over."

"It was meant to be!" declared Silas, nodding in approval.

"But how? When?" asked Tag. He was grateful his sword was returned, but confused as to how she had reclaimed it.

"While you and the Elves were busy excavating the tunnel to access the Sorcerer's lair, I kept myself busy."

"Busy?" Tag frowned in bewilderment.

"Fine! So I was bored waiting about," admitted the Princess. "I had nothing to do, so when I went to the edge of the cliff where the lava flowed to see if I could find any sign of the dragon that fell in, that was when I spotted your sword. It was sitting there, waiting to be rescued."

"Say again!" gasped Rainus. "The three of you encountered a dragon and live to tell about it?"

"On this mission, we encountered more dragons than you can shake a stick at," revealed Rose, shuddering in disgust and fear. "They have been of every size, shape and temperament; even more than you can begin to imagine!"

"In fact, that is how I lost my sword in the first place," informed Tag. "The dragon the Sorcerer kept shackled to his underground lair was mad with hunger and determined to make a meal of us. We were trapped with no way to escape when the Princess lost her footing, almost falling into the river of lava."

"Oh, my! That is quite the adventure!" exclaimed Silas, leaning forward as he listened intently.

"True, but how did the beast meet its end? Not even the mightiest Elven sword can penetrate the scales of a dragon," reminded Rainus, baffled by how these mortals were able to defeat the great reptile.

"The creature's downfall was its hunger," explained Tag. "It was so ravenous, a combination of luck on our part and the dragon's own carelessness resulted in it falling into the lava."

"What an incredible tale!" remarked Silas.

"Oh, this is no tale, Master Wizard," assured Rose. "That dragon was starving. It was so hungry, the creature devoured its own tongue when Tag hacked it off with his sword."

"That is unheard of," said Rainus. "It must have been well beyond starving to willingly cannibalize itself."

"We saw it with our own eyes," confirmed Tag.

"And it was truly disgusting!" Rose added with a shudder.

"That the creature ate its own tongue?" queried Silas.

"That, and the fact it was tasting something that was tasting it back!" answered the Princess, as she grimaced in revulsion.

Tag smiled as he noted, "That definitely sounded like something Cankles would say."

"Hmm… it did," agreed Rose, giving her comrade a thoughtful nod. "I don't know if that is a good thing or bad."

"So, a misstep and the dragon met its demise, burned alive in the ferociously hot lava," determined Rainus.

"Yes," said Tag.

"That explains the acrid smell upon entering the chamber," recalled Silas. "It was much worse than the mere stink of brimstone."

"But we digress," said Rainus. "Master Yairet was inquiring about his sword and how it came to be returned to him."

"What else is there to say?" responded Rose, her shoulders arching up in a modest shrug. "I found it; managed to retrieve the sword before it, too, became one with the lava and cooking dragon."

"But how did you manage to reach it?" asked Tag, wiping off the dirt and smudges before returning the sword to the scabbard. "If it did indeed land where I think it did, not even if I had stretched down, dangling over the ledge, would I have been able to reach the pommel to grasp my sword."

"True, but thanks to my newfound *'resourcefulness'* my Elven longbow was handy in more ways than one. I merely used the length of the bow to reach down, snagging the cross-guard to safely retrieve your sword."

"It must be a good omen; a sign of things to come," decided Tag, nodding in appreciation. "I sacrificed this sword to save you, and the fates decreed it; returning my precious weapon to me. It is a definite sign I must continue on."

"You mean *we*," corrected Rose.

"Whether it is an omen, or not, I suggest that we all get some sleep, for we have a long night before us," urged Rainus. "My men will take turns keeping watch until the sun retires."

"Good idea." Tag nodded in agreement. "We shall rest so we'll be refreshed; have our wits about us to rescue Cankles."

"How do you think he fares?" asked Rose, thinking on their missing comrade.

"I'm confident he's fine," insisted Tag. "Dragonite will do him no harm as long as he believes our friend will provide him leverage in bargaining for what he demands in trade."

"Pssst... Hey, you! Wake up."

These words droned and buzzed, humming like the distant roll of thunder in Cankles' ears as he forced his bleary eyes open.

With his head spinning, he squeezed his eyes shut as he struggled to sit up.

"Bloody well 'bout time you woke up." This voice sounded from the darkness.

Cankles moaned, feeling the cold, damp ground beneath his aching body as he propped his bony back against the hard wall.

"Where am I? What happened?" groaned Cankles, his dry throat cracking as he spoke.

"You are trapped. You have been taken prisoner. That's what has happened."

Cankles' eyes squinted, staring past the glow of the torchlight burning in the passageway as he searched about for this disembodied voice. The words were as foreboding and sinister as anything Parru St. Mime Dragonite would say, but in his heart and mind, Cankles knew it sounded nothing like the Sorcerer.

"Where are you? Better yet, who are you?"

"Here! I'm up here."

Cankles strained to listen, cupping a hand to his ear to follow this voice that echoed, amplified by the acoustics of this subterranean lair.

"Where? I can't see you."

"Look up, you dolt! Up to the ceiling of this tunnel!" This time, the voice snapped in annoyance. "If you cannot see me, then you are as blind as bats are purported to be!"

Cankles stood up on his unsteady legs, staring into the roof of the dim-lit passage. "You must be hidden well and good. All I see is a little bat hanging up there."

The winged creature spread its leathery wings as beady, amber eyes glared at the mortal.

"Ta-ta-da-daaah!" said the Sprite, as though trumpeting his grand arrival. "It is I, Loken!"

Cankles gasped in surprise as the bat transformed under a flash of light. Hovering before this prison, the shape-shifting Sprite assumed his regular form.

"It is you! The Pooka thing!" declared Cankles. His eyes were wide in amazement as his trembling finger pointed accusingly at the Sprite.

"I am not a *thing!* And my name is Loken, if you have not already figured that out."

"What is this place?" asked Cankles, his hands wrapping around smooth spikes of solid crystal that protruded from the cave floor and ceiling, coming together to produce the haphazard bars separating him from the Pooka. Behind him, the walls of Cankles' prison were formed of more crystal spikes; many of them huge columns of crystal, some so large, he'd never get his hands around them. They jutted from the ground, rising up to the ceiling at chaotic angles, some crossing each other to form an impenetrable mesh.

"For now, consider it your home."

"I have never seen such an incredible thing," marvelled Cankles, as he admired the beauty of the crystal formations reflecting the light of the torch. "It'd be quite lovely, beautiful even, if it wasn't my prison."

"This exquisite dungeon is just one of many in Dragonite's secret hideaway," boasted the Sprite.

"Secret?" snorted Cankles, as he scratched his head in thought. "Like the secret passage *hidden* behind the veil of water at the Devil's Tears?"

"Yes!"

"It wasn't *that* secret, you know? We figured out where it was pretty quickly."

"You and your cohorts were just lucky that time," dismissed Loken. "This place is so super secret, if you didn't already know about it, you'd need a special map and a secret decoding device to read it. That's how secret it is!"

"I don't believe you." Cankles' words were blunt.

"Then you are a fool, but that is your prerogative."

"To not believe you, or in being a fool?"

"Either one, take your pick."

"So… we are somewhere under… Crystal Mountain?" surmised Cankles, his eyes taking in the spectacular, glass-like formations all around him.

"How did you know?" gasped Loken, his mouth agape in stunned amazement.

"I didn't. I just took a wild guess. And by the look on your face, I guessed right."

"Damn you! You tricked me." The Sprite trembled in rage as he buzzed about like an angry bee.

"I suppose I did! That was rather clever of me, if I do say so myself," exclaimed Cankles, surprised by this turn of good fortune in spite of his dire situation. "Mind you... I think you're lyin' to me. You're tryin' to trick me into believin' there is such a place as Crystal Mountain! Especially since I just made it up!"

"Enough with these shenanigans! There *is* such a place."

"Yes, and it dwells in my imagination," teased Cankles, his index finger tapping his forehead.

"You dolt! We are smack-dab in the heart of Crystal Mountain," snorted Loken. "Does it look like you're imagining your prison cell?"

Cankles ran his fingertips along one of the smooth bars of crystal. "Feels real enough, but with my hurtin' head, I'm probably imaginin' this whole thing, you included. Never seen such incredible crystal formations... it's got to be in my mind."

"*Argh!*" snarled Loken. "These crystals are real! And so is this mountain!"

"Naw, I think you're just tryin' to make me feel smart, or real dumb, when I just made it up. You're speakin' in jest! A mountain made up of crystal *and* bein' called Crystal Mountain? Can't be real. And if it were, somethin' of such beauty wouldn't be found in a land as desolate as the Fire Rim Mountain range."

"Bloody hell!" cursed Loken, his hand smacking his forehead in utter frustration. "It *is* real and calling it Crystal Mountain makes perfect sense."

"Fine! I'll give you that! But you can't tell me a mountain as grand as this can be found anywhere, but in Fleetwood."

"You puny-minded numbskull! We're just north of the Devil's Tears, well within the mountains that make up the Fire Rim Range."

Cankles shook his head. "You're just messin' with my mind. If I didn't know better, I'd say we're back in the Bad Lands, Dragonite's former stronghold. You're just tryin' to confuse me."

"You are confused enough without my help!" snorted Loken.

"You're right," admitted Cankles. He absorbed the Sprite's angry words, trying to comprehend his exact location based on Loken's argument as he wondered how he came to be here in the first place. "I must have hit my noggin."

"Ha!" scoffed Loken. "According to Dragonite, it was more than just your head that took a hit! By the sounds of it, when the Sorcerer conjured up his powers to escape, he used you as a human shield when the tunnel collapsed during his getaway."

"That's why I was knocked out…"

"You weren't exactly taking a nap by choice," mocked the Sprite. "If anything, it made it easier for Dragonite to get you here than to deal with you had you fought every step of the way."

"I guess I can see that. But what about you?"

"What do you mean?" grumbled Loken. Alighting upon one of the crystal bars, the Sprite slid down the glassy surface, stopping only when his foot came to rest on a bar running perpendicular to it.

Cankles' eyes narrowed in suspicion. "What are you doin' here? I thought you were long gone after deliverin' the magic crystal to the Sorcerer."

"I can ask the same of you. Why are you here?" questioned Loken, his wings rattling with indignation.

"Has your wee brain been addled? Obviously, I was taken prisoner," grunted Cankles.

"Well, duh! I mean to say, why are you here when Dragonite devised a plan that should have caused so much strife between you and your comrades, the silly Princess was to be left fending for herself once you and that young knight-in-the-making abandoned her."

"What are you talkin' about?"

"The infamous 'if-bomb'?" snorted Loken. "I left an ornate dragon egg that was cursed with a spell. Once opened, it was to drive you three mad with doubt and indecision, so much so, you'd abandon the Princess to undertake the quest alone, leaving her to wallow in her own ineptitude."

"The young master was right! You were behind that devious device of indecision!"

"Dragonite was behind that pathetic spell. Had it been me, I would have bombarded you three with something far more potent than a lousy spell."

"Like what?" Cankles dared to ask.

"I had suggested lobbing some flaming canisters of highly volatile oil. That is what I had in mind, but alas, the Sorcerer insisted on tainting your minds with doubt, so much so, you were all second-guessing each other's every word. What *if* we did this, instead of that? What *if* we retreated, rather than advanced?"

"Truth be told, that sounds rather lame," commented Cankles.

"Tell me about it! I wanted to see a hasty end for you three, but *no!* Dragonite insisted on mental warfare."

"Well... I suppose it makes sense, bein' that he is a bit mental to begin with, surroundin' himself with those mimes."

"Do not get me started on his idiot minions!"

"Oooh! Hit a rough patch with the master, eh?" determined Cankles, shaking his head in dismay.

"Fetch off!" snapped Loken, his wings rattling once more. "He is *not* my master."

"If that is so, then why do you still linger? Dragonite claims he possesses the dreamstone. Why do you remain after givin' him that magic crystal?"

"That is for me to know and you to – "

"Find out?" concluded Cankles.

"I was going to say, to mind your own bloody business!"

"My! For one so small, you have a rather foul mouth." Cankles shook his head in disapproval. "It is as though you're compensatin' for your puny size."

"P-puny!" sputtered Loken, his balled fists trembling in rage. "I'll show you puny!"

In a brilliant flash of light, the Pooka morphed before Cankles' startled eyes. Loken's furry head scraped the ceiling as he rose up onto his hind legs. The shaggy coat covering his hulking body blocked out the light of the torch burning on the passage wall.

"Oh, so what? So you're a big, hairy brute of a bear," dismissed Cankles, taunting the Sprite from behind the safety of the crystal bars. "It's not as though you can get me from there."

Cankles' eyes squeezed shut; the dishevelled strands of oil-clotted hair dangling over his eyes were blown aside as Loken's great form bellowed into his face. Before the Sprite could thrust one of his heavily armed paws through a gap in the crystal bars to slash at him, Cankles stumbled back, away from the reach of these deadly claws.

"See! You can't harm me from there," mocked Cankles, daring to taunt the Sprite.

"Wanna bet?" snarled Loken. In another brilliant flash of light, the Pooka transformed.

Cankles jumped with a start as the huge brown bear abruptly morphed into a large snake. Its rough scales bristled as it coiled, poised to strike.

"A single bite and you'll be dead in three heart beats!" hissed Loken, the tip of his forked tongue flickering as he easily slipped his triangular shaped head between the crystal bars. In an undulating, serpentine fashion, his snake form slithered toward the startled mortal.

Cankles' eyes opened wide in fright as Loken's jaws unhinged, spreading apart. The hollow fangs folded against the roof of his mouth sprang into position.

Scrambling on all fours, Cankles retreated to the farthest corner of his small prison. With no escape and no weapon to defend himself, Cankles screamed in fright.

The viper lunged at his legs. With fangs fully extended, they dripped with deadly, amber venom.

3

Forgotten Memories

"Damn!" hissed Loken. His fangs snapped down, just short of the mortal's ankle as a hard yank on his tail sent him flying back through the bars, banging his scaly head along the way.

"What do you think you are doing?" snarled the Sorcerer, tossing Loken's viper form across the tunnel. "I told you to keep an eye on the prisoner, not kill him!"

As the snake bounced off the far wall, Loken morphed once more. Assuming his normal form, he grunted in pain and annoyance. With the obsidian crystal on Dragonite's staff throbbing with light, the Sprite dare not attack, not even in the form of a much larger predator. Though possessing only half the power it was once imbued with, this black crystal was still able to deliver a life-threatening jolt once it had the chance to replenish its magic.

"Who said anything about me killing that moron?" grumbled Loken. In a disgruntled huff, he launched himself into the air. "I was just having a bit of fun with him, that's all; a little scare to keep him on his toes."

"Such insolence!" snapped Dragonite, shaking an accusing finger at the Pooka. "Do you take me for a fool? I understand that wee mind of yours enough to know with absolute certainty you meant to kill my prisoner."

"If you have so little trust in me, then give me what is rightfully mine, and we shall part company. You will be free of my *'insolence'* and I shall be free of *you!*"

"If it were only that easy!" Dragonite gave his head a dismal shake. "Unfortunately for the both of us, you have not outlasted your usefulness to me. When we are done and I finally get what I most desire, then we shall go our separate ways. That is what we agreed to."

"It is what you decided! As if I had a choice!"

"There is always a choice to be made. You can either do as I command, or you will not be receiving what *you* most desire," reminded Dragonite, patting a fold in his robe where he kept a vial of magic potion hidden from Loken's eyes and his eager grasp.

"Excuse me, but if you two do not trust each other, why are you allies?" questioned Cankles, bewildered by this uneasy partnership.

"Shut it!" snarled Dragonite, his staff smashing against the crystal bars.

"It is none of your business!" added the Sprite.

"Sorry," grumbled Cankles, shrinking back from his tormentors. "Just seemed like an odd pairin' to me. You'd both get more accomplished if you learned to get along, methinks."

"Shut the bloody hell up!" growled Dragonite.

The black crystal swelled with light to reflect his mounting displeasure. Pointing the jagged chunk of obsidian at his prisoner, it was enough to make Cankles slap both hands over his mouth as a promise he'd probe no more.

"Yes!" snapped Loken, shaking an angry fist at the mortal. "Just shut that big mouth of yours."

The Sorcerer turned on the Pooka. "And if you have any common sense, you will learn to bite your tongue and follow my orders to the letter, if we are both to acquire what we desire!"

"I suppose a little more trust and cooperation can only help to expedite matters," decided Loken, nodding in agreement.

"Good! Come along then," grunted Dragonite. Flexing his index finger, he motioned for the Sprite to follow him. "We have some critical strategies to discuss and many devious plans to set into motion."

"Any brilliant ideas as to how we proceed?" Tag's words were whispered so he would not wake the sleeping Princess.

He glanced over to Rainus Silverthorn and Silas Agincor as they huddled in conversation under the impending darkness.

"We move on when night falls," responded the Dream Merchant. "Once the temperature drops, enough to hamper the movement of the resident dragons, we shall be on our way."

"No disrespect, Master Wizard, but for one dragon species we've had the ill fortune of encountering, it was apparent the chill of the night did little to slow them down," informed Tag. "The Princess was attacked by the ones you drove off – the very ones that were feasting on one of Lord Silverthorn's men after he fell to his death."

"In light of this new information, that is quite true, young master," agreed Silas. "At least, the majority of dragon species will be taking shelter for the night. It will help reduce our chances of a deadly encounter."

"Speaking of dragons, we should leave this place before the monster we encountered last night returns to discover its nest had been ruined," suggested Denatheen, as he and Halen Ironwood listened in to this conversation. "Believe me; we *do not* want to run into that beast!"

"It was big?" asked Rainus, trying to estimate its size based on the footprints they had seen.

"Even by Elven standards it was *scary big*, my lord. Definitely the largest one I have ever been witness to," stated Denatheen. "It was by sheer luck that Ayden and I were able to escape that creature when it attacked us."

"Do you think I should wake the Princess now? Be on our way well before that dragon returns?" queried Tag, glancing over to Rose as she slept.

Rainus' far-seeing eyes inspected the landscape, from horizon to horizon, searching for possible signs of danger. In the distance to the north, other than the occasional sputtering of volcanoes oozing forth trails of fiery lava, angry bellows and snarls punctuated these sounds. Two juvenile dragons simultaneously attacked a much larger, mature male as they squabbled over a carcass. These scraps, meager remnants of another dragon that had been killed, and then cannibalized by an even larger reptile, were worth fighting for.

"At this time, there is no need for concern, my young friend," reassured Rainus. "I still believe we are safer waiting it out here until night comes, than to venture forth prematurely while the dragons still actively roam about, hunting for fresh meat."

"I'll take your word that we'll be safe for now," decided Tag, removing his sword to sharpen on the whetstone. "But in the meantime, we must devise a plan. How do we even begin to find Cankles and the dreamstone now? There's no telling where the Sorcerer fled to."

"From the entrance of the tunnel hidden behind the Devil's Tears, by my humble estimation, our travels that led us to you and the Princess in the Sorcerer's lair was in a general easterly direction. With the way barricaded by rock fall, there was no way that scoundrel could have doubled back," stated Rainus.

"So he was forced to continue eastward?" assumed Tag.

"Yes," answered Silas. "It is the most logical thing."

"Is there a chance we can intercept Dragonite before he can leave this place?" questioned Tag.

"That will have much to do with your friend," replied the Dream Merchant.

"How so?"

"If Cankles Mayron goes willingly with his captor, there is a chance he, and Dragonite, are long gone. Now, if your friend resists, putting up a fight every step of the way to stymie the Sorcerer's every move, there is a remote chance they are still near to us," answered Silas.

"What is your friend most likely to do, Master Yairet?" questioned Rainus, as he turned to Tag. "Do you believe he will resist or is he more inclined to comply with Dragonite's demands?"

Tag palmed the whetstone as he contemplated this question.

"What say you, young master?" probed Silas. "What are your thoughts on this matter?"

"I believe Cankles will do what he must to keep his friends safe. If he believes his cooperation will guarantee our safety, he will do as the Sorcerer commands."

"So, he is willing to sacrifice the fate of the world in exchange for the safety of two friends, even knowing that in the end, all will be doomed in doing so?" queried the Dream Merchant.

"In all honesty, Cankles is a simple man. I don't know if he has a true grasp of the complexity of this quest nor the ramifications, if we fail. I do sense that if he does, he'd put our safety before his and any cooperation he gives to the Sorcerer will be only done so under great duress. Even at that, I feel it will be so because Cankles firmly believes we will be able to circumvent Dragonite's evil plan before the end."

"Even under the threat of losing his life?" asked Rainus. "He would sacrifice his life to spare yours at this great cost?"

"You can accuse him of being a simple man, but he is a man of honour and great loyalty. I believe with all my heart, Cankles will do what he deems to be the right thing. He would rather die than to betray his friends."

"Your words are spoken with conviction," determined Rainus, as his piercing blue eyes scrutinized the boy.

"Only because I know them to be true. There is no way, under any circumstance, that Cankles will betray me, or the Princess, for that matter. He can be trusted."

"I am sure he can and you speak the truth, but a simple man, no matter how honourable his intentions, can also be *too* trusting," countered Rainus.

"What is that supposed to mean?" grunted Tag.

"I am concerned your friend will be tricked… duped into doing the unthinkable, just because he can be trusting of others, taking them for their word."

"How dare you say such a thing about Cankles?" gasped Tag. "You know nothing about the man!"

"Contrary to what you believe, I know him better than you think, and possibly even more than you do." Rainus' words were matter-of-fact.

"How can that be?"

"Think back to when you and Princess Rose first arrived in the Woodland Glade. Did it not seem odd to you that Cankles Mayron was rather familiar with the enchanted forest?"

"He said he had passed by way of your domain years before."

"That is partly true." Rainus nodded in agreement. "What he failed to mention was that he had resided in my forest for many long days, the passing of four moons to be exact, before he was fit enough to venture on."

"I fail to understand." Tag frowned in bewilderment as he listened to the Elf's foreboding words.

"Surely you must have noticed the many scars that mar his body, from head to toe?"

"Yes… it is hard not to. At one time, Princess Rose believed Cankles was a criminal, severely flogged as punishment for committing a heinous crime. Even Cankles believes he had done something terrible to have been punished as he was."

"There is a difference between being punished and being tortured," explained Rainus. "Cankles was tortured."

"Are you telling me the Princess was right? That Cankles had committed a terrible crime and was tortured to confess his ill deed?"

"Princess Rose possesses an overactive imagination, but the man in question cannot be accused of being a criminal, far from it. He was an ordinary man faced with an extraordinary situation, one that forged him into a true hero of great courage."

"Now I know you speak in jest! Cankles can be honest to a fault, and he is more meek and timid than the heroic type." Tag dismissed the Elf's words.

"I take it he has never revealed to you anything of his past?"

"What had been revealed was vague at best," admitted Tag. "Cankles said he could not remember most of his life; that it must be God's will that whatever happened to him was to be stricken from his memory, either to punish him for a crime or because the brutality of what he endured was just too much for him to bear."

"God's will had nothing to do it. A terrible blow to his head, one that was meant to kill him, was what vanquished from his mind all thought and memory of his previous life."

"Do you know what happened to him?"

"It is obvious what happened to the man," answered Rainus. "What you should be asking is; *why did it happen?*"

"Then I will ask it now. Why was he tortured?"

"His many wounds spoke of *how* he was tortured. He had been lashed with a whip so many times only the combined powers of the Elfkind were strong enough to heal his back that had been shredded to ribbons. And just as traumatic, a great mallet was used to smash his ankle bones."

"He was hobbled?" gasped Tag, his eyes wide in horror.

"Yes, effectively so, to prevent his escape. In fact, his ankles were utterly shattered. The swelling caused them to become one with his calves, hence the name *Cankles*."

"You made light of his serious condition?" Tag was appalled that the Elf would do so.

"Not intentionally," continued Rainus. "But you know how children, even an Elf child, can be."

"Allow Lord Silverthorn to continue," urged Silas, motioning Tag for silence.

"When Cankles refused to divulge pertinent information to his captor, his jaw was broken in retribution. This injury seriously impeded his ability to speak. When he muttered the word *cankles*, we thought he was speaking of his condition. Unfortunately, for the poor soul, the Elf children adopted this name, and so, too, did Cankles when he finally became fully conscious. To this day, the name stays with him. It was as though his mind wanted to leave the past well behind him."

"Amnesia," decided Tag.

"Whether by choice or by divine intervention, he only recalls the hours after waking up from a long sleep I had induced in a bid to heal his physical suffering."

"If he was that brutalized, how could he have had the strength to escape?" asked Tag.

"*Escape?* I hardly think so," disclosed Rainus. "As I said, the blow inflicted to his head was meant to kill him. When it became obvious he would rather die than divulge his secret, a blow to the head was delivered to end his life. By a strange twist of fate, he survived the last assault. He would have died a slow, agonizing death, but he did make his way to the Woodland Glade and into our care."

"But how?" questioned Tag. "With such an injury to his head and his ankles crushed, how could he have made the journey?"

"I believe someone, perhaps one of Dragonite's misguided minions, took pity upon him. When he was left to die, someone with an ounce of mercy in his soul set him on his way here."

"And what was this secret he was protecting?" asked Tag, hanging on the Elf's every word.

"What do you recall of the Battle of Pleno'Gore Fields?" questioned Rainus. "To the east, in the Bad Lands?"

"That was about ten years ago..." Tag searched his memories. "King William's army defeated Dragonite's hordes, but my father still lost his life there."

"Do you recall how your King's army won that battle?" asked Rainus.

"Yes, when the initial fighting had begun, acting on false reports of the number of mercenaries Dragonite had enlisted, my father's army was quickly overwhelmed. When all seemed lost, my father's second battalion arrived just in time. Though most in the first battalion, including my father, had lost their lives, the remaining knights and soldiers were victorious, driving the Sorcerer and his legion of mercenaries far to the north."

"And how was it that the second battalion arrived in such a timely manner?"

"A secret route and the aid of allies made it possible," answered Tag. "But what does any of this have to do with my friend?"

"You really do not know, do you?" asked Rainus.

"Do not answer my question by presenting me with more questions! What are you trying to tell me?"

"No need to get testy, young sir! I just thought you knew, being that you are now in possession of your father's sword."

Tag stared at the weapon he held in his hand. "What of it? Princess Rose returned it to me when we made it back to Fleetwood."

"Think! How did it return to her palace when the owner of that sword did not?"

"Are you saying Cankles returned it? He was a soldier? In my father's army?"

"If the rumours of old hold true, he was *not* a soldier. The man you know as Cankles Mayron was once a young knight in King William's service."

The whetstone slipped from Tag's hand as memories from his past overwhelmed him. He thought back on the sword Cankles kept in his cottage, the one with the stylized initials *MK* woven into the crossguard. It was the sword Cankles had gifted to him at the start of their first quest. "Impossible! As I understand it, all the knights under my father's command were killed. Only a handful of soldiers from this first battalion survived, holding on until reinforcements arrived."

"The passing of time has a way of distorting the truth where history is concerned. That was only partly true."

"If he was a knight that saw action and lived to tell about it, then why does Cankles not speak of this?"

"He had survived a terrible ordeal, one so atrociously savage, he either chooses not to remember or it has been stricken from his memory," continued Rainus. "According to lore, when your father was wounded in battle, Cankles donned your father's helmet, taking up your father's sword and shield. Though the shield was cracked by the blow of an axe, it still bore the markings that distinguished it as the captain's."

"Why would he do that?"

"He knew the enemy soldiers were trained to kill the captain first, a tactical maneuver to guarantee that chaos would ensue in short order. With no leader, the knights and soldiers were easily defeated."

"But that would be suicide. The mercenaries would have done all in their power to kill Cankles, too, especially if they were tricked into believing he was the captain."

"Yes, and he knew that," responded Rainus. "That is why he charged into battle as he did. He bought more time for the surviving men, just enough that the second battalion arrived to engage the enemy. He fled the battlefield with the enemy in full pursuit, never to be seen again."

"He pretended to be my father?"

"He pretended to be the *captain* of King William's army; a clever ploy to spare the lives of his fellow knights and soldiers."

"So he was captured by the enemy?"

"Captured *and* tortured. He survived more than the average man could endure," revealed Rainus.

"How did he come to the Woodland Glade?" questioned Tag, listening intently to the Elf's every word.

"Oddly enough, he was delivered to my domain on the back of a unicorn."

"A unicorn? How can that be?"

"That is a mystery I continue to ponder to this very day. Unicorns by nature are shy, retiring animals. Even for an Elf, it can take years before a unicorn herd will allow us to approach them, however, these animals do what they can to avoid mortal man."

"Then how is it possible that he was brought to your domain by such a creature?"

"Who can say? To this very day, it remains a mystery. All I know for sure is this was how Cankles was delivered to the borders of the Woodland Glade."

"Why did you not reveal this information to us – to *him*, when we were first in your company?" questioned Tag, as he thought back on their initial introduction.

"What was the point? When it became obvious he did not remember me and failed to recognize my wife, Lady Valara, it was evident he recalled nothing of his stay in the Woodland Glade. If he had no recollection of the past, not even fragmented memories, it seemed pointless to remind him of his past ordeal," reasoned the Elf.

"But why did you not say something to me, or the Princess?"

"For what reason? Would this knowledge have somehow changed your opinion of this man?"

"No… I would still trust and believe in him, as well as his sense of honour and duty," stated Tag.

"Then this information would have been shared needlessly. It is only pertinent to Cankles, but why subject him to painful memories of his past when it is obvious his mind is still unable to cope with it?" justified Rainus.

"I suppose I see your point."

"When he left our care, his wounds had healed sufficiently, but his mind was utterly shattered," explained Rainus. "Had he shown an inkling of recollection, then I would sense it was time to reveal these details to him, but until he showed some desire to know of his past, there was no point in bringing it up."

"This explains much about him; his unwillingness to take up arms and yet, when forced to do so, it is undeniable he has skill with the sword," stated Tag.

"That poor soul has seen much in the way of bloodshed during that last battle, but it is evident his skill with the sword is still deeply ingrained in his body and mind," attested Silas. "Even when his mind chooses to forget, his hand still knows how to wield his weapon."

"What good will it do him now?" said Tag, heaving a disheartened sigh. "I returned his sword to him upon receiving my father's. Instead of wearing it at his side as he should, he chose to keep it safely tucked away in his pack."

"In all likelihood, the man you know as Cankles Mayron will be hard pressed to take up his sword to spare even his own life," determined Rainus.

"And now that an old enemy has taken him captive once more, this time, it can prove to be deadly for him," warned Silas.

"Are you saying that the Sorcerer was the one who tortured him the first time?" gulped Tag, his eyes wide in disbelief and horror.

"Yes, and I fear his memories shall come flooding back to him at the most inopportune time," said Rainus. "If so, there is a chance your friend will fold to Dragonite's will, than to summon the courage and strength once more to endure the Sorcerer's treacherous abuse."

"RRAAAARRRR!"

Rose bolted up from her sleep as this thunderous roar shattered the calm of the twilight sky. She glanced about in confusion as the men snatched up their weapons. The blood in their veins ran cold as this terrifying bellow rattled them to their bones and the earth trembled beneath their feet as something of immense size landed with a resounding *boom!*

"Wha- what was that?" stammered Rose, as she stumbled onto her feet.

Tag didn't stop to answer. Instead, he snatched up her cloak, tossing it to the Princess as he whispered, "We leave now."

"To where?" asked Rose.

"Hush! Keep still," whispered Halen, pressing a finger to his lips. He pointed through the cover of foliage. "A dragon… a very *big* dragon."

"The great beast has returned to its nest," warned Denatheen, as he peered through the tangle of branches.

Rose slapped her hands over her mouth to keep from screaming in fright as the creature's wings folded against its body, fanning a great gust of air toward them to send branches rattling and leaves swaying in its wake.

Crouching low in the crater, the dragon eyed the gaping hole that wasn't there before. Though this opening was only big enough for the creature to insert the tip of its snout into, the integrity of the floor was severely comprised. The dragon that had been trapped within demolished many of the stalactites and stalagmites that had fused together over an eon to create the main support pillars in the chamber. As it rampaged about in a desperate hunt for its intended quarry, the beast destroyed these great columns and now, the stability of the chamber's ceiling was seriously in doubt.

The aroma of burned reptile flesh and the lingering scent of a mortal or two tantalized the dragon as its snout probed about, inhaling at the hole in case there was fresh food to be had.

The behemoth stopped sniffing about; cocking its head to one side while large ears swivelled about, listening as the earth beneath it creaked under its immense weight.

Rose and the men in her company watched in stunned surprise as the dragon suddenly bellowed in alarm. It fell from their sight as the fractured crater crumbled away beneath it.

"Maybe the fall killed the beast," hoped Tag. He stood on his toes to peer over the shrub, spying upon a great cloud of dust billowing from what was left of the demolished crater.

Just as abruptly as the creature vanished, the dragon's head reappeared, poking out of the crumbling volcano. Hissing and snarling as it clambered out, the reptile was as hungry as ever, but in a much fouler mood now.

Raising its snout into the air, it sniffed about, trying to catch the scent of those responsible for destroying its nest.

Mortals, Elves and Wizard froze where they stood, barely even breathing as the dragon gazed over to the stand of trees where shrubs concealed them. Tag had his hand clamped over Rose's mouth so she wouldn't scream as the Elves remained motionless.

With a disappointed growl, the dragon turned away; forced to seek a new, warm nest and meal along the way. Just as it fanned out its wings to catch the wind, its ears pricked up; snout lifting skyward as a muffled *'toot'*, followed by an unpleasant stench wafted toward the creature.

All eyes darted over to the Wizard as Silas' face reddened with embarrassment.

"Excuse me!" He whispered, fanning the air with his hand as he apologized. "Just a nervous response, that's all."

Before Rose could groan a disgusted *'Ewww'*, the dragon reared up, wheeling about to face them.

"RUN!" hollered Halen.

He waved off Rainus to escape while he and the others prepared to stand their ground in a bid to hold the dragon at bay.

As Rainus led the way, Tag, Rose and the Dream Merchant rushed behind him.

"Stay close," ordered Rainus. "Do not look back!"

Just as the dragon bellowed, unleashing a torrent of heat and flames from its mouth, Halen and his men dropped low to the ground. They raised a barrier of overlapping shields to protect them from the creature's fiery breath.

The sound was deafening. Fierce, orange tongues of light and heat swirled and raged, engulfing the Elves. Though protected from the flames by this barrier of shields, they could still feel the heat. The rising temperature swelled through the steel boss where they gripped their shields.

All around them, leaves curled and crackled while branches snapped and popped as the flames devoured everything it touched.

"Steady on men!" Halen shouted to be heard above the roar. Watching as the fire's glow dropped from an intense orange to a light amber as the dragon's exhaling breath began to wane, he gave his orders, "Brace yourself! Be ready to attack!"

As tree trunks burned like sticks of kindling and the foliage around them turned to ash, floating down like grey confetti, the dragon's massive head recoiled. As it inhaled, filling its lungs to capacity, the plate-like ventral scales protecting its chest and belly stretched apart ever so slightly to reveal unprotected flesh.

"Go for the exposed areas!" ordered Halen. He dropped his shield and unsheathed his sword. "Choose your weapon! Do so now!"

With swords drawn and arrows nocked, the Elves charged the beast before it could exhale to unleash another deadly blast of incinerating fire.

As dusk surrendered to the coming of night, the diminished light served to impair the dragon's already poor vision. So accustomed to prey fleeing for its life, the blur of movement as the Elves rushed forward only startled and agitated the beast.

Leaping back, the dragon landed with a bone-jarring thud as the puny beings boldly surrounded it, attacking with swords and arrows. Even if they failed to kill the beast, their actions would guarantee Rainus and the others could make good their escape.

"Stay clear of the fire!" shouted Halen, stabbing the tissue exposed between the scales on the chest. He ducked beneath the dragon's body, hearing the gnashing of teeth to produce the spark to ignite its fiery breath.

"The feet!" hollered Denatheen, launching an arrow to blind the reptile's right eye. "Watch out for its feet!"

Halen grabbed Roen-Aldus by his shoulder, yanking him out of the way as a clawed foot smashed down, barely missing him.

"Look out!" cried Ayden, dodging the dragon's tail as it whipped about. He moved in time, but Argon Greenleaf, the young Elf Rose was so smitten with was sent flying into a melting snow bank.

The dragon roared in frustration, enraged by the Elves darting about. They charged from all sides like a small army of ants relentlessly attacking a much larger preying mantis. Shaking its head, the beast tried to dislodge the arrow Denatheen had aimed at its eye. The shaft of the projectile snapped off, but the steel bodkin remained deeply embedded as the dragon clawed at the offending weapon. The nictitating membrane drew obliquely across its wounded eye. This third eyelid was an opaque white, but it quickly turned red from the blood seeping from the painful injury inflicted by the arrow, only to blind it further.

Ducking, dodging and darting to and fro to avoid getting trampled underfoot or lashed by the dragon's wildly writhing tail, the Elves remained dangerously close, a strategy to keep from being burned alive by the creature's breath should it unleash its fire.

Just as the dragon reared up on its hind legs to crush Halen, the Elf saw his chance to strike. Lunging straight up, the tip of his sword pierced through the tissue normally hidden behind the plates of armour. Thrusting the blade forward, Halen shouted in surprise as the dragon suddenly leapt skyward. The powerful downdraft of wind as the creature's great wings lifted it skyward bowled over the other Elves, while Halen dangled from the hilt of his sword. The blade, trapped between the overlapping scales, refused to budge, even as the dragon took to the air with the Elf in tow.

"Let go!" hollered Denatheen. He unleashed an arrow that tore through the dragon's wing.

"Never!" shouted Halen, wedging the blade of his dagger between the scales in a bid to free his sword. "Escape while you can!"

They watched helplessly as their captain was whisked up into the night sky.

4

Evil, with a Capital E

"This way!" ordered Rainus, as he led the charge through the stand of trees, down the sloping terrain. "Follow me."

"Where are you taking us?" asked Rose. Clutching her bow and the quiver of arrows, she tried to prevent the projectiles from rattling about as she dashed after him.

"Away from that dragon, that's where!"

"We should stay! We can't just abandon your men," countered Tag, still brandishing his sword. "That dragon will be the death of them!"

"What they do, they do so willingly. They sacrifice their lives, so we may carry on," reminded Rainus. "They understand the risks they take and the meaning of sacrifice, if the Sorcerer is to be stopped."

"I am confident they will be fine," assured Silas, waving Tag on to follow them.

They froze in their tracks as Halen's frightened scream echoed through the night as the dragon's raucous bellow raked at their nerves.

"*That* does not sound fine!" snapped Tag. "I'm going back!"

"To do what?" Rose grabbed him by the arm to stop him. "Add to the death count? I need you here! I cannot do this alone."

"You are *not* alone," insisted Tag, glancing over her shoulders at the Elf and the Wizard.

"No disrespect to present company, but I can use all the help I can get to rescue Cankles and to reclaim the dreamstone. I hardly think the Sorcerer will be on his own. He'll be surrounded by his mimely minions," argued Rose, refusing to relinquish her grip on Tag.

"The Princess is correct, young sir," stated Silas. "It is not an easy task we undertake. Our numbers grow thin. You have no choice but to come with us."

"But what about them?" Tag listened to the shouts rising above the distant clang of steel bashing against scales as Rainus' men continued to do battle against the monster dragon.

"Those lucky enough to survive will join us when they can," promised Rainus.

"And if not?" questioned Tag, reluctantly sheathing his sword into its scabbard. "If all should die, then what?"

"Then we truly are on our own," stated the Elf. "Now, follow me! If my men fail, it will only be a matter of time before that dragon attempts to hunt us down."

"Let us take advantage of this time they give us," urged Rose. "If they should die, then let it not be in vain."

"Very well." Tag heaved a disheartened sigh. "Lead the way, Lord Silverthorn."

"Come with me," ordered Rainus. "Make haste!"

They raced to safety, sprinting through the forest so quickly, the trees were nothing more than a blur in their passing. Though Wizard and Elf were unaffected by this mad dash, Rose and Tag were huffing and puffing, their ragged breath snagging in the back of their throats as they struggled to keep up with the fleet-footed Elf.

As Rainus cleared fallen trees, bounding over with the ease of a graceful deer, Tag's escape was hampered by the Princess. With each large deadfall they encountered, he was made to stop, lifting Rose over these obstacles that even the old Wizard had relatively little difficulty in clearing. Tag would then rush her on, leading Rose by the hand as they splashed through streams and charged through underbrush.

Adrenaline and fear were now the only things fuelling their desperate flight.

"Come on!" urged Tag, pulling the Princess along as her steps began to falter.

"I am trying," whined Rose, her aching legs feeling as heavy as lead as she fought to gulp down a breath of air.

Tag let go of her hand. He picked up speed as he watched Rainus leap over another deadfall. Just as he neared the toppled tree, Tag's hands slapped down atop of the mossy trunk to thrust him up and over, using the forward momentum to throw his legs to the other side. Landing on his feet, he glanced behind to see Rose was slowing down, instead of using speed to her advantage to clear this obstacle.

Plodding over to the downed tree, rather than vaulting over like Tag did, Rose came to a dead stop. She slumped over the log like a rag doll. Taking a deep breath, she struggled to lift one leg over so she was straddling the tree.

"Get a move on, Princess," ordered Tag, watching as Rose fought to lift her other leg over.

"I *am* moving," insisted Rose.

Just as Tag approached the deadfall to help her over, with about as much energy as a day-old corpse, Rose gracelessly rolled off this horizontal barrier. With legs like jelly, she slumped against Tag, knocking him over with her dead weight.

Landing on top of him, Tag groaned in pain as he fell onto his back, only to have Rose cushion her fall with his body.

"That bloody well hurt!" moaned Tag, pushing the Princess off.

"Good! That's what you get for not being chivalrous."

"I was coming to help you when you decided to bowl me over," complained Tag.

"This is no time for getting cozy, you two," whispered Rainus, as he motioned for the mortals to get up. "We must move on, in case the dragon catches wind of us again."

"I pray your men stay safe, Lord Silverthorn," hoped Silas, glancing over his shoulder up the slope where Rainus' men continued to do battle. His blood ran cold as another scream echoed through the night. The sky erupted in flames, set aglow as the dragon's fiery breath incinerated the surrounding forest.

"The deed is done," announced Loken, brushing the dust from his hands. He greeted the Sorcerer at the mouth of the tunnel where Dragonite awaited his return.

"Did you make it obvious?"

"I left the incriminating evidence in such a way, if the Princess and her cohorts cannot see it for what it is, then there is something very wrong up here with all of them." The Sprite's index finger tapped his forehead.

"Are you sure they will see it?"

"Positive! When I last spied upon them, Agincor and Silverthorn had rescued the mortals from the dragon's keep. They had taken shelter in the forest, on the eastern slope of the old volcano. It was obvious they were waiting for darkness to fall before moving on, and from what I heard, the Dream Merchant intends to direct his search to the east."

"Excellent! But you are sure they will see this sign?" questioned Dragonite. "It is detectable even in the darkness of night?"

"It is so bloody obvious, they'd have to be absolute dolts or completely blind not to see it, especially in the dark! Once they reach the bottom of that old volcano, I made it so conspicuous they will have no choice but to know where they must go next."

"You better be right, or I will – "

"I know… you will kill me," snorted Loken, rolling his eyes in frustration.

"I will pluck those fancy, new wings off your back first, one by one, and then, I will kill you," vowed Dragonite. His bony finger and thumb pinched together, making a quick yanking motion to demonstrate what was in store for the Sprite, if he failed him.

"Brilliant! That way, you'll be left with only your mindless mimes to aid you! A disaster in the making for sure!" scoffed Loken.

"So you say."

"Those idiot mimes will be your undoing if you ask them to do anything more than *pretend* to be guards protecting your little fortress," cautioned the Pooka.

Loken darted away as the Sorcerer, in utter annoyance, thrust the flaming torch in his direction.

"Be warned, once I get that dreamstone working again, my first wish will be to turn you into one of those mimes!" snarled Dragonite. "There will be no back talk from you, then. That's for sure!"

"You hold fast to that little dream of yours, for that's all it will be," dismissed Loken, his wings fluttering to keep up as Dragonite hastened his pace, trudging off in agitation.

"It will be a dream come true, if you are not careful," muttered the Sorcerer.

"Speaking of careful, while I was away, did you complete your task?" Loken's aura paled in the light of the torch carried by the Sorcerer as Dragonite made his way through the crystalline labyrinth.

"Of course I did!" snapped Dragonite, squinting as the flame's light reflected off the shards and pillars of crystal lining the walls of the tunnel that opened into a great chamber. "Everything is as it should be."

"You do realize you had said that the last time? And yet, by some miracle, those meddlesome mortals managed to survive every *deadly* obstacle you placed before them."

"And who told you that my intention was to kill them?" grunted Dragonite, thrusting the torch back into the wall mount next to his crystal throne. He then snapped his fingers, motioning to the shorter, fatter mime standing to the right of this throne to take his position, as the other one continued to stand guard.

Without a word of protest, the mime dropped on all fours. He allowed his back to sway just so, adjusting the curve of his spine so the Sorcerer could prop his legs up, resting them in complete comfort.

"Do you take me for a fool?" grumbled Loken. "I saw the design behind those obstacles you conjured up! You cannot tell me they were created to simply *maim* anyone trying to pass through them. They were meant to kill, but did a poor job of it."

"They were deliberately designed to scare them. If one or two were maimed or killed along the way, so be it. But I designed those obstacles to exact a level of fear that was so intense, those two dolts the Princess fancies as her bodyguards would abandon her on this mission."

"You said you needed the Princess alive. It could easily have been her to be killed along the way."

"I hardly think so," muttered Dragonite, leaning back on his glistening throne as he dismissed this comment.

"You sound so sure of yourself," noted Loken, as he landed on the throne's armrest.

"This is Princess Rose-alyn of Fleetwood you speak of! That coward of a self-serving, self-centred, spoiled princess will always send forth that knave of a knight and that fool of a jester before her, to test the way, before she would even think of advancing."

"I suppose you are right. And as fate would have it, they made it all the way to your '*secret*' lair. So this must beg the question: Were the obstacles you created *deadly-scary* enough? For according to your account, those mortals were rather unfazed when they came upon you, dragon or no dragon guarding your lair."

"I beg to differ!" snorted Dragonite. "In hindsight, they only seemed unfazed, when in reality, they were so shaken by the ordeal they were still in shock. Their actions were rote, merely going through the motions, in a desperate bid to stay alive in my formidable presence."

"Well then, they were a high-functioning, traumatized trio!" Loken shook his head in dismay.

"It is possible," grunted the Sorcerer. He rested his chin on tented fingers, contemplating his latest plot.

"In your dreams!" Loken dismissed Dragonite's words as he slid an index finger across his throat. "I say, outright kill them this time. Nice and easy, be done with them, save for the Princess, if you're still so convinced she is the key to unlocking the dreamstone's powers."

"She *is* the answer! As for doing away with her cohorts '*nice and easy*'? I think not! I have a reputation to uphold, one that has taken years to cultivate."

"So?"

"All it takes is a single, careless moment of ineptitude to destroy what I had worked a lifetime to build."

"Who cares? Everyone, from the citizens of Fleetwood to the

Dwarves in the Land of Big and beyond, knows that you are bad. So what?"

"*Bad?* A child who pulls his sibling's hair is bad... A servant who nicks from his master's wine cellar is bad... I had strived all these years to be *Evil*, with a capital *E!*"

"Oh, like the capital *E* in Egomaniac? Egocentric, Egregious..." offered Loken.

"Egre- what?" sputtered Dragonite, his eyes narrowing in contempt as he glared at Loken.

"Egregious, meaning to be outstandingly bad." The Sprite explained while using a mocking tone.

"*Enough* of your impudence!" snarled the Sorcerer, as he snatched up the tiny being in his hand. His fist clenched, squeezing around Loken's body.

In a swell of light, the Pooka instantly transformed. He disappeared in Dragonite's grip, only to reappear as the Sorcerer yelped in pain, abruptly releasing him.

Using powerful pincers, Loken employed the mandibles of the beetle form he assumed, biting the palm of his tormentor's hand. Landing on the throne's armrest, the Sprite pivoted the rotating, nozzle-like tip of his posterior at the Sorcerer. The noxious chemicals that neared the boiling point in a special abdominal chamber was ready to spray into his opponent's eyes if he was accosted again.

"When will you learn? Do not touch me!" Loken snapped in a tiny insect voice.

"I will learn not to throttle you when you learn not to test my patience!" growled Dragonite, positioning his finger and thumb to flick the beetle of a Pooka off the armrest.

Before he could do so, the Sorcerer's hand sprang back as Loken morphed again, this time, into a sleek, black snake, coiled and ready to strike.

"You try, you die!" hissed Loken, his mouth agape to reveal razor-sharp fangs. "You'll be dead before you can take three steps or conjure up a cure to save your miserable life!"

"That may be so, but not before I can destroy *this!*"

Holding up the tiny vial of potion the Sprite desperately needed, he dared Loken to attack. The Sorcerer threatened to snap it in two, allowing the vial's contents to spill, its powers to dissipate.

"We both act in haste," reasoned Loken. In a swell of light, he assumed his usual form, launching off the throne to hover before Dragonite's scowling face.

"You were the one to act in haste! I acted within reason!"

"Though I am small in size, it does not mean I have a decreased capacity to remember!" argued Loken, his wings rattling with indignation. "As always, you were the one to grab me first! And then, you had the unmitigated gall to try and snuff the life from me in your bony, old hand!"

"I will admit to grabbing you, but it was for good reason."

"You don't say?" The Pooka grunted as he scowled in annoyance. "I'd like to hear it."

"Well, I... I seemed to have developed an involuntary spasm in my hands," lied the Sorcerer, making up an excuse as he spoke. "In times of great stress, my hands have a mind of their own, clenching onto things that happen to get in the way."

"Oh... So, now I'm in your way, am I?" Loken seethed with resentment.

"Not at this very moment, but this action is almost like an involuntary reflex, so you better not cause me undue stress, if you get my meaning?"

The Sprite backed off, hovering a safe arm's-length away from the Sorcerer before commenting. "You manufacture your own stress without any of my help. Which brings us back to the subject of killing the Princess and her cohorts, should they try to rescue their gangly friend and steal away with the magic crystal."

"I say again, the Princess lives...for now. As for her loyal, but foolhardy comrade? Ultimately, the boy is dispensable, so too, any fool Elf or Wizard wishing to aid her on this quest."

"So, killing them is *not* out of the question?" queried Loken, his amber eyes lighting up with hope.

"Oh, rest assured, they *will* die. It is only a matter of how I intend to dispatch them. And, as I said before, I have a reputation, an evil reputation, to uphold. When I decide it is time for them to die, I intend to do so in such a way it will send a swift and chilling message of the mayhem I plan to unleash unto this world. And let us not forget the suffering I shall inflict upon those who oppose my will."

"Then you must have a sinister plan in the works?"

"Sinister *and* diabolical," promised Dragonite, nodding in confirmation as his beady eyes gleamed with malice.

"You do know those two words basically mean the same thing, don't you? Just call it an evil plan and leave it at that."

"They are mere words, but my evil plan is more than just *evil*. It will be diabolically sinister. *Mwa ha ha ha!*"

"You just like to hear yourself talk." Loken rolled his eyes in frustration as he muttered, "And will you stop it with that silly laugh. It makes you sound demented, not sinister."

"I will ignore that comment, and of course I love the sound of my voice! There is good reason I surround myself with speechless mimes." Dragonite took certain delight in poking with the tip of his staff the mime crouched on his hands and knees before him.

The mime merely grimaced, mouthing the word *'ouch'* as he endured the abuse.

"Unlike you, they do not complain, nor do they talk back! And as all you do is constantly snivel and whine, I deliberately choose to block out your *noise*. Therefore, of course I'd enjoy the dulcet tones of my velvety voice, whenever possible."

"Fine! So what is this plan you've hatched?"

"I intend to lure the Princess to my lair."

"And? What about her loyal cohorts and anyone else foolish enough to follow in her footsteps?"

"They will come to understand it is better to hand her over to me, than to endure her shenanigans, and then be on their merry way."

"What is so sinister about that? I thought you said you planned to kill them?"

"Oh… I do and I will! Just when they believe I am letting them go, when their guard is down and they are secure in the thought they are free men, that is when I will strike!"

"Yes!" exclaimed Loken, his tiny fists pumping the air. "Kill them all, nice and easy!"

"No easy-peasy here!" admonished Dragonite, shaking a stern finger at the Pooka. "I have every intention of savouring my victory. I will kill them as I see fit to do so."

"By what means?"

"Torture!"

"Oh, here we go again! You plan to torture them to death?" groaned Loken, his hand smacking his forehead.

"The skills required to torture one's victim effectively is an art unto itself! It will be a slow, lingering but horrible death, I'll guarantee you that! It has as much to do with the unhinging of one's mind as it does with destroying the physical body. This is a challenge I look forward to with great anticipation."

"Well, judging by your last victim, it is an art you have yet to master. In the end, you failed at destroying his body, but you certainly managed to unhinge his mind, enough to make him forget everything you've done to him." As a sign of an addled brain, Loken's index finger twirled by the side of his head.

"What can I say? He was a tough nut to crack, excuse the pun," chortled Dragonite. With a smirk of a grin on his face, the Sorcerer's arms swung as though bringing down an invisible axe. "But this time, not so much. His body is as frail as his mind is!"

"Then where is the challenge in that?"

"Oh, I just wish to torture and kill that git out of spite, for living the first time. The fun and challenge will be in doing away with that knave of a knight the Princess travels with. And do you know what is worse than being tortured?"

"What?" asked Loken.

"Watching your friends, as *they* are being tortured!" responded the Sorcerer, as his thin, drawn lips curled into an evil smile and his gnarled hands wrung together in eager anticipation.

"And if the Dream Merchant is still by their side when they arrive here?"

"Bonus! I will make Silas Agincor suffer as I see fit. When I learn how to manipulate the powers of the dreamstone, irony of ironies, I will use it against him."

"And the Elves? Suppose Agincor travels in their company?"

"If they are foolish enough to do so, then they will become mere casualties of my sinister plan," replied Dragonite, dismissing this matter with a wave of his hand.

"You sound confident."

"I am oozing with confidence," gloated the Sorcerer.

"You're oozing alright, but I don't think that's what it is," Loken muttered as he stared with utter disdain.

Dragonite glared at the Pooka, cursing him with a shake of his fist. "You are a vexation to my spirit! Go make yourself useful, before I take to torturing you."

"What will you have me do?"

"Go see to our *guest*. Check if that stick of a man managed to squeeze through the bars of his crystal prison to escape."

"Suppose he asks for water again?" asked Loken.

"Already taken care of!"

"Well… so much for making him suffer," sighed the Sprite, thinking Dragonite would deprive his prisoner of one of life's most basic necessities.

"Oh, he suffers alright! At this very moment his body continues to shrivel from the lack of water. And guess what the tortuous irony is?"

"The water is poisoned, should he drink it," offered Loken.

"That is *murder*, not torture!" grunted the Sorcerer. "The water is there, he just cannot get to it!"

"Hmph! That is both cruel and clever," praised the Sprite, nodding in approval.

"Indeed! And that idiot would have to be more clever than I am, a regular genius, if he manages to drink even a drop of it."

"I am intrigued," decided Loken, his wings rattling with excitement. "I must see this for myself."

"You do that. And when that fool is delirious from thirst, driven to the point of madness in his despair to drink water he can see, but not reach, perhaps then, I will show him mercy."

"How?"

"I will give him water, just enough to keep him alive so the Princess will see when I kill him."

"He doesn't plan to make it easy for me, does he?" Cankles muttered beneath his breath as he peered down the neck of a giant, crystal decanter that stood chest-high to him. It was just the perfect size, had he been a troll.

The mouth of this vessel was as wide as a large dinner plate, but this flared opening quickly narrowed down to its bulbous body. This is where the cold, fresh water pooled, waiting for him to drink. By the thickness of the crystal and the heaviness of its base, Cankles was sure it greatly outweighed him.

Grabbing hold of the lip of the vessel, he heaved. Pulling it toward him, he attempted to tip it so the water was within reach. Grunting and groaning as he struggled, this container refused to budge. After repeated tries, Cankles put his shoulder against it, once more, pushing with all his might. Still, it remained upright, firmly planted where it first appeared.

With his back braced against the prison wall and his feet propped against the neck of this vessel, Cankles pushed as hard as he could. His muscles quivered from the exertion as he grunted, straining with every ounce of strength he had left to topple over this container. Again, this odd water vessel remained unmoved.

By some strange magic it was either fused to the ground or was exceedingly heavy, so much so, that his repeated attempts to knock it over failed miserably.

This exercise left Cankles exhausted and thirstier than ever. He drew a deep breath, blotting the sweat from his brows, but he had become dehydrated to the point he no longer perspired profusely.

Licking his dried, cracked lips, he peered down the long, narrow neck, staring longingly at the refreshing water that remained out of his reach.

Extending both his arms before him, Cankles eyeballed each limb, determining that his right arm was slightly longer than the left. Pushing up his shirt sleeve, Cankles thrust his hand through the mouth and down the long, skinny neck. His eyes glowed with renewed hope. A small smile curled his lips as his fingertips dipped into the cold liquid.

"Yes!" exclaimed Cankles, curling his fingers to scoop up some water. Just as he lifted his cupped hand, the neck of the vessel impeded his movement. His hand was trapped. The only way to retract it was to relinquish the water so his hand could squeeze back through the narrow opening.

"Damn!" Cankles cursed under his breath.

Like mercury, the liquid slipped through his fingers. Retracting his hand, he pulled it free. Even as this trace of moisture mingled with the dirt and the saltiness from the palm of his sweaty hand, he was not about to let it go to waste, eagerly licking the drops of water from his fingers.

Thumping his head against this object of frustration, Cankles pondered this dilemma.

"Well, I guess if I can't get to the water, the water better come to me."

Picking up chunks of crystal littering his prison, he inspected them, making sure they were of the appropriate size. Brushing the dust from them, one by one, he dropped each down the narrow neck. The more crystals filled the bulbous base, the higher the water level climbed. Eventually, the cold, fresh liquid crept higher, meeting the rim of the vessel.

"Wonderful!" exclaimed Cankles, sighing with relief. He slapped the dust from his hands before dipping them into the water. Scooping up a handful, he raised it to his cracked lips, savouring every drop.

"Aah! So good," whispered Cankles. Blotting his wet hands against his face, he then used the sleeve of his shirt to wipe it dry. "Refreshing!"

"Hey! What do you think you're doing?"

Cankles glanced up, surprised to see the glow of the Pooka's aura shining in the corridor leading to his prison cell.

"I was having a drink," answered Cankles, his bony shoulders arching in a shrug. "I asked the Sorcerer for a drink of water, and this is what he left me. Had to make do."

"But, but –" sputtered Loken, as he landed on one of the slanted crystal bars of this prison. "Dragonite said it was impossible for you to get the water."

"More like difficult, but it wasn't impossible. Do you want some? There's still plenty. Seems to be magic as the level hasn't dropped, even after I drank a whole lot of it."

"But how? How did you get the water?" Loken scratched his head in bewilderment. "It was supposed to be unattainable!"

"Maybe for some, but it wasn't that hard. I just figured that if I couldn't reach the water, I'd make it so I could. I just dropped a bunch of loose crystals into that oversized jug until the water came up, high enough for me to reach it."

"That was brilliant!" praised Loken, stunned by this simpleton's resourcefulness.

"I'd like to think I'm smarter than a bird, but I don't think crows are really *that* brilliant. They can be clever though," commented Cankles.

"What are you talking about? What crows?"

"I've seen a crow do this before. A farmer had some jugs of milk he was goin' to take to market. This crow wanted to steal some, but its beak was just beyond reaching the milk. I watched that bird as it dropped rocks and pebbles into the jug, enough that the milk rose up high enough for the crow to sneak a drink."

"Clever of the crow to figure that out and how humbling it must be for you to admit you had to learn this trick from a bird," scoffed Loken, shaking his head.

"No shame in that! It'd be far more humbling, and kind of foolish, too, to die of thirst than to use whatever means possible to get that water, even if it means learning it from a bird."

"Well, I must admit, I am duly impressed, being that you achieved what the Sorcerer had deemed as impossible," announced the Sprite.

"If that was a compliment, then thank you."

"Oh, don't thank me! Just think of it this way; by figuring out how to get that water, you'll be able to live longer."

"Living longer is good."

"Yes, but in your case, no," stated Loken, his words matter-of-fact.

"What do you mean?"

"It means you have only extended your life. It will be just enough to prolong your agony and horror when you see what Dragonite has in store for you."

"I take it, it won't be pretty," gulped Cankles, taking a tentative step closer to Loken.

"You're bloody right about that!"

Loken jumped with a start, taking to the air as the Sorcerer appeared from the shadows of the long, dark corridor.

Cankles' hands wrapped around the crystal bars that separated him from his captor. Pressing his face through the bars, he stared at the Sorcerer. "You have the dreamstone now. What do you want with me?"

"You are meant to be here," answered Dragonite, giving his prisoner a knowing smile.

"No… no I'm not. I'm supposed to be in Fleetwood. At least, that's where I was supposed to be once this quest was done."

"You are exactly where I want you! In fact, a cruel twist of fate has brought us together once again," said Dragonite, as he pondered his prisoner's desperate situation.

"No, I'm thinkin' it was more like dumb luck," stated Cankles.

"Hush, you dolt! I believe the stars have aligned in my favour this time. You are my prisoner once more!"

"Did you take a knock to your head with that blast you created to escape? I was never your prisoner… until now."

"Yes, you were," sniffed the Sorcerer, nodding in confirmation.

"Are you mad, as in crazy mad, not incensed mad?" grunted Cankles, his index finger spinning by his head. "Until now, I had never been your prisoner, unless you're speakin' of that little dilemma in the dragon's keep that got me here in the first place."

"Oh, stop your inane babbling!" snapped Dragonite, bashing the prison with his staff. "Think back to our very first encounter, long ago."

Cankles scratched his head in thought, recalling when he, in the company of Tag and Princess Rose quite literally stumbled upon the Sorcerer and his army of mimes. The excursion to see the Dwarves in the Land of Big had proven fruitless and the trio was forced to return westward, travelling through Dragonite's domain on their journey home.

"Well, unless you have a different concept about the passin' of time, it was less than a fortnight that we had our first encounter with you, if I remember correctly."

"Unbelievable! You truly are an idiot of the greatest magnitude!" mocked Dragonite, snorting in disgust.

"I'll be the first to admit I'm not the best at rememberin' details, but I'm not so stupid to forget that our allies, the Trolls, Elves and the King of Axalon's army soundly trounced your rabble of mimes, while the Princess handily defeated the shape-shifting Sprite, dragon against dragon."

"I let her win that time!" snapped Loken, forcing Cankles to duck as he dove at his head to yank a fistful of hair.

"You fool!" shouted the Sorcerer. He glared at Loken, motioning for silence as he continued to address his prisoner. "I was not speaking of *that* incident. I was speaking of the one well before it!"

"How much before?" asked Cankles.

"Think back! Think back ten years ago."

"Sorry, but I barely remember what I did ten days ago. How am I to recall something that happened a decade past?"

"Damn you! Think! Think back to your first ill-fated encounter with me!" cursed the Sorcerer, the staff trembling in his grip. "The mere mention of my name should strike fear in your heart."

Cankles rubbed his stubbly chin in pensive thought as he searched his feeble mind for this supposed memory.

"Well?" grunted the Sorcerer.

"Nope! Can't say I remember."

"How about this?" asked Dragonite, turning sideway as he struck a pose. "Surely you remember this dignified profile? It must conjure up overwhelming feelings of fear, does it not?"

"Not really… Unless you're tryin' to tell me you somehow beat me up with your nose. Other than that, with a profile like yours, it actually makes me wonder how you can breathe through that long, skinny, broken schnozz."

"I can breathe just fine! But never mind this proud proboscis," snapped Dragonite. "Focus! How can you forget? You *must* remember me."

"Can't say I do… No offence, but I guess you're just not that memorable."

"Oh, fetch off! Do not raise my ire."

"Sorry, but it's just a fact of life. We're not all the memorable type."

"And yet, I remember *you!* I know who you were, where you came from and what happened to your miserable, lowly life that turned you into the pathetic excuse of a man that you are now," grunted the Sorcerer.

Cankles pressed his face between the bars as he scrutinized those dark, recessed eyes staring back at him.

"What say you now?" asked Dragonite.

"Naw, nobody knows anything about my past," corrected Cankles, "not even me."

He jumped back with a start as the Sorcerer bashed the crystal bars with his staff, snarling in utter frustration.

"Do not test my patience!"

"Then don't test my memory, 'cause where you're concerned, I don't remember a thing. In fact, I think you're lyin' to me." Cankles dared to say. "You're just tryin' to mess with my mind, but too bad for you, it's already been messed up."

"I know plenty!" snorted Dragonite. "And I know how your mind got that way."

"Prove it."

"Oh, you don't want to be asking for that," groaned Loken, his wings rattling as he shuddered.

The Sorcerer's bony index finger flicked Cankles' forehead as he growled at his prisoner. "It is all locked up in here. All you must do is remember; unlock those memories."

"But I don't and I can't remember," insisted Cankles, his shoulders rolling in a shrug. "Nothing to unlock in this old noggin."

"Do you not want to remember who and what you once were?" questioned Dragonite. "Do you not want to know what happened to you? How you received those scars that mar your body?"

"Why would I want to know that? In my mind, I must have done something terrible, truly heinous even, to be punished as I was. If I was a criminal, then I've atoned for my sins. I'm sure of it!" Cankles spoke with conviction while his fingertip traced the scar on his head now hidden by a mop of hair.

"*Criminal?* You were never a criminal, at least in the minds of the free people who opposed me," snorted Dragonite, laughing as his hand slapped his bony thigh.

"What is that supposed to mean?"

"Think, you moron!" The Sorcerer's hand reached through the bars to smack his prisoner on the head.

"Now *that* did not help," grumbled Cankles, rubbing his smarting head.

"Then how about this!" Dragonite heaved a large, heavy disk at him. With a loud clatter, the object landed on the ground before the prison cell.

Cankles peered down at it.

"What say you now? Remember what this is?"

"I'm not daft, of course I know. Anyone can tell you this *thing* is a shield, a crack'd shield at that."

"Yes, but does it not look familiar to you?"

Examining the old piece of weaponry, it was immediately obvious it had seen war on more than one occasion. The steel boss was scratched, dented and dulled by patches of rust or blood while the wood radiating from the boss was faded. Along the edges trimmed with brass, the red paint and the gold leaf that once gilded it were now chipped and flaking off. He could see where the blade of a battle-axe had bit into the wood, cracking the shield right down to the metal boss where the leather strap used to secure the shield to the forearm was mounted.

"It's a broken shield! So what?"

"You are either a complete dolt or your memory has been truly and surely impaired!" sputtered Dragonite.

"It's an equal measure of both, methinks," decided Loken, as he hovered over the Sorcerer's shoulder.

"What must I do to rekindle that spark of a memory?" asked Dragonite, groaning in exasperation.

"No spark. No memory," said Cankles, as his search through the dark vestiges of his mind turned up nothing. "I haven't the slightest idea what you're talkin' about."

"*Argh!* Damn you! You mean to drive me insane with your stupidity," raged Dragonite.

"I'm *forgetful*, not stupid," corrected Cankles, using an index finger to tap his head. "This old noggin is damaged, but it's not completely broken."

"Then let me show you something that will really help to jog that addled brain of yours! Perhaps it will *whip* your feeble memory into shape," cackled Dragonite, laughing at his own pun as he turned away to retrieve a special device of torture.

"Oh my! You're just so eager to die, aren't you?" rebuked Loken, as he hovered before Cankles' confused face.

"Not really… I don't relish the idea at all."

"Then why are you baiting the Sorcerer, pretending you remember nothing of your time spent with him?"

"I think you are mistaken, little Sprite. Parru St. Mime Dragonite is definitely not the type of person I'd socialize with. I'm no genius, but I do know I'd have no desire to spend any time with that madman. It'd be an unlikely friendship."

"*Friendship?*" Loken shook his head in dismay. "There is no love lost between you two, that's for sure. That deranged necromancer tried to kill you back then!"

"Say again!"

"Well actually, Dragonite tortured you first, and then he tried to kill you, but he wasn't very good at it either."

"How do you know this?" asked Cankles, as he frowned in confusion.

"I was there."

"Really?"

"Shall I refresh your memory before the Sorcerer returns and *forces* you to remember?" offered Loken.

"Do you think that's a good idea?"

"It's better than the option Dragonite will present to you." The Sprite's hand snapped an imaginary whip in the air as a sign of things to come.

"You really know about me?" asked Cankles, his fingertip tracing the bare patch on his scalp. "How I received all these scars?"

"I know you are not the criminal you think you were. And yes, I can tell you how you acquired all those nasty scars, including the one on your head."

"Why would you tell me this?" questioned Cankles, staring suspiciously at the Sprite.

"I can be accused of being many things, but the one thing I am *not* is cruel," confessed Loken. "Dragonite intends to kill you. That being the case, I had recommended he do so swiftly."

"You want that madman to kill me? To do so quickly?" gasped Cankles, drawing his index finger across his throat.

"I know it sounds terrible, but believe me, quick and easy is far better than to endure a lingering, drawn out agony," advised Loken. "In all honesty, I don't think I can stomach seeing you tortured again. It was messy business, for sure!"

"Truly? I was actually tortured by the Sorcerer?"

"Allow me to refresh your memory. Once Dragonite's mercenaries captured you, they dragged you back to the Sorcerer's lair."

"Which lair?"

"The one in the Bad Lands. Why? What difference does it make?" questioned Loken.

"Just hopin' for a frame of reference… a small clue that might help me to remember something, anything really. But never mind, carry on."

"As I was saying, his mercenaries dragged you back to his lair. Once there, Dragonite first tried to bribe you to speak by depriving you of food and water."

"Nasty!"

"That was nothing. When you said you'd rather never taste a morsel of food or swallow a drop of water again than to give away your secrets, that's when Dragonite went medieval on you."

"He did?"

"First, he took a great mallet to your ankles so you'd be hobbled; unable to escape. He then strung you up on the racks, taking a whip to you."

"Oh my! Now that *is* nasty!" Cankles' eyes opened wide in horror.

"And it wasn't just any whip he took to your hide," recalled Loken. "He has a special leather whip, one that is tipped with barbed, metal hooks. These hooks are not large by any means, but once the metal bites into skin and muscle just so, it can denude the bones of flesh."

"Say no more!" cried Cankles.

He dropped to his knees as a painful memory seared through his mind. It was as though he could feel the bite of steel-studded leather strips lashing across his back once more.

"You were lashed within a hair's-breadth of your life. When you still refused to speak, Dragonite said, *'If you do not speak to me, then I shall make it so you will never speak again'*. That's when he took the black crystal atop his staff to your face. He bashed you but good, shattering your jawbone."

Cankles' hands slapped over his mouth. His eyes watered as an echo of a memory flashed in the darkest corner of his mind. He shuddered, sobbing as the sharp tang of blood, the taste of copper trickling down his throat, overwhelmed him. It felt and tasted as vivid and real as it did all those years ago.

"When the Sorcerer failed to break your stubborn resolve; that you chose death before dishonour, he granted your wish…"

With his heart racing, pounding in his ears, the floodgate that repressed all of Cankles' forgotten memories burst forth. His mind reeled and his stomach churned as he relived this horrifying ordeal in his mind's eye.

"That was when he took up a great axe to cleave your head," revealed Loken, shuddering as he recalled the grim aftermath.

These words echoed in Cankles' mind. He heaved, retching as the *'crunch'* of a dull axe biting into his head to crack his skull sounded from the inside out, ringing in his ears. His vision blurred, his world spinning into a black abyss as he keeled over unconscious.

"Hey… I was just getting to the best part!" grumbled Loken, hovering over Cankles' prostrate body. "I was about to tell you how I saved your life."

Loken froze as a great shadow swallowed up his form. He gulped down the lump that hitched in the back of his throat, turning slowly to gaze upon the Sorcerer.

"Ah-ha! So you were the one to deliver him to the Elves!" snarled Dragonite. "I knew you could not be trusted."

Before the startled Sprite could transform or fly away from danger, the tip of Dragonite's staff came down, pinning him to the ground.

"I will teach you to never betray me again!"

Loken howled in agony. Brilliant spots of white light danced before his eyes as the world dissolved into black.

5
These are Strange Times

"Well… aren't we the unlucky pair?"

Loken stirred from his unnatural sleep. These words droned in his ears as he opened his eyes, only to squeeze them shut. He winced, accosted by the light of the torch burning overhead. Groaning in pain, he forced his bleary eyes open once more to focus on his crystalline surroundings.

Moaning as he rolled from his side onto his back, Loken bolted upright as a shock of pain stabbed between his shoulder blades.

"Lyin' on your back isn't a good idea at the moment," stated Cankles, speaking in a whisper. "Your wings, at least, what's left of them will probably be hurtin' for a while to come."

Loken's eyes flashed wide open as his hands groped about, feeling his back, high between the shoulders.

"What happened?" asked Loken.

"Well, thanks to you, I passed out," answered Cankles.

"I remember that much."

"Then thanks again to you, I woke up. Heard your tiny scream of pain. Opened my eyes in time to see the Sorcerer marchin' away, leavin' you here like this, in this wretched condition."

The last thing Loken remembered was the crackling, like the sound of crumpling parchment, and then the snap and popping of bone ripped from flesh. Flexing his sore flight muscles, Loken could tell the larger primary wings were intact, but immediately, he felt off kilter. The left secondary wing was still there, but now, the right side of this pair was missing.

"Oh, no…" groaned the Sprite.

"Oh, yes!" Cankles nodded his head. "In my way of reckonin' though, I don't think it's really that bad."

"How can you say that? This is *very* bad!"

"Well, I don't know about that," said Cankles, attempting to downplay the severity of this crippling wound. "When you have your wings closed and folded down against your back, you really can't tell that the smaller bottom one is missin'."

"What good is that?" grumbled Loken. "I am a Sprite, a Pooka to be exact! I was born to fly. And these wings were new!"

Ever the optimist, Cankles chirped up, "You can still fly, maybe not in a straight line right now, but you can still take to the air if you really wanted to. I'm sure of it."

"Oh great! Lovely! Absolutely lovely!" sputtered Loken, as the sarcasm rose in his tone. "I can just spend my days flying in circles. What a bloody waste!"

"Depends."

"On what?"

"Well, if you're spinnin' about, flyin' in real tight circles, then yes, it will feel like you're going nowhere. Now, if that circle is really, really wide," Cankles threw out his arms as far as he could, "it'll feel like you're flying in almost a straight line. You just need to adapt a little."

"You mean adapt *a lot*," sighed Loken. He grimaced in pain as he tried to roll his stiff shoulders that were wrapped beneath a swathe of makeshift bandage. "Did you do this?"

"I tried to do the best I could with what little I had." Cankles sounded almost apologetic, as he fiddled with the ragged hem of his trousers. "I shredded a small piece of cloth, wrappin' a tiny strip around where that wing was plucked off."

"It burns," groaned Loken, his fingertips barely able to reach behind to touch the wound.

"Of course it does. Though it didn't look like much blood to me, for you, it was a lot. The only way I was able to stop the bleedin' was to burn the wound and do so right away."

"You did *what?*" Loken spun about like a dog chasing its tail as he tried to inspect his back. He stopped this spinning when he caught a glimpse of his reflection against a flat shard of crystal.

"I took a burnin' splinter from that torch and used it," replied Cankles, explaining how he cauterized the wound. "Figured that being so puny, you couldn't afford to lose much in the way of blood."

"But what happened to my wing? What did you do with it?"

"I didn't do anything to your wing. I'm guessin' the Sorcerer was gettin' some kind of revenge on you. I woke up to your little scream and to that madman laughin' like the lunatic he is. He had one of your wings between his fingers as he stormed away from here, mutterin' something about teachin' you a lesson."

"Bastard!" cursed Loken, his remaining wings trembling with rage.

"Who? Me?"

"Sure, but I was speaking of Dragonite!" grunted Loken. "I'll get even with that demented soul!"

"Sounds grand, but you best let that wound heal up sufficiently before you go around tryin' to exact any kind of revenge on the Sorcerer," recommended Cankles.

"Then it's a good thing I heal quickly." Loken untied the simple knot Cankles used to secure the bandage. Unwinding the strip from around his body, the Sprite slowly rolled his aching shoulders, gingerly flexing his flight muscles.

Other than the missing appendage, some dried blood and traces of soot from Cankles' attempt at cauterizing the injury, the gaping wound from where Dragonite had snapped and plucked the wing was healed over. There was barely a scab that remained as a testament of the Sorcerer's cruelty.

"I will never fly again."

"You don't know that until you try," encouraged Cankles. "I can help you learn to fly again, if you'd like."

"How?" Loken's voice tightened with skepticism.

"Maybe start with just movin' your wings. Get the blood flowin' through them flight muscles again," suggested Cankles. "It might prickle to begin with, like when my foot falls asleep. It could even be a little painful to do so right now, but it's a start."

Loken gingerly flexed these healing muscles. In response, his wings quivered, flapping slowly at first. Wincing in pain, the Pooka concentrated his efforts. Lifting off, he wobbled about, trying to compensate for the loss of the smaller, secondary wing. Easier than slowing down the stronger side while speeding up the damaged one, Loken adjusted his posture, tilting his body so the weaker side was now subjected to less wind resistance.

With grim determination, Loken laboured to straighten his flight path. Drawing in a deep breath, he calmed his anger and frustration as he veered sharply to avoid a crystal spike jutting from the ceiling. He was so focused on controlling his direction he was able to ignore the pain throbbing in his now-aching muscles. Wobbling to and fro, and then tilting to adjust, the Pooka increased his speed, hoping the force of the forward momentum would help propel him in a straight line.

"Whoa! Slow down!" ordered Cankles. "Nice and easy, does it!"

Forgetting he'd require greater distance to stop now, with a squawk of fright, Loken crashed into the mortal's chest even as Cankles attempted to back away.

"Oof!" groaned Loken. He crumpled into a heap as he fell into Cankles' open hand.

"I gotcha! You're safe now."

"That was neither *nice,* nor was it *easy!* You should've let me fall, put me out of my misery," grumbled the Pooka, his clenched fists pummelling Cankles' palm in frustration. "That was a failed attempt if ever there was one!"

"I beg to differ! To not try at all, to quit before you've begun, is the ultimate failure."

"What do you know?" dismissed Loken, as he dusted off his raiment while mustering his composure and what dignity he had left.

"I know you were most definitely flyin', Master Sprite," assured Cankles. "I admit it wasn't perfect, but I know enough that with more practice, you can do it."

"I can?"

"Of course you can! I suggest for next time, start off slower, so you don't crash into a wall or me again."

"What's the use? My right wing is too weak to fly without a complete set! As I am now, I'll never again fly as I did before."

"True! So you will learn to fly again, as you are now."

"But how?" snapped Loken. He paced dejectedly along this mortal's open hand.

"Trust me."

"I trust no one!"

"That is you're first mistake, little sir! Now, this time, take off slowly. I want to see what you're doin' wrong and together, we'll make it right," insisted Cankles.

"Fine, but it won't make an iota of a difference," grumbled Loken, preparing to take flight.

Priming his muscles, with wings a-quiver with nervous energy, the Sprite pushed off, hovering before Cankles' face.

Angling his body about while adjusting the beating of his wings, Loken gradually steadied himself.

"Now, what will you have me do?"

"Travel, as straight as you can, away from me and toward those bars," ordered Cankles, his finger pointing across the prison.

Without complaint or words to defy him, Loken fluttered to the barrier of crystal, struggling all the way to adjust his flight. Narrowly missing one crystal spike, he slowed down, stumbling as he attempted a landing on another bar.

"So, what do you think?" questioned Loken.

"Well, for starters, you keep veerin' to the right 'cause your left side is stronger; kinda like paddling a boat with just one oar."

"You don't think I know that already?"

"I thought I'd start at the root of the problem," explained Cankles, startled and hurt by the diminutive being's unwarranted eruption. "Anyways, I think you might just need to build up the strength of your lone right wing, or try to rely less on your left wing to balance out the strength."

"Tell me something I do not know," Loken snorted.

"Also try tiltin' your body more squarely to where you want to go, like the way you look toward where you'd want to steer a horse when you're ridin'."

"I don't ride horses!"

"I know that, but just try what I said and see what happens this time."

With a disgruntled huff, Loken launched off the spike of crystal, struggling to level off before flying toward his cellmate.

"Alrighty! Stop glancin' over your shoulder to see your right wing. It's flappin' just fine. Look right at me! That's it! Tip that shoulder, raise the other and…" Placing his hand out for Loken to land on, he praised the Sprite. "There ya go! Not bad at all!"

"You're right… it wasn't bad. It was terrible! I had to struggle every inch of the way."

"So you did!" Cankles agreed with a judicious nod. "But tell me this, Master Loken. When you were a wee one just learnin' to fly for the first time, did it come naturally to you? Was your very first flight graceful and without mishap?"

"Of course not! I had to learn how to control my wings, gauge my speed and adjust my landing so I wasn't constantly crashing into things. It was not something that was learned overnight, you know?"

"Well, then! Just think of this whole exercise as learnin' how to fly all over again," suggested Cankles, giving him a knowing wink of his eye.

Loken rubbed his chin in thought as he rolled his shoulders to loosen the tense flight muscles between the shoulder blades. He drew a deep breath as he considered the man's words.

"I suppose you're right."

"See! It wasn't so bad," said Cankles, nodding in approval. "You keep this up and you'll be flyin' as straight as one of those Elf arrows. Well… at least almost as straight as a slightly bowed one."

"So you say! But I cannot fly like this!" The Sprite's distraught face scowled in frustration. "Constantly fighting to fly in a straight line."

"Give it time and just keep tryin'. In no time, you won't have to fight it, it'll become second nature."

"So you say."

Exhausted by this session, Loken alighted upon the lip of the giant decanter, almost missing the rim as he adapted to his crippled flight. Using his hand to scoop some water, he quenched his thirst.

"It'll take some gettin' used to, but yes, I believe you can, if you put your mind to it," encouraged Cankles, joining Loken for a drink.

"But I have! It's useless…"

"You just have to keep workin' at it. If it's that important to you, then it's worth fightin' for. Just don't give up."

"My ability to fly *is* important to me! It is as vital to me as the ability to walk is for you."

"There you go then. Just think of this as a test, a pothole on the road of life. After all, you can't have a rainbow without a little rain fallin' from time to time."

"Look around you. There will be no escape and no rescue. There will be no salvation for you, nor will there be respite from this suffering for me," grunted Loken. "So, if trouble is a little rain, then we are both caught in the midst of a great deluge."

"But have you ever noticed that no matter how stormy the sky or how much rain comes down, eventually, the sun always comes out," countered Cankles.

Loken shook his head as he wiped the dribble of cold water trickling down his chin. "Who the heck made you so bloody optimistic?"

"Don't rightly know," answered Cankles, his shoulders rolling in a shrug. "Could be that I was born this way. Maybe at the lowest point in my life, when life itself knocked me flat on my back, I couldn't help but stare up at the stars."

"What's that supposed to mean?"

"Well, I'm just sayin' that if you fall in the gutter and you're just lyin' there, at least if you stare up, you can admire the stars. Even from there, things don't look so bad. This alone can make you feel like there's some hope left in this world."

"So it's about being hopeful?" questioned Loken. He studied this mortal's face, seeing the twinkle in his eyes had not diminished, even as the prospect of sacrificing his life was a very real possibility the longer he stayed a prisoner.

Cankles scratched his stubbly chin, contemplating a meaningful answer that would make him seem somewhat intelligent to this minuscule being. "If you don't have hope, then you really have nothing

– nothing to keep you goin', that's for sure."

Loken drew a deep breath as he digested these profound words. "I think you're onto something."

"I am?"

"If I gave up hope, there'd be no reason to continue this dangerous alliance with Dragonite," confessed Loken.

"Why do you associate with that madman anyway, if I may ask? It seems like an odd pairin', if I do say so myself."

"These are strange times that promise to become stranger still. Life as I knew it, is no more." Loken ran a hand down his woeful face. "It is not by choice I am here."

"Well, call me a fool, and I know some do, but am I missin' something? I always had the distinct impression that you chose to be in cahoots with Dragonite."

"To the world it would appear so, but in reality, I am no different from you," confided the Sprite. "We are both prisoners to the Sorcerer."

"You're not trapped like I am." Cankles' hands slapped against the spears of crystal that imprisoned him. "You can come and go as you please. Well, maybe not so easily now, but you can leave if you choose to do so."

"It is true I am not trapped in the physical sense, but believe me, it is not by choice I do the Sorcerer's bidding."

"Really?" Cankles listened intently, eager to learn more.

"I suppose it is better to say, I am here because it is the only way to save the one I love," confessed Loken, his feet dangling over the edge of the water vessel as he rested.

"Love? Hmph! Interestin'… Love can make the sanest of men do the craziest of things, even things they'd never thought possible."

"Grief can do that, too," admitted the Sprite, "especially if it is for the one you loved and lost."

"What happened?"

"Why do you care?" responded Loken, heaving a disheartened sigh as he glanced up at Cankles' concerned face.

"I'm just tryin' to understand."

"What?"

"*You*, that's what! Just tryin' to make sense of all this madness," responded Cankles.

"But why? I'm still trying to figure out why you would help me in the first place. It's not as though I've made your life easy."

"True, you haven't made it easy at all," agreed Cankles.

"If anything, I am the one to blame for getting you in this predicament to begin with," reminded Loken.

"And a dire one it is. But I must make good of a bad situation. There was no pleasure in seein' you suffer, but I did find certain joy in tryin' to fix what I could of your wounded body and broken spirit."

"But that is what I do not understand. If I were you, I would smite me. The first chance I had, I would have done you in," confided Loken, his tiny fist pummelling his hand.

"Truly?" questioned Cankles, staring with raised eyebrows at the Sprite. "And this is behaviour the one you claim to love would approve of?"

"Of course!"

"Are you sure?" asked Cankles.

Loken thought long and hard on this question, pacing to and fro along the rim of the water vessel.

"Well?"

Loken stopped, turning to face the mortal so they were eye to eye. "She would goad me on, demanding I dispatch you immediately!"

Instead of recoiling in fear, Cankles began to chuckle.

"This is no laughing matter!" shouted Loken, his wings trembling in resentment. "I am serious."

"No... you are lyin', most definitely." Cankles' words were decisive.

"I – I am *not* lying!" sputtered the Sprite.

"Yes, you are." Cankles turned his back on Loken, walking to the far corner of his prison cell. "And you're not doin' a very good job of it either!"

"You dolt! Come back here!" snapped Loken, shaking a balled fist at Cankles. "I *am* speaking the truth!"

"You're speakin', but it certainly isn't the truth," scoffed Cankles, dismissing his cellmate with a wave of his hand. "And don't bother with your idle threats. They mean nothing, for you can do nothing to me, at least in your present condition."

"Why you!" snarled Loken. "I'll show you!"

"So you say, but I don't think so, not with that gimpy set of wings you have!"

Instead of morphing into a deadly creature with the power to dispatch this human with a single swipe of a mighty paw, the Pooka launched into flight. Cursing beneath his breath, Loken's amber eyes gleamed with an equal measure of malice and focused intention as his flight muscles adjusted, his shoulder tilting to compensate for the missing secondary wing. Like a barn swallow diving at a skulking cat, Loken swooped down at Cankles' head, yanking a fist full of hair as he passed.

"Owww!" yelped Cankles, ducking as the angry Pooka made another diving pass at him. "Hey! You did it! You can fly almost as well as you did before your mishap."

Loken came to a halt in mid-flight. With a slight adjustment, he hovered before Cankles' face. The pinpoints of fire burning in his eyes faded as he smiled. "You're right! I *can* fly!"

"See! I told you that you wouldn't be condemned to flyin' in circles," exclaimed Cankles, pleased to see his efforts and Loken's hard work had paid off.

Loken landed on Cankles' shoulder, sighing in relief as he came to rest. "You tricked me... You were goading me on, making me so mad I wouldn't think of what I couldn't do. I'd just react and did what I had to."

"And you reacted just the way I hoped you would. Mind you, could have done without havin' my hair pulled."

"You amaze me. I am confounded in ways I cannot even put into words," admitted Loken. He scratched his head in thought as he considered this mortal.

"Amazed and confounded in a good way?"

"I am not sure. I am still trying to figure you out."

"Not much to figure out here," claimed Cankles, a thumb jabbing his chest. "I tend to say what I think and I try to do what I say."

"Then answer me this. Why do you bother with me? I am the last person you should be helping," stated Loken, shaking his head in confusion.

"I don't know. Just seems to be the right thing to do. However, I do know if I were in your position, I'd sure appreciate a show of kindness, no matter how small, no pun intended."

"I can see why your friends are so loyal to you, in spite of some of the odd things you say and do."

"I love my friends, and I'm proud to admit that I tend to say and do what I hold true to my heart."

"Even if it rubs them the wrong way?" asked Loken.

"In my way of thinkin', those who mind, don't matter. Those who truly matter, really don't mind. My dear friends accept me the way I am, even puttin' up with my little idiotsyncrasies."

"You mean, *idio*syncrasies," corrected Loken.

"That, too!"

"So you say, but I am not your friend. There are no bonds that tie us; no reason to show me even a shred of kindness or mercy."

"Well, this might sound insignificant to you, but I believe that it is always better to make a single friend than to make a thousand enemies, or worse yet, a frienemy," explained Cankles.

"A *frie-ne*-what?"

"You know? An enemy who only pretends to be a friend, that kind of relationship can really mess you up. They act all loyal and trustworthy, but when push comes to shove, they'd throw you under a herd of stampedin' horses in a heartbeat."

"I'll grant you that, but isn't this train of thought rather simplistic? Making a friend instead of an enemy?"

"What can I say? I'm a simple man. I like simple. Look at it this way, would you have preferred it if I had killed you instead? Squashed you like a bug when I had the chance?"

"When you put it like that, yes, a friend is the better choice," admitted Loken, as he nodded in confirmation. "Still, you have every reason to turn your back on me, but you didn't."

"True, but I had more reason not to."

Loken shook his head in amazement. "You claim you are a simple man, yet your actions betray you. If I did not know better, I'd say you are complex beyond comprehension."

"And that's bad?"

The Sprite frowned as he stared suspiciously at the mortal. "I haven't decided yet."

"Well, I only know I am what I am, and I believe in makin' friends when I can, and avoid makin' enemies just as much. Plus, I know what my conscience will allow me to do. I felt compelled to help you, so I did. It's as simple as that."

"Aaah… So that is your simple, but devious plan! You mean to kill me with kindness!"

"No… wasn't thinkin' that at all."

"Oh, but by being kind to me, it makes it all the harder for *me* to want to kill *you!* Clever!" noted Loken, giving the mortal a shrewd wink of his eye.

"If it works, then I guess it was clever," agreed Cankles, "so clever, I didn't even know it."

"So why show me compassion?"

"You said you're not here by choice, that you are bound to the Sorcerer to save the one you love," reminded Cankles.

"So I did… What of it?"

"I believe if you have the capacity to love, then there is compassion somewhere in that tiny soul of yours," reasoned Cankles, as he nodded in approval.

"Compassion for another is an emotion that eludes me."

"I don't think so. If you have the capacity to love someone, you must have tremendous compassion."

"I hardly think so. Whatever grain of compassion I had is now buried deep within. It is all but gone now."

"I beg to differ," countered Cankles. "A dear friend of mine once told me compassion takes on many forms. From a token gesture of kindness to grand deeds of selflessness, they are all acts of compassion that mean the most to the recipient."

"And who said this? That dimwitted Princess of yours?" asked Loken, his tone cynical.

"No, in fact, it was a queen; the Queen of the Tooth Fairies to be exact! Pancecelia Feldspar was always quick to offer up some of her wisdom when I needed it."

The colour drained from Loken's face. His wings drooped sadly as he whispered the name, "Celia…"

"Well, even though she is not high on formality, she said none are to address her by that name. She goes by Pance these days."

"You know the Queen of the Tooth Fairies?" asked Loken, his eyes scrutinizing Cankles' face for the truth.

"I know it sounds preposterous, being that she's a queen and all, while I am just a commoner, but we've had marvelous conversations over tea and biscuits. She really is quite the lovely soul when you take the time to get to know her!"

"You are lying," denounced Loken.

"I don't lie, at least, not intentionally."

"Then you are lying now," snorted the Sprite

"No, I'm not. When you lie, you constantly have to remember what you lied about. With a memory like mine, it's easier to speak the truth than keepin' track of lies."

"I suppose."

"It's true. And as I said before, as hard as it is to believe, I know Pance quite well!"

"No… it's really not hard to believe at all. Celia – "

"You mean, Pance," corrected Cankles.

"When I knew her, she was Celia to me. And as I was saying, it is not preposterous at all. It was in her nature to extend a friendly hand to those who were kind and courteous to her," explained Loken, as he nodded in understanding.

"Well, where many grown-ups refuse to believe in Tooth Fairies, I never stopped believin' in them."

"Then you are a rare mortal in this cynical world. With the human race, if they cannot see it, they will not believe it to be so."

"But there are some like me that believin' makes it possible to see what others cannot."

"Like I said, you are a rare one."

As the Sprite grew silent, heaving a weary sigh, a flash of a revelation almost knocked Cankles off his feet.

"Pance was your ladylove!" declared Cankles, staring in surprise at the tiny being.

Loken neither admitted nor denied this revelation.

"She was the one you spoke of! She was the one you mentioned, the one you said you're here because it's the only way to save the one you love."

"What difference does it make?"

"It makes all the difference in the world! We have two threads that binds us, a shared friend in Pancecelia Feldspar and a common adversary in Parru St. Mime Dragonite."

"That is so, but what does it matter? To her, I am but a memory, if that."

"So what? I have more in common with you than you do with that crazy Sorcerer! If he means to endanger her life, then we can work together to save Pancecelia."

"Dragonite is not the one threatening her life, but he does hold the key to saving her, and ultimately, her kingdom," revealed Loken.

"Then we can work together to get that key."

"And what makes you think I can trust you to help me?" grunted Loken, as he stared suspiciously at this mortal.

"I wasn't the one to pluck the wing from your back, was I?" reminded Cankles, giving the Pooka a judicious nod of his head.

"Fine! Then what makes you think *I* am the one that can be trusted? After all, I told you things about your past, terrible things that made you pass out from the trauma of the news."

Cankles fell silent as he slumped down to the ground with the Sprite still perched on his shoulder.

"What say you now?"

"That depends."

"On what?" asked Loken.

"Whether you were the one instructin' the Sorcerer to torture me, or if you were an innocent bystander in the atrocities dealt to me."

"If I still had a conscience, I'd say being a witness to that event would hardly make me innocent, especially if I stood by and did nothing to help you."

"Did you try to help me?" questioned Cankles.

"For my part, I did. I recommended to Dragonite that he execute you with a quick beheading."

"I hardly call that helpin'!" gasped Cankles, fighting against a fragment of a memory scratching at the back of his mind.

"It is, when you consider how long and hard Dragonite took to torturing you. Believe me, a hasty decapitation was a more humane option," answered Loken, his words adamant. "And that was after almost starving you to death first."

Cankles gulped, forcing down the lump catching in the back of his throat. He watched as the Sprite took to the air, correcting his flight as he hovered before his face.

"I like neither option, but given the choices, I guess I'd be beholdin' to you for suggestin' a hasty beheadin'."

"As I said before; I have been called many things. I am admittedly mean-spirited when I want to be, but the one thing I am not is cruel," responded Loken.

"I think I understand."

"Well then, try this one on for size: I was the one to set you free the first time."

Cankles gasped, his brows furrowing in confusion. "Say again!"

"How do you think you got to Silverthorn's domain in the first place?" grunted Loken, offering him a knowing smile.

"Hurry!" urged Rainus, taking Rose's hands to help her down the slope of loose rubble.

"Should we wait here for your men?" asked Tag. Glancing over his shoulder, he could see the flames dying as the fire was pushed along by the winds, forcing it high up the volcano's slope where the sparse vegetation failed to fuel the flames.

The Elf stopped. Cocking his head, he listened. After a lingering moment, he made his decision. "We journey on."

By the look on his face and those decisive words, Tag knew it wasn't good. With such acute hearing, Lord Silverthorn would be able to hear his men, if they had survived the encounter with the monster dragon and were rushing down to join them.

"Are you sure?" asked Rose. The knot in her stomach and the dread in her heart warned there would now be no safety in numbers for them.

"Positive," answered Rainus, pulling her along. "We are on our own."

"This way," ordered Silas, pointing in the direction they were to take. The crystal orb atop his staff glowed, emitting just enough light to illuminate their immediate surroundings as they forged on.

With his keen eyes, Rainus spied something odd at the foot of the volcano. It became more obvious as they ventured down, ever closer.

"Look at that," whispered Rainus.

"At what?" asked Tag, as he and Rose strained to see in the dim glow of the Dream Merchant's crystal.

"This!" said the Elf.

"Can't see what you're talking about." Tag frowned in confusion as he squinted to see in the dark surroundings.

He and Rose jumped with a start as Rainus thrust a tattered note into their surprised faces. "I am speaking of this. It was impaled upon that broken tree branch."

Tag snatched the small piece of parchment from Rainus' hand, studying the smudged words written with the darkened tip of a burnt stick.

"What does it say?" asked Silas, holding forth the light of his crystal for Tag to better see.

The young man read the message aloud:

> *"To find the path to the end,*
> *Light the way to save a friend."*

"Other than being an atrocious rhyme, what is that supposed to mean?" grumbled Rose. "And who left it? It is not even signed."

"We are in the middle of dragon country," reminded Rainus. "Who else would be crazy enough to be here other than us?"

"The Sorcerer?" responded the Princess.

"Yes, none other than Parru St. Mime Dragonite," acknowledged Silas. He studied the scattering of footprints embedded in the ground.

"He was here," surmised Tag, studying the trampled earth.

"Come! Over here," called Rainus. His sharp eyes spied an opening to a tunnel leading into the volcano. "The Sorcerer made his escape from this very place."

"How can you tell?" asked Rose.

"This set of footprints tell the tale of how Dragonite escaped," explained the Elf, pointing to the ground at the mouth of the tunnel.

"Go on," invited Tag.

"The Sorcerer stood over there. See how the tip of his staff bit into the earth where he stepped, using it as a walking stick? A body, presumably your friend's, was dragged along here... Oh, and here is where a dragon or some winged beast picked up the body, taking him into the air, heading... looks like north-east."

"You can tell all that?" questioned Rose, her perfect brows furrowing in curiosity.

"It is all here, if you know what to look for," said Rainus, with a nod of confirmation.

"But what does this message mean?" Tag held up the crumpled parchment. *"Light what way?"*

"Obviously, a light will show us how to find Cankles Mayron," surmised Rainus, as he took the note from Tag's hand. Retracing his steps back to the branch he found it on, the Elf glanced about, searching for other clues.

"But what light? For if that demented soul was referring to the moon or the stars, we can be travelling in circles if we are wrong," warned Rose, stumbling about as she followed in Rainus' footsteps. "And worse yet, while we aimlessly search about, wasting time, Cankles might be forced to reveal to the Sorcerer how the dreamstone works."

"Over here!" said the Elf, pointing to the ground.

In a clearing nestled at the base of the old volcano, there rested a circle of rocks. Within this rocky formation was a small stack of kindling, neatly arranged over a loose clump of dried moss. Rainus knew these rocks were placed here deliberately, not so much to keep a fire from spreading, but to make this conspicuously obvious to all coming by this way.

"The best I can figure is that if we burn the wood, the light it casts shall reveal another clue to show us the way," determined Silas.

"The way into another *trap*," groaned Rose, dreading what was to come next.

"In all likelihood, yes." Rainus' words were matter-of-fact as he nodded.

"Oh, *lovely!*" snorted the Princess, rolling her eyes in frustration. "I thought the idea was to rescue Cankles and retrieve the dreamstone while *avoiding* another trap."

"You knew as well as I did that from the start this quest was not going to be easy," reminded Tag. "Of course there will be traps, probably even more and of far greater danger than the ones we first encountered."

"You are doing nothing to boost my confidence," groaned the Princess.

"The trick is this: proceeding as planned, *without* landing in another one of Dragonite's traps," stated Tag. "That is what we'll do."

"But how is the lighting of these sticks supposed to show us the way?" asked Rose.

"We shall find out soon enough," answered Silas, standing aside as Rainus whipped out a flint and a dagger from the folds of his cloak.

The Elf knelt before the little fire pit. With a flick of his wrist the blade of the dagger struck against the piece of flint. Golden sparks exploded forth, bouncing off the sticks to fade away, but the one spark falling between the pieces of kindling to land upon the tinder of moss below ignited.

Hissing and crackling, the spark glowed with life. A small flame devoured the tinder, growing to lap up at the wood nestled over top. As the fire grew and its light pushed against the darkness, Rainus glanced about, searching for a possible trap to be sprung and rendered harmless before it could be deployed on them.

Nothing.

"Well, that was dumb and rather anti-climatic," groaned Rose, her eyes darting about for signs of danger or another clue yet to be discovered. "Dragonite created this as a diversion! He meant to slow us down by making us play along. Now he is that much further ahead of us."

She yelped in surprise and the men jumped with a start as the stack of kindling collapsed on itself. The burning sticks fell over to one side as the cascading embers floated down, landing on the ground outside the circle of rocks. They watched in amazement as a ring of flames erupted around these rocks, and then spread in a single line, as though magically following an invisible trail. The fire raced up the slope of the volcano, looping and twisting as it burned.

"Well, look at that," marvelled Silas.

"Can't get anymore obvious than this," noted Tag, his eyes squinting from the brilliance as they followed the fire racing along. It revealed a fiery message that read: *Go here*.

The message did not end with proper punctuation. Instead, a flaming arrow pointing to the flat ground directed their eyes to the next clue.

"There is something there," announced Rainus, his eyes catching the glint of light reflecting the dancing flames. "Follow me."

Dashing along behind the Elf, they almost bumped into him when Rainus came to an abrupt stop.

"Look at this," said Rainus, kneeling down for a better look.

"What is it?" Rose peered over his shoulder at the small mound that glistened in the light of the dying flames.

"Shards of crystal," answered Rainus, holding up a large splinter for his comrades to see.

"What are these doing here?" asked Rose, staring at the finger-sized piece that was as clear as glass.

"Obviously, someone placed these here," determined Tag, noticing how the flaming arrow pointed down precisely at this pile of crystal.

"But why? What is it supposed to mean?" Rose wondered aloud.

"This is where we are to go," answered Silas.

"That makes no sense," responded the Princess, staring in confusion at the Dream Merchant, "unless you are saying we are to go to a place marked by a small pile of crystal pieces."

"From our perspective, this would appear to be exactly that," agreed the Wizard. "However, if you were small, as tiny as an ant, this small pile of crystal would look like a mountain."

"So we are looking for a *mountain* of crystal?" assumed Tag, scratching his head in thought. "If so, I hardly think such a thing exists. At least, I've never heard of it."

"Aah, but just because you have never heard of such a thing, that does not mean it is not real," assured Silas, giving the mortal a knowing smile.

"Are you saying there *is* a mountain of crystal? That such a place does exist?" questioned Rose.

"It is very real!" Silas nodded in confirmation. "And it is very big."

"Where?" asked Tag.

"And how can this be possible?" added Rose.

"It is north-east of here, as straight as the raven flies," replied the Wizard, using his staff to point the way. "Long ago, when the entire Fire Rim Mountain Range was still composed of highly active volcanoes, one particular mountain was unlike all the others. Instead of spewing ash and extruding rivers of lava, this mountain never vented. The incredible heat swelling from the bowels of the earth was never released, building up over time."

"So it did not blow up. So what?" asked Rose.

"That pressure, with no release, had to go somewhere," explained Silas. "The combination of intense heat and pressure gave rise to crystal formations."

"Like these shards?" asked Rose.

"These," said the Wizard, with a nod of his head, "and many more as large as the great, marble pillars in the grand hall of your palace."

"No!" gasped the Princess. "That big? Impossible!"

"Bigger! And it is indeed possible! There is good reason why it is called Crystal Mountain. It is one of the true, natural wonders of this world, never before seen by mortal man," answered Silas.

"Then how do you know this to be true if you say it has never been seen by mortal eyes?" questioned Rose, her own narrowing in suspicion as she scrutinized the Wizard.

"Forgive me if I'm wrong, Princess, but the Dream Merchant is *not* a mortal," reminded Tag, as he heaved a disgruntled sigh.

"Oh, how right you are!" Rose nodded in understanding.

"So, our destination is Crystal Mountain," decided Rainus.

"If we mean to steal the dreamstone from the Sorcerer, then yes," said Silas.

"And to rescue Cankles," added Tag.

"Well, if we do not reclaim the dreamstone, then rescuing your friend will be a moot point," reminded Silas.

"Then what are we waiting for?" asked Tag, eager to be on his way.

"How far away is this place?" asked Rose.

"Far enough," answered Silas, gazing to a distant mountain.

"To travel the distance by foot will take a good three days, but here, in dragon country," determined Rainus, glancing about, "I'd say it will be more like four nights."

"Four nights!" groaned Rose.

"Or..." said Silas, in pensive thought as his index finger tapped his bearded chin.

"Or what?" asked the Princess.

"I know of a faster way to get us there."

"How?" asked Tag.

"It involves having a strong constitution and the willingness to endure a sensation that most mortals have described as having a boot to the midriff while spinning in circles so one's mind is momentarily scrambled," warned Silas.

"Magic?" questioned Rose.

"Just enough to get us there in a blink of an eye," answered the Wizard.

"Well, if the sensation is this fleeting, I think I can endure," decided the Princess.

"You misunderstand. Getting there will be fleeting, the sensation... well, it takes a mortal a little more time than that to shake off the discomfort. Yes, that's what it is, an uncomfortable sensation."

"Time is of the essence," decided Tag. "We can put up with a little discomfort, if it gets us there in a flash."

"Let me think on this," said Rose, wary of the Wizard's powers. "When it comes right down to it, I believe my stamina has increased greatly since being made to endure this rough and tumble lifestyle. Walking for three or four nights will not kill me."

"True, but those dragons that roam, unfazed by the chill of the night, could well be your end," cautioned Rainus.

"Oooh… Forgot about those nasty little dragons!" Rose shuddered as she relived in her mind's eye that frightening moment when she dangled helplessly over the cliff at the Devil's Tears while these crazed, ravenous reptiles attacked.

"What say you, Princess?" questioned Silas. "Shall we make the long journey by foot, using the darkness of night to shield us? Or shall we use a little wizardly magic?"

"I am not sure," answered Rose. "Have you transported other mortals by the same means?"

"Not many, but if you have been transported by Pancecelia Feldspar during your first encounter with her, then it will be just like that, but *different*."

"When the Queen of the Tooth Fairies first used her powers on me to transport us from my bedchamber to the palace library, it did not hurt at all. It was a bit disconcerting, but it was not painful."

"Well then, my mistake! So Pance has had much more practice with this magic on mortal men than I have had," grunted Silas.

"Your words do not fill me with confidence," said Rose.

"Ultimately, will it kill us to use this magical method of travel?" queried Tag.

"Him? Most definitely not," replied the Wizard, as he pointed at Rainus. "Being an Elf, Lord Silverthorn has a stronger constitution than a mere mortal. As for the human race? If there is a lightning storm in the immediate area to interfere with the process, then there is a chance of death."

"How much of a chance?" queried Rose. "A five or ten percent chance of meeting a terrible end?"

"It is more like a ninety-nine percent chance of a sudden and excruciating death," answered Silas.

"What?" cried Rose, her eyes wide in terror. "I am not liking those odds, not in the least!"

"Worry not, Princess! There is nary a cloud in the sky," assured Rainus.

"Easy for you to say, *Mister-I-Have-a-Stronger-Constitution*," sniffed Rose. "I am safer walking."

"If we can get to our destination quickly, I say we allow the Wizard to transport us there," recommended Tag.

"Did you not hear the Wizard explain the chances of surviving this means of transportation, if the conditions are *not* perfect?" asked Rose.

"I'm willing to take my chances, especially as we have no time to spare," reminded Tag. "Besides, how bad can it be? If you were unfazed when the Queen of the Tooth Fairy magically transported you, I'm sure it won't be any worse."

"Master Agincor, does this mode of transportation involve the use of a wand and Fairy dust?" questioned Rose, as she scrutinized the Wizard.

"Of course not, being that I am not a Fairy," grunted Silas. "I use this."

He held forth the wizardly staff of wisdom and power before his comrades.

"You use your fancied up walking stick?" Rose's brows arched up in surprise.

"This is much more than just a walking stick! And no, the crystal atop the staff is what I use," replied the Wizard, puffing on the smooth, polished surface to wipe away the condensation with his sleeve.

"Then let us get this over with," urged Tag. "Use your magic, Master Agincor."

"Whoa! Hold on here. Before we go rushing off on this mission, we should take a moment to assess the danger," suggested Rose.

"The danger in resuming this quest, or in employing the Wizard's method of travel?" asked Tag.

"Both," replied the Princess.

"Nothing worth doing is not without risk," reminded Silas.

"Risk is one thing, danger of the deadly sort is a whole other matter," grumbled Rose, as she pondered this dilemma.

"I assure you, Princess, the skies are relatively clear. You have nothing to fear if we go now," promised Silas. "Other than some rattled nerves, I assure you, you will be fine... eventually."

"Then let's do it," decided Tag.

"If the danger is minimal, I suppose we should," conceded Rose, checking the skies for signs of thunderclouds.

"Whatever we do, whether we venture forth on foot or use the Wizard's powers, it is safer than standing here," stated Rainus. "Especially as we do not know what happened to that monster dragon."

"Then quickly," ordered Silas, directing his comrades to an area in the forest where the overhanging branches were well out of the way. "We must do so, unimpeded in a clearing."

Rushing to the Wizard's side, they gathered in a tight circle. Tag, Rose and Rainus watched in amazement as the crystal sphere atop Silas' staff glowed, becoming brighter.

"Steady on," said Silas, waiting and watching the light swelling from the orb until it was strong enough to magically transport them to Crystal Mountain. "Now! Place your hands over the crystal."

As they did so, they screamed in fright, launched skyward while the Wizard's staff fell from his grip, tumbling to the ground.

6

The Past is the Past

The snapping of branches and rustling of leaves came to an abrupt halt. The earth beneath them seemed to spin, while rocking to and fro.

"Mimes! I am beginning to hate them as much as you do, Princess!" Rainus growled as he pushed away Silas' foot from his face. "I should have known they would do this."

"What just happened?" gasped the Princess, as she peered through the netting to the ground below.

"What do you think just happened?" Tag grunted as he squirmed about. "We're trapped! Now get your bow out of my back."

"At this moment, it is pinned under the Wizard." Rose struggled to wrench it free. "The way we are all wedged in this netting, my bow will not budge an inch."

"Sit tight," ordered Silas, struggling to free one of his arms. "Perhaps I can reach my staff."

"From way up here?" groaned Rainus, rolling his eyes in frustration. "I think not! We can barely move."

"How are we to free ourselves now?" asked Rose, wincing in pain as the edge of her quiver jabbed into her hip. "We must get out of here before those mindless mimes return to deliver us to Dragonite!"

"Quickly, Princess, grab it!" Rainus glanced down as he squirmed closer to her. "Pull it out!"

"Pardon me!" gasped Rose, her eyes wide in surprise. She wriggled away from the Elf as he struggled to maneuver next to her.

"My dagger! It is in the holster to my back. We can use it to cut the netting."

"Oh," said Rose, her face flushing with embarrassment. She nodded in understanding as she stretched, straining to reach with her fingertips the hilt of the dagger.

"Can you get it?" asked Tag. He watched from the corner of his eye, as his face was squashed against the net, restricting his movement.

"Just barely." Rose struggled to grip the dagger's polished oak handle.

"How about now?" asked Rainus, writhing about in their tight confines to angle closer to the Princess.

Wrestling the blade free of its leather sheath, Rose exclaimed, "Got it!"

This was promptly followed by: *"Oops!"*

In these cramped confines, as she angled the weapon so the blade wasn't pointing dangerously at one of her comrades, it slipped from her fingers as the hilt snagged on the net. "Dropped it..."

"Well, that was brilliant," muttered Tag, heaving a disgruntled sigh as he peered down.

"Sorry," whimpered the Princess, staring at the dagger that now rested alongside the Wizard's staff.

"All is not lost!" Rainus twisted about to free the scabbard of his sword. "Though it is more cumbersome than the dagger, my sword should do the trick if we are careful of its blade."

Rainus shifted his position, trying to adjust himself so his hand was close to his weapon. As he twisted about, his comrades shrank back in a bid to make more room for him. The Elf compressed his body, exhaling and then holding his breath. Stretching as far as his fingers could reach, he strained to grasp his sword that had gotten twisted about behind him when they first fell victim to this trap. Grunting in exertion, he grabbed the pommel, and then Rainus paused.

"I have a grip on my sword, but it is going to be difficult unsheathing it to cut through the netting."

"Whatever you do, just be careful we do not get hurt in the process," warned Rose.

"I shall take utmost care," promised the Elf.

Rainus slowly unsheathed the sword. As the tip finally came free of the scabbard, he angled the blade just so. Slowly, he sawed through the coarse fibres of this trap.

With the escape hole growing larger, straining beneath their weight, it suddenly tore open. Everyone yelped as they tumbled to the ground.

A disheveled Tag scrambled onto his feet, watching in amazement as Rainus landed on his feet with the natural grace bestowed upon the Elfkind.

"We're free!" declared Tag, lifting Rose onto her feet.

"Think again!" An angry voice snarled at them.

Rose and her comrades froze.

A dozen spears encircled them, the rusty tips thrust into their startled faces.

Rose stared down at their diminutive captors. "Hey… if these are mimes, other than speaking, they are doing a very good impersonation of Dwarves!"

"Don't you go insultin' us!" snapped the leader, the spear trembling in his pudgy hands. "We *are* Dwarves!"

"What are you doing here?" asked Tag, his hand inching toward the hilt of his sword. "Aren't you far from the Land of Big?"

"Who are you ta say?" grunted the Dwarf leader, as a grumble of discontent rippled through his gang. "We've strayed no further than you have. What business have ya here?"

"Our business is our own," responded Silas. Using his foot, he discreetly dragged his staff closer within reach. "We want no trouble! We wish to be on our way, unhampered and unmolested."

"Well, I don't know 'bout that!" The leader tipped the point of his spear toward the old man.

"You are ill-advised to even think of accosting us," warned Rainus, staring down at the Dwarves, "especially while we are in the company of this great Wizard."

"Ooh! I heard that the gizzard from a Wizard is mighty tasty fried up with some onions an' mushrooms," exclaimed the Dwarf standing next to the leader. "Too bad we don't have any onions."

"Or mushrooms," added another.

"What are you talking about?" Rose grimaced in disgust.

"Food! It's time ta eat, boys!" announced the leader of the Dwarves, smacking his lips in anticipation of a long awaited meal.

"We have no food," said Tag.

"You *are* the food," snorted another one of the Dwarves.

"*What?* This is madness!" snapped the Princess. "Even I know your people are vegetarians, lovers of all kinds of root vegetables."

"Oh, we do love our veggies, no doubt about that," responded the leader, "but what we had was stolen by the Sorcerer's minions."

"I knew the mimes were behind this trap!" exclaimed Rainus, his eyes flashed with anger.

"Wrong again, Elf!" snorted the leader. "We set this trap ta catch mimes, but you an' your comrades will do quite nicely."

"Nicely for what?" Rose frowned in bewilderment.

"What's wrong with ya, girlie?" asked the shortest of the Dwarves. "Do ya have cloth ears? *You're* the dinner!"

"Whoa! Hold on here!" ordered Tag. "Are you saying you're *cannibal dwarves?*"

The leader raised his spear in threat as he growled, "In my way of thinkin', the word *cannibal* implies that we eat our own kind, so no."

"Phew!" Rose breathed a sigh of relief.

"We only eat mortals an' Elves when we can't catch a deer or a boar, being that they're so rare in these parts," explained another Dwarf.

"Say again!" gasped Tag, his hand seizing the hilt of his sword. He froze once more as several spear tips were thrust toward his chest.

"This makes no sense!" muttered Silas. "Since when did Dwarves take to eating meat? Human and otherwise?"

"Look around us! We're in dragon country. No root veggies grow well in this volcanic soil an' what we did have, those damned mimes keep stealin' ta feed themselves. We're simply takin' revenge, an' this form of revenge is most definitely best served warm," chuckled the leader. "Now, drop your weapons! You're comin' with us."

"Where?" asked Rose, as she ducked behind Tag.

"We got a big, boilin' cauldron with your name on it, missy," answered another Dwarf.

"How dare you address me so informally, you little... short person? Do you know who I am?" Rose's hand lashed out to slap away the spear from her face.

"I know you'll be mighty tasty in a stew," answered the Dwarf next to the leader.

"I am Princess Rose-alyn Beatrice Elizabeth Wilhemina Pepperton, heir apparent to the throne of Fleetwood! Nobody, especially a Dwarf, is sticking me in a stewing pot to be simmered with vegetables!"

"We don't have no veggies, remember? That's why you an' your friends are on the menu, but a princess?" exclaimed the leader, as a chorus of astonished gasps sounded from his comrades.

"Yes, I am!" declared Rose, her arms crossing her chest in defiance as she stared down at her would-be captors.

"Oooh! We'll be dining *royally* tonight, boys!" chuckled the leader, laughing at his own pun as he used his spear to prod them on.

"Unbelievable!" muttered Rose. "If you are smart, you would eat the Elf first, being that he is probably far more tender and delectable than we mere mortals are."

"Hey, the girl's probably right!" agreed one of the Dwarves, hungrily eyeing the Elf towering before him. "The tall one would be easier ta digest, that's for sure."

"Truth be told, I ain't fussy! I'm so hungry I'd eat a dragon's arse if it was roasted ta well-done," admitted the leader, prodding his dinner on toward their camp.

Rose yelped in surprise, ducking down as Tag and Rainus abruptly brandished their swords. With a flicking action, Silas rolled his staff onto the top of his foot, tossing it up to snatch into his hands.

The crystal orb atop his staff glowed with menacing light, forcing the Dwarves to back off.

"Stand down," demanded the Wizard. "It is far better to *reason* with words than to *fight* with weapons."

"I was hopin' ta *season with salt*, then *bite with these chompers*," groaned the leader, staring wistfully as the promise of a hot meal slipped away. "These are lean times, an' we're just gettin' leaner by the minute with nothing ta eat."

"You want root vegetables? Then you shall have them," promised Silas, nodding to the Dwarf leader.

The diminutive miners jumped with a start as six baskets overflowing with carrots, beets, parsnips, rutabagas, turnips, radishes and potatoes magically appeared at their feet.

Ooohs and *aaahs* sounded from the Dwarves as they dropped to their knees, drooling over the fresh vegetables.

"Glory be! Veggies! More veggies than we can shake a spear at!" exclaimed the leader, trembling with hunger and eager anticipation of a banquet as he eyed this unexpected bounty. "We haven't seen this much food since those damned mimes stole everything we had."

"And this is all yours for the taking," offered Silas.

The Dwarf's eyes narrowed in suspicion as his glance darted between the Wizard and the baskets of fresh vegetables. "What's the catch?"

"The catch is, you allow us to go on our way, and that is without raising the alarum to the Sorcerer or his minions," negotiated Silas, his words were stern.

"Why would we warn the Sorcerer?" questioned the Dwarf, motioning his men to gather up the baskets. "We don't need his bloody mimes ta know about our food. They'd only steal it again."

"Are you not in cahoots with Dragonite?" questioned Silas.

"Are you mad? We try ta avoid that crazy old Sorcerer at all costs. His mimes, too, unless they fall into one of our traps an' we haven't eaten in a while."

"Then what are you doing here?" asked Tag, lowering his sword. "You are far from home."

"Some Dwarves mine for veins of gold and silver, others mine the earth for precious gems."

"So?" responded Rose.

"We've cornered the market on..." the Dwarf used his index finger to motion the Princess to lean closer as he whispered, "crystal."

"Crystal?" repeated Rose, her delicate brows arching up in surprise. "There's only one place in this realm that produces the best quality crystal and that's to the north-east of here."

"But ever since that crazy Sorcerer returned, not only have we been out of food, we've been out of work," revealed the Dwarf standing by his leader.

"So, Dragonite has taken refuge in Crystal Mountain," determined Rainus.

"It's not safe with that Sorcerer there, that's for sure," warned the Dwarf leader.

"An' his crazy mimes," added his comrade. "Mind you, that nasty little Pooka is more of a concern than those fools."

"Dragonite is in the company of a shape-shifting Sprite?" asked Rose.

"We call him a Pooka in these parts, but you heard me! That nefarious little being is hidin' up there with him. Don't know what they're up ta, but whatever it is, it can't be good."

"That is not good at all," groaned Rose, shaking her head in disappointment. "Now we know for sure that the Sorcerer has the *you-know-what.*"

"What I know is, none of us will be safe standin' out here when the sun rises," snorted the Dwarf leader, inserting the staff of his spear through the handles of the basket to carry this bounty away.

"So, we're free to leave?" questioned Tag.

"Of course! Who needs stinkin' meat when we have this beautiful bounty of veggies ta feast on?" responded the Dwarf, as he ordered one of his men to pick up the other end of the spear to lift the basket.

"Before you leave, do you know exactly where in the Crystal Mountain that scoundrel is hiding?" asked Silas.

"We didn't stick around for 'howdy-dos', fleein' as soon as the Sorcerer an' his damned army showed up. But if ya go that way, be careful."

"Of the Sorcerer?" queried Tag.

"Him, and the mountain," cautioned the Dwarf, his voice foreboding. "We were careful not ta delve too deeply, for the lower ya go inside, the temperatures become unbearable, even for an Elf."

"Not ta mention the treacherous crystal formations an' whatnot," added another Dwarf. "Don't want ta fall into a pit, spearin' yourself on pointy spikes of crystal, if ya get my drift?"

"Excellent advice," said Rose, with a nod of her head.

"Then we shall be on our way." Silas held forth his staff before his comrades.

"Please tell me more," requested Cankles, peering down at his shoulder where the Sprite remained perched.

"Why? The past is the past. It cannot alter the present nor change your destiny."

"It is the biggest piece, the *missin'* piece, of the puzzle in my life. For the longest time, I believed I was a criminal... I had done something to deserve the scars of this beatin'."

"*Beatings*, many of them," corrected Loken. "But why the hell do you want to remember now? Knowing will not change the fact you are Dragonite's prisoner, nor will it change what had happened to you."

"I don't *want* to know, I feel I *need* to know. Right now, that is my greatest wish. Before I die, I'd like to fully understand the fragmented dreams that have haunted me for longer than I can remember."

"Even if it means having to relive your worst nightmare, if only in your mind's eye?" questioned Loken.

"Definitely! I believe I am ready now."

"I think being locked away down here has addled your brain even more so," snorted Loken, as an index finger spun by the side of his head.

"So you say, but when I believed I was a bad man, punished for a crime I had committed, I had no desire to know. But now that you say I wasn't a criminal, I must know what happened to me. I must find out the truth."

"And you truly remember nothing?"

"Yes, and whatever flashes of memory played out in fleetin' dreams have been more confusin' than tellin'. You claim to have been there when I was the Sorcerer's prisoner. What exactly happened to me?"

"The first question you should really ask is who you are. Or in this case, were," recommended Loken.

"Then tell me. Who am I?"

"In your former life you were a knight; a great one at that, if I recall correctly, and if the rumours of old stand to be true."

"No... Me? A knight? That's not possible."

"Well then, hit me up the backside of my head and call me a fool! You looked like a knight, dressed like a knight and you most certainly had the attitude and character of a knight."

"The attitude and character?"

"You know? Chivalry, sacrifice for the greater good, death before dishonour... knightly stuff like that."

"*Me?* A chivalrous knight..."

"If not, then you were a bloody convincing imposter!"

"But why would I pretend to be a knight?" asked Cankles. He then yelped in pain as the Sprite, in frustration, yanked on his ear lobe.

"Listen up! I was there! There was no pretending. You stood by your vow about sacrificing for the greater good and all that death before dishonour malarkey."

"I hardly call that malarkey!" Cankles sat a little taller as he digested these words. "These are the things that define a man's good character; that makes a knight a true knight than an ordinary man clad in a stand of armour, bearin' the king's coat of arms."

"Aha! So you do remember!" Loken wagged an accusing finger at the mortal.

"No... not really."

"Well, from what I recall, you were captured because you held a great secret," revealed Loken.

"I don't think so... I don't like secrets because I've never been very good at keepin' them."

"Shut it! Let me continue. Back then, you harboured a secret, one that Dragonite swore he'd pry out of you, even if it meant killing you to do so," said Loken, his hand flashing out as though he was cracking a whip. "When starvation and thirst drove you to the edge of madness, but you still refused to divulge your secret, that was when the Sorcerer really took to torturing you."

"But what was this big secret?"

"As the captain of your king's army, you had knowledge of military strategy and how the second battalion crossed the lands with speed, using a route that allowed them to join the battle and defeat Dragonite and his legion of mercenaries."

"Mercenary mimes?"

"Oh no, these were actual soldiers, hired swords that worked for pay. They had an allegiance to none. Their loyalty lasted for only as long as the funds did. The mimes came into play later on when the Sorcerer realized the mercenaries would think nothing of slitting his throat, if payment through the spoils of war was not made in an expedient manner. Plus, mimes did not talk back the way those unruly, bloodthirsty miscreants did."

"I suppose that makes sense," decided Cankles, "but I was truly a captain? Incredible!"

"Actually, I discovered, much to Dragonite's chagrin, you had only been pretending to be the captain when the real one was felled in battle, unable to lead his men on. It was a ploy you devised to keep your fellow knights and soldiers fighting and to maintain order during the heat of battle."

"So I was a soldier?" asked Cankles, seeking clarification.

"You were a knight, the first officer to your captain, to be exact."

"Oh my!"

"When Captain Yairet was wounded, unable to carry on, you donned his helmet."

"I did?"

"And that cracked shield Dragonite threw at you earlier on in a bid to jog your memory? That was Yairet's, too. You took up your captain's sword and shield. You stood your ground until the second battalion's arrival was inevitable."

"So they made it in time?"

"They did come, but to bolster the chances of victory, you took it upon yourself to lead the enemy away, as many as you could, from the battlefield."

"Wait... Did you say *Yairet*?" asked Cankles, frowning in curiosity as he thought on this name. "As in Oliver Yairet? Tag's father?"

"I suppose, if his father was indeed the captain to King William's army ten or so years ago."

"I was his father's first officer?" Cankles' mind raced as he fought to glean a fragment of a memory from this event in history. "I knew the young master's father?"

"Knew him? As legend has it, you were his first officer *and* his most loyal, trusted friend."

"I am stunned... amazed even," admitted Cankles.

"What is truly amazing is what you did that day. According to those who survived to tell, you sacrificed yourself to give your men a fighting chance. When you were captured and dragged back to the Sorcerer's lair, Dragonite was determined to discover how the second battalion arrived in such a timely fashion. He wanted to know so he could ambush future incursions, stopping them before they had a chance to engage in war on his domain."

"I don't recall this route you speak of."

"Back then, you knew. But even at the cost of your life, you would not divulge this secret, swearing you'd take it to your grave than to ever reveal it to Dragonite, thereby endangering the lives of others."

"And I kept my vow?"

"Right up to the end when the Sorcerer, in a fit of rage, took an axe, albeit a rusty, dull one to your head! But instead of killing you, he had knocked you unconscious."

Cankles' eyes squeezed shut just as Loken raised an invisible battleaxe, swinging it down to reenact the Sorcerer's near-lethal blow. The mortal shuddered, slumping against the prison wall.

Loken darted into the air as Cankles' hands flew up. The colour drained from his face. He clutched his aching head as a splinter of a memory pierced his brain. It was as though a blade had just cleaved his head in two all over again.

Cankles' heart jumped to the back of his throat. It pounded so hard and fast, each beat thudded unmercifully in his head, resonating in his ears. With arms wrapped around his now-throbbing skull that threatened to overwhelm him with a rush of painful memories, his forehead dropped, resting on his bended knees as he groaned.

"You're not looking so well," commented Loken, hovering about as he attempted to peer at his distraught, pained face.

"I don't feel so good," moaned Cankles, his eyes watering as his fingertip traced the scar on his scalp and the permanent dent that was now hidden by hair.

"Well, I did warn you," responded the Sprite, alighting upon Cankles' knee.

The mortal's arms wrapped around his legs as he shook his head to vanquish the pain stabbing and pulsing through his brain to stir up old memories.

"Nothing good can ever come from revisiting the past, especially a past like yours."

Cankles drew a long, deep breath as he fought to regain his composure. "No... I needed to know. If I die now, I can do so with a clear conscience. I can do so knowing I did no wrong or harm to another."

"Say... You sound like a... knight!" noted Loken, staring with raised eyebrows.

"For preferring to die with a clear conscience?"

"That, and the way you speak now! You look the same, but you're sounding like the distinguished, educated, properly enunciating know-it-all you once were."

"What do you mean by that?" asked Cankles, as he rubbed his aching head.

"I mean, not only have you miraculously restored your sense of valour and honour, but your manner of speech... What happened to *knowin'* and *preferrin'*? You used to slur your words, dropping the 'g'."

For a moment, Cankles absorbed the Pooka's comment, slowly sitting upright as he thought back.

"What do you know?" Cankles' brows furrowed in curiosity. "I suppose I am speaking differently."

"You are speaking as you once did, not like the lowly commoner you thought you were," stated Loken.

"I am starting to remember my past now, albeit somewhat fragmented. Could it be that by restoring those lost memories, I have also regained other features that once made me the person I was?"

"It makes perfect sense," decided Loken, giving this mortal a judicious nod.

Cankles shook his head, drawing a deep, cleansing breath. "This is somehow liberating. As horrific as my ordeal was, and as scattered as my memories are at this moment, at least my conscience has been cleared."

"I guess it matters *if* you have a conscience," dismissed Loken, his words were cynical as his tiny shoulders shrugged with indifference.

"But you do have one," countered Cankles, his reeling mind coming to grips with his rediscovered reality. "I know you do."

"You only want to believe it to be so," grunted Loken, sitting cross-legged on this prisoner's kneecap.

Cankles peered down at his little cellmate. "Do not deny it. You do have a conscience. By pretending you don't, you feel you can shield yourself from pain."

"Listen to you twitter on like a mindless bird!" grumbled the Sprite. With a flippant wave of his hand, he denounced the man. "If I did, it was lost when my life changed."

"You know what I say is true."

"You believe it to be so because it's the only thing your feeble *conscience* can grasp, to allow you a grain of hope," argued Loken.

"If it was not true, then you lied to me."

"About what?" asked the Pooka.

"You claimed that you were the one to save me, delivering me to Lord Silverthorn's domain when that blow meant to kill me failed to do the deed," reminded Cankles, as he studied the tiny face before him.

For a lingering moment Loken was silent, mulling over the mortal's words.

"You know it is true. Had you no conscience, you would have left me to die, than to risk retribution from the Sorcerer for saving my life."

"*Conscience?* Bah! I only delivered you to the Woodland Glade because I couldn't stand hearing your incessant cries of agony. Made my hair stand on end, it did."

"Cries of agony? How can that be, if I was knocked senseless?" questioned Cankles.

"I meant to say, cries of agony, if you were to come to. Hence the reason I took the form of a beast of legend to deliver you with haste to Silverthorn's domain before you could drive me mad with your pathetic moans and cries of misery."

"Well, whatever your reason, I must thank you." Cankles nodded in appreciation.

"For what?" grunted Loken. "So you'd live to see this day? Back in Dragonite's custody and awaiting more torture?"

"I believe you felt pity for me, offering some mercy from my suffering by delivering me to those you knew had the power to heal my wounds," countered Cankles. "That is what I am thankful for."

"Believe what you want!" Loken was thoroughly annoyed this mortal chose to give him the benefit of doubt.

"I believe what I know in my heart to be true. But tell me this, how did you get me to the Elves? Did you transform into a great dragon to fly me there?"

"Are you mad? And have every eye on the ground be witness to it? Report back to the Sorcerer what they saw? It would have been the death of me had I taken to the air on the wings of a dragon!"

"Then how?"

"I turned into a creature that was able to bear your weight and travel in secret, and with speed."

"Go on!"

"I became a unicorn," revealed Loken. "As a reclusive and equally elusive creature of the Woodland Glade, even the Elves suspected nothing when I delivered you to their domain."

"That is an awful lot of bother for one with no conscience," determined Cankles, giving the Sprite a thoughtful nod.

"If you don't stop with this nonsense, you'll make me regret ever sparing your life," muttered Loken. "Maybe I'll turn into a great dragon; swallow you up whole!"

"I do not want that. But if you were there to bear witness to my capture and torture, enough to know I was once a first officer to a king's army, then surely you must know my name?"

"For all intent and purposes, as far as the Sorcerer knew, you were Captain Yairet, commanding King William's army. He only found out he had been deceived after the war was fought and lost on his part. You can be sure Dragonite will see to your demise now that you are back in his clutches and he recognizes you for whom you are."

"Well, I suppose that explains why he seems to despise me so much. But it still does not explain you?"

"What is there to explain?" Loken shrugged.

"Why are you in this strange alliance with the Sorcerer? You said it was not by choice."

"For one who claims to have a bad memory, you remember that?"

"I seem to be getting better, and now, I am curious. You were not always bad. What in the world would compel you to form an alliance with that madman?"

"It is *not* an alliance!" insisted Loken, his wings trembling with indignation. "And you are not curious, you are just damned nosy!"

"If wanting to know means I'm nosy, then I suppose I am. But as I said before, I do not believe you were always bad."

"It is just a matter of opinion!"

"In my humble opinion, you really are not as bad or evil as you believe, perhaps a bit mixed up, but I sense there is some good in you."

"You sensed wrong!"

"No, I know what I speak of."

"Daft! That's what you are!" scoffed Loken. "You are so wrong! You know nothing about me."

"I beg to differ... Any person who claims to know Pancecelia Feldspar, or in your case, claiming to *love* the Queen of the Tooth Fairies, can only be touched by Her Majesty's grace. If you love her, you cannot be all that bad."

Loken fell silent as he thought back on his beloved Celia.

"What say you now, my little friend?"

"I am *not* your friend... I have no friends."

"We have a common friend in Pance, so we are at the very least, friendly acquaintances now," reasoned Cankles.

"You and your stinking optimism!" Loken rolled his eyes in frustration. "That is one thing that has not changed about you with the restoration of your memory!"

"So what is your story?" probed Cankles, eager to learn more. "You claim you are not in an alliance with Dragonite, and yet, here you are."

"I am here in body and mind, but not in heart."

"Aha! So you do have a heart!"

"A heart that beats, but feels nothing," insisted Loken, his balled fist thumping his chest in defiance.

"So tell me about your life and what brought you here," said Cankles.

"I do not want to talk about my life!"

"Fair enough... Then how did you come to know Pancecelia Feldspar, or were you lying about knowing her?"

"I was not lying where Celia is concerned. She means too much to me to trivialize what we had with a stupid lie."

"Go on then! Tell me, how do you know her?"

"Celia and I had a long history. I started out in her service, but through uncompromising duty and loyalty, it evolved into a true friendship that eventually blossomed into love."

"Tell me more."

Loken closed his eyes, drawing a long, deep breath as he collected his thoughts. "It feels like a lifetime ago, but we were once lovers."

"She is a Fairy. You are a Sprite," noted Cankles, rubbing his stubbly chin in pensive thought. "Is that allowed?"

"True love knows no boundaries," sighed Loken, a small smile crept across his haggard face as he thought back on some of his fondest memories. "Many were opposed to our relationship, both Fairies and Sprites, but we cared not. If anything, Celia believed it was a way to unite our peoples as one, if we were to wed."

"You were betrothed to wed?" Cankles' eyes sparkled with wonder at the prospect.

"Yes, but it wasn't meant to be," said Loken, giving his head a dismal shake.

"What happened?"

"We were about to make a formal announcement of our intention to marry, when a devious, contemptible soul did everything in his power to see me undone! When he failed to besmirch my good name and reputation, he destroyed me by murdering my mother and siblings, falsely accusing me for those murders."

"That is outrageous!"

"Celia's mind was poisoned against me with a spell that remains to this day. And for me, I was exiled, lest I be captured and executed for murders I did not commit."

"Oh my! I lived my life believing I committed a heinous crime while you had lived yours innocent of these murders, but having the one you love believe you did commit them. I do not know which fate is worse."

"You were never certain of your guilt or innocence. I knew I was innocent from the start, but nobody believed me, not even my precious Celia, once the spell took hold of her heart and mind."

"Tragic... absolutely tragic," groaned Cankles. "Who would do such a terrible thing?"

"At first, many were opposed to our union, but as those on Celia's council grew to understand the relevance and benefits of uniting our races, there was one who vehemently opposed our betrothal. He was sly; clever in hiding his opinions to Celia and the others, but he made it perfectly clear to me that he was going to do everything he could to force the Queen to abandon her love for me."

"So she was tricked?"

"Celia is a smart one. When my foe discovered she could not be easily swayed and sought to uncover the truth about my family's death, he resorted to employing a spell to taint her heart and fog her mind."

"So, it was someone close to her that undermined you both?" questioned Cankles.

Loken breathed a weary sigh as he nodded in confirmation.

"Devious! Devious *and* evil!" exclaimed Cankles, feeling pity for the Sprite.

"Yes," agreed Loken. "I never believed he was capable of such ruthlessness, but Firestar did everything, and more, that he promised he'd do if I did not relinquish my love for Celia."

Cankles' face blanched. *"Firestar?* As in Sparks Firestar?"

"The one and only! That snake of a Fairy continues to plot while he ingratiates himself to the Queen. He means to dethrone Celia during the eve of the summer solstice, when her powers are at their weakest."

"But why? I always thought Master Firestar was a very likeable fellow, charming and sincere."

"It is nothing more than a ruse. He's *likeable*, as long as you do not cross him or question his beliefs," stated Loken, his voice taking on a bitter tone. "Before an audience, he was always civil to my face, but alone, he made his opinions perfectly clear. He denounced me, stating he would never allow a Sprite, especially a shape-shifter, to be the consort to the Queen of the Tooth Fairies."

"Hmph," grunted Cankles, scratching his head in thought. "Who would have thought he was capable of such evil?"

"So you are like all the others. You don't believe me."

"I never said that. In fact, it would explain why that Fairy was so eager to see us leave the first time I took the young master and Princess Rose for an audience with Pancecelia in the Fairy's Vale."

"Of course," said Loken, nodding in agreement. "He did not need some mortals snooping about, getting close to discovering the truth."

"So Sparks Firestar is doing this to spite you? Because he cannot tolerate a Sprite being married to the Queen."

"At first, I thought that was it, but Firestar's plans are far more sinister."

"Is it more than just hate for you, or does he despise the Sprites in general?"

"Indeed! It is much more than that! His hate for me is deep rooted, but I recently discovered his plot to usurp Celia, to steal away with her powers."

"How do you know? It could just be hearsay," countered Cankles.

"Hearsay? I think not! I heard with my own ears what that deviant soul is plotting to see my Celia dethroned and disgraced."

"Oh my!" groaned Cankles. "Poor Pance."

"Poor indeed! At this moment, my dear Celia has no idea, not even an inkling, of what Firestar is up to."

"And you were saying that this is the reason you're here; to save the one you love. But how?"

"The Sorcerer has a potion, one that will break the spell Celia is under. If I aid him, I will be rewarded with it." Loken pulled a tiny square of cloth that was tucked in his sash. Peeling it open, he revealed what was inside.

"What is that?" asked Cankles, staring at the specks of glitter.

"Fairy dust, from Celia's wings. When mixed in the potion, it will work specifically on her. But the difficulty is in getting that vial from Dragonite to begin with."

"I think I understand," said Cankles, as he nodded in sympathy. "You are not here by choice. You are here because you feel you have *no* choice. To claim that vial of potion to undo the spell Pance is under means you are forced to do the Sorcerer's bidding, even if it is the last thing you want to do."

"Yes…" admitted Loken. His head lowered in sadness.

"In my life, I have seen bad men do good deeds and good men forced to do bad. Your hand was forced."

"I would do anything to save my Celia and clear my name."

"Oh, my! The summer solstice will be upon us sooner than we think. We don't have much time to put things right."

"*We?* There is no *we* where the two of us are concerned," muttered Loken. "In fact, I must work all the harder now to ingratiate myself to the Sorcerer once more to earn his trust and win that vial of potion."

"I think you have a better chance of getting that vial working with *me* than trying to reason with *him*. Just keep in mind, you angered him enough to have him pluck off one of your wings, something I would never do," reminded Cankles.

Loken frowned, staring up at the mortal's earnest face. "Your intentions are good, but you are a bumbling, useless fool, trapped in this prison with no hope of escape."

"But I was once a knight, if my memories continue to be restored, then surely my courage will be, too. Together, we can get the potion and help the one person we both greatly care for."

"That was another lifetime ago. You are a knight no more, lacking in both courage *and* skills," mocked Loken. "I am better to rely on my own abilities to get what I want."

"So you say, but it hasn't gotten you very far at all, has it?" responded Cankles.

"I must change my strategy. It is as simple as that," decided Loken. "As time is of the essence, I must work with speed rather than be encumbered and hampered by a fool like you."

"Remember what I said," whispered Cankles, watching as the Sprite morphed into a little brown bat clinging to the bars of this crystal cell. "We can work together to escape, even defeat the Sorcerer."

"I think not," grunted Loken, fanning out his leathery wings before launching into flight.

"Please, you must at least consider it!" Cankles pressed his face between the crystal bars as he stared at the Sprite hovering before him.

"Sure! Of course I can consider it, but it does not mean I will choose to do so."

"Wait!" called Cankles, shouting as Loken's bat form flitted away down the tunnel. "Come back! Please come back…"

7

Far From Home

"Oh, my! That was much worse than I had first anticipated," groaned Rose. She squeezed her eyes shut as her mind reeled from the ordeal. Digging her nails into Tag's shoulder, she struggled to keep from toppling over.

"I warned you this mode of transportation was not for mortals with a poor constitution or those faint of heart," responded Silas.

Rainus hopped out of the way just as Tag dropped to his knees, retching as his mind spun and his stomach churned.

"Lovely," muttered Rainus, shaking his head in revulsion as the boy vomited while the Princess toppled over, disoriented by the dizzying ride. "Perhaps giving in to this magic rather than fighting it would have made it less stressful for you."

"Easy for you to say." Tag wiped his mouth using the back of his hand as he slowly stood upright. "And I wasn't fighting it; the Princess was the one who was so bloody reluctant to use this magic."

"Can you blame me?" grumbled Rose, as she wobbled, swaying to and fro before falling over once again.

"Take a slow, deep breath in through the nose, and then just as slowly, exhale through the mouth," instructed Silas, pulling Rose back onto her feet. "It seems to help the uninitiated. Do this several times and you should be as good as new."

"Thank you," wheezed the Princess, between deep breaths. "At least I fared better than Tag did."

"I think not!" muttered the boy, only to crumple to his knees once more to heave like his stomach was turning inside-out on itself.

"Oh, I *do* think," mocked Rose, as she stared down at Tag. "And now I know I have developed a stronger constitution than you!"

"Hush," whispered Rainus, pressing a finger to his lips. "Keep your voices down. We are only paces from the mouth of the tunnel leading into the mountain."

"This is Crystal Mountain?" Rose wondered aloud, staring up the treed slope. "There is no crystal here. It looks likes any other mountain we have encountered. I believe you delivered us to the wrong destination, Wizard."

"Look again, Princess!" Silas lifted a clump of moss. Beneath this primitive vegetation and the loose dirt it clung to, he exposed a large chunk of crystal, the largest she had ever seen.

"So I was wrong," admitted Rose, seeing that through the ages the crystal formations were now concealed by a blend of earth and volcanic ash from which trees and other plants found a roothold to grow from.

Tag unsheathed his sword. "Let us venture forth; see to recovering our friend and that dreamstone."

"You should be commended for your eagerness to proceed, my young friend," praised Rainus, using the broad edge of his blade to impede his movement, "but not so fast. There is no telling what hidden dangers await."

"We do not need to fall victim to another trap, that is for certain," agreed Rose, her hand resting on Tag's shoulder to prevent him from rushing ahead.

"Fine, but we cannot loiter about, waiting for Dragonite to appear for a confrontation," stated Tag. "We should take him by surprise; catch him unawares so he won't have a chance to use his magic against us."

"True enough, but you have yet to gain your bearings," whispered Rainus. He noticed how Tag and Rose both teetered to and fro like drunken sailors wobbling about on the deck of a ship being pitched about on a stormy sea. "Allow me to advance first. See if it is safe to move forward."

"A wise idea, Lord Silverthorn. We shall wait for you here," promised Silas, pulling Tag back into the bushes that concealed them at the base of the mountain. "Proceed with due caution."

"And speed," urged Rose, glancing to the eastern sky where the impending sun threatened to vanquish the moon and the stars. "We must move before the sun rises and the dragons begin roaming about again."

Cankles peered up. The sounds of footsteps echoed through the long corridor, growing louder. By the gait and the rhythmic, dull '*thud*' as the end of a staff impacted the ground he knew it was Dragonite, not one of his minions or the shape-shifting Sprite coming his way.

The Sorcerer's distorted shadow jerked and twisted about at the mercy of the light cast by the torches as the flames danced in his wake.

Cankles' eyes squinted as he stared at the many reflections shining off the wall of crystal. Even before the Sorcerer rounded the bend in the tunnel that would deliver him to this prison, he could see it was his foe, coming to dispense more torment on him.

"I see I have finally succeeded in driving you to the brink of madness," noted Dragonite, scrutinizing this trapped mortal.

"I'm not exactly happy bein' held here, if that's what you mean?" Cankles slipped back into his regular manner of speech the Sorcerer was used to, so he would not rouse suspicion.

"I was speaking of your present state of mind! I heard you talking to yourself, babbling like the fool that you are."

Cankles could make out Dragonite's dark, recessed eyes searching about for signs of the Pooka.

"I always talk to myself. But I'd be more concerned if I began answerin' my own questions, especially since I don't usually have any real good answers."

"Shut it!" snarled Dragonite, threatening to take a jab with his staff at Cankles. "If you were not speaking to yourself, then who were you talking to?"

"I was speakin' to…" His voice trailed off as he considered the most appropriate answer that would cause him the least amount of grief.

"Go on! To whom were you speaking to? I demand to know."

"My… shadow. Yes, I was talkin' to my shadow. It gets lonely in here all by myself."

"Excellent! You *are* losing what little mind you have left!"

"Yes… I was callin' for it to come back to me when you heard me earlier," lied Cankles, his hands clutching his midriff as it suddenly rumbled, demanding to be fed.

"My timing is impeccable!" delighted the Sorcerer, hearing the growling of his empty stomach. "You must be hungry."

"Starving, really," admitted Cankles, nodding in confirmation.

"I have some food for you."

"For me?" Even as his eyes narrowed in suspicion, Cankles' mouth watered involuntarily.

"Of course, for you! What kind of host would deny his guest of a meal?"

"What kind of host keeps his guest imprisoned behind bars, albeit crystal ones?" questioned Cankles.

"I am truly disappointed," snorted the Sorcerer. "Now you are making me out to be some kind of monster."

"I don't think my opinion of you is that far off the mark!" Cankles' words were matter-of-fact.

"Come now! Would a monster of a host offer water to a thirsty man?" Dragonite glanced at the giant decanter he had conjured up in the middle of the cell.

"A considerate host would've made that water easily accessible," argued Cankles.

"Never mind that! Would a monster offer a meal to a hungry man? I think not!"

"Sure he would, if it was poisoned. You could have tainted it with some kind of deadly potion meant to kill me."

"You dolt!" cursed Dragonite. "Why would I do that? I need you alive, at least for the time being."

"Then prove it. Whatever it is you're plannin' to feed me, you take a bite first." Cankles dared the Sorcerer.

"Very well," conceded Dragonite, fishing about through the folds of his great cloak. Presenting the large, leather bag he had confiscated from his prisoner upon first capturing him, the Sorcerer plunged his hand inside. Pushing aside an old tunic, a well-worn pair of wool socks and the old sword Cankles carried, but refused to wear at the ready after it was returned by Tag, Dragonite groped through the contents of the bag until he found what he was looking for.

"Here we go! A scrap of bread removed from *your* pack" announced the Sorcerer, holding it up for his prisoner to see, only to drop it. Snatching it up from the ground, he continued, "Unless you had poisoned it yourself or those stinky, old socks somehow contaminated it, this food should be safe to consume."

"I know the bread was gettin' stale, but it was safe to eat when I put it in there. However, between then and now, who can say what you've done to it."

"I've done nothing," insisted Dragonite. He angrily tossed away Cankles' bag against the far wall, well away from his prisoner's reach. "Unless you count dropping it, but I did make a concerted effort to pick it up within a few seconds of hitting the ground, in case it mattered."

"Prove it," ordered Cankles, refusing to take the Sorcerer's words as the truth. "If it's as safe as you claim, you'll have no problem eatin' some of it."

Dragonite snorted in disdain as he scowled at his prisoner. "Fine! A bite, it is!"

"Go on then." Cankles peered through the bars to see if his captor was going through with this taste-test challenge.

Dragonite's sharp features became all the more severe as his nostrils flared, his nose wrinkling in disgust. Like a snarling dog bearing its teeth, he drew back his thin lips, pulling them away so they would not touch the crust. Cavity riddled, dull, yellowed teeth protruded to gnaw on the bread.

A small piece of crust snapped off. The Sorcerer held it between his teeth to show Cankles the evidence.

"Now, chew it up and swallow," demanded Cankles, waiting to see if Dragonite was about to spit it out before the poison took hold.

The Sorcerer's beady eyes gleamed with malice as he glared at his prisoner. The piece of bread disappeared in his mouth. Hard and dried, it instantly absorbed what saliva there was, but it was still impossible for him to swallow it without choking. Using his tongue, he pushed the desiccated morsel to one side where it formed an obvious bulge in his usually sunken cheek. With a look of utter disgust clearly etched on his gaunt face, Dragonite began to chew, his molars grinding together to pulverize the piece of bread.

Cankles watched with interest, and sure enough, he heard the Sorcerer swallowing hard, forcing down the petrified crust.

"Satisfied?" snapped the Sorcerer.

"Aha! By the look on your face, that bread was indeed poisoned!" declared Cankles.

"You fool! I find all this grainy goodness to be absolutely detestable! It is fine for you mortals to partake in, but I do not take well to foods your type find appetizing!"

"Not so fast. Open your mouth. Let me see if you really did eat that piece of bread."

"What?" gasped the Sorcerer.

"You heard me. Now, open your mouth. Let me see if you actually swallowed it."

"You are testing my patience!" snapped Dragonite.

"Hey, if you really want me to stay alive, if I don't eat, I won't be alive for long. It's the only way to convince me it's not poisoned, so you best do as I demand."

"I am the one to make demands, not you!" growled Dragonite, his feet stamping in annoyance and frustration.

"Well, you can either have another bite or you can show me that your mouth is empty, then maybe I'll believe you."

"Fine!" snapped the Sorcerer. His jaw dropped open for this mortal's inspection.

Cankles peered inside and sure enough, the bread was gone. All that remained were masticated bits and pieces sticking to the ridges and pits of decaying molars.

Dragonite's mouth snapped shut as he grumbled, "Happy now?"

"Happy that you swallowed, but not so happy about bein' here," corrected Cankles, extending a grimy, open hand to accept what was left of the bread.

"Damn you!" cursed the Sorcerer. He sputtered as he trembled with rage. "You have tested my patience for the last time."

Throwing the stale offering to the ground, he used the toe of his boot to nudge the bread oh-so tantalizingly close, but just out of his prisoner's reach.

"As your punishment, I will make it so this is as hard to acquire as that drink of water," mocked Dragonite. Spinning about on his heels, he stormed off.

Before Cankles could tell him the water was not that difficult to obtain, the Sorcerer was gone. Dragonite stomped away; thoroughly agitated by the thought this fool of a prisoner had succeeded in making a fool out of him.

For the longest moment, Cankles stared at the bread, licking his lips in hunger.

Crouching down, he leaned against the crystal bars of his prison. Wedging his shoulder against this gap, he thrust his right arm through, straining to reach the food.

"*Strrr---e--tch*," Cankles whispered beneath his breath as he struggled to claim the piece of bread. Every time his fingertips just grazed by the crust, he groaned in disappointment as the bread moved a little farther from his grasp with each attempt.

Cankles slumped to the ground, his lanky legs sprawling out before him. With a disheartened sigh, he gazed longingly at the offering, wondering if a rat would devour it before he had a chance to claim his meager meal.

"I wish my arms were longer," lamented Cankles. Leaning forward, he stretched his sore back, his fingertips touching the tips of his toes. "Maybe not as long as my legs, but just long enough to reach that bread."

Then it suddenly dawned on him. He stared at his outstretched arms, mentally measuring them against his straightened legs.

"That's it!"

With newfound determination, Cankles scooted over, pressing close to the bars of his cell. From this sitting position he slid his right leg between the two bars that provided the greatest space and direct path to the bread. Just as he did so, a hungry rat peeked out from the shadows. It was as though fate was deliberately conspiring against Cankles once more.

He cursed himself for even thinking such a creature would appear at this very moment to steal away with his meal, but it was too late to dispel this negative thought.

Sitting up on its haunches, snout held high as whiskers nervously quivered, the gaunt-looking rodent sniffed the air.

"Oh, no you don't!" Cankles frantically waved his hands about in hopes of shooing away the rat.

Instead, the brazen creature advanced, skittering forward with jerky stop and go movements as it assessed the threat this mortal posed.

In desperation, Cankles thrust his skinny leg between the bars until it was wedged through up to his thigh. This awkward position allowed him to flex at the knee and ankle, but no more than that. With the crook where foot joined leg, bending his knee, Cankles dragged the chunk of bread closer to the bars of his prison. All the while, the rat, driven by hunger, refused to flee. Instead, it inched ever closer, following the tempting scent of food.

"Scat! Go away!" ordered Cankles, dismissing the animal with a wave of his hand. "If you leave, there may be a crumb or two left for you."

Hunger overrode fear as the rodent crept right up to Cankles, crawling over his foot to sniff at the bread.

Cankles' first instinct was to flinch, flinging the rat from his foot, but he was forced by his own hunger to remain composed, enduring the tiny paws armed with sharp claws clambering about on him.

As he drew his knee up, bringing the bread closer, the rat lunged, diving at the food.

Just as it was about to flee with his meal, Cankles' hand darted through the bars. It slapped down, trapping the rodent by its scaly, bare tail.

Squeaking in fright, the rat dropped the bread, twisting about to bite the hand pinning its tail down.

With a flick of his wrist, Cankles knocked the animal away while lunging forward to snatch up the food before the rat could make off with it.

"*Yes!*" exclaimed Cankles, retracting his arm and leg through the bars to enjoy his small victory over an even smaller meal. "I did it!"

Retreating to the centre of his prison, Cankles rested his back against the giant decanter of water. Blowing off the dust and dirt from the bread, he proceeded to nibble on the crust, savouring the morsel as he used his fingertips to collect the crumbs that fell, gathering on his chest.

Though this scrap of bread was a far cry from a decent meal, he was grateful to have something in his stomach. Brushing up the last of the crumbs, he popped them into his mouth, using the tip of his tongue to lick any trace of food from the palm of his hand.

For a lingering moment, Cankles sat on the ground, imagining he had just dined on a three-course meal. With a contented sigh, he stood up, speaking to himself. "Now, to top it off with a hearty pint."

Pretending he was drinking the best ale made in Cadboll in the County of Wren to be served up at his favourite haunt, the Gelded Pony Inn, Cankles swallowed down handful after handful of water, hoping the liquid would be soaked up by the bread to make him feel full.

Hearing the scratching of clawed feet, Cankles glanced up to see the rat had returned, sniffing about where the bread had landed, searching for leftovers.

"Sorry, rat," apologized Cankles, "but I am far from home and trapped behind these bars, not even able to reach my bag to see if there is anything left in there to share with you. You have the freedom to look for food; I do not. If I am still here in a day or two, perhaps you can return with a plump friend."

The rat sat up. It stared in his direction upon hearing this voice.

"Yes, in a pinch, I am sure you're as tasty as any water rat when roasted just so over an open fire." Cankles decided if desperation should force his hand, this scrawny rodent was an option. He sighed in disappointment as he watched the animal scamper away in search of another food source.

As the rodent disappeared down the tunnel, Cankles shouted behind the rat, "If you should see that little Sprite in your travels, send him down this way, will you? I desperately need to speak to him."

"Bloody hell!" squeaked Loken. He made the mistake of letting his guard down.

His heart raced; his leathery wings flapping madly. Twisting about through the air, he narrowly dodged the talons of a great horned owl. The bird swooped down from the night sky, the soft, ragged edges of its feathers helping to muffle the sounds of its approach. The only thing that saved the Sprite was his erratic manner of flight. Flying dangerously close to Loken, the turbulent wake produced by the owl as it missed him caused his little bat form to tumble, head over tail, through the air.

"That was stupid of me!" Cursing beneath his breath, he glanced about, searching for the bird of prey in case it was returning for another assault.

He managed to elude Dragonite as the Sorcerer made his way down the corridor to torment his prisoner. The Pooka made sure none of the mimes spotted him as he winged his way to the mouth of the tunnel leading from the Sorcerer's lair, even taking precautions to make sure there were no dangers lurking at the entrance into the mountain as he made his escape.

Having avoided detection by any dragon lurking about as the chill of the night waned, Loken was overly confident his flight to the northern reaches of the Dimbolt Forest would go without danger or delay. With the stark silhouette of the trees against the predawn sky in sight, it gave him a sense of security, so he was caught completely off guard. This momentary lapse in awareness was enough that he failed to detect the owl's silent approach.

Pumping his wings to fly through the air as fast as he could, Loken twisted about, then suddenly dropped and swerved as the owl circled around, swooping down on its intended meal.

Spinning and tumbling through the air, the Sprite dipped, ducking beneath those sharp talons as the owl dove at him.

With clever, aerobatic maneuvering, Loken proved elusive. His haphazard, unpredictable flight delivered him to a tall fir tree where a flock of crows perched, sleeping peacefully until the coming of the sun.

Ducking between the boughs, Loken avoided capture.

The owl, so focused on this meal, tried to follow but was forced to abort the attempt as the startled crows burst into the dark sky, cawing in agitation and surprise by the raptor's sudden attack. The ebony scavengers' raucous calls broke the tranquil pre-dawn sky, echoing across the lands as their wings beat in frantic, confused flight to avoid this bird of prey.

Outnumbered by the crows, the great horned owl immediately lost interest in the bat, electing to beat a hasty retreat than to face being mobbed by these harassing birds.

"Aah! The joys of shape-shifting," sighed Loken.

Without this ability, had he been a typical Sprite rather than a Pooka, the difficulty coming with being crippled by the Sorcerer when Dragonite plucked off one of his wings would have made it nearly impossible to fly as he did. And in Loken's mind, a Sprite that couldn't fly was as good as dead. He sighed in relief, watching as the owl winged northward while the crows flew east, coming to rest on a distant tree as they waited for the sun to peer over the horizon.

Perched on a high bough of this fir, Loken's bat form clung to the limb as it swayed with the impact of his landing. With the impending sun he could now adopt another form better adapted to daylight and capable of moving with far greater speed. Clambering about, using the thumb on the apex of each wing, he made his way from the flimsy end toward the more stable tree trunk. For a moment, Loken dangled upside-down, using the opportunity to catch his breath as he surveyed his surroundings.

With no sign of the owl returning and the flock of crows already busy nattering and pecking at each other, Loken felt at ease, enough to morph. In a show of bright light, Loken took on his usual form, but he was forced to seize a twig to steady himself. His missing wing momentarily threw him off balance as he wobbled about on the branch.

"This will take some getting used to," muttered the Sprite, annoyed he had forgotten about his new *condition* while flying unhampered as a bat.

Drawing a deep breath, he gazed southward. With the start of a new day, he could set a straight course. If everything goes as planned, he'll be home, back in the Fairy's Vale well before the sun is high in the sky.

"The way is clear," whispered Rainus. With a wave of his hand, he motioned his comrades to join him at the mouth of the cave.

With the impending sun leaching away the darkness, Rose didn't know which was worse; being out in the open with dragons actively on the hunt in search of an easy meal, or venturing deep into the tunnel that would lead them to the Sorcerer's secret lair.

"Come on, Princess," urged Tag. "Quickly!"

Before she could protest, he seized her hand. Pulling Rose along to follow the Dream Merchant, he rushed her on before they could be spotted by a hungry dragon or a menacing mime.

"Hold on!" grumbled Rose, yanking her hand free as they ducked into the tunnel.

"For what?" asked Tag.

"I will not blindly rush into danger!" Rose drew an arrow from the quiver to nock the projectile onto her bow. "I recommend you do the same. Draw that sword of yours. Keeping it safely sheathed will be your undoing, if we are caught unawares."

"I'll do that, but if you think any of us are crazy enough to venture forth with you taking up the rear with an armed bow, nervously sneaking along behind us, then think again."

"No offence, Princess, but the young master is quite right," stated Silas. "Use your sling if you must, but we will all be safer if you put that arrow away for now."

"I suppose my sling will do for this occasion," conceded Rose. She placed the arrow back into the quiver as she patted her never-ending supply of steel balls she carried in a pouch tied to her sash. Slinging her bow over her shoulder, she wound one end of the leather sling around her hand, just in case.

"Your aim is becoming legendary, Princess," said Silas, nodding in approval. "With Lord Silverthorn taking up the rear as I lead the way with my trusty staff, the three of us shall keep you safe."

"Hmmm... the four of us against an army of mimes, a crazy little Pooh-do thingy, and a deranged Sorcerer?" snorted Rose. "I am not liking the odds."

"This is no time to be cowering in those fancy little shoes of yours, Princess," warned Rainus, as he stared down the passageway. "There is no turning back now."

"I know," whispered Rose. "I just wanted to make sure all of you are perfectly aware of what we are getting ourselves into."

"Believe me, we know," grumbled Tag. Unsheathing his sword, he motioned for the Princess to stay behind him. "We move, now."

"I will lead the way, Wizard. Follow me," whispered Rainus. Removing a torch from its wall mount, he pressed a finger to his lips as he whispered, "And keep your voices down. The crystals lining these tunnels seem to amplify every little sound."

Rose nodded in understanding as she crept behind Tag.

With measured steps, they tiptoed along the passageway. Even as Rose and Tag attempted to muffle their footsteps, trying to be as silent as Rainus as he led the way, their subdued footfalls still amplified against the walls of the tunnel, echoing with every cautious step.

The flames of Rainus' torch twisted about, swirling in chaotic dance, buffeted by their wake as they advanced. This fire burned brightly, reflecting off the crystal walls to cast a stunning, rainbow prism of light all around them.

Rose gasped in surprise as she stumbled, accidentally kicking a chunk of crystal to send it bouncing and tumbling along. They froze, grimacing with every 'click', 'clack' and 'clatter' the fist-sized quartz made as it travelled on what seemed to be a neverending path. Finally, it stopped. Only its sounds continued to echo down the tunnel before gradually fading away.

Rose's comrades turned to face her, scowling with a menacing 'are *you serious'* look of reproach.

She cowered beneath their unforgiving gaze.

"It is not like I meant to!" she whispered in her own defense.

"Please try to be more careful, Princess," urged Tag. "We don't want to attract any unwanted attention. Step lightly. Lift your feet so you don't send another rock or crystal tumbling ahead to announce our presence."

As the tunnel narrowed, Rose, Tag and Rainus gasped in surprise as the passage abruptly opened up into a massive chamber. Their eyes took in the natural spectacle as the many crystal facets reflected the torch's light. All around them, clear columns of crystal jutted from the floor and protruded from the ceiling, all leaning at sharp angles. Each column was easily six-foot in circumference, and far taller, towering higher than the eighteen-foot-tall marble pillars gracing the main hall of Pepperton Palace.

"How is this even possible?" marvelled Rose. Her eyes were wide-open in amazement as they glanced about, only stopping to admire her reflection in the flat facet of one of the columns. "I thought the crystals lining the passageway were impressive, but this is…"

"Magnificent!" concluded Tag.

"There are many wondrous things in this world you have yet to witness, Princess Rose," assured the Wizard. "Just because you cannot conceive how it is possible, it does not mean it is impossible."

"Never mind her," said Tag. "She has a limited imagination to begin with, restricted to what she knows and sees within the confines of her palatial residence back in Fleetwood."

"It is rather dazzling, you must admit," explained Rose. "I am just a little awestruck."

"I wish you were more dumbstruck," whispered Tag, motioning the Princess to lower her excited voice. "Your words really carry in here."

"No more than yours," argued Rose, tiptoeing behind Silas as the Wizard advanced. "I just think it would be the perfect accent for my bedchamber back home."

"Home is the farthest thing from here, and it should be the furthest thing from your mind at this moment," scolded Tag. "Focus on the here and now, will you?"

"I admit this is an amazing thing, for even I have never been witness to such a spectacle in all my years, but we cannot loiter here," said Rainus, his sharp eyes surveying their surroundings. "We should move with haste, advance before Dragonite or his minions show up."

"I thought the plan was to confront and defeat the Sorcerer," commented Rose.

"As there is a very real likelihood that we will be vastly outnumbered, I believe the prudent thing to do is to sneak in, steal the dreamstone, and then rescue your friend. Be in and out before Dragonite knows we are here," explained Rainus.

"Prudent indeed, I like your plan!" praised Rose, nodding in agreement.

"This way." Silas waved his comrades on.

With silent, measured steps they advanced, creeping through the chamber, their every move mimicked by the facets of crystal that also served to reflect the torch's light.

"Are you sure we are going in the right direction?" questioned Rose.

"At this moment, this is the only way," answered Silas. "Just be grateful we are not faced with choosing between two passages."

"You spoke too soon, Master Agincor," groaned Rainus. "If my eyes do not deceive me, I see we are faced with four possible tunnels to choose from."

"Lovely!" grunted Rose. "Which is the correct way?"

"Hush! Do you hear that?" asked Rainus, his head cocking to one side.

"Hear what?" whispered Tag, cupping a hand to his ear as he listened for what the Elf heard.

"I hear nothing," said Rose. "It must be those Elf ears of yours."

"Listen," urged Rainus, as he motioned for the Princess to be silent. "I hear noise…"

"Noise?" whispered Rose. "That is rather vague? What kind of noise?"

"The kind mimes makes when they are trying to move in silence," answered the Elf. "That is why you cannot hear them, but my keen ears can."

"How many?" asked Tag, taking Rainus' words at face value. "Do you have a sense of numbers? Are they heading our way?"

The Elf raised his hand for silence. Closing his eyes, he focused on the distant drone that sounded from the mouth of the tunnel that delivered them to this chamber.

The crystals not only amplified the faint sounds detected by his sensitive ears, but they served to distort them as well.

"What say you, Lord Silverthorn?" questioned Silas. "What do you hear?"

"Footsteps! Many of them!" answered Rainus, rushing toward the far side of the chamber. "Hurry! Follow me."

"But which tunnel do we take?" asked Rose, as she rushed behind the Elf.

Rainus stopped, studying the four passageways that looked identical except that one tunnel, the one farthest to the right, was lit by torches while the others remained dark.

"How about this one?" suggested Rose, tugging Tag toward the dark tunnel farthest to the left. By the ragged cobwebs draping over half the entrance, she could tell none had entered the passageway for quite some time. "It looks the least used."

Before Rose could use the tip of her bow to knock down the web, Rainus stopped her.

"Now what?" asked Rose.

"Duck *under* the web," ordered the Elf, tossing the torch aside so it's light would not betray their presence, "so none will suspect we went this way."

"Brilliant!" exclaimed Tag, giving the Princess a nudge. "Now, go!"

"But –" Rose's protest came to an abrupt halt before it even started, as Tag pushed her head down and under the half curtain of webbing.

He, Silas and Rainus crept behind her as she inched her way forward in the growing darkness, hands extended before her so she wouldn't run into a wall of crystal or more cobwebs.

"I cannot see a thing," whispered Rose, shuffling along just in case the cave floor dropped away beneath her feet.

"Just be careful," urged Tag, following the sounds of her voice in front of him.

"Ouch!" yelped Rose, her hand slapping over her forehead as she bumped into a crystal jutting from the low ceiling of the tunnel.

"Allow me," offered Silas. The orb on his staff glowed, shedding just enough light to illuminate their immediate surroundings without revealing their presence in this tunnel.

"Much better," whispered Rose, pressing her hand against the fresh contusion.

"This way," ordered the Wizard. "We shall venture on, just to be on the safe side."

Following the dim glow of the Wizard's crystal, it was sufficient light for the Elf to see with relative confidence. Rose pushed by Tag to cling to Rainus' arm. If a crack in the earth big enough to swallow them up should appear, he would see it first.

"Do you mind?" grumbled Tag.

"I mind falling into a great big, gaping hole," whispered Rose.

"No fear of that," assured Rainus. "Just keep your eyes on the ground before you."

"Easy for you to say," grumbled the Princess, inching along in the darkness. "You are like an owl with those magic Elf eyes."

"A little further, and then silence," ordered Silas, "until we are confident the danger has passed."

Venturing deeper, they came to a dead-end as they entered a small cave, its ceiling so high there was only an all-consuming blackness above them.

"Keep still... Quiet now," whispered Rainus. His comrades could tell he was listening for sounds of the enemy as they marched into the large main chamber.

They stood silent, barely breathing as Silas doused the light of his crystal orb so they were smothered by the darkness, shielded from the enemy's eyes.

Tag and Rose could now hear what Rainus had heard in the distance. From where they hid, the sounds of footfalls echoed toward them from the cavernous chamber.

With the distortion created by the massive crystal columns, even for the Elf it was impossible to ascertain numbers. Their best and only strategy was to bide their time in the black void of this cave until danger passed.

As the footsteps gradually faded, Rose glanced up to the ceiling of the chamber. To her surprise, dots of light, like tiny, pale green stars, began to glow against a backdrop darker than any night sky in the dead of winter.

"What is that?" whispered the Princess. "Those cannot be stars, not in here."

Tag's eyes glanced high overhead. "Stars don't move, at least, not like that."

"Those things cannot be fireflies," stated Rainus, squinting to see as more and more dots of lights filled the ceiling.

"How beautiful," commented Rose, admiring the spectacle as the entire cave overhead glowed with thousands of greenish spots of light that swelled and dimmed, only to glow brightly again.

"Whatever they are, those things are alive," ascertained the Elf.

"Do my eyes deceive me or are they getting brighter?" asked Rose, staring at this phenomenon.

"They are not getting brighter..." determined Rainus. "They are coming closer."

"But what are they? If not fireflies or Fairies, what glows like that?" asked Tag. "It's very odd."

"Worms," whispered Silas, speaking with utmost certainty. "Glow worms to be exact."

"Worms! Ewww! I hate worms!" shrieked Rose, as Tag slapped his hand over her mouth to stifle her scream.

As her voice boomed, echoing through the cave, revulsion filled her heart. As the sound waves created by her words accosted the sensitive, soft-bodied grubs, they began to fall. The patter of worms raining down from the ceiling to pelt her head caused Rose to panic all the more.

Her mind reeled as her heart raced. The popping of squishy grubs crushed underfoot made Rose's stomach churn. All she could remember seeing in the darkness were smears of sickly green light everywhere she stepped as the silken threads produced by the worms brushed against her face and hands as she dashed away.

"Bloody hell!" cursed Tag, "Come back, Princess!"

Using the broad edge of his blade, he swept away the glowing worms dangling on their silk tethers before him.

More disgusted than terrified, Rose had no intention of hiding in there for one second longer.

Tag, Silas and Rainus gave chase, following her form that was illuminated by the worms that had landed on her head and shoulders. The trio caught up to Rose in the main chamber.

Like a girl gone mad, she thrashed about. Jumping and frantically brushing away the worms and the threads they produced, she whipped her hair about to fling off the grubs clinging to her tresses.

"Ewww! Disgusting!" groaned the Princess. Her skin crawled as a worm dropped down her back from all this frenetic movement.

"Have you taken leave of your senses?" scolded Tag, as Rainus and Silas motioned Rose to quiet down.

"I hate worms, glowing or not!"

"It's not like these worms will eat you!" rebuked Tag, flicking off the one clinging to her shoulder.

Rose shuddered in repulsion.

"Oh, no!" groaned Rainus, staring down the lit tunnel the mimes had entered. "They are returning!"

"Not again," muttered Silas. "Quickly, back into hiding!"

"I am not going back in there!" insisted Rose, digging her heels in.

"Then we'll go down this one," suggested Tag, using the tip of his sword to point to the dark tunnel next to the one they had just evacuated.

"But there could be even more worms," responded Rose.

"Those worms did not start falling until you screamed," reminded Rainus.

"Can you blame me? They were utterly disgusting!"

"Better disgusted than dead!" Silas used the tip of his staff to prod her on.

"*No!* No dark, worm-infested tunnel!" protested Rose, her feet stamping the ground in stubborn defiance. "I refuse."

"If those mimes catch us, Dragonite will kill us for sure this time!" countered Tag.

"This is no time to argue," snapped Rainus. "Move!"

Just as the first in a row of mimes appeared at the mouth of the illuminated tunnel, Rose shrieked as Tag steered her on to escape into the black hole.

"Hurry!" shouted Silas, following right behind them.

With her arms outstretched before her, the Princess blindly rushed forward, stumbling into the consuming blackness.

"Slow down!" snapped Tag, his heart pounding in his chest as he raced after her.

"Wait!" ordered Rainus. "Something is not right."

"What do you mean?" asked Silas. He dare not use the crystal orb for light as it would give away their precise location.

"Those mimes, why did they not give chase?" whispered the Elf. Staring down the dark passage, he could see their stark silhouettes. They congregated at the mouth of the tunnel. He could tell they were staring into the passage, but not one made an effort to come after them.

"This *is* strange," noted Tag, squinting to see down the dark tube.

"Why did they not follow?" wondered Rose, perplexed by the lack of retaliatory action on the mimes' part.

"Maybe they know it's us and they're more afraid of us, than we are of them," offered Tag.

"That's being highly optimistic, young sir, considering we are greatly outnumbered," said Silas.

"There is a reason they did not pursue us," determined Rainus, growing suspicious of the mimes' reluctance to give chase.

"Oh, no…" groaned Rose.

"What?" asked Tag, turning toward her voice.

"Suppose there is something worse in here than those glowing worms?" whispered Rose, her eyes anxiously darting about, searching for signs of danger.

"Like what?" Tag's hand gripped the sword's hilt all the tighter.

"You know… like maybe some big, ugly, humongous spider," whispered Rose, her eyes growing wide with dread. "Maybe that is why those mimes did not follow. There is a monster spider lurking in here, waiting to trap us in a great, big web, and then suck the blood from our bodies until we are dead."

"You have an overactive imagination," scolded Tag. "Such a

creature does not exist, at least, not in our world."

"Could be conjured up by someone dabbling in the forbidden arts," countered the Princess. "After all, we are sneaking about in the Sorcerer's lair."

"Oh, hush! That's crazy talk! A giant spider? I think not," rebuked Tag, shaking his head even though none could see.

"Then why did they not follow?" asked Rose. "Answer me that!"

"I sense the Princess is right," whispered Rainus, his keen eyes struggling to focus in the darkness.

"What? There is a giant spider in here?" whispered Tag, turning toward the Elf's voice.

"I never said that. But something is preventing those mimes from following."

"Perhaps they are just as disgusted by the glow worms as the Princess is," surmised Silas.

All eyes turned toward the ceiling of the tunnel as the dozen or so mimes that had clustered at the mouth of this passageway, refused to enter.

"Do not scream this time," ordered Tag, his voice in a whisper. "If you don't want a cascade of glow worms coming down on you, keep your voice down."

Immediately, Rose bit down on her lower lip to mute a scream if grubs should start falling on her.

"We must hide deeper in this tunnel," whispered Silas, "only until those mimes leave."

With eyes cast upward, waiting for points of pale green lights to glow, the Wizard and his comrades slowly backed away, further into the darkness.

Hanging onto Tag's arm as she retreated, Rose continued to stare at the ceiling, waiting and watching for the first sign of the luminescent grubs to light up the tunnel.

Nothing… only blackness.

Rose gasped, screaming in terror as she stepped back. Tag yelped in surprise as her hands seized his arm, pulling him down with her.

"Help!" shrieked Rose.

Just as Silas' crystal glowed with light to illuminate their surroundings, Rainus lunged down. He grabbed onto Tag as he toppled into the gaping hole as the tunnel abruptly terminated, dropping straight down.

"That is why the mimes did not follow," determined Silas, as he helped the Elf to drag Tag onto solid ground as the boy clung on to the Princess. "They believed we would fall to our death in that hole."

"This hole is really not that deep," stated Rainus, as he reached down, helping Tag to pull Rose to safety. No more than ten feet from below her dangling feet, there were rows of jagged rocks that decreased in size as the pit narrowed into a fist-sized black hole in the centre. "Unless you knock your head on one of those rocks, the worst that can happen is a twisted ankle from a hard landing."

The Wizard's eyes opened wide in horror as he shouted, "Quickly, get out! Those are not rocks!"

8
Dark Magic

Rose screamed as she glanced down. The rocks below suddenly shifted, but none tumbled down as an eerie rumbling resonated from the depth of the dark hole in the centre of this pit.

"What is that?" gasped Tag, staring at the ground that seemed to come alive beneath Rose's dangling feet.

"They're teeth!" warned Silas, pointing at what appeared at first glance to be nothing more than rows of conical shaped rocks. "And they're attached to a very large mouth!"

"Get me out of here!" shrieked Rose. She panicked as the black hole suddenly expanded, unleashing a loud, vile stench of a belch as those giant teeth moved in an undulating wave toward her.

Rainus and Tag hauled the Princess out, yanking her from the pit as the rumble sounding from the depth of the black abyss became a deafening roar that drowned out their own screams of surprise and fright.

"*RUN!*" hollered Rainus, not even waiting for the Wizard's crystal orb to light the way.

Ahead, he could see the silhouettes of the mimes as they mouthed a silent scream, scattering in fear as the bellow echoing from the deep overwhelmed Rose and her comrades as they raced forward. Tag seized Rose's hand, pulling her along while the Wizard used his staff to steady himself as the creature's roar rattled the tunnel. Its huge body was thrust from the pit, stretching like a monstrous earthworm. Rows of bristling hairs adorning rings of sinewy, undulating muscles helped the creature to advance as it squeezed through the tunnel in pursuit of a meal.

As the Elf ducked to exit the tunnel that narrowed as it opened into the main chamber, Silas, Tag and Rose dove forward, bowling Rainus over as they leapt from the opening to escape the huge, snapping maw of the killer worm. Its forward movement came to an abrupt halt, impeded by the smaller opening.

"What is that thing?" Rose recoiled in horror as Rainus and Tag jabbed at the gaping orifice armed with rows of teeth.

"A worm!" explained Silas, taking up his staff. "A very large and hungry worm!"

"How can that *thing* be a worm?" gasped Rose, ducking behind the Wizard as Rainus and Tag battled the behemoth grub. Hacking and slashing, their swords did little to drive the beast back.

"A little dark magic can conjure up such monstrosities," answered Silas.

Snatching the burning torch from its wall mount, the Wizard thrust it into the monster's gaping maw. As though the light itself burned as surely as the flames of the torch, it was enough to repel the beast.

Rainus and Tag breathed a sigh of relief, dropping to their knees in exhaustion as the worm abruptly withdrew, disappearing into the black abyss from whence it came.

"Phew!" exclaimed Tag, drawing in another deep breath.

"That was too close!" exclaimed the Elf.

Rose screamed, yanking back on Rainus and Tag as the worm burst forth once more. Bashing against the columns of crystal, it attempted to widen the opening of the tunnel to snap them up.

The three scrambled, ducking low to the ground as Silas unleashed a blast of energy from his crystal. Whether it was the brilliant show of light or the pain from being struck directly in its throat, the creature retreated. With a nerve-wracking bellow, its body shrunk back, slipping into the blackness to wait once more, its mouth agape, hoping for a meal to drop in.

"What is this crystal house of horrors? A sanctuary for worms of all shapes and sizes?" groaned Rose, shuddering in disgust.

"The glow worms are common enough in these parts, but that monster worm was an anomaly," assured Silas. "I am quite certain Dragonite had a hand in conjuring up that beast!"

"And what a beast it was!" exclaimed Tag, snatching up his sword from the ground as he clambered onto his feet. "If it wasn't so freakishly large and armed with all those teeth, it would have been amazing to behold!"

"*Amazing?* Give your head a shake! You do realize that beast wanted to eat us alive!" snapped Rose. "Only a hungry fish as monstrously large as that worm would have reason to find it worthy of *beholding*."

"Hush!" ordered Silas, as he raised his hands for silence. Glancing around the empty chamber, it was evident the mimes had fled in fear.

"Have you forgotten the enemy?"

"Hey... where did they go?" whispered Tag. "You'd think those mimes would have stayed to make sure that monster worm killed us."

"I have a feeling those fools believe that is just what happened," assessed Rainus. By the distant scampering of the many feet that he alone could now detect echoing from the illuminated tunnel, they had been abandoned to their fate.

"Whether they departed from here because they believed we were killed or because they feared for their own lives if that giant worm was able to enter this chamber to kill them, I recommend we forge on," suggested Silas. "Let us be on our way before they can report to Dragonite."

"And before the Princess can protest, we will *not* be venturing down dark tunnel number three," said Rainus, as he pointed to the black opening next to the tunnel lined with burning torches.

"Brilliant!" praised Rose, nodding in approval. "If tunnel number one had a host of worms and number two had the single, large monster worm, I am betting number three will have a terrible surprise worse than the first two combined."

"That is not the reason I suggested avoiding the last dark tunnel," responded the Elf.

"Truly?" Rose's brows arched up in surprise.

"My first thought was that there were no fresh tracks leading in or out of that tunnel, so there was no point in venturing down that way in search of Cankles or Dragonite," revealed Rainus. "As such, the Sorcerer, and what we seek, both alive and inanimate, must be some-where down this well-used, lighted passageway."

"That sounds all very logical to me," agreed Rose, as she stared down the dark tunnel, "but I still believe there is something terrible hiding somewhere down there in that blackness."

"Then it's a bloody good thing we are not going that way," grunted Tag. "Now, stop wasting time. Let's be on our way."

"Fine," grumbled the Princess. She followed behind Rainus as he listened first, checking for sounds of approaching danger before venturing on.

"This way," urged the Elf. "And remember, keep your voices down. If those mimes believe we are dead, let them continue thinking so."

"It is too bad there is not some kind of dark magic I can call upon to make Sparks Firestar believe I am dead," Loken muttered beneath his breath. He morphed back into his usual form from the one of the falcon that delivered him with speed to the Fairy's Vale. "If he believed it was so, he'd let his guard down. I'd have a chance to speak to Celia, warn her of his devious plot to usurp her."

Glancing about, he sighed with longing as he watched the warming sun glisten off the beads of dew bejeweling the leaves and blades of grass. It was during moments like this, when the tranquil morning was greeted by the dazzling sun filtering through the tree canopy, that he missed this place the most. It was enchanting when the golden sun beamed down on the Fairy's Ring in the meadow, the dappled sunlight dancing about as a calming breeze whispered through the treetops.

This was a far cry from the dark, wretched caves Dragonite took refuge in. Even the dazzling crystal caves and tunnels could not compare to the natural beauty of the Fairy's Vale, day or night.

Loken drew a deep breath, fighting to compose himself. His heart tightened as he fought the old feelings of anger and frustration. It was like standing on the threshold of one's home, but not being able to step inside. And if he did, he knew he would not be greeted with warm salutations. Knowing Sparks, he would do everything in his powers to have him executed on sight, before his beloved Celia could learn the truth from him.

But how was she to discover what really happened with Sparks Firestar standing in his way, impeding his every move? He unleashed a disheartened sigh as he pondered his plight.

"I must get closer," whispered Loken, peering down at the hole in the tree trunk where the Queen of the Tooth Fairies resided in her gleaming, dentine palace. "At least close enough to find out what that devious soul is plotting against her now."

Searching about, other than the wrens and thrushes chirping in the trees surrounding the meadow, Loken could see the resident squirrels that dwelled in this great oak were nowhere to be seen this morning.

Had the acorns on this tree been ready to harvest, the squirrels would be noisily chattering as they went about their business, warding off hungry crows, jays and other strange squirrels hoping to plunder from their treasure trove of nuts. At this moment, it was obvious the squirrels that had staked out this oak as their own were forced to forage elsewhere. These rodents searched for berries and mushrooms and were made to hunt about to uncover their hidden cache of acorns until this tree provided them with an ample food supply in the autumn when the nuts ripened.

With a snap of his fingers and a glow that was dulled by the brilliance of the morning sun shining through the boughs, Loken morphed into a red squirrel. Listening for sounds of danger; his ears swivelled about, the long tufts of hair tipping them quivered with nervous energy. He had to make certain the squirrels residing here were away; otherwise, his presence in their territory would cause the bushy-tailed rodents to raise the alarm with their noisy chatter.

In the distance, he heard the telltale alarm chirps as the squirrels drove off a raccoon that was getting too close to a store of acorns hidden beneath the leaf litter.

For the time being, Loken knew he'd be safe and would go unnoticed by the resident squirrels as he made his way along the boughs and branches of this giant oak tree.

With ankles that allowed his hind feet to rotate backwards, Loken's squirrel form nimbly advanced down the tree trunk, climbing down head first as he used the stop and go, skittering motions typical of these furry bundles of nervous energy.

Loken easily made his way to the large tree hollow, always watchful of predators seeking an easy rodent meal and mindful of potential guards stationed before the palace.

Cocking his head and pricking up his ears, Loken listened. Faint voices carried across the courtyard, drifting outside of the hollow.

"What is the matter with Firestar?" muttered the sentry, as he shuffled about restlessly, waiting for his long shift to come to an end.

"What do you mean?" asked the younger Fairy, standing guard next to him.

"I swear his codpiece is all bunched up or something. He's been in a foul mood of late, more so than usual."

"I'm guessing he has a lot on his mind. That's all."

"Well, if you ask me, this is bloody waste of time. We've yet to see the return of the snake that invaded the palace, and if Sparks Firestar was so convinced it was that cursed Pooka, and I highly doubt it was, we've seen neither hide nor hair of either since that serpent trapped him in the queen's bedchamber."

"He just means to keep our queen safe and the palace free of vermin," responded the younger Fairy.

"Well, if he wants to keep it free of vermin, he should see himself out of the palace," complained the older one, speaking in a whisper in case Sparks was in earshot. "Since he took over as the personal aide to the queen, he's gotten all high and mighty, flaunting his title and abusing his powers before us. And you know how bad he gets when the queen is on her nightly teeth gathering forays! He becomes a regular tyrant, a spoiled brat who thinks we should all be at his beck and call because of his higher station, when to me, he's nothing more than a glorified manservant."

"It is his business to flaunt his title, if he wishes! Remember, we're nothing more than palace guards. We always do what we're told," argued the younger Fairy, still standing at attention.

"That's just it! When Loken gave us orders, at least we were told why. We didn't blindly follow. If anything, he gave me a sense of purpose, while Firestar, he's just plain, old bossy. And these days, he's become a pissy bugger!"

"He's bossy, I won't argue that, but at least we are getting our orders from a fellow Fairy and not from a *you-know-what!*"

"Oh, so you'd rather be bullied about by one of your own than made to feel like a valued member of the queen's guards by a Sprite?" questioned the older Fairy, staring with raised eyebrows at this junior sentry. "You must get your priorities straight, young sir, or at least have the scruples to know when right is right and wrong is wrong!"

"Oh, bite your tongue! What you say *and* think are both wrong! Have you taken leave of your senses?"

"My senses are fine, thank you very much! You're just too young to understand all the inner workings of what's at play here. When Loken was the queen's aide and advisor, and saw to the daily business of running the palace, at least he treated us with respect; a sense of decency and dignity. Even when the queen was away on her nightly expeditions, unaware of what was happening in her absence, he still treated us fairly, even though we differed in race. You cannot tell me Sparks Firestar does the same."

"Yes, the Pooka treated us with respect until he went all loopy in his head, killing his mother and siblings in the process," reminded the younger Fairy, his index finger spinning by his ear. "My mother always warned me that a Sprite couldn't be trusted, especially a shape-shifting Pooka."

"Well, before he went all crazy in his head, I always thought he was a decent bloke in spite of his odd abilities. He was fine up until the night of the murders. I sense that something made his mind snap."

"His mind snapped, indeed!" snorted the younger Fairy. "Like Master Firestar said, the fool Sprite was out of his mind with too much drink! Indulging in too much fermented honeydew will make the average Fairy inebriated, while a Pooka like Loken just goes crazy when he's had too much."

"So you say – "

"Master Firestar claims it to be the truth. I'll take the word of a bossy Fairy any day, than those of a drunken, insane, shape-shifting Sprite," retorted the younger Fairy.

"That is what I could never understand… Loken never drank before, not like that, not even in Queen Pancecelia's absence."

"Maybe the presence of so many Fairies is what drove that Pooka to drink," offered the junior guard, his shoulders rolling in a shrug of indifference.

"Your smart attitude would be enough to drive anyone, mortal man, Fairy or Sprite, to drink."

"At least being *'smart'* it is better than having a fool of an attitude," countered the younger sentry.

"I was being sarcastic!"

"And I wasn't."

"Then it's a bloody good thing our shift is coming to an end," grumbled the senior Fairy, as he sneered at his partner.

"At least we agree on that!"

"Imbeciles!"

Both Fairies snapped to attention; their backs erect, chest thrust out and shoulders pulled back as an angry voice barked at them.

"You are supposed to be guarding the palace, not chatting like gossipy old women!" Sparks stormed down the stairs of the keep as two fresh sentries followed close behind him.

"Sorry, Master Firestar," apologized the older Fairy, as his partner stood at attention, pretending he was not the one engaged in any kind of conversation while on duty. "We were just having a little discussion, nothing of importance, sir."

"Odd," grunted Sparks. "I swore I heard mention of my name, as well as other words that were far from flattering."

"No, Master Firestar! We were just discussing how the queen's nightly forays have been quite successful. Just look at the sheen of the palace. Absolutely stunning," commented the older Fairy. Stiff as a plank of wood, he pointed at the dentine edifice. He then discreetly elbowed his partner, gesturing him to back up his words.

"Yes, it is quite the wonder! I doubt Queen Pancecelia would be so successful without you by her side, to aid her as you do," added the younger Fairy.

Sparks' eyes narrowed in suspicion as he growled: "Do you take me for a fool? I know what I heard! How dare you besmirch my good name and reputation?"

"We did no such thing, sir!" yelped the senior guard, grimacing under Sparks' scathing tone. "Just sharing opinions, Master Firestar."

"You were sharing *your* opinions, not me!" corrected his comrade, retaliating by nudging him back.

"In the future, I recommend that if you have issues with the way

I conduct the queen's business, or any business for that matter, air your grievances to me! Do not set tongues a-wagging by spreading falsehoods about me, for I know how to deal with malcontents and usurpers. And be warned, it will be in the harshest manner and with the cruellest of hands!" rebuked Sparks, eyeing the guards with obvious contempt. "Is that understood?"

"Yes, sir!" The guards answered in unison, snapping to attention once more.

"Very good! Now, let it be known that I am a fair and just leader, I mean to say, aide to the queen. I am willing to overlook this one indiscretion, but there will be no second chance for you two."

"Absolutely, Master Firestar, no second chance," gulped the senior guard, his eyes staring straight ahead.

"If I should hear even a whispering of disparaging words about me or how I conduct the queen's business, I will be forced to encourage Pancecelia to undertake cost-saving measures, beginning with job cutbacks, if you get my meaning?" snarled Sparks, as he seethed with anger.

"We are very happy with the way business just humms right along! No need for change here!" exclaimed the older Fairy, attempting to secure his position.

"Although we could do with shorter hours, as well as a break for little snackies every now and then," suggested his younger partner, believing the threat did not apply to him.

"You ungrateful ne'er-do-wells!" cursed Sparks, shaking an angry fist at them. "You should consider yourselves lucky that I allowed you to take the night shift!"

"Lucky, indeed!" conceded the older guard, nodding in agreement.

"And even more so because I am feeling generous on this day," announced Sparks. "I shall steady my tongue this time; forego reporting the both of you for your lackadaisical attitude where your duties are concerned to our queen!"

"Thank you, sir," said the younger guard, bowing his head to appease the irate Fairy.

"Just remember, the next time, you will both be made to stand guard through the light of day, rather than sleeping as most Fairies would be doing."

"Yes, Sparks – " The senior Fairy's back stiffened as he was interrupted.

"It is Master Firestar to you!" Sparks bristled with indignation. "I demand respect!"

"Yes sir, Master Firestar, sir!" acknowledged the guard, as he joined his younger comrade in bowing repeatedly to pacify him.

"It will not happen again," promised the younger one, watching as Sparks darted back into the keep, slamming the double doors behind him.

'Busybody of an idiot! Respect is earned, not given freely,' thought Loken. The keen hearing provided by his sensitive squirrelly ears allowed him to hear every word exchanged between the two guards as well as Sparks' angry rebuke.

His fur coat prickled, standing on end just hearing this Fairy's grating voice. It lay flat once more as he thought on the conversation shared by the guards. Loken took some comfort in knowing a handful of Fairies were still of like mind as their queen; indifferent to his race and understanding it was his actions, words, and his treatment of others that defined his true character.

Loken also appreciated the fact that although the Fairies were forbidden to talk about him since his exile, it was evident there were some who defied Sparks Firestar's edict. A few still questioned Sparks' need to rush to justice, to have him executed without trial, citing that if he had indeed murdered his family in a drunken rage, would it not stand to reason that once the alcohol-fuelled madness wore off, he would be fit to be reasoned with? At the very least, he'd be able to explain his actions, if nothing else.

Whatever the case, Loken knew Sparks incited fear by telling one and all that he would morph into a huge and terrible creature, one that would destroy the palace and go on a murderous rampage once again to kill the Fairies of the Vale, including their queen. He was certain the fear Sparks instilled was sufficient, enough that any Fairy coming across him now will not hesitate to kill him on sight.

For a moment, he listened intently. All Loken could hear were the sounds of the two fresh guards assuming their stations as they prepared for the next watch. With pikes at the ready, the Fairies were set for sentry duty.

In spite of their presence, Loken knew he had to find a way in, a way to get closer to Sparks Firestar to discover what he was plotting and if, in the wake of his last surprise return as a snake, this Fairy was planning to move up his plot to steal away with Celia's powers, thereby usurping her from the throne, or worse.

Loken drew a deep breath as he considered his options.

In a glow of light dulled by the radiance of the morning sun, his squirrel form disappeared. To the untrained eyes, the shape-shifting Sprite had all but vanished; however, for a minuscule hummingbird or bushtit seeking a small morsel, Loken's newly adopted form would be a tempting treat.

Using his wings, Loken flew down, alighting upon the entrance of the tree hollow. Checking first to see if his presence went unnoticed, he used his three pairs of legs working in synchrony to deliver his tiny fruit fly form into the hollow. With stealth, he crossed the ceiling. His compound eyes situated just so on his insect head allowed him to detect danger approaching from all angles as he skittered along while his muted colours let him blend into the shadows.

As he passed above the two Fairies guarding the keep, they remained stock-still, staring straight ahead through the opening of the tree hollow as though waiting for uninvited guests to appear and launch an assault to storm the palace.

'Unnoticed and unchecked! It should be easy enough to gain entry into the palace,' thought Loken, as he used his wings to alight upon the turret of the main watchtower.

Employing the tiny, barbed hairs on the pad of each foot, the smooth, polished surface of the teeth making up the walls of this dentine edifice proved tricky, but not impossible to climb. Making his way down, he pushed off against this wall. Fluttering down, he landed on the balcony of the royal bedchamber.

Peering through the window veiled by a gauzy spider web bejeweled by beads of dew, he spied upon Pancecelia Feldspar. She was nestled in her bed, the quilt drawn up under her chin as she slept peacefully until the coming of dusk.

For an instant, Loken's heart skipped a beat as it raced in his chest. Even sound asleep, he could see and feel the radiance of her loveliness; an ethereal quality that was all the more beautiful because of her kind and fair heart that had won him over. He studied her delicate features, the slow rising and falling of the counterpane as she gently breathed while she dreamed. He longed to touch her; to speak to her again, but he knew whether he reappeared to her in his now cursed form of a Pooka or as this harmless fly, Celia would only recoil in fear and disgust. It was another rejection he just could not bear.

Stealing away with one final glance, with a disheartened sigh, Loken moved on, scurrying across the balcony. He inched his way down the palace wall toward the high window of the main hall. From this vantage point, and with this pair of compound eyes at his disposal, it was easy for him to keep a look out for Fairies arriving and leaving this palace, as well as the guards posted to the stairs of the keep.

Peering through the tall window, Loken's eyes searched about, seeking signs of Sparks' whereabouts. The grand entrance and main hall were quiet, and would have been cloaked in darkness had it not been for the glow of fireflies spaced at regular intervals along the walls.

In the gloom, Loken spied a seam of golden light seeping beneath the doors of the main library. By the intensity of the glow, he knew this chamber was occupied, undoubtedly by his nemesis, Sparks Firestar, as this Fairy plotted his rise to power.

"So this is it, my love?"

Loken morphed back to his usual form. He listened, hearing this female voice whispered through the crack between the double doors.

Peering through this narrow gap, Loken watched as Sparks held up a dark, cobalt blue bottle for the Fairy maiden to see, but not touch.

"Yes! Is it not clever?" responded Sparks, holding it up to the chandelier where a cluster of fireflies glowed brightly so he can see its contents against the light. "It looks like any old bottle of honeydew cordial, but four drops diffused in her chalice of water, and the queen's heart will slow to the point she will lapse into a coma.

"So, it will take more than that to kill her?" questioned Iris, staring intently at the bottle of poison.

"According to Dragonite, the Sorcerer claimed four, undiluted drops taken straight from the bottle will mean instant death, thereby raising suspicions of murder."

"I see," whispered Iris, as she nodded in understanding. "So if she falls ill, none will be the wiser to her eventual demise."

Loken's heart quickened, realizing now that Sparks had sought the Sorcerer's counsel, seeking advice and the necessary poison to do the deed.

"Yes, and it was a bloody good thing that wretched Sorcerer was willing to strike up a bargain with me," said Sparks, with a satisfied grin. "One would never have thought that necromancer would ever find use for that miscreant of a shape-shifting Sprite."

"I still cannot think of what use Dragonite would have for that vile Pooka." Iris shuddered at the thought of Loken.

"When your powers are as stunted as his, thanks to the council of his brother Wizards, of course Dragonite can use the magic of a shape-shifter, one desperate enough to do his bidding just for a vial of potion to break the spell Pancecelia is under. When surrounded by an army of idiot mimes, at least the Sorcerer has some might behind him when Loken becomes a fearsome dragon or some other deadly creature."

"Tis the irony of all ironies," noted Iris. "Loken was always so clever! And yet, he lacked the vision or wisdom to know the very spell you had placed our queen under was accomplished by the Sorcerer's dark magic, and it is now Dragonite's potion that Pooka seeks to undo this very spell!'"

As Sparks' dastardly secret stabbed at Loken's heart and gnawed at his conscience, the Sprite fought the urge to transform into a creature swift and deadly to destroy his enemy. His heart thundered in his chest, pounding in his head as he listened to the Fairy's confession.

"Never mind that," dismissed Sparks, placing the bottle onto the table before him. "My hand has been forced. Though my intentions were to administer this poison on the day of the summer solstice when the queen's powers are at the weakest, it begins tonight. I will administer the first dose, one so small it will slowly sap her strength. As the solstice draws near, I will increase the dosage until she lapses into a coma, and eventually, death will take hold."

"Can you not speed up the process?"

"Not without arousing suspicion. If orchestrated just so, with no heir to succeed her, the elders on council will see fit to transfer her powers to me before the end, but this can only be done when her defenses are down and she is unable to resist or defy me."

"Then let me get her chalice of water now, so it will be by her bedside when she wakes," offered Iris.

Sparks' face suddenly darkened with concern. His eyes darted to the double doors. He stared suspiciously at the barrier separating this chamber from the great hall.

"What is it?" whispered Iris.

Pressing an index finger to his lips, Sparks motioned for her silence as he crept to the entrance of the library.

Loken's heart jumped to the back of his throat as the seam of light beneath the door was cast in a dark shadow growing larger as it moved his way.

Sparks stopped. Pressing an ear to this barrier, he listened for footsteps or voices on the other side. Drawing a deep breath as though calling upon his courage, Sparks flung the door wide open, leaping forward with wand in hand. His eagerness to confront his enemy was dampened by a sense of confusion. Glancing about, there was no one to be seen. The hall was empty, all except for the fireflies glowing softly along the walls. This late in the morning the members of the palace staff, like the queen, were all soundly asleep. Sparks knew the only Fairies to be up and about at this time of the day were those appointed to sentry duty or those plotting something evil.

His eyes scanned the shadows of the great hall as his ears listened intently for a whispering of voices or faint footsteps echoing in the distance.

Nothing.

"Well? What is it?"

"Nothing more than my paranoia," stated Sparks, shrugging off his concern. "Fill the silver chalice."

Iris picked up Pance's favourite goblet, topping it with fresh water before placing it on a tray.

"How many drops do I dispense?" asked Iris, calling to Sparks as he took one final look for unwanted intruders.

Instead of an answer, she was met with silence.

"Sparks?"

Again, she was greeted with a foreboding silence.

Placing the blue bottle onto the table, she crept toward the open door. Standing at the entrance of the library, she peered around, searching for her accomplice in crime.

The main hall was empty.

She could not even hear the sounds of Sparks' footfalls, if he had wandered off, nor could she hear the thrum of his wings if he had taken flight upstairs.

"Sparks? Where are you?"

Iris' eyes scanned the shadows of the hall as she listened. Her heart raced, for immediately, she knew something was terribly wrong.

"Sparks, where did you go?" Her words were whispered, as she waited for his response.

Stepping forward to begin her search, she jumped with a start as a body fell before her, landing at her feet with a heavy *'thud'*.

Mummified in a sticky shroud of spider webbing with barely one eye peeking from this stifling silk jacket, Iris didn't even know who this was until she recognized the angry, muffled words sounding from this writhing form.

"What the…?" She knelt down by Sparks' struggling body trapped within.

Before she could tear away the silk threads from his mouth, she yelped in surprise. A big, black and yellow orb-weaver dropped from the ceiling, hovering over Sparks' prostrate body as the Fairy maiden scrambled away on her hands and knees.

Retreating into the library, her scream snagged in the back of her throat as panic filled her heart. Kicking the door closed behind her, Iris' bid to place a solid barrier between her and this massive spider proved futile. Several powerful legs pushed it open before she could latch the door.

Rushing in, Loken's new spider form easily bowled her over once again as he rushed to the table to snatch up the bottle of poison.

Darting out of this chamber, with his many legs almost trampling the struggling, cocooned Fairy, Loken scrambled up the stairs with his prize.

Collecting enough of her wits to take action, Iris rushed out of the library, falling to her knees by Sparks' side. Instead of tearing at the webbing wrapped around his mouth and head that kept him from talking, she rushed to free his hands. Yanking away at the worst of the tough, sticky strands, it was enough for Sparks to sit up and use his arms to struggle free. Using his one free hand to tear away at the web on his face, he sputtered in rage, "You idiot! I was trying to tell you that spider was Loken!"

"The Pooka?" gasped Iris, her eyes wide in shock. "No! If it was Loken, he would have killed you, not wrapped you in webbing."

"You silly girl! He didn't kill me because I fought him off!" growled Sparks, dignifying his situation with a lie as he tore at the strands to free his legs. "Fetch the guards! *Now!*"

Iris scrambled to her feet. Launching into the air, she flew off to summon the guards while Sparks peeled away the last of the spider web. Free at last, he flew across the grand hall, snatching up his wand that was sent flying when Loken attacked from above, hoisting him to the ceiling to restrain him in silk.

As Loken reached the top of the stairs, he charged down the corridor, morphing in a glow of light as he darted away. Transforming into his nemesis, Sparks Firestar, he was identical in every way, right down to the Fairy's lopsided, smug grin.

Loken knew this was his one chance to save Celia. Standing before the door to the royal bedchamber, he smoothed back his hair and adjusted his vest, making sure he looked respectable. Down below, he could hear Sparks shouting, his words echoing from the grand hall as he ordered Iris to hurry in summoning the guards.

With not a moment to lose, Loken crept into the bedchamber and just as silently, closed the door behind him. Drawing the cloak's hood over his head to shield his amber eyes in shadow, he advanced. Tiptoeing to the side of the bed, before the Queen of the Tooth Fairies could sense his presence, he slapped a hand over her mouth to keep her from screaming.

Pancecelia woke with a start, struggling to wrench this hand from her face.

"I am sorry to wake you like this, Your Majesty, but I come with terrible news!" whispered Loken, hoping his transformation into Sparks was sufficient enough to fool her. "You will not scream?"

Pance stopped her momentary struggle as her eyes focused on her personal aide standing over her. She nodded in understanding as the

Fairy pressed an index finger to his lips for her silence.

"There is danger! You must come with me, immediately!"

She sat up, the fog of sleep rapidly fading from her mind as the urgency in his voice alone warned her of the level of peril.

"Why? What is happening, Sparks?" asked Pance, throwing back the counterpane as she swung her legs off the bed.

"An intruder! There is no time to explain! He wishes you dead! Just trust me. We leave, now!"

Just as Pance reached over for the bell to sound the alarm, warning the guards of this impending danger, she gasped in surprise as it was snatched from her hand.

"What is the meaning of this, Sparks?"

"Trust no one!" He pressed a finger to his lips for her silence. "There is one within your inner circle who means to kill you. Come! I will explain in due time!"

Just as he pulled Pance onto her feet to rush her out the door, it flew open. There stood the real Sparks Firestar, wand trembling in his hand as he snarled at his doppelganger, "Get away from her! Come to me, Pancecelia."

Standing between these identical Fairies, Pance's heart raced as she glanced with suspicious eyes at the one poised to attack and the one standing slightly behind her, ordering her to come with him.

"What is going on here?" she demanded to know.

"I am the real Sparks Firestar," declared Loken, a fist thumping his chest in defiance as he pointed an accusing finger at the Fairy. "He is an imposter!"

"No! *He* is the imposter!" insisted Sparks, his wand glowing in threat. "Now step toward me! I shall kill this vile Pooka before he harms you."

"I am Sparks!" argued Loken, as he pointed at his nemesis. "*That* conniving fiend is the Pooka, not me. He even stole away with my wand!"

"Liar!" growled Sparks. "Trust me, my queen. Step away from him!"

"Can you not see? Look at him! He is a mess!" denounced Loken, pointing at the real Sparks. "His clothes are crumpled; his hair, disheveled. Since when have I ever taken to sleeping in my raiment?"

Pancecelia glanced at the Sparks next to her, noticing his tunic and hair in pristine condition, and then she stared at the deranged looking Fairy standing at the door, attempting to inch closer.

"You are a mess!" noted Pancecelia, taking a wary step away from him.

"He did this to me!" snarled Sparks. "*He* attacked *me!* Demand that scoundrel drop the cloak's hood. His eyes will tell all."

"Do not listen to him, Celia! He is a liar! That fiend wishes you dead!"

Pancecelia turned with a start. Peering into the shadow cast by this hood, she whispered, "No one calls me Celia, no one except... Loken!"

"A-ha!" snorted the real Sparks, as he aimed his wand at the queen and the Sprite. "*He* is the imposter!"

Realizing Sparks was prepared to sacrifice her life just to kill him, Loken suddenly morphed. Pancecelia screamed in fright as the Pooka transformed into a huge spider once more. With eight powerful, dexterous legs, he used three to battle Sparks, knocking the wand from his hand as he shoved the Fairy out the door, slamming it closed behind him.

Before she could reach for her wand on the nightstand, Loken seized Pancecelia. A single prick from one of his fangs into the nape of her neck injected just enough venom to dull her senses and paralyze her muscles. She wilted in his arms. As Sparks ranted, ramming his shoulder against the door to gain entry, Loken worked with speed. Using his front pair of legs, he rolled Pancecelia in webbing so she'd be easily restrained and carried.

"Get in there!" bellowed Sparks, his angry words accosting the arriving guards. "Break the door down!"

Just as the guards rammed against this barrier, Loken removed his spider feet. With this sudden lack of resistance, the door flew open, sending the Fairies tumbling to the floor. In a mad scramble to reclaim their weapons and gain their bearings, they were blinded by a flash of light as the Sprite transformed once again.

"*Get him! Kill him!*" demanded Sparks, watching in dismay as Loken, this time as a dormouse, snatched up the queen in his jaws as he burst through the double doors to escape over the balcony. With great, bounding strides, Loken dashed across the courtyard to flee through the entrance of the tree hollow. He disappeared from sight as the two guards stationed at the stairs of the castle keep took to the air, flying after the swift moving rodent.

"Bloody hell!" cursed Sparks, pushing through the tangle of guards as his nemesis escaped with Pancecelia.

"This is like a bad dream," gulped one of the sentries, staring at the empty bed, and then the open doors of the balcony.

"A regular nightmare," groaned Sparks. His eyes gleamed as his trembling hand eagerly claimed the powerful wand Pancecelia had left behind.

"Hey… Time to wake up."

These words whispered in Cankles' ears caused him to stir. It was a voice so familiar it was like a ghost from his past, come to life.

"Come now, if not your eyes, then at least have the courtesy to open your mind."

Cankles slowly sat up, propping himself on his elbows as a man's form, backlit by the burning torch on the far wall, took shape, towering before him. For a split-second, fear gripped his heart, but just as suddenly, Cankles sensed this stranger meant him no harm.

"Fear not, my friend. In your hour of need, I am here to offer words of counsel and comfort."

"Who are you?" asked Cankles, sitting upright, as the man knelt before him.

"Do you not remember me?"

"Should I?" questioned Cankles, his eyes adjusting to the torch's light that prevented his cell from being bathed in utter blackness.

"I would certainly hope so!"

"I mean no disrespect to you, and I will admit your voice is vaguely familiar, but your face? Not so much," admitted Cankles, as he scrutinized the facial features distorted by light and shadow refracted by the crystal prison.

"Good God! What has the Sorcerer done to you to addle your brain? I am your friend!"

"Tag? Tag Yairet? How many years have I been here?" Cankles scrambled onto his feet. "You've changed! You've aged so much!"

"Aah! To be a youth again! Alas, I would even settle for old, but still alive."

"Say again!" yelped Cankles, shrinking back in fear as he struggled to comprehend these strange words. "Are you telling me that you are a gh- ghost? If so, what dark magic conjured you up?"

"No dark magic involved whatsoever, my friend. And if I were truly a ghost, do you not think I would make it my business to haunt you during your waking hours than to appear in one of your dreams?"

"I'd say it would depend on your manner of business," answered Cankles, as confused as ever. "So, are you saying that I'm only dreaming and you are but a figment of my imagination?"

"Only dreaming… A dream is not merely random, rambling thoughts that pop into one's mind when sleeping. It can divulge a man's greatest desires or his most desperate secrets; it can even reveal his true character."

"Well, it is no big secret that I desire to be free of this place, and to warn my friends of the dangers if they should try to rescue me, but that probably doesn't say much about my character. In fact, if anything, talking to you, whether you're a ghost or not, it is reason to question my sanity."

"You, my friend, are saner than most," assured the stranger. "But do you truly not remember me?"

"Let me think on it. It was not long ago that I discovered my own forgotten memories. As fragmented as they are, only now are they making some sense to me."

"I know it's been many years, but surely I look familiar to you?"

Cankles searched this seemingly friendly, but dignified face, spying the broad, affable grin peering through the neatly trimmed beard and moustache. Failing to recognize the facial features, he studied the man's dress of steel armour worn over a vest of mail, the ornately embroidered double boiled leather vambrace adorning each forearm, down to the articulated steel gauntlets protecting his hands.

"What say you now?"

"Hmm… no. Can't say you look familiar at all," responded Cankles, shaking his head in doubt. "Why? Are you going to tell me something outrageously bizarre; like you're my father?"

"No! Mind you, had it been so, I would have been proud to have called you my son."

"Well, I do not mean to be rude, but if you are supposed to be someone I know, I'm still not remembering you, not at all."

"How about now?" asked the man, as he spun on his heels to show his back to this prisoner.

Cankles jumped with start, stumbling back as a gasp snagged in the back of his throat. He stared at four arrows, each fledged with black feathers, protruding from this man's broad back. The metal bolt of each projectile launched by crossbows had penetrated his armour to stab deep into flesh and shatter the bones of his ribcage wherever steel made contact. The fine wool cloak he wore darkened, turning almost black with blood seeping from the puncture wounds.

With his mind reeling in horror, a gasp of surprise finally wheezed from his mouth as Cankles dropped to his knees. He trembled, daring to gaze upon this knight bearing the heraldic symbol of Fleetwood embroidered with golden threads on this tabard as blood oozed from his back to stain this surcoat.

"Stand before me, Sir Myron Kendall," ordered the knight.

"Say again?" These two words were barely a whisper from Cankles' lips as he peered up at the man.

"Hmph!" grunted the knight. "It is obvious Dragonite failed to break your will, but took great pains to destroy your mind."

Placing his left hand on Cankles' scarred head, the knight whispered, "Let what once was yours be restored. You will remember, but you will feel no pain in doing so."

As the wall that held back the memories of his past life came crashing down in his mind, Cankles collapsed, falling onto his back as flashes of memories, as vivid and real as the day they happened, flooded his brain to overwhelm his heart.

Warm, but fleeting memories of his childhood in Cadboll in the County of Wren nourished his soul. These were followed by recollections of his training as a squire, the tutelage falling to a man other than his own father when he became crippled in battle, unable to teach his son the time-honoured traditions of the knighthood.

His heart filled with joy as he recalled memories of when his father proudly handed him the family sword as he entered the knighthood. This joy was tempered by his mother's tears as she stood on the stoop of the cottage he now occupied, bidding him farewell as he prepared to go to war for the first time.

As though his mind raced through a million fractured memories, pulling all the missing pieces of his life together and arranging them in chronological order, Cankles glanced up as the knight spoke to him in a commanding voice.

"Stand before me, Sir Myron Kendall, for that is your name, my friend."

His eyes suddenly widened in surprise as recognition set in. "Captain Yairet! You live!"

"Yes, albeit only in your heart and your mind," confirmed Tag's father, as he smiled at his old friend. "Do you remember now?"

Squeezing his eyes shut, he thought back to another place and time. In this memory, he was caught up in the heat of battle, mercenaries storming in from all sides as he waged war by this man's side. A flash of a memory sparked in his mind as he shouted for his captain to beware as the enemy soldiers armed with devastatingly powerful crossbows let their arrows fly. Horror gripped his heart once more as the whine of these projectiles hissing through the air, followed by the sickening *'thunk'* as the metal bolts pierced through armour and flesh to fell this captain. He watched in stunned disbelief as the one man he believed to be invincible tumbled, mortally wounded, from his steed.

Scrambling over fallen bodies to protect him, he stilled his racing heart as Captain Yairet whispered his final orders to his trusted first officer. "Save them... You know what to do..."

This first officer nodded in understanding.

Donning the captain's feathered helmet and taking up his sword and shield, the first officer unleashed a blood-curdling war cry. It drew the attention of every eye and ear on the battlefield.

"Now you remember," determined Captain Yairet, giving his loyal friend a knowing smile.

"I do... but why now?"

"It was obvious you were not ready to learn the truth until this very moment," answered Captain Yairet.

"You are a welcomed sight, but a lot of good it does me now. Why do you come to me at my darkest moment when it is too late?"

"I came to you when your need was the greatest," revealed Captain Yairet, his head bowing in humility, "as mine is now."

"Yours? What need have you? You are dead!"

"True, however, my son is not. Before the end, he will need your help to save the Princess, but you must do what you can to spare his life!"

"Spare Tag's life?" this prisoner muttered in disbelief. "Do you speak in jest? It is not as though I was any good at sparing yours when we last went to battle. If anything, I'm feeling bloody guilty now, knowing that I failed you."

"And that is why those memories were undoubtedly stricken from your mind, my friend. The guilt you bore would have been your end, even though it was never your fault and you did everything in your powers to spare the lives of your fellow knights and soldiers until King William arrived with the second battalion."

For the longest moment, he absorbed these words as this one memory threatened to swallow him up, allowing him to drown in despair.

"Do you hear me, my friend? Your service was exemplary, right to the very end. You *never* let me down."

"Never?"

"Yes! That is why I ask you now, rise up and find the courage you once had. Though my life was not spared by the Sorcerer's cruel ambitions, I ask of you... no, I beg of you, do what you must to spare my son's life."

"But what can I do? I am trapped... a prisoner!"

"You must learn to believe and trust once more," urged Captain Yairet. "There was good reason I appointed you as my first officer. You were always skilled with the sword and stout of heart, but I swear on King William's good name, you were smart; smarter than most men! You will find a way. You always did, and you always will."

"But how?" he asked once more.

"Believe and trust..."

"Who am I to believe? You? Me? You *and* me? I need something more to go on!" he cried out as this apparition faded like mist, disappearing through the crystal bars.

As his hands smacked his head in frustration, his eyes snapped open. He slowly sat up. The fog of confusion lifted from his mind as he rubbed the sleep from his weary eyes to glance about his prison cell. His sense of reality, knowing that he had been dreaming, did nothing to comfort him as he sat alone in the numbing silence, wide awake in this nightmare he was trapped in.

9
Take That!

"Do you see or hear anything?" whispered Tag. Though the crystals lining this tunnel seemed to amplify sound, aside from their own footsteps, his mortal ears could hear nothing out of the ordinary.

"Either the mimes fled, moving with utmost speed to place greater distance between us and the gargantuan man-eating worm, or they have exited this tunnel altogether," determined Rainus, his keen ears hearing nothing untoward to warn him of potential danger.

"Or," piped in Rose, as she crept along behind the Elf, "those idiot mimes have been devoured by another one of those freakishly large worms and that is why we can no longer hear them."

"Nonsense," admonished Silas, taking care that his staff, which now doubled as a walking stick, did not thump noisily against the ground to announce their presence. "The way is well-lit. That monster worm we had encountered had a strong aversion to light."

"So you say, Master Wizard," responded Rose, blotting the beads of sweat from her forehead. "But suppose we encounter another hideous worm, this time, one that takes to light? And that crazy Sorcerer is using it to guard the way?"

"We shall cross that bridge if, and when, it comes," answered Silas. "For now, we venture on."

"We must be travelling deeper into the earth," assessed Tag, feeling a trickle of sweat roll down his chest. "It's getting warmer."

"So it is not just me feeling this?" Rose wiped the clammy palms of her hands on the skirt of her frock. "I thought that perhaps I was becoming delirious, imagining this heat, as Lord Silverthorn seems rather unfazed by it."

"I am an Elf. I can endure extremes of heat and cold far better than any member of the human race."

"Oh."

This was the only word Rose could think of as she noticed Rainus appeared his usual, dapper self; not a single strand of platinum hair out of place and no fine patina of sweat glistening on his forehead as on Tag's.

"This tunnel is coming to an end," whispered Rainus, his eyes squinting as he stared ahead.

"How can you tell?" asked Rose, staring down the length of the tunnel. "I see nothing."

"Our voices are not echoing back to us as before," revealed the Elf, "therefore, logic dictates that it must open up into another chamber."

"Sounds logical," said Rose, with a shrug of her shoulders.

"Just keep your voice down," urged Tag. "If this tunnel should terminate into a chamber, there is a bloody good chance that's where we'll find the Sorcerer."

"Right!" Rose pressed a finger to her lips, reminding Silas of the need for silence, as if the Wizard required it. "Careful now, the last thing we want is to fall into another trap."

Racing out of the hollow, Loken scurried up the tree trunk as the urgent shouts of the guards stationed at the front of the keep echoed behind him. He abruptly dashed down the other side of this great oak. With his precious cargo carefully clutched between his teeth and the bottle of poison tangled in the silk strands restraining his prisoner, his little dormouse form dove into the tall grasses. He disappeared into the deep shadows cast by the dense forest of overlapping blades of grass.

With his heart thudding madly, Loken listened to Sparks angrily reprimanding the guards on duty.

"You incompetent fools! How dare you allow that blasted Pooka to infiltrate the palace again? Find him!" snarled Sparks, frustrated that the guards had failed him once again. "Hunt him down! Kill him on sight!"

"But sir! What about our queen?" questioned a guard.

"Forget about her! She is dead. The cursed Sprite injected her with venom. We shall mourn her passing when time allows it, but for now, we must avenge her murder!" Sparks railed, the anger and contempt coursing through his veins.

From this hiding place, Loken watched in silence, one paw pressed firmly over Pancecelia's mouth to ensure she remained quiet. He spied upon the two guards that were appointed to watch the entrance of the tree hollow. They led the charge and behind them, a league of Fairies, their wings a-buzz like an angry swarm of bees, followed close behind. Breaking formation, they spread out to hasten the search for Loken and their queen, knowing that every second wasted placed more distance between them.

Flying over the grassy meadow, they scanned for signs of movement that would betray Loken's presence. They ventured on to the surrounding forest, all the while searching for evidence of the Pooka and their deceased queen.

Feeling secure, Loken darted away, stopping every now and then to make sure his pursuers were not following him.

Ducking under a large leaf, he narrowly escaped the watchful eyes of several guards circling back around as they scoured the meadow for him.

"That was close!" gasped Loken, peering through the forest of grass as he morphed back into his usual form. Though the layer of webbing he used to contain the Fairy was not thick, the strands were incredibly resilient, tough enough to keep her restrained if she had the will or the strength to attempt an escape. Masking her mouth to stifle her screams should she suddenly regain full use of her faculties, Loken's cupped hand pressed firmly over her mouth in case she cried out for help.

Though Pancecelia was completely lucid, aware of what was happening and what this shape-shifter was saying, the minuscule dose of spider venom he had injected into the nape of her neck was just enough to render her muscles useless. The most she could manage was to swallow, breathe and blink her eyes as the terror of being in Loken's presence sent her heart racing in panic. Lying limp and helpless, she watched through the canopy of grass as Sparks hovered at the mouth of the tree hollow, condemning Loken to a hasty execution should he be caught.

"I want him dead this time! No excuses! Just kill that damned Pooka!"

"But how will we know it's him, if he's changed into another kind of animal?" questioned one of the guards.

"Kill *any* creature with amber eyes that you should encounter! Take no chances, kill as many as need be! That Pooka must die this time."

"Bastard! Now he incites hysteria and invites a murderous rampage. I fear many innocent creatures will die because of him," Loken cursed beneath his breath as he crouched low in the grass by Pancecelia's side. "He is a liar. Every word that fear-mongering miscreant speaks is a lie! He continues to deceive every Fairy in the Vale, and beyond, so they will not hesitate to kill me, no questions asked."

Peering into Pancecelia's terrified eyes, he whispered to her, "I must get you to a safe place. Somewhere Firestar will never think of searching for you."

All efforts to plea for her freedom failed as even her vocals cords were temporarily paralyzed, but Loken knew by just a single glance at her fiery eyes, she was just as angry as she was frightened. It was better for him to reason with her sooner than later, when she is fit enough to hurl venomous words of contempt and loathing.

With the Fairies now scattering far and wide while Sparks continued to rage as he wove through the boughs of the oak tree to hunt him down, Loken decided to make his move. With his wings damaged by the Sorcerer, even compensating for the loss of one secondary wing, Loken knew he'd never be able to fly safely with his prisoner in his arms. Morphing into Sparks' double once again, with a full set of wings and a disguise like this, should he encounter other Fairies, with any luck, he would pass by unmolested, even welcomed for the safe return of the queen.

Scooping her up in his arms, Loken glanced between the overhead foliage to make sure there were no unwanted eyes spying on him and that his nemesis was well out of the way, completely unaware of his presence.

"I am truly sorry it has come to this, my dear Celia," apologized Loken. "Though it does not seem like it now, I do this for your own good; to keep you safe from harm."

All he got in response was an angry glare. Her eyes burned with contempt, pinpoints of fire that threatened to sear through his soul if he locked eyes with her for any longer.

"Trust me. I will make a believer of you, yet," vowed Loken, taking to the air with his reluctant passenger safely in his arms.

Tag brandished his sword, gripping it tightly as Rainus armed his bow. Together, they crept forward, moving in silence.

Ahead, the tunnel opened into another crystal chamber, even bigger than the first.

"It is getting hotter," whispered Rose, peeking over the Elf's shoulder to see.

"The deeper underground we journey, that is what can be expected," responded Rainus, motioning his comrades to join him against one side of the tunnel as he neared the cave. "It will only get worse; bearable to an extent for an Elf, but not so much for a mortal, that is for sure."

"Let us hope we don't have to venture too far," whispered Tag, listening intently for signs of the Sorcerer or his minions.

Rainus inched closer to the mouth of the chamber. Raising his hand, he motioned them to stop. He pressed an index finger to his lips for silence.

Listening first, Rainus then peered around the corner to his left. Seeing nothing but the burning torches lining the walls of this vast crystal cave, his eyes scanned the expanse, searching for signs of danger. Directly ahead, torches marked the entrance to a tunnel. Glancing to his right, he noticed another passageway.

"Well?" whispered Silas, creeping up to the Elf's side.

"We have two options," responded Rainus, staring at the tunnel across this great chamber, and then glancing over at the one to his right. "For now, both ways are not being guarded."

"Which one do you think will lead us to the dreamstone and our friend?" questioned Tag.

"There is a chance both are hidden away in two very separate locations," answered Rainus.

"Or they can be in the same place," added Rose, hoping for the best.

"We can only pray for that," said Tag. "But how do we know which way to go?"

Rainus listened and watched for a moment. Taking silent, measured steps, he crept into the huge chamber, arrow drawn and all his Elf senses on high alert.

"I would say it is safe to assume the passage that is more difficult to travel will be the one protecting the dreamstone," assessed the Elf.

Rose stared across the way at one tunnel, and then at the one to the right that was nearer to them.

"I think they both look easily accessible, and equally so." Rose searched about for the obvious.

"Think again," said Rainus, waving his comrades over to join him on the floor of this cave that tilted up ever so slightly. "Does that tunnel look easily accessible now?"

As Tag, Rose and Silas approached, Rainus used the tip of his bow to point before them. "That is why it is getting hot down here."

Separating them from the tunnel at the opposite end of the chamber was a wide chasm. Far below, a river of molten lava churned, bubbling and roiling as it cast the overhead spikes of crystal in an eerie red glow.

"It makes sense to protect the dreamstone by making it as difficult as possible to acquire," stated Silas.

"If it is on the other side, down that tunnel, how do we even cross over?" asked Rose.

"We can use my powers again to transport us there," offered the Wizard.

"Will it be less physically taxing on us because it's only a short jaunt?" asked Tag, staring across to the other side of the gorge of lava.

"No, for you and the Princess, it will be just as uncomfortable as the first time, unless of course, you have suddenly developed a stronger constitution for this method of travel."

"Based on the aftermath of that first attempt, we do not have time for them to recover from the state of nausea that ensued," reminded the Elf. "I think it is better to find another, perhaps more earthly method to clear this gap."

"What do you have in mind?" asked Tag.

"I have an idea I believe will work," answered Rainus.

"Oh, no, no, no!" gasped Rose, studying the Elf's face. She watched as he pulled a grappling hook from the depths of his cloak. "I do not like that look on your face!"

"You must trust in me," urged Rainus, testing the knot that secured the grappling hook to one of his arrows as he searched the ceiling.

"You want us to *swing* across?" groaned the Princess, shaking her head in disapproval as her eyes opened wide in disbelief.

"Well, I am an Elf and even I know I would not be able to leap across this distance, not even with a running start." His words were matter-of-fact.

Rose stared across to the other side that dropped slightly lower than the edge she stood on.

"You truly want us to swing across this deadly chasm on that flimsy, little rope?" asked Rose.

"Not all at once," replied Rainus, nocking the augmented arrow onto his bow.

"But it might not support Tag's weight," argued Rose.

"I weigh more than you, but it's not like I'm all that heavy," grunted Tag, holding the coil of rope Rainus had handed to him. "And besides, this rope was strong enough for us to climb out of that old volcano. It will be more than adequate."

"Ah, but that was for climbing, not swinging," reasoned the Princess. "These are two completely different actions."

"Believe me when I say this rope will hold," assured Rainus, taking aim at a jagged formation of crystal protruding from the ceiling to jut over this chasm.

"I will believe it when I see it," gulped Rose, staring at the burning red ooze churning below.

"If it helps to put your mind at ease, I will go first," offered the Elf. With confidence, he let the arrow fly as Tag held fast onto the end of the rope. The coil unravelled, rapidly shrinking in his hand.

The arrow sailed up and over the crystal formation to ricochet off this protrusion. The deflection caused the projectile to snap on impact. The grappling hook dropped, the forward momentum causing it to wind about several times before two of the three prongs of this hook bit into the crystal, setting it in place.

Giving the rope a hard yank to ensure the grappling hook was securely anchored, Rainus slung his bow over his shoulder. Grasping the rope, his grip tightened around the line.

"Are you sure about this?" asked Rose, staring across the formidable divide.

"Quite!" The Elf spoke with utmost confidence.

With no hesitation, Rainus ran to the edge of this gorge, launching his body across the heat and the river of lava churning below. Landing on the other side with the grace afforded to the Elfkind, Rainus set to work. He created a ball of a knot near the end of the rope. This was to add weight to the line so when he threw it back to his comrades, it was easy to direct this throw. Also, it was easier to catch the rope by this knot than to chance the line slipping from their fingers to dangle uselessly over the fiery chasm where none could retrieve it.

"Catch!" hollered Rainus, swinging the rope back to the others.

Tag easily caught the rope, handing it to the Princess.

"You're next," stated Tag.

"No, I'm not!" responded Rose, her words concise.

"You can do it!" Tag thrust the rope into her reluctant hands. "You crossed those hexed pillars to make it over the river of lava in Dragonite's other lair, this will be easy in comparison."

"I almost died that time!" snapped the Princess, pushing the rope away.

"Then just think how easy this will be," urged Tag.

"I think not!"

"Princess Rose, time is of the essence! We must forge on," insisted the Wizard.

"See! I am safely on the other side," reminded Rainus, waving Rose on. "There was nothing to it!"

"Yes, well there is nothing to your weight either. You are much lighter than Tag, perhaps even me!" argued Rose, refusing to grasp the rope.

"Time is wasting away, Princess," grunted the Wizard. "Allow me! Though I can easily use magic to get from here to there, I will do this now to show you a safe crossing by this means is possible."

Snatching the rope from Tag's hands, Silas backed up from the edge. Taking a running leap, the forward momentum propelled him over this perilous gap. As he reached the other side, Rainus grabbed his arm and the rope to assist with the Wizard's safe landing.

"See! Even an old man can do it," called Silas, waving her over. "Come! Join us on the other side."

Rose peered down the gully of flowing lava and then across to the Wizard. "Never! Not even if you had biscuits!"

"Oh, come now, Princess! Be done with it," urged Tag, catching the rope by its knot that Rainus sent back.

"Suppose I wait here, while the three of you go on without me?" offered Rose.

"And what will you do if the Sorcerer's minions should come by this way?" asked Tag. "Do you intend to use that bow with the full intention of protecting yourself this time?"

Rose glanced over at the opening of the tunnel the mimes had no doubt entered.

"But they might not come back. They could be completely preoccupied with other matters," reasoned the Princess.

"Or they can come back any time and catch you here alone," cautioned Tag, gripping the rope as he threatened to cross without her.

"Hey!" called Rainus. Cupping a hand to an ear, he cocked his head to listen. "Make up your mind quickly! I hear footsteps – many of them, coming from that tunnel behind you!"

"Right!" snorted Rose, shaking an angry fist at the Elf. "You are trying to trick me."

"I promise you, it is no trick! They are coming, Princess!" Rainus waved her over.

Before she could volley more words of protest at the Elf, Tag's hand slapped over her mouth as he snapped at her. "If you cannot hear them, surely you can feel their approach."

As Rose pried his grubby, sweaty paw from her face, the first thing she noticed was a cloud of dust rising up at the edge of the precipice where the tremors radiating from the tunnel terminated. These shockwaves sent loose dirt tumbling into the fiery abyss below.

Immediately, Rose knew Rainus was telling the truth as mimes poured forth from the tunnel to fill the chamber. Though they were silent, armed with spears, she knew this time they could be deadly.

"Here, Princess! Go!" urged Tag, as he shoved the rope into her trembling hands.

"I – I can't do this," stammered Rose, her eyes wide with fear, "not on my own!"

"Then we'll go together!" offered Tag. "I won't let you fall. But whatever happens, don't hesitate this time when we make the leap."

She managed to nod a quick response.

With her arms wrapped around his neck and shoulders, and Tag's strong arm around her waist, they prepared to swing across as the front line of mimes hoisted their spears to throw.

Just as Tag held tight to the rope to leap across to the other side, Rose stopped him. For that split-second, when their gaze locked, the motes of her lavender eyes seem to vanish. The dark flecks were lost in the sparkling radiance, as though trapped within jewels of amethyst. Its beauty took him by surprise.

For that single moment, with her face so close to his, he could feel the warmth radiating from her dewy, rosebud lips. Tag's heart raced as he pursed his lips together to meet hers.

"Take that!" grunted Rose, her hand slapping his startled face.

"What was that for?" Tag groaned, wincing with the sharp pain.

"For luck, and because you're always getting me into dangerous situations! Now, go!"

As the mimes hurled their spears at the couple, Silas unleashed a powerful surge of energy from the orb atop his staff. It burst forward, shattering the spears to send shards of wood and twisted metal flying in all directions as the mimes leading this incursion were bowled over by the magic.

While many of them retreated with this assault, taking refuge in the tunnel they had come from, just as many stepped forward. Dashing to the edge of the chasm, they flung their spears as Rose and Tag swung across the divide.

So terrified, the Princess screamed all the way, her eyes squeezed shut as she clung for dear life onto Tag. Not once did she glance down. Feeling the sweltering heat rising from below, she knew they were still somewhere over this river of doom, sailing through the air as a volley of spears followed.

As Silas discharged another bolt of energy to deflect and destroy the projectiles coming for Tag and Rose, he realized too late they would be caught in the wake of his magic.

Rose gasped in surprise, feeling Tag's weight suddenly shift as he flung his feet forward to increase their momentum. She then screamed long and loud, feeling the terrifying sensation of falling as Tag released the rope, pushing her away as he threw her toward Silas and Rainus.

Trying to catch her as she landed on the other side, Rose bowled the Elf over. Glancing over her shoulder, she watched in horror as Tag, arms and legs flailing through the air in a desperate bid to propel his body forward just a little more, landed on the very edge of the precipice just at Silas' feet. The jarring impact of his landing caused the earth beneath him to give way, crumbling into the lava below and taking him down, too.

"NOOO!" shrieked Rose. She scrambled on her hands and knees to the ledge as Rainus lunged forward to keep her from tumbling down after Tag.

"Damn!" cursed Sparks, his eyes scrutinizing the shadows of this long-abandoned tree hollow. "They are not here."

"Where to now, Master Firestar?" questioned one of the guards in his company.

"How the bloody hell am I to know?" snapped Sparks. In frustration, he kicked at a broken mug to send it tumbling across the floor, splintering into even smaller fragments of earthenware.

"Meant no disrespect, sir, but you seemed confident the Pooka would be returning here, of all places," responded the guard. "There is nothing here, with the exception of the ghosts that haunt this place after the ill deed done when they were living. Other than that, this place is empty."

"I know!"

"Then where would you have us concentrate our search," asked the guard, hovering just above the floor so his feet wouldn't touch the layer of dust doing a poor job of hiding the bloodstained floor.

"Anywhere, but here!" growled Sparks, his nerves on edge as he dismissed the three guards with a wave of his hand. "Now, get out! Find that murderous fiend!"

In single file, they departed; flying through the small knothole of the elm tree to resume their search, abandoning Sparks Firestar to stew alone in his misery and foul mood.

Concealed by the slender, vine-like branches of the elegant willow growing across from this elm tree, Loken watched in silence, one hand pressed firmly over Pancecelia's mouth as the other held onto her as she still lacked the coordination to sit upright on the tree branch.

Beyond the knothole, within this tree hollow, Sparks yanked down the tattered remains of a curtain that drooped sadly over a small window. The Fairy squinted as a dazzling beam of sunlight penetrated the gloom. Waving his hand about, he tried to dispel the cloud of dust swirling around him.

Glancing about, Sparks could still see the chaos of the deadly night that happened just over ten years ago. The overturned furniture; the remnants of destroyed dishes hurled in self-defense remained untouched. Even the pools of blood that had long since coagulated and dried, remained after all this time; a haunting reminder of events that led to the demise of the last Sprite family to dwell in the Fairy's Vale.

At least the sharp scent of blood no longer hung heavy in the air as it did the last time he was here. Flying up to the loft, he momentarily hovered as he stared at the empty, overturned beds; the mattresses stiff and black with blood that had soaked through to eventually dry.

It was evident not even a dormouse or squirrel had ventured through this threshold to take residence in this tree hollow, as though they knew something evil had befallen the former occupants.

Settling down onto the main floor, the Fairy heaved a weary, disgruntled sigh as he glanced about one final time.

As he made his way to the knothole, Sparks stopped.

He stared at the tapestry hanging on the far wall. For the longest moment, he gawked at the one remaining thing in this home that had stayed in place in all this time. His head tilted as he scrutinized it, not so much to study the composition of the faded threads woven together to form an image that was now splattered with dried blood, but to determine how straight this tapestry hung.

Floating over a toppled table, the broken chairs and other wall hangings that were ripped down during a terrible struggle, the Fairy hovered before the wall. His eyes fixed on this dusty, stained piece of art.

After careful consideration, Sparks adjusted the tapestry, raising the right corner ever-so slightly so it was perfectly straight once more.

"Better…" he muttered cynically beneath his breath. Without taking a second look back, Sparks exited the hollow, taking to the air to catch up to the other Fairies on the hunt for the Pooka.

Loken's heart raced as he watched Sparks disappear over the tree-tops, shouting orders at the guards to spread out in a bid to widen the search radius.

"Perfect," whispered Loken, waiting to make sure his nemesis was well on his way, with no intention of returning. "He'll have no reason to come back now to snoop about."

Scooping up Pancecelia in his arms, still in the guise of his enemy, Loken left the cover of the willow tree to head for the knothole in the old elm. Turning sideways so he would not bump her head or feet, he ducked into the tree hollow.

Loken almost dropped her as a tidal wave of emotions overwhelmed him. He forced down the lump catching in the back of his throat as he stilled his racing heart. Taking in the sight of his abandoned family home, long forgotten, happy memories were abruptly swallowed up by the tragedy that had unfolded in this very place.

Drawing a deep breath, Loken struggled to compose himself as he propped Pancecelia against the wall. Taking the only chair that hadn't been smashed; he positioned it upright, gently lifting her onto this seat. By the tenseness of her body, Loken knew she was regaining her ability to move.

Spying the fire in her eyes, he knew she was just as incensed now as she was when he first made off with her. Any hopes he had that she would cooperate, willingly listening to his words, were non-existent at this point while still under the spell Sparks had dispensed on her.

Under a glow of light, Loken assumed his usual Sprite form, ignoring the uneasy feeling that she was staring at his disfigurement at the hands of the Sorcerer. Tearing a long strip from the tattered curtain that lay on the floor, Loken wound it around her waist; tying her to the backrest of the chair he had seated her on.

"I will remove this webbing from about your mouth, Celia," said Loken, "but you must promise you will not scream."

She responded with the weakest of nods, as though she barely had the strength or coordination to lift her head.

"Very good," whispered Loken, offering her a gentle smile to put her heart at ease as he knelt down to strip away the silk strands from her mouth.

"Take that!" snapped Pancecelia, her forehead butting against his as her feet came up, striking the Sprite in his groin.

Wheezing out a gasp of pain, his eyes watered as his hands cupped his manhood. With a loud moan, he fell over on his side.

"Still as fiery as ever, eh, Celia?" groaned Loken, wincing in agony. "If I were not in so much pain, I'd be laughing about now."

"You come near me again and I will happily dispense more of it!" She struggled against this webbing to be free.

Snatching up the remnants of the curtain, Loken tore off another long strip. Using one arm to shield him from the blows of her kicks, he used the other to pin her bound legs down against the chair as she tired from her frantic actions.

"Now, if you do not wish for me to use this last strip as a gag, you best listen up, my lady."

Before she could issue an angry tirade, Loken dangled the strip of cloth before her as a warning. "You really do not want me to do this."

"I dare you!"

"Do not dare me, my dear Celia, for I have nothing to lose in gagging that pretty little mouth of yours. However, in doing so, I will gain some much needed silence. The choice is yours. What will it be?"

"My choice is to be set free. Untie me! Do so now!"

"That was *not* one of your choices. I ask again, do I have your cooperation if I do away with using this gag? All I ask is that I have your ears for just a moment."

"You are free to have them once you kill me, hacking me up as you did to your mother and poor siblings!"

Loken slumped back onto the floor, fighting to control his anger as voices, distant echoes from the past whispered in his ears. He could still hear his mother's cry for help, his name ringing out into the night as she screamed for him. This memory haunted Loken to this very day. He cursed beneath his breath, mentally flogging himself for not coming to the aid of his family sooner.

"Listen to me, I beg of you," pleaded Loken. "I did not kill my family! I was sent on an errand, one that Sparks Firestar had conveniently appointed to me. It was one that would see me return here just as the killings were done. From the distance, I thought my mother was calling me home. It was not until she screamed did I understand the true urgency of her cries, but I was too late."

"A likely story!" snapped Pancecelia.

"I speak the truth! Their bodies were still warm, the spilled blood still fresh when I raced back here, only to be confronted by my accuser. Firestar had been waiting all along for my return."

"I doubt that very much."

"That conniving Fairy had it all planned out. You can only imagine my horror to see the blood of my mother and siblings splashed across Firestar's face and raiment. I knew right away what he had done, but before I could confront him, the guards arrived and he ordered them to kill me before I could transform and escape."

"The innocent do not run," insisted Pancecelia. "You would have stayed to clear your name and reputation."

"And the dead, no matter how innocent, cannot prove it to be so. I was forced to flee!"

"So, you want me to believe you are innocent of these murders?"

"Yes! But if you do not believe me, then look upon this," ordered Loken. He marched across the room, yanking down the only tapestry left hanging on the wall. Concealed behind it, scrawled across the wall in bloody letters was one sentence: *I am innocent.*

Pance stared at this cryptic message. "Well, if this does not scream of your guilt, I do not know what does."

"But I *am* innocent!" insisted Loken. "To my final day and with my dying breath I will swear it to be so."

"Using the blood of the dead – the blood of your murdered family is the act of a deranged killer, not one who claims to be truly innocent."

"It was an act of desperation. When I found my loved ones, I quickly realized Sparks meant to trap me, to have me blamed for their deaths. With no time to find ink and parchment, I resorted to using the only thing I could find."

"So you used blood? How utterly vile!" She stared in horror into these amber eyes that were no longer familiar to her.

"Yes, the spilled blood of *my* family. I left this message in hopes that you would see it, but in my desperate bid to escape, the guards in Sparks' company assumed the blood on my hands meant I killed them. That blasted Fairy worked them into such a frenzy to get revenge, in the darkness, they failed to notice the blood splattering his apparel."

"Sparks told me you had smeared the blood on him in a struggle, when he tried to apprehend you."

"I mean no disrespect, but are you mad, woman? I am a Pooka!"

"So?"

"I could have easily overpowered that Fairy; turning him in for the crimes he had committed against my family. If he hadn't already condemned me to death by ordering his men to kill me first, then ask questions later, I would have done so."

"If you were so innocent, then why hide that bloody message behind the tapestry," probed Pancecelia.

"I didn't! When Sparks re-entered my family home while the guards gave chase, he was quick to hang this tapestry up once more so none of his men would see these words when they returned."

"And you expect me to believe this?" grunted Pance.

"The Celia I once knew and loved would have believed me."

"Then I am not the gullible person you once knew. Thanks to Sparks, I am wise to you and your evil ways!"

"You are still the just and kind Celia I always knew, but Sparks uses dark magic, one that blinds you to the truth and blackens your heart where I am concerned."

"Sparks warned me that should you return, you would say such things to trick me. He said you do the Sorcerer's bidding so that demented soul can reign with unrestricted powers over this realm, cloaking it in his misery and dark magic."

"Of course he would say such things! Firestar is a liar. He has deceived you and your people from the start. He is the one plotting with that wretched Sorcerer, not me. He is a traitor, a usurper of the worst kind! He means to win your confidence, trick you into trusting him, only to manipulate you so he can denounce you as being unfit and unable to rule, thereby having your powers transferred to him."

"Sparks Firestar is a loyal and trusted friend, my personal aide," argued Pance, refusing to accept what Loken deemed so obvious. "He would never undermine me!"

"Undermine you? He means to *kill* you!" Loken thrust into her face the cobalt blue bottle he stole from Sparks.

"Liar!"

"I heard him say this not once, but twice, the first time was when I returned to the Fairy's Vale almost a fortnight ago."

"You were here?"

"You did not know?" asked Loken, frowning in confusion. "Firestar never told you why he suddenly felt compelled to post guards at all hours to protect the palace?"

"He said a serpent, a great snake, had invaded the hollow, but there was no need for concern as he and the guards managed to drive the creature off. He means to keep that snake from returning."

"*I* was that serpent in question! I overheard your treacherous aide speaking of his plot to see you undone when I was there to steal away with something."

"You meant to *steal away* with my life!"

"Then why would I come in the dead of night when I knew you were away on your nightly foray to harvest teeth?"

Pancecelia's mind raced as she tried to understand.

"I will tell you why, my dear Celia. I only risked my life to return to the Vale to steal away with this!" Loken fished out a small square of silk that was tucked away in his belt. Peeling back the corners of this tattered cloth, its contents glimmered in the sun's light that shone through the window. "I needed to sneak in to steal this, dust; Fairy dust from *your* wings."

"You risked your life, returning to the Vale just for a memento of me?" gasped Pancecelia, staring at the iridescent scales shed from her wings.

"It is more than that. This is needed to complete the potion that will break the spell you are under, the one Firestar received from the Sorcerer."

"I refuse to believe you, spell or not. Sparks Firestar would never undermine me. I trust him with my life."

"He means to *take* your life!" snapped Loken, holding up the bottle to remind her. "He planned to use this poison to gradually kill you."

"Say what you want! I will never believe you."

"When I returned today, as you slept, Firestar and that little trollop he's been having dalliance with behind your back have been plotting against you! I heard him; I heard them both. Sparks planned to use this, a poison given to him by the Sorcerer, Parru St. Mime Dragonite.

He planned to administer the first dose tonight, increasing it until you lapsed into a coma by the height of the summer solstice, thereby stealing away with your powers when you are at your most vulnerable."

"If this is true, then why did you not just kill Sparks when you had the chance to?" questioned Pancecelia.

"As tempted as I was, if I had acted on my need for revenge, then I'd be no better than that fiend. If the spell that still grips you prevents you from believing my words, I need you to hear them from that murderer's own mouth! If you refuse to believe me, then a confession from Firestar is sure to suffice."

"Ha!" scoffed Pancecelia, struggling against her restraints once more. "I hardly think a confession made under the threat of death can be held as true. One can be made to say anything, whether true or not, if it means to survive."

Loken slumped back in defeat as he absorbed her words. He now understood that to capture and parade Sparks before her, forcing him to confess his sins were doomed to fail. Even if the spell she was under waned just enough for logic to set in where he was concerned, Loken knew the odds were stacked against him. Knowing Sparks, he'd dramatically crumple to his knees, begging for his life. He'd admit his guilt, but he'd twist the truth somehow, so Celia would believe his admission was forced and merely said to spare his life.

"Bah!" cursed Loken, his hand running down his woeful face in utter frustration.

"See! You *are* a liar!"

"Even when I speak the truth, you fail to see it. Your heart has been tainted by Firestar."

"And you are so tainted by evil, you do not even look as you did before," countered Pancecelia, staring with disdain at the Sprite.

"It is the spell Firestar uses on you!" insisted Loken. He pleaded to her on bended knees. "Search your heart, Celia. Remember the love we once shared. Remember how things used to be."

Pancecelia gazed upon his face. He looked nothing like the Sprite she loved. His once handsome face was now gaunt, haggard as though his exile aged him rapidly while those amber eyes now shone of evil. Even his muscular physique had changed; gangly as if suffering from malnutrition and now, with crippled wings, he was a mere shadow of his former self.

"Please remember what we once shared," pleaded Loken.

"Before you went on a murderous rampage? I think not! If you mean to kill me, then do so now."

"*Firestar* means to kill you, not *me!* That is why I spirited you away from your palace, to keep you from harm's way."

"I do not believe you."

"Then who would you believe?" asked Loken.

"Anyone but you!"

"Would you believe an old friend? How about Cankles Mayron?" questioned the Sprite.

"I would believe *him* over *you* any day," sniffed Pancecelia. "But what would you know of this mortal?"

"He can help me – us, for he knows the truth and how Sparks Firestar conspires with the Sorcerer."

"What? That is absolutely ludicrous! Besides, he is not here. There is no telling where Cankles is at this very moment."

"I know exactly where he is! I will free him and he will help me to have you see the truth!"

"Free him? What do you mean?"

"The Sorcerer holds him captive! I will free him and he will help me to get the potion that will break the spell you are under."

"You are cracked in the head!" denounced Pancecelia. "There is no spell, you are lying to me. Just as you lied about your innocence, you lie about Cankles Mayron. The last I heard, he was safe with his friends, trying to catch up to Dragonite."

"Catch up to that necromancer? He trapped and caught your mortal friend! Cankles is safe no more, not while the Sorcerer holds him prisoner."

Loken jumped onto his feet. Taking the strip of cloth, he tied it around her mouth as he apologized, "I am sorry to do this, but I need you to wait quietly for my return."

Pancecelia clenched her teeth together, turning her head to and fro to fight his efforts to gag her, but in the end, Loken succeeded in stifling her angry words.

Kissing her forehead, he made a promise, "I will return. In due time, you will know the truth, but for now, you will be safe from Firestar as long as you remain here."

As he dashed off, with a parting glance he vowed to her, "I do love you, my dear Celia. If I should fail, remember, I always loved you."

Using his crippled wings to launch his body from the knothole, Loken morphed into an inconspicuously tiny, ruby-throated hummingbird, flitting his way northward with utmost speed.

10

A Touch of the Crazies

"TAG!"

Rose screamed as Rainus yanked her back from the crumbling ledge as he disappeared from sight.

Silas crouched low to the ground, leaning back. His heels dug in as he held onto his staff. He groaned from the exertion as he called out, "A little help, please!"

Rainus glanced over the precipice, and to his surprise, Tag dangled from the end of the Wizard's staff, his hands snagging onto it just as he went down. Lying on his belly, the Elf leaned over, grabbing the boy by the wrist, and then by the collar of his shirt.

"Look out!" shouted Silas, watching as spears launched their way came progressively closer as the mimes fine-tuned their aim.

"Why you... you... *mimes!*" cursed Rose, unable to think of another derogatory name to use to belittle them. "I'll show you!"

Arming her leather sling with not one, but three steel balls from the magical, never-ending supply she kept in the pouch tied to her sash, Rose unleashed her fury. With unerring aim, she launched an assault, striking the mimes lining the edge of the cliff. The Princess was so enraged, she did not even stop to admire her handiwork as one mime, opening his mouth at the most inopportune moment, shrieked in agony, only to be choked into silence. His front teeth shattered as he gagged and coughed on one of her steel balls that continued on, flying undeterred to hit the back of his throat, only to be swallowed.

Another unlucky mime reeled from the blow. He toppled forward; sinking into the river of lava after a steel ball struck him spot-on between the eyes to knock him unconscious, while the third stumbled back. His hand slapped over his right eye that now stung with searing pain like it had been jabbed with a sharp, burning stick.

Screaming like a woman gone berserk, Rose vented her wrath like never before. She continued pelting the enemy, her aim so precise, the mimes began to retreat even though a river of lava separated them.

"I think you can stop now," said Tag, as the Elf and the Wizard hoisted him onto his feet. They watched in amazement as the Princess single-handedly succeeded in driving off the Sorcerer's minions.

Rose trembled with rage, her hands quaking as she lowered the sling, its cradle now empty of ammunition. Her chest heaved, rising and falling with each deep breath while her eyes burned with resentment.

Tag brushed the dust from his raiment as he asked, "How do you fare, Princess?"

Rose said nothing. She just seethed with rage.

"You're looking a bit out of sorts at this very moment," continued Tag. "Got a touch of the crazies?"

Her nostrils flared while her eyes burned; pinpoints of fire as she glowered at him.

"Hello! I'm speaking to you!" Tag waved a hand before her face to break this angry trance.

Her silence was broken as she erupted in a volcano of furious emotions. A flurry of fists pummelled his chest as she vented her wrath on him. "You fool! You idiot! I hate you! I hate you!"

"Whoa! Settle down, Princess!" Tag seized her by the wrists to end this angry assault.

"I hate you…" sobbed Rose, her arms going limp in his grip as the tears welled in her eyes. "You could have died."

Tag was at a loss for words as she threw her arms around him, embracing him in a great hug. Holding her close, he could feel Rose's heart hammering against his chest as she trembled, overwhelmed by fear, anger and grief over what could have been.

As the tears tumbled down her dirt-smudged cheeks, Tag held her in his arms, holding her tight as she sobbed, her face buried in his chest as she wept.

"I'm fine! See? I'm far from dead," assured Tag, lifting her chin to gaze upon her tear-streaked face.

"But you - you could have d- died," whimpered Rose, stuttering as she exhaled on a sob. "I could not have continued this mission, had you died."

"I made a promise to your father to keep you safe on this quest. I have no intention of dying, not just yet!"

"I'm alive! You're alive. We're all alive," interjected Silas, his hands flapping about impatiently. "We really must be on our way."

"Yes, this tender moment must wait," agreed Rainus, tapping Tag on his shoulder to gain his attention. "Before those mimes deliver word to the Sorcerer that we are here, we should move on."

"Oh – oh, yes! Of course," responded Tag. Both he and Rose released their embrace. They jumped apart as though one thought the other had contracted the plague and were about to pass it on through this close contact.

"We should go," said Rose, hastily wiping away the tears as she drew a deep breath to compose herself.

"This way, my friends, follow me," ordered Rainus, waving his comrades on toward the mouth of the tunnel.

Removing one of the burning torches from the wall mount, the Elf led the way. The flames twisted about, flaring and dancing in the wake of his movements as he ventured into the passage. The light of the torch pushed back the darkness, reflecting off the many facets of the crystal formations lining the walls of the tunnel.

"We must move with speed, but be cautious of potential danger," warned the Wizard, as he took up the rear.

"So we tiptoe quickly?" asked Rose, peering over Rainus' shoulder to see what perils awaited them.

"Yes, while we keep our eyes open for dangers that lurk, so do not rush ahead of me."

"Oh, believe me, I have no intention of doing that, Lord Silverthorn," stated Rose. "Go on then, show the way."

As the light of the torch illuminated their surroundings, Rainus crept ahead, brandishing his sword in the other hand as he advanced.

No more than forty paces into this tunnel, the Elf came to a halt. He raised his weapon as a sign for the others to stop.

"What is it, Lord Silverthorn?" asked Tag. "What do you hear?"

"It is not what I hear that concerns me, it is what I see," whispered the Elf, as he stared ahead.

"So what do you see?" questioned Rose. "More of those crazy mimes?"

"No mimes, not at this moment," answered Rainus, pressing a finger to his lips so she would lower her voice.

"What is it?" asked Silas.

"I am not sure," answered Rainus, his eyes darting to and fro as he studied the strange reflection of light. He noticed how the glow of the torch would refract and intensify against the facets of crystal, creating a series of light beams that bounced from wall to ceiling to wall in a dazzling kaleidoscope of rainbow colours.

"This is absolutely beautiful!" declared Rose, her eyes taking in the splendor of this light show.

"It is downright odd, that's what it is," corrected Rainus, staring at the beams of light transecting the tunnel from every angle imaginable. "Something is not right about this."

"Do you think this tunnel is under some kind of enchantment?" questioned Tag, moving over as Silas made his way to the Elf's side.

"We are deep within the Sorcerer's lair," reminded Silas. "It is a very real possibility."

"It is only light; beautiful, harmless beams of pretty light," rebuked Rose, her tone dismissive.

Before she could push past Rainus and the Wizard, the Elf seized her by the arm, yanking her back. As Silas raised the tip of his staff to intercept a beam of light, Rose shrieked in fright as this broken stream of light caused a deadly reaction. Pointy spikes and shards of crystal flew across from one wall to shatter against the other.

"What the?" gasped Tag, staring in disbelief as Silas yanked free a sharp splinter of crystal that had become embedded in the tip of his staff.

"Oh, my!" exclaimed Rose. "I would have been riddled with holes, more holes than a peasant's tatty old trousers!"

"Well, at least we know we are on the right path," determined the Elf. He watched as new spikes replaced the crystal formations that were deployed forcefully across the passage. These sharp crystals gradually protruded from the walls, waiting to be unleashed once more by dark magic.

"How so?" questioned the Princess.

"Dragonite would not bother with this unless he had something worth protecting hidden down here," replied Rainus.

"So we venture on?" assumed Tag.

"I recommend we find another way, one that is easier than to chance getting impaled by deadly spikes of crystal," suggested Rose.

"We cannot turn back now," countered Silas.

"Yes, if you retreat those mimes will either be making their way across that fiery divide as we speak, or they are already waiting for you at the mouth of this tunnel," cautioned Rainus.

"Yes! Like hungry cats waiting to pounce on a helpless mouse as it comes out of its hole," added Tag.

"Better to proceed," urged Silas. "We cannot turn back now or –"

"I know, I know!" grunted the Princess, rolling her eyes in frustration as she finished his sentence. "Or we will be doomed; the end of the world as we know it shall be imminent, and blah, blah, blah. Well, need I remind you that we have a more immediate problem? If we proceed along this same treacherous tunnel, we are likely to get skewered many times over; to die a horrible death, and then there will be no saving the world at all."

"This passage was made to keep others out, but it is clear the Sorcerer can run the gauntlet, reaching the other side unscathed," determined Rainus.

"Yes, he probably does something like this." Rose snapped her fingers in demonstration as she chirped, "Magic on! Magic off!"

"Perhaps in another time before we, being my brother Wizards and I, had stripped him of his great powers," revealed Silas. "That is why he desires the dreamstone now. He believes if he can unlock its magic, his powers can be restored by many fold and our situation will become more dire."

"Are you saying that any trap or obstacle he creates with magic cannot be manipulated with more magic?" asked Tag.

"Dragonite has the ability to concoct potions and create hexes, even conjure short bursts of power from that black crystal of his to do terrible damage, but magic to this extent requires great concentration, time and energy, all of which does not come easy to him these days. He cannot just turn it on and off, as simply as that."

"So how do we overcome this magical, but deadly obstacle?" questioned Tag.

"It is a matter of outsmarting that fox to defeat him at his own game," answered Silas.

"And just how do we do that?" grumbled Rose. "We have no idea how far this deadly obstacle course runs, nor do we know how to avoid being hit by a barrage of flying crystal as sharp as broken glass. We will come out the other side looking like minced beef or a bloody, crystal pincushion if we survive."

"I believe I know how to do this," replied the Wizard, taking the torch from Rainus' hand as he watched the crystal formations magically replenish themselves along the walls. Holding forth the burning torch, the light of the flame was refracted by the facets of crystal, shining in beams of light that would be the envy of any rainbow. "We must move with speed, timing our advance just right so the crystals that explode forth ahead of us are rendered harmless, but moving before the ones that have been replaced aren't triggered by the torchlight, to go off on us."

"It is all a matter of timing," confirmed the Elf. "If we remain close together and move accordingly, we should be fine."

"Are you ready, Princess?" asked Tag.

"Of course not! But why do you even bother asking me? It has never prevented you from traipsing ahead, dragging me along with you, right into the heart of danger."

"Good point," agreed Tag. "So let's be on our way."

With the torch in one hand and the Elf's sword in the other, Silas advanced. Holding the light before him, the crystal formations closest to the torch refracted its light, scattering narrow rainbow beams criss-crossing through the tunnel.

Slashing the blade of the Elven sword through the passage to disrupt the beams of light, this action was immediately followed by the explosion of shards and spears of crystal being jettisoned across the way. The larger spears impaled the wall while smaller, but just as deadly shards disintegrated, shattering on contact without a soft, yielding body to absorb the impact.

"Do not lollygag, my young friends. Keep up, unless your intention is to be the recipient of random, and deadly, body piercings," warned Rainus, urging the mortals in his company to remain close on the Wizard's heels as Silas rushed ahead to set off more crystals to explode against the opposite wall.

Methodically making their way forward to avoid certain death, the four comrades pressed on, timing their advance just so.

"Halt!" ordered the Wizard, raising the Elf's sword so none would venture before him.

"This is no time to stop. The flame of the torch begins to wane," cautioned Rose, watching as the fire wavered, continuing to shrink.

"More deadly crystals ahead?" asked Tag.

"Yes!" Slashing through the diminishing beams of light, only the crystal projections nearest to the Wizard where the torch's flame was the strongest were set off. "But these are not the only obstacles that concern me."

"What is it then," queried the Elf.

"The way is marred by another impediment," answered Silas. Holding up the torch, it cast its light further down the tunnel for him to see. "I stand corrected. There are *many* impediments. The floor of this tunnel is riddled by great holes, probably not unlike the one before us."

"Oh my!" gasped Rose, peering down. "Is that what I think it is? A skeleton?"

Silas lowered the torch, its unsteady light illuminating the pit below to better reveal what the Princess had spied on.

It was a sad sight to behold. The skeletal remains were suspended above the floor of the pit by the crystals jutting out from what was left of the husk of a body. The spikes protruded from a multitude of places, including what was once his manhood, to add insult to an already deadly injury. So riddled with spikes of crystal, the tattered remains of clothing clinging to this skeleton was like a beautifully bedazzled piece of art, but horrifyingly so.

By its size, it was obvious this was once a dwarf. Scattered near this corpse were old mining tools liberally coated in a layer of dust and cobwebs. A burned out torch lay broken nearby.

"The poor soul," lamented Silas, with a sad shake of his head. "What a terrible way to die."

"At least death was instantaneous." Rainus noted how the pointed tip of a crystal had pierced through the right eye-socket to protrude from the back of a fractured skull.

"I was not liking this before, I am liking this even less now," groaned Rose, inching away from the edge.

"Whether you like it or not, we must venture on, Princess," responded Tag. "Now hurry before we lose the light of this torch.

Just as they were skirting the edge of this pit, a draft of air swirled around them, buffeting the dying flames to extinguish the torch.

"This is bad," whimpered Rose, her hand groping about, searching for Tag's arm. "It is now blacker than black."

"Bloody hell… Is it just me? Or does this always seem to happen to us at the most inopportune moment?" questioned Tag, his eyes blinking hard in this consuming darkness.

"Believe and trust…" mumbled Cankles. He inhaled deeply, unleashing a great yawn as he rubbed the sleep from his eyes. Glancing about, he could see no one, not even the Pooka, in or near his prison cell. "Either I am losing my mind or I just had a very odd dream, much odder than usual."

Cupping his hands to his mouth, he called, "Hello! Is anyone here? Captain Yairet, are you still about?"

For a lingering moment, he listened, waiting for a reply. All he could make out was the faint echo of his voice resonating off the spikes and columns of crystal. It was followed by the steady, dull thud of his heart beating as he fought against the despair awaiting him in his waking hours.

Standing up, Cankles stretched his aching back before shaking the fog from his head. Scooping up some fresh water from the giant, magical decanter the Sorcerer had conjured up, he drank first to quench his thirst, and then to fill his hungry stomach. When he was done, Cankles splashed some water onto his face.

"Ah! Much better," he muttered to himself as he used the sleeve of his shirt to blot his face dry.

"Perhaps I *am* losing my mind. It was such an odd dream, after all… Believe and trust!" snorted Cankles, his words tainted with cynicism as he tried to shake the memory of Tag's father from his mind. "I *believe* I am trapped and I *trust* that this time, I am as good as dead."

As Cankles reflected on his dire situation, the glimpse of torchlight dancing off the brass detailing on the old, cracked shield Dragonite had tossed aside in frustration caught his attention. The only comfort he found was in knowing his true name and identity, thanks to Captain Yairet.

Pressing his face between the crystal bars, he stared at the shield that once belonged to his dear friend and captain.

"You said you came to me during my darkest hour… well, Captain Yairet, that hour stretches on and it has only grown darker still. Why show yourself, if it was not to help set me free of this hell? Instead, you leave me with horrific memories that are useless to me now and I'm left without hope of ever escaping this place."

Despite these desperate words, Captain Yairet failed to manifest before him. All he saw was his reflection many times over, staring back at him on the surrounding crystal formations.

"So what would you have me do?" He slumped to the floor of his prison. "What *can* I do?"

Again, he listened for an answer, but there was none.

"If I was smarter than most, as you had once claimed, I would not have gotten myself in this predicament to begin with. I would be able to devise a cunning plan that would lead to my escape, thereby enabling me to warn my friends of danger."

With arms wrapped around his legs and his forehead resting on bended knees, his mind churned, provoked by the captain's audacious words.

"If I was so smart, I would think of a way to make the Sorcerer drop his guard, even use his magic to remove these bars. But the only way he would ever do that is if he had reason to… like if he believed I was dead. Now, there's a grim thought. If he believed I was dead, that would give him good reason to come in here to see if I truly had met my demise, as I am no good to him as a corpse. Once he steps near enough to me, I can overpower him; perhaps even steal away with that staff of his."

Mulling over these words, he muttered to himself, "Mind you, how do I go about this business of looking convincingly dead? I can only hold my breath for so long, after all."

He unleashed a dreary sigh, contemplating the possibilities as he spoke aloud, hoping against hope Captain Yairet would reappear before him once more, or at the very least provide him with some guidance as a disembodied voice from the beyond.

"Perhaps that is the most logical thing to do. If I were to die, the Sorcerer would have nothing to bargain with, as his desire was to trade my life for the Princess'. There would be no honour in trading my life for hers... However, there is some honour to be restored in sacrificing mine, so she may go on. Princess Rose can still turn back, leaving Dragonite with a dreamstone he cannot use."

He stopped his plotting to internally flog himself.

"I am an idiot, the village idiot at that! What am I thinking? I can't even escape from a wet burlap bag, let alone a fortified prison imbued with dark powers."

Squeezing his eyes shut, he tried to ignore these negative words. Drawing a deep breath, a powerful revelation cleared his mind.

"No... I am Sir Myron Kendall, a knight of Fleetwood, first officer to Captain Oliver Yairet. I cannot... I will not hide from my past any longer."

Standing up to his full height, an air of dignity and purpose filled his heart as a determined resolve seeped into his mind. "Instead, I shall embrace my destiny. If it means to sacrifice my life, then so be it. I shall do so with honour."

He spun about, turning to face the applause from a single pair of hands.

"At last, you finally remember who you are," grunted Dragonite, kicking aside Captain Yairet's damaged shield.

"I remember everything! I even recall the atrocities you subjected me to."

"Oh, my! That surely must have been soul destroying, knowing what I had reduced you to!" scoffed the Sorcerer.

"I beg to differ. All it did was confirm my resolve. You did not break me before. You will not do it again."

"Break you? I will not waste my precious time trying to *break* you! Oh, no! Instead, this time, I will out and out kill you."

"Then do so now. I am a knight of Fleetwood. I do not fear you, nor do I fear death."

"You should, for I will be the one to dispense it!"

"Then do it! To die unarmed, killed by a necromancer like you will reveal to the world just how truly pathetic you are."

"*Necromancer?* Now I am truly impressed! The former you would not even know the meaning of this word."

"I know this and a whole lot more. If you do not kill me first, then you have fated yourself to a terrible end."

Dragonite scowled in contempt, taking a step back as his prisoner rushed up to the bars that separated them. "I preferred you more as the lowly, snivelling Cankles Mayron, with an addled brain and the backbone of a spineless worm."

"Only because it is *you* that now fears *me!*"

"I *fear* that you are sadly mistaken, *Moron* Kendall. Your time in captivity has inflicted your wobbly mind with a good dose of the crazies," growled Dragonite, his words curdling with malice as the obsidian crystal perched atop his staff glowed with his growing rage. "*You* are my prisoner. *I* am the one who will control your fate, not you!"

"My name is Myron Kendall, *Sir* Myron Kendall!"

Rather than backing away from the power waiting to be unleashed from this black crystal, Myron's hands lunged through the bars. Seizing the Sorcerer by his robe, he rammed him against the prison. He made no attempt to grapple the staff from Dragonite's grip, instead, he held on. Fighting to maintain a hold on the flowing robe as the Sorcerer struggled to be free. If there was a way to pull this deviant soul through these bars, even if it were in small, bloody pieces, then this former knight was going to find a way. He slammed his nemesis against the crystal barrier once more.

Myron's frantic attempt came to a halt as the Sorcerer thrust the obsidian crystal against his throat.

"Do you wish to die?" snarled Dragonite, the crystal throbbing with light.

"Do it! Kill me now!" In defiance, Myron pressed his neck harder against the jagged chunk of obsidian. The sharp edge pierced through his skin to draw a trickle of blood as he dared Dragonite to end his life where he stood.

Neither adversary backed down.

The knight remained steadfast; hoping his bold act of defiance would drive Dragonite to either slash his throat with the keen edge of the crystal or discharge a surge of energy powerful enough to claim his life.

"I know what you attempt, but even at this, you fail!" cackled Dragonite. His eyes gleamed with malice as he mocked his prisoner, removing his weapon from Myron's neck.

Before the knight could hurl words of insult or dare his captor to steal away with his life, the Sorcerer's eyes gleamed with evil intent.

Dragonite unleashed a burst of energy from the black crystal.

Myron groaned in pain, his breath hitching in the back of his throat. He flew across the prison cell to bounce off the opposite wall.

Collapsing to the ground, his right shoulder caught the edge of the giant water urn, knocking him onto his back. With teeth and fists clenched and eyes squeezed shut, his trembling muscles seized under the powers of this debilitating magic. Convulsing, his back arched with excruciating pain as blue lights, like miniature bolts of lightning, danced and crackled across his stricken body. He gasped for air, his ragged breath catching while his heart raced, pounding so hard and fast, it felt as thought it would explode from his chest.

"You will die when I decide it is time for you to die!" snarled Dragonite. The tip of his staff merely bounced off this mortal's midriff, the muscles still contracting and stiff from the shock of the energy coursing through his body. "For now, you will suffer for your noble, but foolish gesture. When the Princess arrives, you *will* die. In fact, you and all your friends will most certainly die by my hands."

These words echoed and hummed in the knight's ears, the light of the torch fading to black as he lost consciousness.

11
Change of Plan

"This is bad! So very, very bad," whimpered Rose. Her eyes ached to see in this utter blackness as she clutched to what she hoped was Tag's hand. "Of all the times for that torch to burn out... I swear! You are doing this on purpose!"

"What you are babbling about, Princess?" muttered Tag. "I had nothing to do with it! It was either a bad torch, bad timing or both!"

"So you say!" Rose gave him a dismissive grunt.

"Our situation appears to be dire, but actually, it is not such a bad thing, Princess," assured Rainus, his words were matter-of-fact as he sensed the panic rising in her voice.

"I mean no disrespect to you, Lord Silverthorn," countered Rose, "but those are sounding to be the words of a man gone mad."

"How so, Princess?"

"Have you lost your mind? Need I remind you that we are standing here in complete darkness? We only now discovered this tunnel of doom with the projectiles of crystal waiting to be unleashed has the additional obstacle of gaping holes along the way, waiting to swallow us up with one misplaced step."

"What I mean to say is, without a source of light, those jagged, deadly pieces of crystal cannot be launched at us, plus, the dying flame was snuffed out by a draft," explained the Elf.

"*A draft?* What is the big deal about a draft?" The Princess frowned in confusion though none could see.

"It means this tunnel must be coming to an end, opening into another chamber or even the world outside."

"I can understand your optimism, Lord Silverthorn," said Tag, "but you forget; without light, how do we negotiate this tunnel? As the Princess said, the floor of this tunnel is riddled with who-knows-how-many of these pits, each lined with spears of crystal for the unlucky sod that should fall in, becoming impaled upon them."

"We must be strong," urged the Wizard. "Carry on through the gloom that is this tunnel."

"*Gloom* is the understatement of the century! It's darker than dark in here, if that is even possible," reminded Tag. "In fact, it is so black, it's hurting my eyes staring at this suffocating nothingness."

"At this moment, yes, the darkness is undeniable, but we must forge on," responded Silas. "This is neither the time nor the place to just up and change our plan. We must advance."

"But how? Through a process of elimination?" Rose's tone was cynical. "Each time one of us disappears, screaming as we fall to our death, we are to assume there is pit before us to be avoided by the survivors?"

"I have an idea," replied the Wizard.

"One that will not get us killed, I hope," prayed Rose, staring toward the sounds of Silas' voice that hung in this blackness.

"If we are careful, we shall be quite fine."

"Then what is this plan you have, Master Agincor?" asked Tag, struggling to be free of a clammy grasp in case it wasn't Rose's hand that had latched onto his.

"My orb! I will simply use the glow of my crystal to light the way!" explained Silas.

"Hold on!" cried Rainus. "If you light up that orb, I can pretty much guarantee the crystal formations that were deployed as we came to this very spot have been magically restored by now. They will be ready to launch as soon as you set that thing aglow."

"Worry not, Lord Silverthorn," assured Silas. "I will use just enough power to see in our immediate area, or at least *you* will be able to do so. It will be so diffused it cannot cast those hazardous beams of light as the flames from the torch did."

"But how will you know if it will not be so strong as to send these crystals hurtling at us?" questioned Rose.

"Well, there is only one way to find out how much is too much," stated the Wizard. As the orb on his staff glowed ever-so dimly, Tag and Rose immediately ducked; dropping to the ground in hopes of being out of the line of fire should the crystal spikes and spears be launched. They remained frozen in their places, hands over their heads just in case, as this light grew brighter by tiny increments.

"That is sufficient," said Rainus, motioning at the Wizard to desist. "I can see just enough to know what is what and where these pits are, without triggering these crystals."

"Are you sure?" asked Silas. "I can make it a little brighter."

"He's positive!" shouted Tag, his hand frantically waving about for the Wizard to stop with his magic. "Lord Silverthorn, with the exceptional sight gifted to the Elfkind, can lead us from here on."

"Very well then," conceded Silas. Holding his staff before the Elf, the orb glowed, casting just enough light for Rainus to see in front of him.

"There better not be any more surprises in the way of deadly traps," groaned Rose, "or someone will hear about it."

"I'm sure we'll *all* hear about it," muttered Tag. "Now move on."

"Hey… wake up!" shouted Loken. Grabbing a fistful of hair, he tugged on the strands to send a sharp pain through the mortal's scalp. It was just enough discomfort to stir him from this unnatural sleep.

"Come on, Cankles, my man! You must get up. There is much to be done."

The only response the Sprite received was a low moan from this crumpled and disheveled form sprawled out on the ground, flat on his back.

"Get up! You cannot sleep your entire life away!" grumbled Loken.

With another sharp tug, it was enough to make the unconscious man open his bleary eyes. For the longest moment, he lay on the ground, just staring at the Pooka as the muscles in his arms and legs twitched involuntarily. Tensing them up, the tingling sensation, like the pins and needles in one's foot that had fallen asleep, began to subside.

"You came back…" he finally spoke, struggling to prop himself up on his elbows to look upon the diminutive being pacing to and fro across his chest.

"So I did, but what happened to you?" questioned Loken, noticing the blood that had trickled down his neck only to dry and mat into his hair. "Did you try to slit your throat on the dull edge of a crystal?"

"Now there's a thought."

"What happened?" probed Loken. Seeking the truth, he stared into this mortal's eyes.

"I had a confrontation with the Sorcerer. It did not go quite as I had anticipated. He hit me with a surge of power from his black crystal."

"Are you mad? If he wanted to, Dragonite could have easily killed you with one blast! Do you have a death wish or something?"

"Yes… In fact, that was what I was counting on, to have that madman end my life. With my demise, he will have nothing to bargain with, in his hopes of capturing Princess Rose."

For a moment, the Sprite was taken aback, unsure if he heard this mortal correctly. "Hey… I thought it was just a momentary phase and you'd slip back to your old ways."

"What do you speak of?"

"Your manner of speech, it continues to improve," noted Loken. This mortal spoke with clarity; each syllable of every word was properly enunciated rather than Cankles' usual habit of speaking quickly and slurring his words by dropping the 'g's when he said 'counting' and 'capturing'.

"I suppose it is better to say that this is the way I used to speak and it is coming back to me, now that I remember what I had long forgotten."

"Amazing!"

"Never mind that! Did you not hear me? If I am to save Princess Rose, I must die."

"Well, that is downright noble of you... crazy, but noble nonetheless," decided Loken, nodding in approval. "But whether you live or die, it matters not to the Sorcerer. He is intent on capturing the Princess."

"So you say."

"It is what I *know*, but what brought this on? Why all this willingness to sacrifice your life for hers?"

"I told you, I remember everything."

"*Everything?*" Loken frowned in confusion. "Even more than I had disclosed to you?"

"Yes! I know who I am and I have not forgotten my fealty to King William. I have taken a solemn oath to protect my liege and his family. I know what I must do to protect Princess Rose."

"And that is to die?"

"Yes, and I am willing to make it so, if it gives her and my friends a chance to survive this quest."

"Hey, what is going on here?" Loken backed away, and then he launched into the air as he scrutinized the man struggling to sit upright before him. "You look like Cankles. You even smell like Cankles. But you certainly do not sound or act like him!"

"As I said, I know who I am now. I am Sir Myron Kendall, a knight of Fleetwood, first officer to Captain Oliver Yairet."

"I knew you were a knight, but what kind of name is Myron? Why not Byron or something else more befitting a noble knight?"

"Myron suits me just fine. It was my grandfather's name, after all. I am just grateful I remember now."

"Oh… you *do* remember, even more than I thought possible,"

commented Loken. "So, I take it, from henceforth, you will not be answering to Cankles Mayron?"

"Only because I know my true name is Myron Kendall. I have no desire to hide from my past, not anymore. I know my purpose and I will not hesitate. In order to save Princess Rose, I must die."

"So you say, but you're no good to me as a corpse."

"What do you mean? What do you care if I live or die? After all, you even confessed you had, at one time, suggested the Sorcerer have me beheaded."

"That was before... in the past! And it is jolly good to see you believe your purpose in life is to die, but there is more at stake here than just Princess Rose's life, you know?"

"What do you speak of?"

"There are other lives in peril, if you do not help me. Your knightly attitude is exactly what I'll need to expedite your escape from this glittering, crystal hell."

"My escape? *You* plan to help *me* escape?"

"Yes, me! And why the hell not? It's not as if you have a lot of options at your disposal at this very moment, Sir Myron Kendall!"

"You had no desire to help me before."

"I can understand your apprehension, but now that you are *not* Cankles the *village idiot* and you can recall, at least in mind if not body, whom you once were, I can use a knight with the will to right a wrong, if that's what knights are supposed to do."

"Of course it is! My sense of justice remains intact. It is as strong as ever, if not more so."

"Good, that will take you a long ways. But if I aid you, you must promise to help me take from the Sorcerer something he promised to me long ago."

"If this is merely to spare your life, for Dragonite is quite prepared to kill you on sight, then I must think on it."

"Tell me this, Sir Myron Kendall; is your duty as a knight to protect the innocent from harm?" questioned Loken.

"Yes, but you, little sir, are far from innocent."

"There are times when even the good are forced to do evil and vice versa, but never mind about me! I am speaking of Pancecelia Feldspar, the Queen of the Tooth Fairies. You can help me to save her life and her entire kingdom, too."

"*Me?*"

"You claimed she was a dear friend. Did this change since we last spoke?" questioned Loken, staring suspiciously at the mortal.

"No, but what can I do? I am here, trapped in this crystal prison while she is in the Fairy's Vale."

"So you would help, if you could?"

"You, I am not so sure of, however, Pancecelia... she is a whole other matter. I just cannot see how I can be of service to her. And if I can, she will be made to wait until I can figure out how to be free of this subterranean dungeon."

"This cannot wait!" snapped Loken, his voice tightened with frustration. "As we speak, Sparks Firestar is plotting her demise."

"Say again!"

"You heard me! Everything I told you about him and his dastardly plot are coming to fruition as we speak!" declared the Sprite. "That deranged Fairy is going to kill her! I made off with Celia, hiding the queen from Firestar to keep her from harm."

"Why would she suddenly accompany you? I thought you said she no longer sees you as you once were? That she now spurns your every attempt to reason with her."

"That, I did. I was forced to take her against her will, for Celia's tainted perception continues to cloud her every thought and judgment where I am concerned. If I had not done so, as surely as the seasons come and go, she will be brought to her ruin by Firestar, if I had not intervened when I did."

"Do you have evidence? Some kind of proof he means to murder her?"

"I have this!" Loken pulled out a tiny blue bottle from his cloak. "I stole it from that wretched Fairy. It contains poison Dragonite concocted for Firestar so he could steal away with Celia's powers and eventually, her life."

"Good gracious! So you were never really conspiring with the Sorcerer! It was Sparks Firestar from the start."

"That's what I've been trying to tell you all along! Although it would appear I am in alliance with Dragonite, as I said before, I had no choice. I heard that deviant soul confessing he had struck a deal with the Sorcerer."

"What kind of deal?"

"He knew Dragonite had a weakness for his lowly mimes, unwilling to part with them. The Sorcerer understood his minions were nothing more than actors, bad ones at that in my opinion, not worthy as soldiers capable of fighting and winning his wars. With his powers wanting and no longer trusting the mercenaries he failed to compensate after losing his last big battle, he became desperate. Dragonite knew if he could employ the powers of a shape-shifting Sprite like me, his bid for world domination was possible."

"He was merely using you."

"I allowed it, if it meant a chance to save my love, to put things right in Celia's world once more, I would have sacrificed anything – *everything* to see it done."

"This is not good."

"Tell me about it! Now, if you can find it in your heart to help me, and if not me, then my dear Celia, I can break the spell that grips her. At this moment, she cannot understand the very real danger Firestar poses to her life. I just need you to help me get the one thing from the Sorcerer that will see this spell undone."

"You mean this?" asked Myron, opening his hand to reveal a tiny vial to the Sprite.

Loken's eyes grew wide in surprise as he stared in awe at the vial of magical potion.

"But- but- How did you get this?" stammered Loken, dropping to his knees as he alighted upon Myron's hand. The Sprite's mind struggled to grasp how this simpleton of a man was able to do what he could not in all this time. "I've spent years trying to secure this from the Sorcerer, but not once have I succeeded in doing so! You must have performed a great miracle to possess it now."

"Yes… if you can call *stealing* a miracle."

"With all I've endured in my attempts to acquire this vial of potion to save my Celia, yes! It is a miracle indeed! How did you accomplish the impossible?"

"It was quite easy, really. Once I had the Sorcerer in my grasp, daring him to kill me, it was easy to take this vial. Being so small and light, I doubt Dragonite even realizes that it's gone."

"I am truly astounded! You did what I could not. Even with all my abilities and numerous tries, I had failed."

"Take it," offered Myron, handing the tiny container to the Sprite.

Loken glanced suspiciously at the vial, and then at the man offering it to him. Instead of gleefully or graciously accepting it, he considered this 'gift'.

"What is the catch?" questioned the Sprite.

"If you believe this will help Pancecelia, take it! Go! Be away from here before Dragonite returns, for he has every intention of doing away with you now, if he should catch you here."

"And what about you?"

"After all these years, it is time to rise up as the knight I once was. I am prepared to die to help my friends. It is the right and honourable thing to do."

"You are truly set on this, aren't you?" asked Loken, stunned by this man's unwavering conviction.

"It is something I must do."

"Well, if you are so intent on dying, I can help you," offered the Sprite.

"What do you speak of?"

"This!" Loken held up the bottle once more.

"The poison you stole from Sparks Firestar?"

"Yes!"

"I hardly think that tiny bottle of poison, even if I drank the whole thing straight up, is enough to kill me. Perhaps make me slightly ill or numb my tongue so I am unable to speak, but kill me? I think not!"

"Perhaps not in this quantity," responded the Sprite, nodding in agreement.

Myron jumped back with a start.

In a show of light, Loken morphed before his eyes, appearing before him as his likeness.

"Amazing!" gasped Myron, in awe as his eyes scrutinized his doppelganger, "but I assure you, I am not as gangly as this."

"Yes, you are. Your mind is trying to remember how you once appeared when you were a knight," reminded the Pooka.

"Oh... I suppose you are right."

"Now this should do," announced Loken, holding forth the bottle that had also transformed in proportion to his new size.

"We can do a trade."

"And I am the one getting the better deal," assured Loken, handing the bottle over to the mortal.

"So you say," responded Myron, as he accepted the poison. "In my heart and in my mind, this is for the best. I only pray my death will not be in vain."

"In my opinion, it will be, if you do not get revenge on the Sorcerer first," stated Loken. He morphed back into his usual form. Pushing off the ground, he adjusted his damaged set of wings as he hovered before Myron's face.

"My revenge will be in preventing Dragonite from harming my friends."

"How about a little change of plan, my friend? For there is a better way to get revenge on that murderous villain," suggested Loken.

"Whether I was Cankles or as I am now, with total recollection of who I am and what I represent, I am not the vengeful type."

"You should be! But if vengeance is not to your taste, I am hoping your sense of justice prevails."

"It does. So, go on... tell me more," urged Myron.

"To die so Dragonite cannot manipulate you, to prevent him from using you as a pawn to capture the Princess, is a grand way to foil his plan. However, what would drive the old bugger absolutely stark raving mad is if you were to come back to life: Return from the dead, so to speak; to bring chaos to his order. This would see that crazy old coot completely undone, and you can do so without ending your life so dramatically!"

"So you say, and I would be the first to agree, but there is no coming back from death. That is impossible!"

"It is *possible* with that bottle of poison you hold, if you know how much to take," revealed Loken.

"What do you mean? Poison is poison. It is created to kill."

"This special poison concocted by the Sorcerer himself, if taken in the proper dosage, will *simulate* death," responded the Pooka, pressing an index finger to the side of his nose as he gave the mortal a knowing smile. "Undiluted, it will kill, absolutely! However, several drops added to a cup of water for a man your size? To drink it as such, the poison will work to slow the heart and your breathing drastically, enough for the untrained eye or the unwitting fool to stumble across your body to believe it to be a corpse."

"So I would only *appear* to be dead?" asked Myron, considering the bottle now in his hand.

"You will appear to be *very* dead, so much so, you will not be able to fight, even if your life depended on it. Your muscles will be non-functioning until the poison wears off."

"So, if I understand correctly, my muscles will be temporarily paralyzed, to add to the effect?"

"It will be as though your body has lapsed into a deep coma, but your mind will remain alert. Your body will be as limp as a wilted piece of kale, but you'll hear everything happening around you."

"Brilliant!" exclaimed Myron, nodding in approval.

"I know! When Dragonite finds your *dead* body, he'll have his mimes take you away."

"He will?"

"Of course! He won't want a corpse lying about, rotting away here. It will foul up the air he breathes and that will not do, especially when this is where he plans to imprison Princess Rose." informed Loken.

"Where will they take me?"

"He will have his idiot mimes drag your carcass out of here and dump you off at one of the many openings to his crystal fortress. No burial, no funeral to mourn your passing. They'll just leave you there."

"Are you sure they will not toss me over the edge to my real death? Throw my body into an abyss just to be rid of it?"

"Well, they are mindless mimes that tend to do what they're told, but there is always a chance one of them might get it in his head to discard you instead of leaving you as a treat."

"A *treat?* What are you talking about?" questioned Myron.

"You know? A morsel… a snack! Think of yourself as a little appetizer," answered the Sprite.

"For what, pray tell?"

"For one very large dragon," replied Loken, "hence the use of the word *'morsel'*. If this behemoth catches a whiff of fresh meat lying about, that beast will be here to feed faster than a starving man hearing the dinner bell at a beggar's banquet."

"They will toss me out as dragon food?" gasped the knight.

"Like scraps for a hungry pig, but no need for despair. If it should come to that, take comfort in knowing the dragon will be done with you in one swallow."

"That is not exactly what I wanted to hear."

"Yes, but it is a fact of life, or in your case, death, if the dragon is hungry and in the immediate vicinity. Just pray the creature is not about and you will regain full use of your limbs to make your escape."

"But why bother with keeping a dangerous reptile close to his fortress?" asked Myron, scratching his head in thought.

"Watchdogs, no matter how big the mutts to keep intruders at bay, will not survive in these lands. They'd be picked off like defenseless lambs by starving wolves with these dragons roaming about. The Sorcerer tosses out an occasional *offering* to keep those beasts near to this mountain fortress. Consider it a visible warning to stay away; that if he doesn't kill you, a dragon surely will."

"Lovely," groaned the knight.

"Using dragons for watchdogs? I'd say it's practical and it works to keep the average, unwanted visitor well away from here."

"Unfortunately, my friends are far from average. I hardly think a few dragons will deter them at this point of the quest."

"I sense you are right," agreed Loken. "You best do what you must, if you're so intent on saving them."

"Yes… So, if I *'die'* and I am placed out there and the poison does not wear off as expected, I am likely to be eaten by a dragon?"

"That is why you must use the precise amount of poison and drink it at just the right time," explained Loken. "Fool Dragonite into thinking that you are dead; have his idiot mimes drag you out of here as dragon fodder; then once those fools have deposited you outside of his lair, the poison should have run its course. You can escape before that dreaded beast shows up to feed on your bony carcass and Dragonite will be none the wiser to it. To the Sorcerer and his minions, as far as they will be concerned, you are dead and digesting deep within a dragon's belly."

Myron rubbed his stubbly chin in pensive thought as he stared at the bottle of poison that could spell either his release or a sudden and tragic demise.

"Are you having second thoughts now?" questioned Loken.

"I am not... I am thinking on how best to set my plan into motion."

"So you'll not be reneging on our deal?" asked the Sprite. "I can still keep this vial of potion for Celia?"

"By all means," answered Myron, extending his open hand to Loken. "Time is of the essence. Go save her. Take it!"

"Thank you!" gasped the Sprite, clutching the vial in his trembling hands. "Now, just make sure you use that poison as intended. My dear Celia will not be pleased with me if you do yourself in with poison I had provided to you."

"Indeed, but now the trick is to dispense the right amount of this toxic brew into that supply of water," said Myron.

"Just remember, if you put in too little, your ploy at feigning death will be ruined. If you put in too much, you will linger in this state, wishing you were dead until death makes its claim."

"I understand perfectly," acknowledged the knight, his head nodding to the Sprite in appreciation. "You should go now, while you still have a chance. You have what you need. Save Pancecelia, if you can."

"I will," vowed Loken, his hand over heart in solemn promise. "Even if it kills me, I will save my love."

Myron squinted, shielding his eyes from the glow as the Pooka assumed a new guise. Knowing Dragonite would mostly likely kill him upon spying his aura glowing through the shadows of the gloomy passageways, Loken transformed into one of the denizens of this subterranean lair. Circling the prison cell twice, he banked about in mid-air, flying through the gap between two of the crystal bars.

"Good luck," offered Myron, wishing him well.

Loken did not answer, nor did he look back.

For a lingering moment, even after he lost sight of Loken's bat form and could no long hear the flapping of those leathery wings echoing through the passage, Myron continued to listen.

Silence.

Loken was gone, carrying with him, Pancecelia's hope for salvation from impending doom and his own redemption should she finally learn the truth.

"So... several drops in one cup of water," said Myron, glancing over to the crystal container that remained filled to the brim no matter how much he drank. Drawing a deep breath as though to steady his resolve, he muttered beneath his breath, "I must do what must be done."

Myron scrutinized the giant decanter, trying to gauge the quantity within. His eyes kept shifting from the decanter to the dark blue bottle, trying to figure out how he should approach this. As he estimated the portion of poison to use, Loken's warning flashed through his mind: Too much, and he would die. Too little, and it would not be effective enough for his plan to work.

Holding the bottle against the light of the torch, Myron could see the poison filled it almost to the bottom of the cork seal pressed firmly into the mouth of this vessel. Clamping his teeth around the cork, he wrenched it about, twisting it free. He peered down the slender neck of the bottle to see inside. The poison was as crystal clear as fresh, glacial water.

Taking a whiff of the poison, he sensed it would at least release a hint of something noxious that the Sorcerer would be able to detect, even recognize. Instead, it was odourless.

Myron's mind began to reel as he thought on this dilemma. *'It looks like water... it is odourless like pure, clean water. Could it be nothing more than that? Perhaps the Pooka had lied to me; maybe he deceived me in his desperation to save the love of his life?'*

Drawing in a dreary sigh, in his heart he knew Loken's history and his penchant for lying to get what he desired. The Pooka could have just devised this clever scheme, fooling him after gaining his trust. There was a good chance this was nothing more than plain, old water.

Bringing the bottle to his lips, he considered tempting fate by tasting it to see if it was indeed poisonous. He stopped short; realizing that there was a definite chance it could also be real. Hastily, he pulled the bottle away from his mouth, realizing in doing so, it could be his last and most deadly mistake.

Siding with caution, he meticulously counted out the drops per estimated cup that filled this giant decanter. When he was done, he waited to see if the water would somehow transform; becoming cloudy or assuming an unusual colour as the toxic potion mingled, thereby betraying its presence to the Sorcerer.

Instead, the drops of poison became one with this crystal clear liquid. Dragonite would have no way of knowing it was tainted, not unless fate conspired against him and the Sorcerer drank it himself.

"I hope this works," prayed Myron, as he resealed the bottle. For a moment, he stared at this potentially deadly concoction. Suddenly, he popped off the cork, throwing in an indiscriminate splash of poison into the water. "For good measure... just in case."

Without sufficient poison in this solution, his effort to appear dead was doomed to fail. Too little will not have the desired effect; too much was sure to kill him, or worse; it would slow his heart beat and breathing for too long, causing irreparable damage to body and brain. This concern was tempered by his desire to make sure that if he had miscalculated on his measurements and the proportion of poison to water, he was confident the extra dose would be enough to kill him. The idea of poisoning himself to the point of permanent disability, but not attaining death was unthinkable. Better to die by his own hands than to be eaten alive by a dragon, unable to fight for his life, if he wanted to.

"That should do," decided Myron, as he nodded in approval. Concealing the bottle between spikes of crystal on the far wall, the Sorcerer would not find it unless he knew to look for it.

"Now, I wait."

With the precious vial of potion clutched firmly in his grip, Loken's little brown bat form moved with ease and single-minded determination. No longer hampered by his damaged set of wings, at this size and gifted with the ability to navigate in total darkness, the Pooka winged his way through the labyrinth of tunnels, the tips of his leathery wings not even grazing the crystal formations as he maneuvered about. Ducking into the shaft that had delivered him in secret to Myron's prison cell, Loken ventured on, his wings pumping in frenetic flight as he swerved, dipped and careened though the darkness.

The high-pitched squeaks he emitted to bounce off of solid objects to be collected by his sensitive ears formed a mental image of his surroundings. The faster these sound waves returned to him, the closer he was to a spike of crystal protruding into the passage or where the tunnel would take a turn to the right or left.

Loken was able to determine exactly where the walls flared out and where they narrowed, in some sections so small that a grown human would barely be able to squeeze through on his belly. Navigating the pitch black with confidence, he ventured on, a distant blur of dim light beckoned him forward.

As he advanced, the passage opening to the outside world beckoned him on. The dazzling blue sky shining through the entrance grew brighter. Loken transformed again, shedding his bat guise to adopt the form of the swift-flying falcon. He burst from this narrow tunnel into the light of day, only to '*screee*' in surprise, twisting through the air to escape the waiting maw of a dragon.

Like a cat waiting for a rodent to appear at a mouse hole, the mace-tailed dragon pounced, pushing off the mountain to give chase as Loken rushed skyward, gaining in altitude.

As this beast's powerful jaws snapped shut, the displaced air forced Loken away, pushing his sleek, feathered body from the teeth that smashed together. Twisting through the air to escape, Loken winced in pain as the dragon's fangs snagged several tail feathers; still the Pooka managed to escape with the help of the winds.

As much as the thermals helped to carry his falcon form higher, so too, did this bank of warm, rising air deliver the dragon into the blue, aiding in its vigorous pursuit.

Loken glanced down. In a glow of iridescent green scales that shone in the sun's light, the Pooka could see the dragon's powerful wings were thrusting the creature through the air, quickly closing the distance on him.

With greater agility than the much larger dragon, Loken began weaving to and fro, climbing higher into the sky as the winged reptile drew ever closer.

If this dragon were to attempt to take aim, using a blast of fire in a bid to down this prospective meal, Loken's erratic flight pattern would make it difficult.

With leathery wings that billowed like the sails of a tall ship as the dragon pushed through the air, the creature closed the gap as Loken hovered with his wings fully extended. Just as the dragon's mouth opened to snap down on its prey, Loken folded his wings. Diving straight down, he spread his wings open once more, levelling out as he glided between the mountains.

The dragon's bellow of frustration thundered through the air, echoing off the landscape below as the reptile wheeled about, resuming the hunt.

Loken glided southward, gaining altitude as the mace-tailed dragon followed. The thought of morphing into an even bigger dragon to confront his pursuer did cross the Pooka's mind, but depending on how hungry and belligerent this creature was, instead of retreating, there was a very real chance he'd be engaged in an aerial battle. The likelihood of defeating the pursuing dragon was not a concern, but wasting time to return to the Fairy's Vale was more pressing to Loken. His best option was to out-maneuver and out-fly this reptile, while still maintaining his flight southward.

Glancing down, the dragon was nowhere to be seen. Loken breathed a sigh of relief, only to pivot sharply, banking to his left as the unnerving sensation that something wasn't right seized his heart.

Loken tumbled through the air as the dragon flew by. Missing him by a feather's-width, the turbulence of the creature's powerful wings rushing by sent the Pooka spiralling out of control. With the wind rustling through his fully extended wings and his tail feathers fanned out, Loken slowed this rapid descent, allowing the rising thermal to catch him. Gliding south toward the protective cover of the Dimbolt Forest that was still so far away, he began flapping his wings, driving his body through the air.

Glancing above, and then below, the dragon was nowhere to be seen. Loken pushed skyward, climbing toward the feathery bands of cloud pushed along by the wind's design. That was when he spied upon the dragon in eager pursuit. It had been following directly behind him all along.

"Damn!" cursed Loken, tilting his head to see the reptile ascend and gain on him, unwilling to give up. Racing on, this falcon flew toward the closest patch of forest. Knowing the stands of trees would create an effective obstacle, one he could easily negotiate, it would prove difficult for a beast the size of this dragon to maneuver through.

Just as Loken dove downward, the dragon, already fooled once before by this tactic, acted swiftly. As this falcon eluded the snapping jaws, the dragon twisted backward, its spiky tail swinging up as Loken dove down.

Veering away from the bony spines arming the tip of the tail, the Pooka dodged this weapon, but a sudden flick of this appendage as the dragon levelled out to resume its pursuit clipped the edge of Loken's wing, sending his falcon form tumbling through the air.

Though it was just feathers that were impacted by this blow, it was easier to roll with the percussion than to immediately correct his flight in the turbulence created by the dragon's wings.

Catching the wind once more, Loken spread his wings wide open, riding the thermal as the dragon bellowed in rage, clawing at the air as though it would somehow move it closer to capturing its prey.

"Too bloody close!" gasped Loken, folding his wings as he dove toward the trees.

Dodging branches and weaving between the treetops, his deadly flight was followed by the sounds of crashing foliage and boughs as the dragon continued this chase, its club-like tail smashing everything it touched as the beast winged its way just over the forest.

Ever determined to journey southward, Loken's tree cover abruptly ended at the edge of a narrow river. Instead of veering left to duck back into the forest, he dipped down, flying low over the water.

The dragon followed, the tips of its wings and heavy tail skimming the turbulent surface.

Up ahead, Loken could see the water becoming choppier as it picked up speed, smashing against boulders jutting from the river. As the thundering of water grew louder and plumes of mist swirled through the air, Loken suddenly folded his wings, diving over the edge of a waterfall with the dragon in full pursuit.

Lacking a falcon's agility and slowed by the chill of the rising mist, the dragon struggled to keep up. Before the beast could maneuver up and away from the rocky formations at the head of the waterfall, the dragon bellowed in pain. The spiky protrusions arming the end of its tail snagged between two boulders. The forward momentum threw the creature over the edge. Its desperate cries to be free were drowned out by the coursing water as it thundered over to unmercifully pummel its wings and body; the icy cold sapping the dragon's strength and will the longer it remained trapped.

12

Expect the Unexpected

"We are almost there," whispered Rose, as she followed close on the Wizard's heels.

After journeying on for what felt like an eternity, there was quite literally a light at the end of the tunnel. The glow of Silas' orb waned the closer they advanced toward it.

"Yes, not too much further to go now," agreed Rainus, his keen eyes detecting the unsteady light of burning torches ahead.

"Oh, hoorah!" exclaimed Rose. Though her words were tainted with sarcasm, she was anxious to be out of this crystalline death trap.

"You cheer now," admonished Tag, shaking his head in disapproval, "but you do so prematurely."

"And just what was that supposed to mean?" grunted the Princess.

"We are in the heart of the Sorcerer's fortress, a stronghold teeming with who-knows-how-many of his mimely minions," reminded Tag. "We made it here thus far, but you'd be a fool to let your guard down now."

"*My* guard down? You are supposed to be protecting me. You are the one who should not be letting *your* guard down."

"I'm just saying that we should be prepared; expect the unexpected," cautioned Tag, as he crept along behind her.

"How dare you dampen my spirit? You are worse than a wet blanket," pouted Rose. "In fact, you are a downright soggy quilt!"

"The young sir is quite correct, Princess Rose," whispered Silas, turning off the glow of his orb as they neared the end of the tunnel. "It would be prudent to keep our wits about us. There is no telling where the next trap or snare awaits."

"But suppose there are none?" questioned Rose.

"Then that would make for the ideal situation," responded the Wizard. "However, we are where we are, hence, the need to proceed with due care and attention, for it is highly probable Dragonite will have other devious methods in place to prevent us from reclaiming the dreamstone."

"I mean no offense, Master Agincor," said Rose, "but you are like Tag. He is the wet blanket and you are the equally soggy sheets beneath it, both conspiring to undermine my spirit."

Tag merely rolled his eyes in frustration upon hearing the Princess whine some more.

"Say what you will," dismissed Silas. "I know Dragonite. I can promise you, he will not make it easy for us."

"Your words ring true, Wizard," acknowledged Rainus, as he peered into the small chamber. "Look at this."

As his three comrades stepped forward, the tunnel opened into a crystalline room that was illuminated by two torches burning brightly at the opposite end. The ceiling was several hand spans higher than the top of the Elf's head when he stood upright and only just as wide.

"Watch where you tread," warned Rainus, his hand resting on Rose's shoulder to halt her advance. "You do not want to end up in there."

"What is down there?" Rose squinted as she peered into the perfectly rounded opening that dropped away into a black abyss.

Silas set his orb aglow once more, pointing it down so they can see into the depth of this dark hole in the ground.

Glittering shards and splinters of crystal lay scattered about at the bottom of the pit.

"That is not so bad," decided Rose. "At least if one of us should fall in, there are no deadly spikes of crystal waiting to impale a body."

"Forgive me if I am wrong," said Rainus, "but I do believe those sparkling bits and pieces smashed across the floor of that pit were once deadly spikes. The question is; how did they get that way?"

"Oh, lovely! I will add you to my collection of soggy bedding! You can be the damp, stinky mattress to go with the wet blanket and sheets!"

"Merely stating the obvious, my lady," responded the Elf, gazing across to the other side.

"I'm having a very bad feeling about this," remarked Tag, as he studied the small chamber. "What do you make of the smooth walls, ceiling and floor? It looks like a cylindrical tube of sorts that terminates into this pit."

"Cylindrical? Oblong? Equilateral triangle? Who cares? I see possible freedom; an end to this quest on the other side."

"Hey, I never thought you even knew what an equilateral triangle was," commented Tag, staring in confusion at the Princess.

"I don't. It just sounded fitting for the occasion."

"I agree with Master Yairet," said Rainus, scrutinizing the path on the other side of this pit. "Throughout this journey, we had encountered every shape and size of crystal imaginable. Why now are the walls as smooth as glass, like they've been polished to this fine finish?"

"Maybe the Sorcerer wanted to change up the décor a bit?" offered Rose, her fingertips brushing lightly where the walls were worn, and then along the tunnel where she and her comrades stood. There was a definite contrast to the jagged protrusions surrounding them.

"What are you babbling about?" Tag frowned in confusion at the Princess.

"You know? Perhaps he wanted a change of scenery," explained Rose. "Even crystal, no matter how sparkly in its regular form, can become boring after a while when it is over done. He just wanted to change it up a little."

"That's what I love about you, Princess," commented Tag.

"My great sense of logic and impeccable taste in fashion?" asked Rose, blushing upon hearing his words.

"No, I was speaking of how intelligent you look, and yet, some of the loopiest things come out of that mouth of yours."

Before the two mortals could engage in a full-blown verbal fisti-cuff, the Elf intervened, gesturing for quiet as he knelt down.

"Hush! You heard him," ordered Rose, pressing a finger to her lips as she turned on Tag. "Lord Silverthorn is on to something."

The young man merely rolled his eyes in response as he unleashed a dreary sigh.

"What is it?" queried Silas, peering over the Elf's shoulder.

"I could be wrong, but I highly doubt it," replied Rainus, as he scrutinized the floor of the chamber.

"Doubt what?" asked Tag.

"If my eyes do not deceive me, the ground from the mouth of this pit toward the entrance where those torches burn appears to be at a very slight incline," noted Rainus. "It is barely visible, even to the most discerning, trained eyes."

"What are you speaking of? I know one is required to train their eyes to detect a fashion calamity in the making or when white gold is merely silver, but since when does one need training to discern if something is crooked or slanted?" Rose knelt down next to the Elf, squinting her eyes to see if that would help her to see what Rainus saw. "I do believe your eyes are deceiving you, Lord Silverthorn. I do not see it."

"Princess, if it is not too much of an imposition, may I have one of your steel balls?" asked Rainus.

"My supply is endless. You can have as many as you like," offered Rose, her slender fingers digging into the suede pouch. "Do you want the sling, too?"

"One ball will suffice," answered Rainus, extending his hand to accept the projectile. As Rose removed one, another magically replaced it to keep the pouch constantly supplied.

Holding it up to the light of the torch, the Elf examined the cold, hard sphere. It was perfectly round, polished to a silvery finish and bore the engraved image of a single rose twined around a dagger.

"A rose and a dagger?" questioned Rainus, staring quizzically at the Princess.

"You know? It symbolizes me: beautiful, but deadly. But never mind that, what will you do with it?"

"Watch," answered Rainus.

He tossed the steel ball. With a sharp 'clack' it bounced on the smooth ground only once. As it settled in the middle of the floor, the ball began to roll toward them; slowly at first, but picking up noticeable speed as it neared. They watched as the steel ball rolled right into the pit, disappearing into the blackness, leaving in its wake more shattered crystal down below.

Rose stood up, rolling her slight shoulders in a shrug as she asked, "So I was wrong? There is a slight tilt to the floor. Now, other than wasting a perfectly good steel ball that could have been used to do away with a mime or Dragonite himself, what was the point of that little exercise?"

"Lord Silverthorn was trying to demonstrate that the floor of the chamber is tilted ever so slightly toward this pit," answered Tag.

"And?" The toe of Rose's shoe tapped impatiently on the ground as she awaited an answer.

"It is a trap," explained Rainus, his words spoken with confidence.

"So you say," argued the Princess. "But you cannot convince me that the floor is so tilted, if we attempted to head through that opening we will only slide backwards, disappearing into this pit that is not even very deep nor is it armed with crystal spears waiting to impale us."

"I am more than confident we can easily manage this barely noticeable incline," stated Silas. "However, did you not notice how that steel ball of yours gradually gained in speed as it rolled down?"

"Yes, but it is not as though any of us are as round as that ball," reminded Rose. "If one of us should slip, it is not as though we will all go tumbling down like chicken eggs rolling off a slanted table top."

"True, but a perfectly round ball certainly can," stated Rainus.

"What harm can a little round ball do to us?" countered Rose, as she dismissed the Elf's concern. "Unless you tread on it to slip, landing flat on your back, cracking your noddle in doing so, what is the big deal?"

"Look around you, Princess," urged Rainus. "Can you truly not see what I speak of?"

"See what?"

"Lord Silverthorn is talking about a *massive* ball," explained Tag, staring at the opening of the pit. "One that can fit through here to crash down on what were once crystal spikes."

"Are you sure?" asked Rose.

"The condition of this chamber explains it all." Silas' eyes studied the smooth surface of this chamber that took the form of a cylindrical tube. "A sphere that just fits, its form polishing smooth the walls and floor through abrasion, did this."

"Fits? How much of a *fit* are you speaking of?" questioned Rose, as she tried to imagine the size of a boulder to accomplish this.

"It is safe to assume that it would take a boulder of such size to fill this chamber from top to bottom, and side to side, in order to wear our crystalline surroundings smooth like this," answered Rainus.

"Oh my!" gasped Rose.

"Indeed! If one of those boulders should come rolling down through this chamber and we're in its path, we'd be nothing more than smears against the walls and floor," stated Tag.

"Now there's a lovely thought," said Silas.

"But – but, I am too young and beautiful to be a smear on anybody's wall," whined Rose, dreading what was to come next.

"If I am correct, aside from where we stand now on this side of the pit, the far wall where those torches are mounted offers the only safe refuge for us should a boulder come crashing through here," determined Rainus.

"That is good to know, but first, we must clear this gaping chasm," reminded Rose.

"Not a problem," responded Rainus. "Stand aside."

Taking several steps back, the Elf took a running start, pushing off against the edge of the pit to land safely on the other side.

"Stay where you are," ordered Rainus. "I will first make sure there is no boulder rolling our way before we proceed."

"Brilliant! We wouldn't want that now, would we?" The Princess waved the Elf along. "We shall remain where we stand."

Rainus rushed forward, pressing his back against the far wall. As the flames of the torches swirled and flickered, twisting in the wake of his movements, he waited. As the fire burned steady once more, the Elf's ears pricked up as he listened. From the shadows of the connecting passage there was only silence. There was no loud rumble of a huge boulder crashing forward to annihilate them. Nor was there the clatter of footfalls to indicate the enemies' approach.

For the count of thirty heartbeats, Rainus waited, listening for signs of danger.

There was only numbing silence other than the occasional *'Tap! Tappity-Tap!'* as Rose tossed a crystal pebble or two into the pit. It was not so much to determine how deep or long it was, instead, her actions were motivated by sheer boredom as she waited for this miserable quest to lead them onward to another misadventure.

When Rainus felt at ease; his senses and intuition determining there was no impending danger lurking in the passage ahead, he joined his comrades at the gaping hole.

"It is safe to advance," advised the Elf, waving his comrades on.

"Excellent," said Tag.

"I see no place where you can use a grappling hook so we may swing across," noted Rose, staring at the ceiling overhead that had been worn as smooth as her own perfect complexion.

"You are going to jump, as I did."

"No, seriously," said the Princess, as she glanced about, "there is nowhere for you to use a hook. It looks like you will have to proceed without us."

"No need for that," responded Rainus, dismissing her words. "You will jump the distance on your own."

"Say again!" Her eyes were wide open in fear.

"Jump! It can be done. With a little bit of energy and effort on your part, you can clear this pit."

"Yes, if one is an *Elf* gifted with height and those leggy legs," argued the Princess, prancing about on her toes like a nervous, newborn fawn. "Surely you do not think we are capable of clearing this great chasm."

Rose gasped in surprise. In a blur of movement, she watched in surprise as Tag raced forward, pushing off the earth to propel his body forward, over the mouth of the pit.

As his foot landed on the other side, Rainus snagged him by the shoulder, pulling the mortal onto solid ground.

"Are you crazy?" cursed Rose, shaking an angry fist at Tag. "You must want to die!"

"Not at all," countered Tag. "I knew I could do it, so I did."

"You know nothing! You *are* crazy."

She shrieked in surprise as the Wizard flew by her. Sailing over the pit, his gaudy robe, a smear of vibrant colours, billowed behind him as he made the leap. Before he could fall short of a safe landing, Tag and Rainus seized him by his outstretched arms, pulling him and his staff to safety.

"You, sir, are crazier than that rapscallion of a would-be-knight!" snapped Rose, pointing an accusing finger at the Wizard, and then at Tag.

"Nonsense! I merely proved that if an old man can make it, so too, can you."

"Have you taken leave of your senses, Master Wizard? You just barely made it to the other side!"

"If you take a running start, there is nothing to it!" insisted Tag, waving her on to follow. "Now move! We haven't got all day. We must advance with haste. This is no time to lollygag about."

"And you'll be running with haste for your life when I get my hands on you!" cursed Rose, stamping her feet in defiance.

"Hark!" shouted Rainus, cupping a hand to his ear as he stared down the darkened tunnel behind her. "Quickly, Princess! It is coming!"

"What?" asked Rose. She glanced over her shoulder as her heart jumped into her throat. "What is coming?"

"Mimes!" shouted Rainus.

"Giant worm!" Silas cried out at the same time.

"Say again?" gasped Rose, staring in confusion at them.

"It sounds like *mimes* being swallowed alive by that *giant worm,*" corrected Tag.

"Oh, no!" yelped Rose, her body freezing in panic.

"Hurry, Princess!" shouted Tag, waving her over. "The monster worm must have followed us."

Before he could tell Rose to back up so she can build enough momentum to help propel her over the pit, the Princess leapt from where she stood. A look of sheer panic was etched across her face as she sailed over, landing easily on the other side without assistance from the others.

Dashing past her comrades, she headed straight for the end of the chamber, struggling to remove a torch she could use to drive back the beast. Turning to call for assistance, Rose's eyes were greeted by the strangest sight.

There, in a row, stood Tag, Rainus and Silas, all in shock by what they just bore witness to. Mouths agape, eyes wide in surprise, they stared at the Princess. This feeling of mute shock suddenly gave way as the three burst out in a fit of laughter.

"What? What happened?" Rose frowned in confusion. She ceased her struggle to remove the torch as she stared at her companions.

"You should have seen your face!" howled Tag, slapping his thigh as he laughed.

"She was like a rabbit being scared out of its warren by a vicious hound on the hunt!" Silas snorted as he guffawed. "Jumped like there'd be no tomorrow."

"The way you sailed over, you could have made it across with me on your back!" chortled the Elf.

Realizing they had tricked her, Rose marched over to confront them.

Before Tag could say: *'Uh-oh'*, Rose slapped his face as she declared: "*You* are evil."

Punching Rainus in his midriff, she denounced the Elf: "*You* are mean!"

Stomping down on the Wizard's left foot, she growled at Silas: "And *you* are a troublemaker!"

Then stomping down on Silas' right foot, she added, "You are also evil and mean to boot! How dare you trick me? That was a cruel thing to do!"

Between moaning in pain from the unexpected assault and trying to stifle their laughter, Tag and Rainus stopped upon seeing the incipient tears. They welled up in the Princess' eyes as she turned away, sobbing.

"Whoa! Hold on, Princess! We were just having a bit of fun," explained Tag, feeling guilty they had reduced her to tears. "Just trying to ease the tension of this trying situation."

"At *my* expense!" sobbed Rose, pushing him away as he tried to console her.

"It was a fleeting instance of levity, brought on by the stress of the moment," justified Rainus, now feeling as badly as Tag did.

"It was funny as hell, and it got you across, did it not?" snorted Silas, struggling to refrain from laughing aloud once more.

The Wizard's unrepentant response generated a chorus of sobs and *'boo-hoo-hoos'* as the Princess openly wept, dissolving into the *ugly cry* Cankles and Tag dreaded the most.

Tag and Rainus gave Silas the *'eye'*, using unspoken words to urge the Wizard to apologize, if that's what it was going to take to make Rose stop weeping.

Instead of complying with their wishes, Silas refused to express regret for his involvement in the scheme to get her to cross over, as well as his fit of laughter in watching her do so.

With a heart-wrenching sob that sent her body shuddering uncontrollably, Rose crumpled to her knees. Burying her eyes in the crook of her arm, she unleashed a torrent of bitter tears. She was truly a pathetic sight to behold.

"Go on!" insisted Tag, speaking in a whisper as he prompted the Wizard on. "Apologize to Princess Rose."

"And you better be sincere about it," added Rainus, as he nodded in agreement with the mortal.

"But she slapped you and went on to punch you," reminded Silas, pointing at Tag, and then the Elf. "Plus, she stomped on not one, but both my feet."

"Come on, Wizard," urged Rainus. "Man up! Do the right thing and we shall be on our way."

"Very well," groaned Silas, his eyes rolling in frustration. Standing before the Princess, the Wizard made his peace. "I am truly sorry, Princess Rose."

Instead of accepting his apology, Rose shuddered as another long, hard sob wracked her body.

"Now, now my dear girl! No need for tears. I am truly sorry I behaved as I did. Meant no disrespect!" promised Silas, as he knelt down before her.

Again, his words were met with stuttering sobs and loud sniffles as the Princess refused to even look at him.

Joining the Wizard, Tag and Rainus were humbled. They knelt before Rose as all three began to apologize profusely for their unbecoming conduct.

"I speak the truth, Princess, I'll never do that again," vowed Tag. "We will never laugh at you again; with you perhaps, but never at you, if you take such offense."

"Sweet Mother-of-Pearl!" groaned Rainus, wanting nothing more than for her to stop with the tears. "I will cut off my beautiful tresses in penance, if it will make you stop weeping, my lady."

"I will help to cut-off his hair while I apologize yet again, if it pleases you," offered Silas, hoping to close this floodgate of tears.

The three were bowled over as Rose suddenly hopped up onto her feet. "*Ha!* Got you all!"

As quickly as she had whipped up these phony tears, she stopped crying.

"What the?" gasped Rainus, startled by her performance.

"You were just pretending?" groaned Tag.

"It is called *acting*, great acting by your sorry response!"

"Well, I'll be!" grunted the Wizard.

"The three of you deserved that," rebuked the Princess, her arms crossing her chest in defiance as she stared at the men, giggling at the stunned expression on their faces. "And now, I laugh as I embrace the levity of *this* moment, brought on at *your* expense!"

"Fair enough," conceded the Wizard. Wallowing in humility, he brushed off the dust from his hands. "Lesson learned, Princess Rose."

"Good! We journey on," said the Princess, nodding in approval as she waited for Silas to lead the way.

As the minutes stretched into hours, Pancecelia Feldspar's hopes of struggling free of her restraints began to wane as her fear began to grow in equal increments.

Without her wand in hand, it was impossible to just vanish as though she were in a child's bedchamber to steal away with a tooth. And to cry out for rescue was not an option either. The gag Loken had secured around her mouth refused to budge, reducing her screams for help to nothing more than stifled moans and sad whimpers that were inaudible beyond this tree hollow.

Knowing Sparks, and those desperately looking for her, would not be back having already searched Loken's family home, Pancecelia knew she would either die by the Pooka's hands should he return or languish, fated to suffer a lingering death waiting for rescue that will never come, if something prevented Loken from coming back to do the deed himself.

Either way, neither option was sitting well with the Queen of the Tooth Fairies. She always believed if she were to meet an early demise, it would be beneath the pillow of a child tossing about in restless sleep, squashing her as flat as a trampled cow patty. She never dreamed it would be through the actions of the one she once loved. That, to her, was the cruellest of all ironies.

With all the composure of a true, regal queen, she gathered her will and determination, drawing a deep breath as though it would somehow help. Exhaling with a stifled scream, Pancecelia thrashed about, fighting with all her might to break the resilient strands of silk. Panting in exhaustion, the gag remained around her mouth, while the tangle of webbing that mummified her body did not break, let alone loosen.

It became apparent that no matter how frantically she struggled against these bonds, freedom was impossible. Fighting against tears of despair, she knew she had only one option left to her. If she waited until nightfall, her golden aura, dimmed by the light of day would swell, growing bright as darkness engulfed the Vale. If she saved her strength, she'd be able to glow brightly, enough that perhaps, should Sparks be in the immediate vicinity looking for her, he'll be able to see her aura shining from the entrance and windows of this tree hollow, glowing like a beacon to summon his help.

With nothing left to do but wait until nightfall, Pancecelia was left to wallow in her misery. Staring at the cryptic message scrawled in blood on the wall, her only companions were her thoughts and Loken's troubling words that Sparks Firestar was the one she was to be cautious of.

'The world has gone crazy, or perhaps I am the one who is crazy now. I do not know whom or what to believe anymore. If what Sparks said was true, how could I ever have loved Loken? I believed he truly cared for me, but was it nothing more than a clever ploy to weasel his way into my heart? Was it nothing more than a trick to seize the throne for himself?'

Pance shook her head trying to dispel this disturbing thought from her troubled mind.

'How could anyone fake that kind of love? And if he did, only someone coldhearted, cruel and calculating would do that, someone like a... murderer.'

She groaned, trying to wrap her head around this mindboggling situation. Now she was forced to choose to believe between the one she once loved and the one she always trusted. With none present to share in her thoughts, Pancecelia's mind struggled to sort through everything she knew in heart to be true and everything she was told to believe was the truth, as explained by Sparks Firestar.

'Well for one, Sparks has been someone I have trusted from the start, and his reasoning always made perfect sense. He is always helpful and reliable. Even while Loken was in the process of kidnapping me, he had the guards search for me, dispatching them immediately.'

As she combed through her thoughts looking for explanations to justify Sparks' actions, things just did not add up.

'Sparks has been trying to protect me from Loken this whole time. I am sure of it... His actions have always been loyal. There is no way he could have strayed.'

Then Loken's warning of Sparks' duplicity, his warning that her trusted aide had tricked them both, gnawed at her conscience.

'Loken is lying. He must be in alliance with the Sorcerer, pretending

*his innocence by writing it in his family's blood. He does not even look
the same; he is but a ghost of his former self. And he had the audacity
to kidnap me in a bid to keep me away from Sparks and the truth! How
could I have ever loved such a horrible being? But then, why was
Sparks so quick to tell the guards I was dead? To instruct them to kill
Loken on sight...'*

Her anger and frustration mounted the more she thought on this.

'Stupid me! Stupid, stupid me!'

These angry words played over in her mind as she thought on her
predicament and how she could have ever fallen in love with a Sprite,
a shape-shifting one at that. The terrible feeling that Sparks Firestar
was right, that she should never have trusted a Pooka to begin with,
wreaked havoc on her heart and mind.

*'I loved him with all my heart! I trusted Loken with my very life!
Now I am doomed to die by his hands, already bloodied by the murder
of his poor mother and siblings.'*

Fighting back her tears, she stared at the bloody message on the
far wall, and then at the tattered remnants of the family portrait. It lay
amongst the chaos on the floor near her feet. The painting featured
Loken's mother sitting dignified upon a stately chair, while her two
youngest children stood on either side and Loken stood proudly behind
his mother. His hand rested lightly on her shoulder as the four smiled
politely for the artist commissioned to create this portrait.

For the life of her, Pancecelia knew that everything Sparks told
her of that murderous night in this very tree hollow cried of Loken
committing a deed most foul. And yet, staring at this family portrait,
unless the painter used creative license to portray a scene of devotion
and familial bliss, behind that smile and those kind eyes, there lurked
the heart of a ruthless, calculating killer.

Glancing about, by the level of destruction and the telltale sprays
and pools of dried blood left by a madman on a murderous rampage,
she knew the killer was driven by unadulterated hate.

According to her trusted aide, it was a crime motivated by pure
bloodlust. It was not committed by a petty thief in the night, caught in
the act of pilfering and merely wanted to do away with witnesses. It
was a heinous act performed by a demented soul out for revenge.

But why would Loken seek revenge against his own family? That
was the one piece of the puzzle she could never seem to quite fit into the
scheme of things. Loken's mother did not oppose, neither in her words
nor her actions, of their impending betrothal. In fact, she was jubilant
about the news, hoping it would unite their races in this realm.

Perhaps rumours that surfaced immediately after the horrific murders, that Loken had been on a drunken rampage were true. It seemed highly unlikely to her, but it made more sense than him seeking some kind of revenge against a family he so loved and respected.

The longer Pancecelia sat, trapped with the ghosts of Loken's past, the more her head hurt. Logic dictated that all the things Sparks was able to explain away about that fateful night made sense to her. After all, why would her loyal aide lie? And yet, an unsettling feeling clutched her heart. It was as though the voices whispering in the shadows of this once happy home, restless spirits trapped in this realm by tragic events, served to haunt her.

It was not a sense of terror or revenge she felt weighing heavy in the musty air, closing in around her, it was the overwhelming feeling of sadness; one so palpable, she was sure it would swallow her up whole, sucking her soul into a black void of emptiness if she were to die here.

She stared at the painting, blinking back the incipient tears as she gazed at the image of Loken as she once remembered him.

Back then, before he was tainted by his evil alliance with the Sorcerer, Loken's eyes were as blue as the most perfect sapphire. They would sparkle, outshining the brightest stars on a winter's night whenever he smiled and laughed. They shone of wisdom, honesty, virtue and kindness, all the qualities she loved about him. It had been just over a decade now, but this one memory of Loken remained deeply embedded in her heart and in her mind.

Perhaps it was wishful thinking on her part; a desperate attempt at justifying to others why she loved him back then. Or maybe it was her pathetic way of clinging to a happier time in her past, a time she was never able to recreate with another. Whatever the case, she just could not comprehend Loken's tragic fall from grace.

"There you are!" exclaimed Sparks, appearing at the entrance of this tree hollow.

Pancecelia jumped with a start, her heart racing until she realized it was a friendly and familiar face.

"I have been searching everywhere for you, Your Highness."

As Sparks stepped into the room, she sat upright, attempting to salvage her dignity as she drew in a great sigh of relief.

"I should have known that demented Pooka would bring you here. He was never bright to begin with, but I suppose had I been smarter, I would have suspected this much from the start. It is like hiding you in plain sight!"

Rather than racing over to free her, Sparks casually sauntered over.

"My, my, my! What a sorry state Loken has left you in," commented Sparks, rubbing his chin in pensive thought as he scrutinized her.

Pancecelia struggled about, waiting for him to cut her free. Instead, he paced to and fro, stopping on occasion to consider her situation.

"What am I to do with you, my queen?"

"Free me!" She sputtered through the gag as she writhed about.

"Free you?" repeated Sparks, interpreting her muffled words. "I think not!"

"What?" gasped Pancecelia. She stared in confusion at her personal aide and trusted confidant.

"I have other plans for you, my dear!" Sparks wrung his hands in eager anticipation as he considered his sudden turn of good fortune. "This is perfect! Now all will believe that nefarious Pooka has come full circle, returning to the Vale to finish what he had started, and of all places, to do so here!"

A horrible revelation finally came to light, squeezing her heart with an all new level of fear. She glared at him, then cast her gaze to the bloody words scrawled on the wall.

"Oh, I see you read the note! Well, my dear, I am *not* the one who was innocent. That damned Pooka left that message for you. Alas, when he needed you to see it the most, you were too distraught to witness this scene of murder; lucky for me!"

"It *was* you!" mumbled Pancecelia, her words stifled by the gag.

"I like you, too! Even respected you at one point in my life," muttered Sparks, as he misinterpreted her words. "However, I never *loved* you the way that wretched Pooka did. Mind you, I could have put on a convincing show, if it meant ruling the Fairy's Vale, but no! You had to whine and pine for a lost love that went so tragically wrong to begin with. The only way to snap you out of that pitiful grief was to set an enchantment on you; one that would force you to see Loken in a terrible light, to drive him from your heart, forever."

"You murderer!" cursed Pancecelia, frantically struggling against the gag and the silk webbing that bound her.

"Ew murmurer?" repeated Sparks, frowning in confusion. "Oh! You mean to say, *you murderer!* Oopsy! I suppose now that I have confessed my sins to you, there is only one way to deal with it. I will have to kill you."

"Please, no!" begged Pancecelia, her desperate words wheezed through the gag. "Let me live! I shall see you set free. Escape now, so you can avoid punishment."

"Oh, how odd that I understood what you said this time!" snorted Sparks, his attitude was cavalier as his brows arched up in mock wonder. "Thank you, but no! I believe your reign is about to come to a hasty end, and my rule is about to commence. However, this will not happen if I am forced into exile, living on the run. And the last thing I need is for your guards, and heaven forbid, that crazy Pooka to come after me. I will be as good as dead, but there will be nothing good about it! Therefore, your early demise is imminent."

"No!" shrieked Pancecelia, thrashing about to be free.

"Oh, yes! It is a pity you were not able to see my point of view when it came to Sprites, particularly that shape-shifting Pooka, sitting by your side in the throne room; dispensing orders like he was above us. Now, things will be as they should be. Fairies living here in the warm, more hospitable climes to the south; while what remains of the Sprite population remains banished, lingering in the cold, somewhat barren north, guilty by their association to that *murderous* Pooka. And now, they will be forced from this realm altogether, once they receive the ill news that one of their own returned to murder the Queen of the Tooth Fairies."

"Please, no!" whimpered Pancecelia, struggling against the strip of cloth Loken used to secure her legs to the chair. No matter how hard she fought, she couldn't lift her feet to kick him away.

Standing before her, a cruel smile curled his lips as he pulled her wand from his holster.

"See this? If I use it against you, in a blink of an eye I can reduce you to a shimmering pile of Fairy dust. It would be fast, easy and far less messy for me, but I am no fool."

"No... Please, don't do this!"

"But I must! Now, I shall do unto you, what I did to Loken's family. To keep it consistent with the other killings, I shall slit your throat and believe me, it will be far less messy if you do not put up a fight like those foolish Sprites did," whispered Sparks, dragging the tip of the blade down her cheek and along her neck. "And do you know what the lovely thing will be about this tragedy, Your Majesty?"

Sparks grasped her chin, forcing her to stare at his face. "Everyone will suspect the devilish Pooka once again. All eyes will be cast his way as they search the lands for Loken, to bring him to justice while I sit on the throne, donning a splendid crown as a new dawn breaks over this realm!"

Pancecelia's eyes opened wide in horror. Her mind raced, trying to comprehend Sparks' menacing words and her last moment in this world as the touch of the cold blade kissed her throat.

"Once I am king, I foresee grand changes." Sparks leaned in to taunt her. "Expect a great many things to happen in your absence!"

Her eyes squeezed shut, only to snap open as her nemesis gasped. His weapon fell from his grasp as he dropped to his side, hitting the floor with a heavy *'thud'*.

"Didn't *expect* that to happen, did you now?" grunted Loken, yanking his dagger from Sparks' back. "That was for my mother, my sister and my brother! I pray their souls can find some peace now that they have been avenged!"

Kicking aside the Fairy's still body, Loken untied the gag, carefully peeling it from Pancecelia's aching mouth.

"I am sorry it had come to this," apologized Loken, using his hands to tear away the silk threads from her body.

"You saved me!" Her eyes were wide open in astonishment as she stared at the Sprite.

"That was always my intention, my dear Celia."

"Say it again."

"My intentions?" asked Loken, as he used his dagger to cut her free of the tangled webbing.

"No… my name. Please say my name again." She pressed his hand to her face.

"Celia… You were always my dear Celia," whispered Loken, his fingertip brushing the tears from her cheeks.

She threw her arms about his neck, embracing him in a great hug.

"I would have gladly died a thousand deaths if it meant that you would see me as I once was and believed me as you did before." He breathed a sigh of relief as he hugged her back, feeling the familiar beating of her heart against his.

"So it is true, what you have been trying to tell me all along; that Sparks had placed me under an enchantment?" She stared into his eyes, searching for the truth.

"Yes, but that was the very nature of the spell. You had no reason to believe me. No matter what, you would only listen to Firestar. He manipulated you by manipulating the truth."

"But now, I have heard the truth with mine own ears! Sparks confessed, telling me everything he had done to you – to us."

"Everything?" asked Loken, gently rubbing her numb hands to restore circulation in them.

"Yes, even how he murdered your family, and did so in such a way the blame would be cast on you."

Loken dropped to his knees. His sad face rested upon her lap as he wept, apologizing to her.

"There is no shame in tears shed for those you grieve over," said Celia, as she gently stroked his head in sympathy.

"These are tears of joy, for you are finally safe from Firestar and I have found salvation and redemption in your eyes once more."

"That is so, and this spell should be broken now that I know the truth." She stared at Loken's face. "But why do you appear as you do? You remain unchanged."

He still looked haggard; aged beyond his true years and his eyes still burned bright amber in colour.

"It is not yet broken, not completely." Loken presented to her a small vial.

"This is the potion you spoke of?"

"Yes! Cankles helped to steal it away from Dragonite. We must act quickly, if I am to return the favour," urged Loken.

Removing the scrap of cloth he had tucked into his belt, he peeled back the corners to reveal the iridescent dust he had collected when he had stolen into the palace. "You need to add this to make the potion your own, to make it work for you."

Tipping the glittering scales shed from her wings into the vial, he placed his thumb over the top, giving it a vigorous shake.

"Here, now take a sip, my love."

Without hesitation, Celia accepted the vial. Closing her eyes, she swallowed a sip of the tepid, bland liquid. Drawing a deep breath, she slowly opened her eyes. Her smile faded from her face as she gazed upon Loken.

He stood before her, looking expectant, but remaining unchanged; damaged wings and all.

"It is not working," groaned Celia. Before Loken could instruct her to drink a little more, she gulped down the entire contents of the vial.

"And now?" asked Loken, his heart racing in anticipation.

The look of disappointment was evident on her face as she opened her eyes again.

"No…" gasped Loken.

He fell onto his knees before her, groaning in defeat, frustration and utter disappointment.

"Dragonite lied to me. All along, he had been lying to me! All the wrong deeds I had committed to make one thing right, and all the while, the Sorcerer had tricked me!"

"Just as Sparks Firestar had tricked and manipulated me, for I, too, have done you wrong, blindly dispensing justice on you because I trusted in him."

"But he deceived you! He had you under a spell concocted by the Sorcerer," argued Loken, his trembling hands ready to tear the wisps of hair from his head in utter frustration.

"We have both been deceived, manipulated by the ones we most trusted."

"I never trusted Dragonite. I was just so desperate to do something, *anything*, if it would help to save you; to have you know I am not the monster Firestar accused me of being."

"Fret not, my love," urged Celia, embracing Loken in a consoling hug. "I care not that the Sorcerer's curse lingers on you. It is your heart that remains unchanged, that is what I loved about you first and foremost, even though you are a Sprite with a special gift, I always saw beyond your physical appearance."

"You cannot love me now," whispered Loken, as he turned away, "not like this."

"Yes, I can," promised the Fairy, "just like this."

As her soft lips pressed against his, Loken's heart raced as all their shared memories of a happier time flooded his being, filling him with joy. The heavy burden of his tragic life and existence he had lived until now melted away as he kissed her back.

Enveloped in the glow of her golden aura, enraptured by her loving embrace, Loken was transformed. His dull glow was radiant with renewed life and energy by this one kiss.

"But how can you still love me like this?" Loken frowned in bewilderment.

"Now that I know the truth, I love you no matter what, but with our kiss, you are now as you once were," revealed Celia, her hands caressing his familiar face as she stared into the sapphire eyes she so loved.

Her very words made his heart lift with elation, only to realize he was floating above the floor. He had his full set of wings again, and they were no longer ragged and tatty. He stared at his hands. No more were they gnarled and liver-spotted. Touching them to his face, his sunken eyes and aged skin were gone. He then ran his fingers through a full head of hair. The limp and wispy strands were gone. He was once again the Sprite he was, in all his former glory.

"I *am* me again!" gasped Loken, clasping Celia's hands as he twirled about in joy, pulling her up into the air to join him in celebration.

"I think I prefer the other you… those amber eyes were beginning to grow on me," teased Celia, joyfully hugging Loken.

"Really?" asked the Sprite, searching her eyes for the truth.

"As long as your heart, the one that made me fall in love with you, remains the same, it matters not."

"Where you are concerned, my love for you has remained unchanged," assured Loken, smiling at her with adoration. "But for now, I must head north. There is one more wrong I must right, if your friend Cankles Mayron still lives. I must do what I can to save him, and if not him, his friends."

"Cankles is in danger?"

"Very much so! Now, return to the palace. Let your people know what has become of Sparks Firestar so his body can be dealt with accordingly," urged Loken, as he kissed her forehead.

"My *trusted* aide is going nowhere. It is time for me to right a wrong as well. We will do this together.

"Are you sure?" asked Loken.

"I am positive," answered Celia, as she reclaimed her wand from Sparks' holster. "Take my hand. Hold on tight!"

13

A Very Bad Place

"I wish all the tunnels through this crystal fortress were like this one," whispered Rose, admiring their sparkly surroundings as she traipsed along behind the Elf.

"Like what?" questioned Tag, creeping forward as he traced her footsteps.

"You know? Nice and straight, not all twisty and windy. And all smooth and shiny, too," replied Rose, running her fingertips along the wall of the long, cylindrical tube they had been trooping through, "not jagged and nasty with gaping pits along the floor that are lined with spears of crystal waiting to impale a body or two should you fall in."

"Do not be lulled into a false sense of security, Princess Rose," warned Silas, the glow of his crystal orb casting great shadows before him as he took up the rear. "Remember how this passage came to be this way?"

"Oh, yes… How can I forget?"

"And the straightness of this worn passage is only because one that has twists and turns only serves to slow down the speed of a rolling sphere," added Rainus.

"Yes, don't forget that, Princess!" added Tag. He plastered his body against the polished wall, pretending he had been smeared like a squashed fly, flattened by the passing of a massive boulder rumbling through.

Rose's eyes narrowed in resentment as she scolded him, "I do not find your shenanigans to be humorous at all. And I was merely making conversation to liven things up; lessen the monotony of this trek."

"The monotony of conversing with you will make this trek even more boring and arduous," teased Tag.

Before the Princess could throw a fit, Rainus intervened. "The young master means to say, we are better not to speak. We should be listening for danger in whatever form Dragonite sees fit to dispense on us."

"Yeah, what he said," agreed Tag, realizing the Elf meant, in his own civil and eloquent way, to keep quiet. It was said not only to preserve them from possible danger, but it was to spare them from her wrath for being the recipient of his insult in the first place.

"Look! Up ahead," announced Silas, pointing before him. "I see light."

"I sense *danger*," cautioned Rainus, as he advanced using stealth.

"Light, indeed, but it is not the light of torches that burn up yonder."

"What do you mean?" whispered Rose, increasing her pace to keep up with the Elf.

"The light's intensity is constant... unchanging; unnatural to say the least. If it were from a torch, it would be unsteady; ever changing in intensity as the fire burns and wanes," explained Rainus.

"Perhaps it is light from the outside world?" offered Tag, longing to feel the warm sun on his face once more.

"It may very well be a trap," warned Silas, rushing along behind the others as this tunnel came to a sudden end.

"The dreamstone!" Rose pointed to the bead-like object balanced atop a slender crystal pedestal. She rushed ahead of her comrades.

"Halt!" demanded Silas. "Do not touch it!"

The Princess froze. She stood before the alcove housing this crystal stand. With absolute certainty, she recognized the filigree bead-cap that attached the magic crystal to the fine strand of gold. "It *is* the dreamstone, I tell you!"

"Now *this* is a trap if I've ever seen one," declared Tag, glancing about nervously as he stood at the entrance of this chamber. The small room was flawlessly circular, except for the alcove at the opposite end. High above, instead of a flat or domed ceiling, this one was convex.

"Well now, it is evident where the boulders originated from," noted Silas, "the ones that rolled through the passage we just came from to polish it smooth as glass."

"Where?" asked Rose, frowning in confusion as her eyes darted about, searching for what the Wizard was speaking of.

"Up there!" Silas pointed to the globular ceiling, its most central point bulging down ominously over them.

Rose gasped, glancing up to where a smooth crystal, like the bottom half of a perfectly round boulder of quartz appeared to be magically suspended above them.

"Aaah!" shrieked the Princess. She raced across the floor, leaping into Tag's arms as she yelped, "This is bad! This is a very bad place to be!"

"Get a hold of yourself, young lady!" Silas motioned Rose to calm down as Tag deposited her on the ground. "We do not know what will trigger that boulder to fall, setting it on a path of destruction through this tunnel to crush us."

"Stepping into this chamber did nothing, nor did dashing back across its floor," determined Rainus, the toe of his boot pressing gingerly on the ground before him.

"Neither did her hysterical screaming," pointed out Tag.

"Yes, but I believe I know what will," said Silas, as he crept up to the alcove.

The dreamstone glowed invitingly. Its light intensified against the crystal facets of its surroundings to create a steady, brilliant show of light. Scrutinizing the pedestal it sat upon, the Wizard examined its design from top to bottom. When he was done, Silas shared in his insight.

"It is safe to say Dragonite conjured up some dark magic to safe-guard the crystal. To remove the dreamstone will cause that massive ball of solid quartz to come down. And as you can see, once it does, unless you are immediately crushed, you will be eventually. There will be no outrunning it."

"This is not good, not at all!" groaned Tag, pressing his back against the wall, and then glancing up to see if he was thin enough to avoid being pinned or crushed. Alas, he discovered if he was as wide as the thickness of his pinkie finger, he might have a chance of surviving.

"I know! Once I have the dreamstone in my grasp, I can wish us out of here," offered Rose, never so glad to see the bane of her existence once more.

"Are you mad?" gasped Tag, shaking his head in response. "You lack that kind of focus!"

"Before you even have a chance to conjure up an image of how and where we would escape to, it will be over," cautioned Silas, his eyes studying the hairline cracks spreading out like a spider web from the center of the polished floor where boulders crashed down before rolling through the passage to disappear into the pit at the far end.

"Then how about this? As soon as I snatch away the dreamstone, we can escape, using your magical powers," suggested Rose, looking hopefully to Silas.

"I can disappear on my own instantly, but for all four of us to do so simultaneously?" Silas shook his head. "I would have to summon all my powers plus, you three must place your hands on this staff at the precise moment, which will not be quick enough."

"That will take too long," agreed Rainus. "If that boulder does not immediately come crashing down, I have a feeling it would be just enough time to flee from this spot, but not much more than a few paces before it comes rolling down the passage way to flatten us."

"What about here?" asked Rose, pointing to the narrow gaps in the alcove housing the pedestal the dreamstone was perched on. "I am sure we can fit, if we squeezed in. If, and when, that boulder should come down, we will be safely out of the way."

"There is no way two of us on each side can fit, not even if we shed our weapons, stripped down to the bare necessities and all held our breaths could we squeeze in there," argued Tag.

"There is room enough for two though," stated Rainus, glancing at Rose, and then Tag. "You can fit in there, one on each side.

"And then what?" asked Tag, his eyes narrowing in suspicion as he gazed at the Elf.

"Master Agincor can use his magic to disappear to safety at the precise moment," replied Rainus.

"But what about you?" asked Rose.

"I am prepared to run the gauntlet. It is a straight path to the pit at the other end of this tunnel. If that boulder does not come crashing down immediately, and if it does not increase its speed greatly until near the end, there is a chance I can outrun it, leap over the pit to land safely on the other side, while the boulder drops away to fall into the chasm."

"That is two *'ifs'* too many!" declared Tag, shaking his head in disapproval. "What happens *if* you trip and fall?"

"I am an Elf. That is not possible," responded Rainus. His words were matter-of-fact as he stood tall and proud before the mortal. "No offense to you, young sir, but I have far more grace and agility than the average human being. I have a far better chance of surviving this dash than you do."

Tag sensed Rainus was making this claim not because it was true, but more because there was no other option and no time to debate his stance.

"But that is so far to run," gasped Rose. Her eyes filled with dread. The thought of a huge quartz boulder chasing the Elf through the tunnel, only to catch up and flatten him, played havoc with her mind and sense of guilt. "How can you possibly make it?"

"It is like anything else in life," replied the Elf, his shoulders rolling in a modest shrug, "I can only try my best; do my utmost to escape and pray it is enough this time."

"Well, you must be commended, for it is a brave and noble gesture on your part, Lord Silverthorn," praised Silas. "However, I believe I have a possible solution."

"You do?" responded Rose, as she gazed hopefully at the Wizard.

"Go on then!" urged Tag. "What is it, Master Agincor?"

"It appears Dragonite uses a simple spell to make this pedestal sensitive to pressure," answered the Wizard, pointing to the crystal bead. "If the dreamstone is removed, the displacement or removal of its weight will trigger that boulder to come crashing down."

"So, in theory, if we can find something of the identical weight, placing it on there just as the dreamstone is removed, we should be safe from harm," assessed the Elf.

"That is exactly what I am saying," responded Silas.

"That is bloody brilliant!" praised Tag, nodding in approval.

"Brilliant? It is bloody diabolical!" snorted Rose. "But what do we have that duplicates the weight of the dreamstone? I have no other crystal bead on me just like that. Do any of you?"

"It need not be another crystal," explained Silas, "it merely needs to be an object of the same weight."

Glancing about, even though they were surrounded from floor to ceiling by crystal, all Rose and her comrades could find in the immediate area were the fine splinters and minute shards where boulders had previously crashed down on this quartz floor to mar its polished surface, sending fine cracks radiating outward from the initial point of impact.

"I hardly think any of these will do," determined Tag, using the toe of his boot to scrape up fragments from the slight indentation in the centre of the chamber.

"I'm afraid not," said the Wizard, as he continued to search about.

"Too bad the only thing I have mirrors the dreamstone in shape, but nothing else," lamented Rose, heaving a weary sigh as her hand patted the suede bag housing her never-ending supply of steel balls she used to arm her sling with.

Silas' eyes gleamed upon hearing her words. Thrusting a hand toward her, he made his demand. "Why did you not say so? Let me see one of those balls."

"I say again, it is not the identical size, nor is it the same weight," warned Rose, her fingers fishing about to remove a steel ball from the pouch. "If anything, it is noticeably heavier."

She presented it to the Wizard, holding this ammunition forth in the palm her hand.

Uttering an incantation while pressing the crystal atop his staff to the steel ball, it magically transformed. It remained of steel, but now, it was smaller, even smaller than the dreamstone perched on the pillar.

"Amazing!" marvelled Tag, staring in wonder.

"It is too small," protested Rose, holding it up between her finger and thumb to examine.

"Aah, but does it not weigh the same as the dreamstone now?" questioned Silas, giving the Princess a knowing smile.

Rose scrutinized the metal sphere, palming it to better determine its weight. Bouncing it in her hand, she fumbled. The steel ball hit the crystal floor, adding to the cracks before rolling away. Rainus stood ready to intercept it before it could roll down the passage to disappear, but instead, it came to rest in the slight depression in the very center of the room.

The Elf approached, picking up the shrunken steel ball to return it to the Princess. "Here you go, my lady."

Rose reluctantly accepted it, taking it up between her thumb and index finger.

"Come over here, Princess Rose." The Wizard flexed his finger, motioning her to join him at the alcove and the hexed pedestal.

"What must I do?" Her voice tightened with nervous anticipation that she almost squeaked out her words.

"Snatch the dreamstone up with one hand; place the steel ball down with the other," instructed Silas.

"Sounds easy enough," decided Rose, as she nodded in understanding.

Rainus and Tag's eyes darted from the Princess over to the Wizard, waiting for Silas to explain the significance of this one, simple action.

"Indeed, it sounds easy," agreed Silas, "but here is the catch, Princess: to prevent that boulder from crashing down, you must have *impeccable* timing to do this simultaneously."

"Wait a minute…" Rose studied the rounded ceiling that waited to drop. Glancing over at the dreamstone on the pillar, she then stared at the steel ball pinched between her finger and thumb. "Are you telling me I must remove the dreamstone *and* place this atop the pillar, at the same time?"

"That's what *simultaneously* implies," reminded Tag.

"That is why perfect timing is absolutely critical for this to work," reiterated Silas, as he nodded in confirmation. "You must replace the dreamstone before it can trigger that boulder to fall."

"And don't even bother to ask what will happen, should you fail to do it just so," cautioned Tag, his hand slapping down hard on the other as a visual demonstration.

"Thank you for that!" snapped Rose, as she glared at Tag.

"You're welcome, now get to it," he urged her on.

"I was being sarcastic."

"So was I," grumbled Tag. "Now focus; get this done without getting us killed."

"I must make ready first."

Knotting back her golden tresses and tossing the edges of her cloak over her shoulders so nothing could accidentally land atop of the pedestal other than the steel ball, Rose drew a deep breath. Slowly exhaling, she prayed it would calm her madly beating heart that was pounding so hard and so fast it caused her hands to tremble.

"Steady on, Princess," cautioned the Elf. Rainus backed away toward the entrance of this chamber, bracing himself to run for his life, for this time, it really would depend on it.

"I am trying," whispered Rose. She fought to control the tremors that seemed to worsen the more she had time to deliberate on this dire situation.

"Maybe I should try?" offered Tag, wiping the sweaty palms of his hands dry on his trousers.

"No," said the Wizard, as he waved him off. "It requires a delicate touch, one that neither of us possess. Just give her a moment. Allow the Princess to concentrate on the task at hand."

"No offense, Master Agincor," said Tag, "but at this moment, her hands are shaking so badly, it can start an earthquake if she touched them to the wall of this chamber."

"Never mind the young sir, Princess Rose. Do not allow yourself to be distracted," ordered Silas. "Focus on what must be done."

Rose drew another long, deep breath, exhaling just as slowly in hopes it would calm her rattled nerves.

"Very well… I think I can do this." Rose's one hand hovered over the dreamstone, preparing to pluck it up as the other readied to replace it with the steel bead.

"Do not *think!* Just do it," urged Tag. "There is no room for error this time."

"Will you stop it?" snapped Rose, as she glared at him.

"Just saying!" grunted Tag. Throwing his hands up in surrender and frustration, he prepared for the worst possible outcome. Squeezing in to one side of the alcove, he made sure he did not touch the pedestal in doing so.

"There is no pressure, my lady," called Rainus, from where he stood, ready for the run of his life as he shot a *bite-your-tongue, say-no-more* look of reproach in Tag's direction to make him stop harassing her. "Just make no mistake."

"Concentrate, Princess," coaxed Silas, directing her gaze back to the magic crystal. "Take all the time you need to get this done, for you will have but one chance."

"I know! I know!" whined Rose, shaking off her rattled nerves as she closed her eyes, envisioning exactly how she'd make this switch.

With the Elf poised to make his dash while Tag and Silas anxiously hovered over her, watching her every move as they held their collective breath, Rose snapped in disapproval. "I cannot do it with you both staring at me! Look away!"

"The Princess is quite correct," said Silas, motioning Tag to avert his eyes while he did the same.

"Just do the deed," urged Tag, staring at the top of the alcove. "On the count of three, swap one for the other."

"I will do that," decided Rose, as she gathered her courage. "Now... one, two, and then swap on three? Or one, two, three, then swap?"

Resisting the urge to snap in frustration at her, Tag answered, "Whatever pleases you, Princess. Just see it done."

"Fine! One... two... two and one/quarter... two and one/half... two and three/quarters... *THREE!*"

In a blur of movement, Rose snatched up the dreamstone as the steel bead swooped in to take its place.

She ducked into the alcove and Silas prepared to vanish while Rainus raced off to beat the boulder. Instead of a thunderous crash or even a slight tremor to herald the unleashing of the giant sphere of quartz, there was only numbing silence.

"Miracle of miracles! What do you know?" marvelled Silas. "It worked!"

Tag and Rose breathed an audible sigh of relief. Careful not to bump against the pedestal to displace the precariously balanced steel bead, they came out of hiding.

"What happened?" asked Rainus. He poked his head back into the chamber to see the ceiling was still intact and his comrades were not flattened like a wafer of dried beef jerky.

"Nothing happened," answered Rose, proudly dangling the dreamstone by its gold chain before the Elf. "I did it!"

"Well done, Princess!" praised Rainus. In glee, he scooped her up in his arms to triumphantly spin her about.

Seeing the sparkle of gold, Tag was suddenly overwhelmed by a tidal wave of dread. "Hey... should we not have taken the weight of the bead-cap and gold chain into account as well?"

The colour suddenly drained from Silas' face as he realized his miscalculation. "I thought I had..."

All four stopped in their tracks, staring at the shiny steel bead perched atop the pillar. They then glanced up to the giant quartz boulder still hovering overhead.

"Phew! I suppose the steel ball still weighed the same as the magic crystal and all its finery," noted Silas, sighing in relief.

"Thank goodness for that!" exclaimed Rainus, as he dropped Rose back to the ground.

Now, it was unclear whether it was this simple motion of setting the Princess back onto the floor or if a tremor deep within the earth was to blame, but the four comrades cried out as that small bead of steel began to roll. None were close enough to prevent it from falling off the top of the pedestal. As it tumbled off the surface, Tag hollered at the Elf, *"RUN!"*

Shoving Rose into one side of the alcove, Tag wedged himself into the other side. The boulder suspended high above came crashing down just as Silas vanished in a great show of light.

The erratic, loping gait of a mime pretending to be a lame, hunched-back minion echoed through the gloom as he led the way. He held the torch on high so Parru St. Mime Dragonite need not waste his energy or magic on his obsidian crystal to illuminate their surroundings.

This mime's footfalls were followed by the steady, rhythmic march of *'step, step, thunk; step, step, thunk'* echoing through the long corridor as the Sorcerer followed. Behind Dragonite, a procession of a dozen mimes took up the rear. Each one bore a scowl, their brows knitted in a frown of disapproval, as they mimicked the Sorcerer's every move, right down to his stiff, measured gait, while only pretending to have a staff in their hands as they marched along behind him.

Blissfully ignorant of their mocking performance, the Sorcerer was entrenched in his thoughts, wandering in the happy places of his mind, if there was such a thing for him.

Reality faded into fantasy as Dragonite imagined bounding through a lush, green meadow bejeweled with a plethora of wild flowers blooming in every colour possible. With the energy of a spry lamb in the springtime of its youth, he pranced about, leaping effortlessly, albeit in slow motion. His usual dour frown was replaced by a snide grin as he gleefully hoisted his staff. Sweeping it before him, the obsidian crystal worked like a scythe, slicing through the delicate stems to send decapitated blossoms flying through the air in reckless abandon.

In his mind's eye, he pictured each bloom as bearing the head of those he regarded his enemy. The Sorcerer pouted in feigned sadness as blossoms resembling Silas, Rainus, Tag and Princess Rose issued a silent scream as their flowered heads tumbled through the air, succumbing to the swipe of his mighty staff. The sad pout transformed into a maniacal grin as he watched their demise, his heavy boot slamming down to grind these doomed 'flowers' into the earth.

From this delightful, sunny meadow, Dragonite was seamlessly transported to another one of his happy places, deep within the bowels of this secret crystal fortress. This time, he imagined he was torturing the Princess, using a method she most feared and detested! To extract the secrets of activating the dreamstone, the Sorcerer delved into an equal measure of miming and maiming.

To weaken her resolve, Dragonite ordered the best of his performers to demonstrate the classic mime act of *'tug of war'* and then the infamous *'I'm stuck in a box'* routine. Rose was forced to watch, and when she failed to divulge the dreamstone's secrets, the Sorcerer took up a pair of dull shears. Half pulling and half hacking, the dull blades gnawed at a fistful of her luxurious, golden tresses.

Forced to endure a bad case of ugly hair that only promised to get worse if she did not cooperate, the Princess broke down in tears as Dragonite urged his mime to put on another performance. As Rose wept, he and his minions applauded and cheered, but did so in the most appropriate fashion: silently.

The Sorcerer's thin lips curled into a sneering smile as he daydreamed, thinking up of other terrible punishments to exact on the Princess while he marched on to antagonize his prisoner.

As Myron Kendall awaited his fate, he thought on the irony that his life would end ten years later, as Dragonite's prisoner once again, and as the knight he once was. This was the last place he ever suspected he'd meet his demise, deep inside a mountain of crystal. Staring at the flickering flames of the nearby torch, he had lost track of the days, and when he last felt the warmth of the sun upon his face.

He drew a weary breath, longing for the place he most wanted to be; wandering through the lush, green hills, vales and the freshly ploughed fields of Cadboll in the County of Wren, perhaps on the way to his favourite pub, The Gelded Pony, for a pint of ale.

Glancing over his shoulder at the toxic brew waiting for him in the crystal urn, he wished he had a pewter mug brimming to the top with his favourite dark ale. It would be one final cup of cheer to celebrate his life and the memories that came to him too late to fully appreciate all he had accomplished, and all that could have been.

Closing his eyes, Myron gathered his thoughts and steeled his nerves for what was yet to come. Though he did not relish the thought of dying, his only comfort was in knowing that this time, he would be the one to determine his end, not the Sorcerer. He already knew and accepted his fate. Unwilling to submit to torture, whether it be physical abuse or a slow, lingering death due to starvation, Myron was willing to chance the poison. If his estimates were wrong, he believed it was better to die an honourable death than to be used as a pawn in exchange for Princess Rose. This was his only chance to save her life, even if it means losing his.

'*Step, step, thunk! Step, step, thunk!*'

Myron opened his eyes. Before he could see the light of the advancing torch, he heard the faintest of sounds; that distinct gait punctuated by the end of a staff striking the ground. These sounds were carried and amplified by the crystal surroundings. It echoed through the length of the corridor, coming ever closer to this prison.

Listening intently, Myron made sure it was indeed the Sorcerer heading his way.

There it was again: '*Step, step, thunk! Step, step, thunk!*'

As this unmistakable noise Myron had come to recognize drew closer, he made his move. Dashing over to the giant urn of water, he scooped several handfuls, drinking deeply. Though laced with poison, he could not smell or taste it. For a moment, he panicked, thinking the lethal potion had dissipated, somehow evaporating as he waited for the right moment to drink it.

Within seconds, he felt his tongue grow numb as his chest tightened. It was working! Taking a few more gulps, Myron drank to make sure it was more than sufficient to see him through to the end, whatever that end be.

Staggering across the prison, Myron's trembling legs gave out, his knees buckling beneath him. Slumping against the crystal bars, his arms fell limp as his head lolled onto his chest. He could feel the poison stealing away with his breath as his heart beat slowed. It felt like a great weight was crushing down on his chest. Panic filled his mind, but just as quickly, a sense of calm buoyed his soul as he welcomed this fate. He thought there would be one final, defiant gasp, but there was none as his eyelids fell heavy, closing to immerse him in blackness.

"Stand aside!" snapped Dragonite, motioning for the mime leading the way to set the torch into the wall mount near the prison. Each time the Sorcerer turned to gaze upon the two rows of mimes that marched along behind him, they stood at attention, like perfectly disciplined soldiers. However, each time the Sorcerer looked away, all twelve mimes tried to out do each other's impersonation of Dragonite.

Catching a glimpse of their shenanigans from the corner of his eye, the Sorcerer snarled, "Now is not the time to honour my greatness through mime! There will be time for a grand performance when your work is done and my reign over this realm begins."

For each mime that nodded in agreement, there were two that shrugged in bewilderment upon receiving this scolding. They pretended they had no idea what Dragonite was speaking of.

"Enough!" shouted the Sorcerer.

With the threat of his staff, the two rows of mimes, six men deep, snapped to attention once more.

"Better! Now, let us see who can act the most like a well-trained soldier awaiting his next order," challenged the Sorcerer, tricking them into following his command.

All twelve stared ahead, standing perfectly still at full attention; chest thrust out, shoulders pulled back, feet together.

"Excellent! Now, the first one to mess up will die," warned Dragonite, as he turned his focus to the prison cell.

"Wake up!"

The Sorcerer waited impatiently to be acknowledged, but instead, his prisoner remained still. Dragonite slammed his hand against the crystal bars as he shouted, "Wake up, I say!"

Again, he received no response.

Staring at the mortal slumped against the bars of the prison; he used the end of the staff, giving his captive a sharp jab between the shoulder blades. Rather than jumping to his feet in response, the limp body tipped over, his right temple hitting the ground with a dull 'thud' as the torso followed the dead weight of the head.

"This is not good," muttered the Sorcerer. He crouched down to reach through the bars. Grasping a fistful of hair, he pulled on his prisoner's head, trying to lift it to better inspect the face. There was no yelp of pain or protest, no resistance whatsoever.

Touching the obsidian crystal to the bars of the prison cell, they magically retracted into the floor and ceiling, allowing Dragonite to step inside. Armed with his staff in case this was some kind of trick, the Sorcerer used the toe of his boot, prodding the body to elicit some kind of response.

Nothing.

Stepping on the splayed hand, his foot twisted about as he ground the fingers into the floor of the prison. Still no response; not even a fleeting wince of pain appeared on the face that had taken on a pale, sickly pallor.

Tilting the head in his direction, Dragonite pried open one of the eyelids, peering in to see the pupil was dilated, remaining unchanged with the glow of his crystal as it intensified. Holding the palm of his hand to the nostrils, the Sorcerer waited to feel a warm breath of spent air.

There was no hot, moist exhalation; no obvious rising and falling of the chest to indicate breathing.

Picking up the prisoner's left wrist, Dragonite released it, watching it flop to the ground as limp and useless as the rest of this body.

"Bloody hell… He was in worse shape than I thought. Perhaps I should have fed him more than that crust of bread," decided Dragonite, giving the corpse another sharp poke, this time in the ribs.

When it was obvious no amount of poking or prodding was going to resurrect the dead, Dragonite chewed the hangnail on his index finger as he pondered his next move.

"You weakling fool! Had you lasted a day or two longer you could have died in the company of your friends."

The mimely minion that had led the way scratched his head in bewilderment, taking a moment to gesture to the Sorcerer how silly it was for him to stand there, having a conversation with a dead man. It made as much sense as trying to engage a mime in conversation.

"Yes, yes!" snapped Dragonite, swatting at the man to get out of his way.

The mime then pinched his nostrils shut, fanning the air with his other hand before pointing at the corpse.

"Yes, he is still warm, but get him out of here before he begins to rot and stinks up my sanctuary!" ordered Dragonite. He motioned for two of the largest mimes to step forward and remove the body.

"Take him away! Leave this corpse outside to appease the resident dragon," demanded the Sorcerer, watching as the mimes ducked into the cell.

One mime grabbed the body by the ankles while the other picked him up by the wrists. As they attempted to squeeze through the opening at the same time, they struggled to fold the corpse in half so the head lolled between his knees. With barely enough space for two men to fit through, shoulder-to-shoulder, the mimes got stuck.

"You idiots!" snapped Dragonite, waving an angry fist at his useless minions. "You must fit through one at a time."

Allowing his comrade to exit first, the mime that had a hold of the wrists maneuvered about, dropping his load. He then motioned to his partner, offering to take one of the ankles so they could easily drag the body outside than to be made to carry this dead weight.

"Perhaps if we are lucky we shall witness a battle supreme as the mace-tailed dragon that had been sniffing about of late, waiting for one of you to die, is made to challenge the grand old beast of the north," hoped Dragonite, motioning the mimes to follow behind him. "It would not make for a long battle, but it should still prove to be entertaining."

The two men burdened with the task of corpse removal took up the rear, unceremoniously dragging their load behind them.

"Halt!" commanded Dragonite, raising his hand for the procession to stop as a frantic mime came charging toward him.

"What is it?" asked the Sorcerer, not even waiting for this, his most vertically challenged minion, to catch his breath.

The diminutive mime tugged on his earlobe.

"Sounds like…" said Dragonite, as he watched intently each move this performer made.

The mime used an index finger to point at his eye.

"Sounds like eye… *I?*"

The mime nodded as he gestured the next word, frantically pretending to saw a piece of wood.

"Sawing?"

Using his hands, he motioned Dragonite to shorten this word.

"Saw! *I saw*… What did you see?"

The mime pranced about, daintily holding up the hem of an invisible gown. He then proceeded to pretend he was sniffing a flower, plucking the petals off.

"You saw a girl picking a flower?"

The mime stopped, looking momentarily flustered. He then adjusted an equally invisible tiara on his head before touching an index finger to his nose.

"What? You saw a well-dressed girl *picking her nose?*"

The mime tugged at his earlobe again.

"Sounds like…" said Dragonite, urging him to continue with this charade.

He then resumed sniffing a flower, plucking at a few petals before touching his index finger to his nose.

"Sounds like nose… *rose!*"

The mime nodded.

"You saw a girl with a rose," concluded Dragonite.

The mime's hand slapped his head in frustration as a booming baritone bellowed from his small body, "You're no bloody good at this! I've been tryin' to tell ya, I saw Princess Rose!"

"What?" snapped the Sorcerer, quivering in rage. "Why was I not informed?"

"Have ya even stopped to check your messages today?" questioned the little mime with the big voice.

"Of course not! I am in the throes of world domination! I have been busy of late."

"There ya go then! It's not my bleedin' fault if you keep forgettin' ta check."

Dragonite unleashed a dreary sigh as he lightly pressed the obsidian crystal against the wall.

Being an excellent conductor of sound waves, the rhythmic taps vibrating through the crystal walls were carried along the length of his staff to his hands. He could feel every tap, thud and drag of a small iron mallet beating out a code the Sorcerer was able to decipher.

"Intruders… enemies breach lava... Princess and company… on the move… Stop," Dragonite read aloud. He then tapped the black crystal mounted to his staff once against the wall to have the messenger delete the transmission of this particular message.

Pressing his crystal against the wall once more, the Sorcerer waited to receive the next message. Through his gnarled hands he felt every tap reverberating through the wall, carried along the staff. It came swiftly, the code waiting to be picked up and deciphered.

"Urgent! Running low of… milk and… eggs!" Dragonite sputtered in anger, hitting the wall to have the messenger refrain from transmitting this message again. "Bloody hell! I am drowning in a sea of incompetence! Good help is so hard to find these days."

His mimes merely nodded in agreement while the one that broke miming protocol by talking, spouted off, "See! You were warned. When ya failed ta respond, that's when I came lookin' for ya."

"Better late than never, I suppose," snorted the disgruntled Sorcerer. "So, where are they now?"

"Didn't you pay attention to that message?" asked the mime.

The small man's retort was met with a thump on the head as Dragonite hit him with his staff.

"I meant ta say, the Princess is here, with her cohorts; the boy, the Elf lord and the Dream Merchant, Silas Agincor! We tried ta capture them, but they managed ta clear the river of lava, escapin' from us," revealed the mime.

"I do not care about the others, but the Princess, is she still alive?" questioned the Sorcerer.

"If she is, she's bloody lucky! They managed ta escape your giant *'pet'* worm and were last seen enterin' the tunnel with the trap."

"Which tunnel with what trap? There is one in practically every single passage leading to the heart of my fortress."

"The one with the spears of crystal that fly at ya if you travel through it with a blazin' torch," answered the mime.

"Oh… that one."

"Yes! That one!" snorted the mime.

"The orders were to capture her before she went that far!" snarled the Sorcerer, his hand balling into a quivering fist of rage. "You have failed me!"

"Hey, it's not my fault if she gets killed because of those traps *you* set."

"Yes, it is! Those traps were intended to keep greedy Dwarves and foolish mimes from attempting to steal the dreamstone from me. And you and your mute friends were supposed to capture her alive before she ventured that far."

"What can I say? She proved ta be a greater adversary than any of us had anticipated."

"You mean to say her comrades proved to be the greater adversaries," corrected the Sorcerer.

"No, I do mean the Princess. She was a force ta be reckoned with! At one point, she single-handedly launched a deadly assault; one that caught us by surprise. She was like a woman gone mad! Totally mental, I tell ya!"

"How? Was she gifted with magic? Did she use unearthly powers to repel all of you?"

"Well…"

"Well, what?" snapped Dragonite, the toe of his boot impatiently tapping the floor as he waited for an explanation.

"She used her sling… mind you, there's a good chance it had been deeply entrenched in magic, for her aim was unerring."

"I preferred it when you did not speak!" growled Dragonite, using the end of his staff to smack the mime on his head once again.

"Ouch!" groaned the mime, rubbing the growing goose egg sprouting from his noggin. "But maybe there's a chance she's still alive."

"How so?"

"She does not travel alone," reminded the mime, hoping to pacify his master. "I have a feelin' it is the Wizard's powers that keep her an' her cohorts alive."

"Perhaps you are right… Glory be! That means I still have a chance to unravel the secret of tapping into the dreamstone's powers, plus, I will be able to kill them all with my own hands!"

Dragonite yelped in surprise while his mimely minions cried a silent scream of fright as a loud *'BOOM'* sounded through the tunnel as the walls of crystal rattled all around them, shaking them to the bones.

"What the?" gasped Dragonite, feeling the weight of a massive boulder crashing down to reverberate through the mountain.

"Oops! I spoke too soon," gulped the diminutive mime, as he cowered before the Sorcerer.

14
So Close!

In that brief, harrowing moment, Princess Rose swore she saw her short, but privileged, life flash before her frightened eyes as the quartz boulder crashed down. The *'whoosh'* of displaced air as this massive crystal filled the room was powerful enough to thrust her and Tag hard against the far wall of the alcove.

This thunderous sound as the boulder impacted against the solid, crystal ground echoed throughout the mountain, rattling it to its very foundations. The resulting shockwaves resonated, shaking the floor of this chamber like a great earthquake.

Their hearts raced, pounding madly in their chests. Their breath snagged in the back of their throats as Rose and Tag pictured poor Rainus Silverthorn engaged in the race of his life as the boulder proceeded to roll after him, catching up only to crush the Lord of Elves as flat as unleavened bread. As the quaking subsided and the sound faded away, they were left in complete and utter silence.

There were no sounds, like the deafening roll of thunder, as the great boulder began to travel from the chamber into the passage that led them here. Instead, this latest impact served to add even greater cracks to the floor, a myriad of hairline fractures radiating from the point of initial impact. This latest strike also made for an even greater indentation that the massive crystal sphere came to rest in.

When she finally dared to open her eyes, Rose could barely make out Tag's form in the cloud of dust swirling in the shadows of their tight confines.

"What just happened?" asked the Princess, blinking hard as her eyes squinted, adjusting to the gloom and veil of dirt and dust particles that gradually settled on and around them.

"The giant crystal fell, but it didn't roll away like we thought it would," answered Tag.

"Thank goodness for that! So, now what?"

"At this moment, we are good and trapped," responded Tag. Struggling about on his side of the alcove, he pressed his shoulder against the boulder to test how solidly it sat in place.

"We're trapped?" gulped Rose, her hands pushing hard against its polished surface.

"Just calm down, Princess! Stop that or you might just send this boulder on its way, rolling off to crush Lord Silverthorn," warned Tag.

"So what will you have me do? You said we are trapped."

"Not for long! Just wish us out of here."

"I would if I could, but it is not possible." Rose unleashed a disheartened sigh.

"Believe me, it won't be a wish wasted. And remember, you'll still have two more at your disposal after that."

"I know!"

"Then what are you waiting for, Princess?"

"When you stuffed me in here, I accidentally dropped the dreamstone."

"You dropped it?" groaned Tag, his hand slapping his forehead in frustration.

"Yes! I can see it though, I just cannot reach it." Rose pointed to the ground.

She could make out the glow of the magic crystal against the wall over to the left of the alcove. It rested in the space created by the roundness of the boulder and the straight edges where the wall met the floor. "It is so close, and yet, so very far. I can see its chain, but it is not within my reach."

"Hello? Any survivors?" These words echoed through the chamber. "Princess Rose? Master Yairet?"

"Lord Silverthorn!" called Tag. He stared through the opaque boulder that was now riddled with fine cracks from the solid impact of striking the floor.

"Yes! Are you safe?" shouted the Elf, as he stood at the entrance of the chamber. "Are you alive and well?"

"We're both alive," answered Tag. "But how well we are shall depend on if we can be freed. We're trapped in the alcove."

"And the Wizard? He is not crushed beneath this, is he?" asked Rainus, as he knelt down to see if there was an unfortunate victim pulverized beneath the weight of the massive crystal boulder.

"Master Agincor managed to escape before the boulder came down," replied Tag.

"Excellent! Now, all the Princess must do is wish for the two of you to be standing here, next to me, so we can move on."

"I wish!" lamented Rose. Struggling to crouch down, her fingers strained to drag the gold chain closer to her, but it was well out of her reach. "I dropped the magic crystal. I can see it, but I just cannot get to it."

"Well, I certainly did not anticipate this happening," hollered Rainus, staring through the glassy boulder that did not roll after him. "Can you try to use your foot to draw the dreamstone closer to you, so it is within your grasp?"

"Only if I were double-jointed or my knuckles dragged on the ground when I walk. It is a feat I am sure Tag is capable of, but the dreamstone is closer to me than him."

"Your humour remains intact in spite of our dilemma," noted Tag, heaving a disgruntled sigh.

"Who said I was being funny?"

"Focus, my friends! Where exactly is the dreamstone?" questioned Rainus.

"It is to the right of me. At least the chain is, but I am confident the crystal is still attached, for I can see its glow in the darkness."

"To your right, Princess?" asked Rainus, attempting to ascertain its location.

"It is better to say that from where you stand, it is just to the left of this alcove where the Princess is trapped," informed Tag, as he searched for a rough surface or handhold on the boulder he could use to prevent it from rolling over top of the Elf, should it shift about.

"Perhaps, with a bit of work, I can reach it," said Rainus. He crouched down, inspecting the space between the curve of the boulder and the right angle of the floor and wall.

"Unless the Elfkind have the ability to stretch to unusual lengths, I hardly think your arm can reach all the way," countered Rose.

"I was speaking of squeezing my entire body, not just my arm, into this gap."

"Is it possible?" asked Tag, watching Rainus' blurry shape through the boulder.

"If I squeeze in, my back to the corner where the floor and wall meet, I should manage it. The only thing that would prevent me from making my way to you and the dreamstone is if this boulder is damaged, or has damaged the wall or floor, obstructing the way."

"And if it is?" asked Rose.

"Then I shall withdraw; try my approach toward Master Yairet's side," answered Rainus.

"Can you even fit in there?" questioned Tag.

"With shoulders as broad as mine, it will be an exceedingly tight fit, but I am confident it can be done."

"Perhaps we should wait for the Wizard to reappear," suggested Rose, "just in case you become trapped, too."

"No need for concern, Princess Rose," assured Rainus, as he prepared to enter this narrow passage. "And there is no telling how long it will be before Master Agincor makes his presence known to us. I might as well be proactive and make an attempt."

"Just be very careful," cautioned Tag. "We've come this far and we have survived so much, there is no point in taking unnecessary risks."

"I believe the risk will be minimal, but if I should succeed, whatever the risk, it will be well worth it."

"I agree, Lord Silverthorn!" said Rose, urging the Elf on. "Now, go to it!"

Crawling on his hands and knees, Rainus inspected the space and considered his best approach. Following the contour of the round boulder, he decided to wedge his body in headfirst. With his back and shoulders rolled in to better fit against the right angle formed by the floor and wall and his chest pressed against the boulder, he squeezed in. It would allow for some mobility so using his feet, and a little traction, he'd be able to crawl forward. Rainus was confident he could do the deed, thereby securing the dreamstone and their freedom in the process.

Allowing for shallow breaths so his lungs would not fill completely, thereby taking even less room in these already tight confines, the Elf proceeded to make his way toward his trapped comrades. Inching his way along, the soles of his boots provided some grip against the floor and wall. Using his hands against the smooth surface of the boulder, Rainus made slow, but gradual progress.

"How is it going?" questioned Tag.

"It goes, but not quickly," answered Rainus. "I must admit, this is the one time I wished I had the hands of a mortal."

"Strong and powerful?" asked Rose.

"No, rough and sweaty! It would make for better traction against the boulder's polished surface."

Each time Rose and Tag spied upon his distorted face plastered against the giant orb, they knew he was in a tight spot, forced to use his right or left cheek for additional traction to drag his body forward.

After agonizingly long minutes, Rainus called out, "I see the glow of the dreamstone!"

"Huzzah!" cheered Rose, her hands clapping together in glee.

"Can you reach it?" asked Tag, noticing how the Elf's form became more visible the nearer he came to this light source.

"Patience, Master Yairet," responded Rainus, as he inched his way forward. "I will do so soon enough."

Rose and Tag listened as the squeaking and squealing of bare skin against crystal grew louder, as did the Elf's grunts and groans as he forged on.

"There it is!" shouted Rainus, as he basked in the dreamstone's luminous glow. "I see it now!"

"Is it broken?" asked Rose.

"From where I am, it looks fine. Just a little farther now..."

"Hey... what happened to this boulder? So much for it rolling away," said Silas, as he reappeared in a flash of light.

Rose and Tag glanced up, to see the Wizard balanced on top of this huge, crystal sphere.

"You've returned!" exclaimed Tag, relieved to see the Dream Merchant was safe from harm.

"Of course!" responded Silas, just as relieved to find his comrades were spared a horrific death. "It just took a little longer than I had first anticipated."

"Why? What happened?" questioned Rose. She could see his form silhouetted against the glow of his crystal through the quartz boulder he stood on.

"I had the ill fortune of escaping from here to materialize far from Crystal Mountain to avoid an untimely encounter with Dragonite and his mimely minions."

"What is so bad about that?" asked Tag. "That would have been the wise thing to do, for the last thing you needed was to be captured by the enemy."

"Very true, however, I had the misfortune of materializing before a very large, very hungry dragon!"

"What?" Tag and Rose gasped in unison.

"Fear not, my young friends," assured the Wizard. "It took some evasive action and the conjuring of magic on my part, but I managed to elude the beast to return intact. And it would appear that I did so just in time to save the day. Speaking of, where is our dear Elf friend?"

"I am here, Master Agincor," hollered Rainus, "beneath this boulder!"

"Heaven forbid!" gasped the Wizard, his eyes wide in horror. Immediately, he used his magic to hover above the boulder as though relieving it of his additional weight would somehow make a difference on the pinned victim. "And yet you live… You are very resilient for an Elf, Lord Silverthorn."

"I am very uncomfortable at this moment, that's what I am! I've never been in such a tight spot."

"I'd say that is the understatement of the century! If you were a girl, you'd be a carpenter's dream!" remarked the Wizard, marvelling over how much pain Rainus could endure in this flattened state.

"How so?" asked Rainus, baffled by Silas' comment.

"You know? As flat as a board and as straight as a nail!"

"I think I understand, Master Agincor."

"So, are you suffering much?" inquired Silas, staring through the crystal as he searched about for the squashed Elf.

"I am quite fine," assured Rainus, as he squirmed his way forward.

"Lord Silverthorn is not crushed beneath this boulder," corrected Tag. "He is using the narrow gap between the wall and the boulder to maneuver toward us."

"So he can become just as trapped as you two are?" questioned Silas, hovering closer to where Tag's voice squeezed out from the alcove, between the top of the boulder and the wall.

"I am merely trying to retrieve the dreamstone; return it to the Princess so she can wish us out of this predicament," explained Rainus, as he paused to rest for a moment.

"Well then, thank goodness you are safe, my friend. In the meantime, perhaps I can be of assistance."

"I have the situation under control now," responded Rainus, collecting the magic crystal and the strand of golden chain it was suspended on. "I just need to maneuver closer; within Princess Rose's grasp."

"There is an easier way to do that," said Silas, ready and willing to call on his magic.

"Here you go, Princess! Can you reach it now?" asked the Elf, straining to lift the dreamstone to Rose.

Wedged sideway into the alcove, the Princess knelt down as far as she could, her knees banging against the pedestal. With her back to Rainus as he lay on his side, right arm outstretched with the magic crystal dangling from his hand extended toward her, Rose could barely see the dreamstone from the corner of her right eye.

With just barely enough room to bend her knees and lower her stance, Rose struggled to blindly reach about behind her.

"Can you inch a little closer, Lord Silverthorn?" asked Tag, watching as they repeatedly missed each other's hand.

Rose wriggled about, struggling to get lower as the Elf wormed about, fighting to get closer to her, but a jagged chunk of quartz protruding from the damaged floor impeded his forward movement.

"How about now?" asked Rainus, flicking his wrist to send the crystal swinging like a small pendulum toward Rose's opened hand.

"Again!" urged Rose. She felt the cold, smooth surface of the dreamstone glance by her fingertips. "Do it again! I almost had it."

"I can help," insisted Silas. Staring through the boulder, he alighted upon the massive crystal to watch this desperate exchange.

Just as Rainus tossed the dreamstone into Rose's hand, she screamed in fright. There was no warning creak or groan as the massive boulder crashed straight through the compromised floor, taking the Wizard down with it.

Rainus and Tag's screams of fright joined Rose's as the floor continued to disintegrate. With nothing to hold onto, the trio fell, disappearing into the black hole.

15

The Fortress of Ineptitude

"Now what the bloody hell was that?" snarled Dragonite. He shoved aside the mime he was accosting. Using his staff, he steadied himself. This second thunderous boom was even louder than the first; the ensuing tremors rattled his gangly body, jarring him to the bones.

"If they weren't dead before, methinks it's safe to assume they're really dead now," gulped the mime, falling to his knees as the walls and floors of the tunnel shuddered around them as this deafening *'boom'* sounded from the heart of the Sorcerer's secret lair. These tremors stopped as quickly as the first round of shaking had.

"That did not sound right," assessed Dragonite. "If the Princess and her cohorts made it all the way to the chamber where I stored the dreamstone, we would have heard a *'boom'*, followed by a stifled scream of anguish or two, then the *'rattle, rattle, splat'* as the boulder rolled through the tunnel to finish off those escaping its initial crushing fall. The second *'boom'* that followed was much louder, more devastating than if it had merely rolled away, falling into the pit."

The mime standing closest to the Sorcerer gave his robe a tug to gain Dragonite's attention.

In the fashion of a true performer, he mimed the act of boldly venturing forth to investigate this mystery.

"Of course, I must see for myself. Perhaps, if the Princess is just severely mangled, but still clings to life, she will gladly share the secret of the dreamstone in exchange for a swift and relatively painless death."

The mime that had broken the code held dear by all in his vocation by speaking slipped back into his role, nodding and gesturing that he would volunteer to throttle the Princess with his own hands if it pleases the Sorcerer.

"I commend you for your enthusiasm," praised Dragonite, as he nodded in approval to this mime, "however, I will be the one to deal with that wretched mortal."

The mime snapped his fingers in feigned disappointment.

"Pity for you, but if you had done your job properly, there'd be more prisoners to go around," grunted Dragonite, dismissing the mime with a wave of his hand. "But this is no time to whine about what could have been; I must investigate that commotion."

The Sorcerer gestured for the mimes taking up the rear to come with him, accompanying the others as there was safety in numbers and if anything, they were expendable, he was not.

"Forget about that useless body for now, there is something of greater urgency to contend with."

To accompany their master, the corpse the mimes had been dragging along by the ankles was unceremoniously dumped, abandoned in the middle of the passageway.

"Be ready to fight, my mimely minions! Find your courage, summon your strength and be prepared to do battle, if need be," ordered Dragonite, as he rushed through the tunnel to investigate the source of this quake, and if indeed there were any survivors.

In response, this small army of mimes adopted angry sneers. With chest puffed out and pretending their arms were bulging with great knots of vein-popping muscles that were so large they were unable to rest them alongside their body, they acted like hulking, big warriors capable of ripping off their foes' heads with their bare hands.

Now, with the messenger joining in, they marched in two rows, seven-men deep behind the Sorcerer, lumbering along like behemoth warriors prepared to do battle.

Standing atop the boulder, Silas was the first to disappear as the shattered floor abruptly disintegrated beneath the massive crystal. Rose screamed in terror as Rainus followed.

As the quartz floor continued to crumble away toward the alcove, just as Rose was about to tumble in, Tag seized her by the hand, holding her by the wrist with one hand while the other grabbed the pedestal the dreamstone was once perched on.

"Don't let go!" Rose screamed as she dangled into the dark abyss waiting to swallow her up.

"Never!" promised Tag. He could feel her fingernails digging into his wrist as Rose clung to him for dear life. She dared not glance down to see what horrors awaited her below.

Just as he hoisted her up, the floor beneath him broke away under his weight. His scream of fright was drowned out by Rose's as they tumbled down.

Still clinging to each other's wrists, they groaned with pain as they landed on their backs against the boulder, only to slide off the curved surface to land on their feet.

"I can't believe you let me fall!" snapped Rose, her hand smacking his chest as she glared at Tag.

"You said '*don't let go*' and I didn't!" he grunted, raising her hand to show he still had a grip on her, even after they landed safely on solid ground.

"How do you fare?" questioned Silas, as he and Rainus rounded the boulder to join them.

"All considering, we're fine," answered Tag.

"*You* are fine! *I* am severely traumatized," countered Rose, shaking off Tag's hold.

"Are you able to move on?" asked Rainus.

"Yes, I believe so," replied the Princess.

"Good, the trauma must have worn off," said the Elf. "Now quickly, use the dreamstone to wish us out of here."

"Good idea!" agreed Tag. "Let us be free of this place before the enemy hears and that crazy Sorcerer shows his ugly face."

"Call me daft if you want, but I am positive when that boulder fell the first time every person, from here to the Dimbolt Forest, heard and felt it," grumbled Rose. "And if the Sorcerer did not, then he is more daft than I am!"

"That is highly unlikely, but we really should be on our way," urged Tag.

"What is unlikely?" snapped the Princess, as she glared at Tag. "That I am more daft than the Sorcerer?"

"Those were your words, not mine!" grunted Tag.

"Focus, my friends!" urged Rainus. "There will be time for bickering later. I recommend we leave this place now, if you wish to rescue Cankles Mayron!"

"Oh, yes!" agreed Rose, as she gave Tag another smack on his chest for good measure.

"All you must do is envision your friend, and wish for him to be by your side," instructed Silas, eager to rescue their missing comrade so they may vacate this lair as quickly as possible.

"Right!" said Rose, extending her hand to the Elf. "The dreamstone, please, Lord Silverthorn!"

"Pardon me?" Rainus' perfectly groomed brows furrowed in

confusion. "I passed it on to you! You have it, Princess."

"*Me?* I do not have it. I thought you still had it."

"I distinctly remember tossing it to you, just before the floor caved in on us."

"You tossed it to me? Well! There you go then!"

"What do you mean?"

"I am a girl – and a princess at that! I am not accustomed to things being thrown at me; nor am I used to catching things that are thrown!"

"Never mind that," said Silas, as his glanced about. "We need to find the dreamstone, and do so quickly."

"Spread out," ordered Rainus, as he dug through the rubble that was once the floor from the chamber above. "Look everywhere."

Rose and Tag dropped to their hands and knees, sifting through the broken crystal as they searched for the dreamstone, while Silas called upon an incantation. It set the orb atop his staff glowing brightly to illuminate the large cavern.

"If not the dreamstone, search for its gold chain, for it should lead to the magic crystal," said Rainus.

"It shouldn't be that hard to find if it's still glowing like it was before," said Tag, pushing aside a chunk of quartz.

Rose paused for a moment, looking to the Wizard, "Master Agincor, why was the dreamstone glowing as it rested upon the pedestal? It never did that on its own when I wore it around my neck."

Silas straightened his aching back as he answered, "We are deep in the heart of Crystal Mountain, Princess Rose."

"Meaning?"

"The finest samples of quartz crystal found in this realm are extracted from this very place. It is a substance that has a power and energy of its own. Imbued with magic, the dreamstone, when surrounded by crystal such as this, draws on that energy."

"Hence, the glow," surmised Rose, as she nodded in understanding.

"Yes, do not be surprised that its powers are now greatly enhanced," warned the Wizard.

"So I can have more than three wishes per day now?" queried Rose.

"In your case? No, definitely not! But now, it has the power to do great things well beyond the realms of your imagination. At the same time, in the wrong hands, it has the power to destroy, even more thoroughly than ever before."

"All the more reason to find it now," recommended Tag. "Get to work, Princess. We need to claim that crystal before Dragonite does."

"I know, but as far as that vile soul is concerned, we can be anywhere in this mountain of crystal," stated Rose. "The Sorcerer will have his work cut out for him. It will probably take him forever just to figure out exactly where we are."

"Think again, Princess," responded Silas. The orb atop his staff glowed to push against the darkness. "It is not as though we are hidden away in a little-known corner of his fortress."

Rose, Tag and Rainus gasped in surprise. Their eyes opened wide in awe as the glassy floor checkered in perfect squares of black obsidian and white quartz patterned the entire length of this great chamber. Above, the stalactites of crystal suspended from the ceiling reflected the Wizard's glowing orb of power and light. Rows of magnificent quartz pillars lined this long, rectangular room and between these pillars and the walls, a narrow gully dropped down into a stream of lava. At one end, the crystal formations lining the wall glowed red, reflecting the light emitted by the bubbling, oozing lava collecting in a natural cauldron big enough to swallow up a carriage and a team of horses to pull it. The lava pooled here before spilling off on either side to fill the streams, bathing the entire chamber in an eerie red glow.

At the opposite end, on a raised obsidian platform, a magnificent crystal throne sat empty. Exquisitely carved and etched, it was majestic in appearance and colossal in size, its back extending all the way from the floor to the ceiling.

"Incredible!" gasped Tag, glancing about their beautiful, but menacing surroundings.

"Incredible, indeed!" agreed Rose, staring at the most lovely throne she had ever seen in her entire, young life. "Who would have thought the crazy Sorcerer would have such refined taste in furnishing?"

"Never mind that," snapped Tag. "Don't you know where we are?"

"I can hazard a guess, and it probably will be right, so I'd rather not say," gulped Rose, as her eyes glanced about.

"It would appear we had the misfortune of landing in the middle of Dragonite's throne room," determined Rainus.

"Yes, no doubt one of the busiest chambers in his mountain hide-away," responded Silas, dimming the glow of his orb so they could resume the business of searching for the dreamstone without alerting the enemy of their presence. "Thank goodness it is empty at the moment."

"Darn!" Rose cursed as she snapped her fingers. "I knew I was right! But why have this grand throne room way down here?"

"I suppose Dragonite finds certain solitude deep in his subterranean fortress."

"An underground fortress for solitude?" grunted Rose, glancing about their glistening surroundings. "It is more like a fortress of ineptitude, if you ask me! Who in their right mind would even consider taking refuge down here?"

"Who said the Sorcerer was in his right mind?" Tag's index finger spun by his head to demonstrate Dragonite's level of craziness.

"I'll grant you that," agreed Rose. "But at least, at this very moment, that crazy bugger knows not where we are."

"I hardly think so," contested Rainus. "When that crystal boulder initially fell, only to smash through the floor to land here, disturbing this fortress' solitude, it will only be a matter of time before Dragonite or one of his mimely minions figures out exactly where we are."

"All the more reason to work with speed," urged Tag, his eyes staring at the scattered debris radiating out from the impact of the quartz boulder.

"You do not suppose the dreamstone was crushed in this mishap?" asked Rose, pointing at the great sphere. "Suppose it has been pulverized beneath it; destroyed beyond recognition?"

"I doubt that very much," replied the Elf, using the toe of his boot to sift through the rubble. "This boulder came down first, we, and the dreamstone followed."

"I suppose that makes sense," responded Rose, as she nodded in understanding.

"More searching; less talking, Princess," ordered Tag, pushing aside a large chunk of flooring to search beneath it.

"I can do both at the same time, if I put my mind to it," insisted Rose.

"I know you can, just focus on the task at hand," urged Tag, tossing aside a spear of crystal. "We need to be out of this place as quickly as possible."

"Fine!" grunted the Princess, walking away from her comrades toward the throne and where the debris was smaller and thinly scattered. "I will concentrate my efforts over here; work my way in to where you are."

With a degree of reluctance, she dropped down on her hands and knees. Rose slowly inched away as she feigned her search for the dreamstone. Her hands swept before her in large, circular motions, skimming the surface of the floor to lend emphasis that she truly was involved in the act of hunting for the magic crystal.

Stealing a furtive glance over her shoulder, Rose could see her comrades were deeply engrossed, searching with great concentration as they delved into the task at hand. Turning her head to see in front of her, she kept her eyes on the prize. There before her, at the far end of this great hall, was the most exquisite throne she had ever seen. It waited all alone and empty. Rose could swear if it were alive, that throne would be *begging* to be sat upon by her royal bottom.

The crystalline throne, in all its grandeur, sparkled in the slow, steady glow of the surrounding lava. Its beauty was bewitching, so much so, in the Princess' mind it called to her, seductively whispering so only she could hear: *'You know you want to sit on me. Just think of how you'll look... You are beautiful now, but seated upon me, you will truly be the fairest in all the lands! I'm the perfect accessory for one with such exquisite taste. You will be the envy of every monarch from Fleetwood to Axalon and all the kingdoms well beyond!'*

"Princess! Any luck where you are?" called out Tag, not even glancing up as he continued his search.

Rose froze. Her trance was momentarily broken as she answered him. "No, not yet! I see a pile of crystal over here though, the dreamstone could have been sent flying this way!"

"Fine! Just keep looking until we do find it!"

Rose relaxed, breathing a small sigh of relief to see her comrade continue to turn over broken flooring in his diligent inspection. Scrambling, she made short work of the little distance that was left between her and this magnificent throne.

Standing up, she dusted off her hands. Taking a deep breath, she composed herself as she stepped up onto the raised obsidian platform that played host to this seat of power.

Tucking the wrinkled skirt of her frock underneath her, Rose slowly sat down. Adjusting her posture so she sat upright and as regally as her mother always did, in the most dignified manner, she surveyed her surroundings. Her eyes came upon Tag, Rainus and the Dream Merchant on their hands and knees, searching for the dreamstone. For a moment, it seemed like they were nothing more than lowly peasants grovelling before her and now, seated upon the most beautiful throne ever, the Princess felt even more powerful than she thought possible.

"What do you think you're doing?" asked Tag, staring with raised eyebrows at the Princess as she perched regally on this crystal throne.

Rose drew a deep breath as she returned to her sorry reality. "I am just resting for a moment."

"I hardly think so! You were testing it out, weren't you? You want a throne just like that, don't you?"

"Nothing wrong with looking ahead, should we survive this quest. So what if I think this lovely piece of furniture would make a striking addition to Pepperton Palace? And just think how it will be even more perfect with me seated upon it!"

"Now is not the time to think of redecorating the palace," ordered Tag, as he waved her over. "Get back to work! Find that bloody dreamstone."

"Fine!" Rose snapped with a disgruntled huff as she hopped off the magnificent throne. "I will do just that."

Crawling along on her hands and knees, the Princess noisily tossed aside debris to make it apparent to all in her company that she was indeed hard at work, so there was no need to harp at her.

"Lord Silverthorn! Master Yairet," called the Wizard, waving his comrades in. "Spread your search out from this vicinity forth. Follow the spray of debris, for I am confident the dreamstone was caught in the wake of the floor's collapse."

"Good idea, Master Agincor," agreed Tag. He dropped onto his knees, sifting through the rubble as the Elf and Wizard fanned out to hunt about for the missing crystal.

Ignoring Rose's half-hearted attempts to search for the dreamstone, Tag decided his time was better spent focusing on the task at hand than to waste anymore time coercing the Princess to concentrate.

Tossing aside the larger chunks of shattered crystal with one hand while the other skimmed lightly over the smooth floor, Tag hoped to feel what his eyes might miss in the limited light emitted by the surrounding lava. As his meticulous search took him farther from the boulder, the spray of debris cast in its wake became smaller and finer.

"Where the bloody hell did it go?" Tag grumbled as he wiped the dust from his hands. "It's not as though it could have magically grown legs and just walked away from here."

"Maybe it did," said Rose, stopping her search to address Tag.

"Are you mad?"

"The Wizard did warn us that within this mountain of crystal the energies herein has made the dreamstone more powerful. Perhaps it did do just that."

Silas, overhearing this exchange, chirped in: "More powerful, yes, but it would still require the wielder of the dreamstone to wish for it to be bestowed with appendages to do so."

"Point well taken, Master Agincor," Rose acknowledged with a curt bow of her head as she resumed her unenthusiastic hunt for the missing crystal.

Drawing a weary breath, Tag's eyes probed about in the gloom of this great chamber. The farther he worked his way from the boulder and the closer he inched his way to the churning lava flowing along the perimeter of this throne room, the better the illumination of the floor.

Glancing about, he could see that his comrades, at least Silas and Rainus, were still deeply absorbed in the task while Rose continued to clamber about on all fours, working her way toward the boulder.

It was just as his gaze scanned across the floor from the Wizard to the Princess, that Tag saw it: the dull but familiar glow of light shining from the polished surface of a tiny object! As the light flared from the belch of lava, it reflected on the dust-covered dreamstone.

This small sphere of crystal was still anchored to the beadcap and its chain of gold. There it sat, perched precariously on the very edge of the floor where it dropped away to the molten lava below. The only thing that kept it in place was the necklace that streamed behind the crystal when it was sent flying by the percussive blow of the boulder crashing down.

"I found it!" declared Tag, jumping onto his feet.

"Where?" asked Rose, as Silas and Rainus turned to look at the small object Tag was pointing at.

"There! Over there!" shouted Tag, as he ran toward the dreamstone that waited to be reclaimed.

Just as the percussion of his jarring footfalls reverberated though the crystal flooring, it caused the bead to quake, and then roll. Disappearing over the edge, the dreamstone was followed by the gold chain. It trickled over the edge to the lava below.

"*NO!*" shrieked Rose, her eyes wide in disbelief and horror as she watched the magic crystal vanish from view.

Tag raced forward. With a heart-stopping lunge, he dove toward the dreamstone. He came to a skidding stop, his head and shoulders hovering over the brink as he snagged the last inch of necklace before it could slip away. His grimy, sweaty hand slapped down, trapping the fine, gold links before the weight of the crystal could take it down to be swallowed up by the roiling lava.

Peering over the edge, Tag could feel the scorching heat that swelled, radiating hotter than the heat exuded from any blacksmith's furnace.

"*Yes!*" cheered Tag. He snatched up the magic crystal in triumph before it could disappear forever. "Got it!"

"Now, give it to me!"

He spun about, gasping in surprise to spy upon the Sorcerer. The jagged edge of his obsidian crystal pressed against Rose's throat.

16
Double the Duplicity

"Wake up! Wake up now! I command you!" Celia shouted this order as she pushed up on the mortal's eyelid to peer into this glassy, vacant orb that seemed to stare right through her. This eyelid snapped shut as she lost her grip. "Bloody hell! I am the Queen of the Tooth Fairies! I should be wishing for Cankles to stay asleep, not ordering him to wake up!"

"He now insists on going by his true name, Sir Myron Kendall," corrected Loken, as he tugged on a fistful of hair in a bid to rouse him. "And he is not asleep."

"*EWWW!* He's dead?" gasped Celia, wiping her hands on her gown as though she was attempting to be rid of some invisible film of death that may be contaminating this corpse.

"It would appear so," answered the Sprite. He alighted upon Myron's stubbly chin as a barely discernible breath wheezed through the slightly agape mouth. It sent Loken's wings trembling ever so slightly in its wake. "But looks can be deceiving, my love."

"You are speaking in riddles, Loken. I fail to understand."

"This man was once a knight of high standing in his king's army. He decided that he would do the most honourable thing; sacrifice his life so he could not be used as a pawn against his friends. I gave him the potion that Sparks was going to use on you."

"*What?* You allowed him to poison himself? How could you do this to him?" she demanded to know, the toe of her shoe tapping impatiently on the mortal's face as she waited for Loken to explain his part in this man's demise.

"Hush, Celia! Worry not. Remember what I told you? How Dragonite had concocted this poison so if it was taken alone, the potion will deliver a swift and certain death? It is obvious Myron had diluted it with water and the right amount was administered. He drank just enough to bring on this death-like state. By his appearance, he looks to be dead, but the toxins only simulate death. So you see, he is still very much alive."

"He is breathing, but just barely. What dark magic did the Sorcerer evoke to make the living seem dead to the world?"

"Many things in this world seem impossible and yet, they exist. This is just one of them. From what I overheard from Sparks when he was planning to administer this poison to your chalice of water was that, when diluted just so, it paralyzes the muscles. The mind supposedly remains alert, but the body is rendered useless. The lungs and heart slow dramatically."

"Enough to feign death," concluded Celia, as she nodded in understanding.

"Yes! In fact, I am amazed he was able to accurately determine how much of the poisonous potion to pour into that large water vessel to result in this condition, than to outright kill himself."

"Perhaps we should try to get him on his feet again," suggested Celia "Before the Sorcerer or his mimes should return to find us here."

"Definitely!"

Celia braced her feet against Myron's lower lid, using her hands to push against his upper lid. Slowly, she pried his eye open; enough to peer into his pupil that remained fixed and fully dilated.

"Hello, Sir Myron Kendall! It is I, Pancecelia Feldspar! Loken and I are here to aid you. Now, rise up before me."

As the Fairy launched into the air in preparation for this mortal to miraculously sit upright, the only physical action he could muster was involuntary. His eyelid merely snapped shut upon her release.

"Get up, man!" Loken yelled into his ear as he tugged at Myron's hair. "You have places to go, lives to save! Now, get up!"

The Fairy and Sprite unleashed a disheartened sigh as Myron Kendall failed to respond to their verbal demands and physical prodding.

Exhausted by their futile attempts, they alighted upon his chest, feeling its very slight rise and fall as he continued his shallow breathing that was the only indication he truly was still alive.

"Celia, could you perhaps undo the magic that besets him?" questioned Loken.

"I am sorry, but no. I am not able to undo the magic of a Wizard or Sorcerer with more magic."

"So we must try again, using conventional methods," conceded Loken. Taking to the air, he landed on Myron's forehead. Grasping a fistful of hair, he tugged again while Celia alighted upon the tip of his nose, stomping up and down to elicit some kind of response.

"This is utterly useless!" declared Celia, slumping against the mortal's nose. She glanced over at Loken as he sat in defeat, his feet dangling over Myron's chin. Each time this giant exhaled, his breath caused the Sprite's wings to rattle in its wake. "There is no telling when he will be revived. We do not even know if his mind is fully functioning so he can act in the capacity of a knight, once this potion runs its course. Suppose his mind has gone totally wobbly and the damage is permanent?"

"We must hold on to hope," decided Loken, running a hand down his woeful face as he pondered this dilemma.

"Hope? There is no hope left at this point, my dear Loken! Suppose the poison has completely and permanently addled his brain? Then what are we to do?"

"Then this poor soul will only wish for his demise, but I am not ready to give up, not just yet. We must be resourceful and think of another way," determined Loken, offering Celia a confident smile as she wrung her hands in despair.

"I understand that, but what if his mind no longer works? Suppose he is completely oblivious to everything and everyone, forever? Wobbly beyond reckoning or repair?"

As another slow breath wheezed from Myron's mouth that was slightly agape, this subtle breeze sent Loken's wings a-trembling. The Sprite's eyes shone brightly and the tips of his pointed ears pricked up as an idea took form in his mind.

"I know that look! You have a solution to this dire predicament," noted the Fairy, staring with raised eyebrows at Loken. "What are you thinking?"

"I am thinking you are absolutely correct! As sure as I am about the very depth of my love for you, so too, am I confident this man's mind is alert and fully functioning although his body, at least his muscles, are not."

"How do you know for sure?"

Loken stood up on Myron's chin, scrutinizing this mortal's limp form and expressionless face. Even beneath these closed lids, his eyes remained unmoving, staring into this enforced darkness. "I will make him respond... make him answer my questions. If he can do so, we'll know that all hope is not yet lost!"

"He cannot even open his eyes to blink a response. How do you hope to make him answer your questions?"

"He cannot blink, but he is breathing," stated Loken. "I pray he has enough control over this faculty that we can take advantage of it."

"Is it possible?"

"We shall soon find out," answered Loken, as he leaned over to his downed comrade's right ear. "Pssst! Myron, if you can hear me, breathe a single, short breath for yes."

To their surprise, without hesitation, the mortal released a short, quick breath, and then resumed his long, steady pattern of breathing once more.

"Well, I'll be!" gasped Celia, her hands clapping together in delight. "If anything, he *can* hear you!"

"Good! Very good!" praised Loken, patting Myron's cheek in encouragement. "I will ask you questions and you shall answer. One short breath for yes, two short breaths for no, my friend. Do you understand?"

Again, the knight exhaled with purpose a short breath, this one more powerful than the first.

"Excellent!" Loken nodded in approval.

"My dear friend, other than this potion laying claim to your body, are you hurt otherwise?" questioned Celia, hovering by his right ear.

Myron released two short, deliberate breaths.

"He's not hurt!" confirmed Loken. "Thank goodness for that. And thanks to you, I was able to save Celia in the nick of time. We are here to help you."

"Yes, we are here to help you escape and to save your friends, if we can," added the Fairy.

"How did you get out of your prison?" asked Loken. "Did you find a way to finally escape?"

Myron exhaled two short breaths in response.

"So Dragonite had his minions remove your body, thinking you were dead?" probed the Sprite.

One short breath escaped the mortal's lips.

"This is bizarre. Why did they leave you here in the middle of this passage?" asked Celia.

Unable to answer this question with a 'yes' or 'no', Myron just lay there; unresponsive, breathing as he normally did considering the condition he was in.

"Did something happen? Is that why you were abandoned here?" queried Loken, rewording Celia's question.

Myron issued a single, short breath.

"Yes!" deciphered Celia, as she nodded in understanding.

"Your friends! Have they come? Is that why Dragonite abandoned you here as he did?"

Again, Myron answered with a short puff of a breath.

"They are here!" Loken nodded to Celia. "Are your friends still safe?"

Two quick, urgent breaths denoted the level of peril Rose and those in her company were in.

"They're in danger," said Celia. "Do you know where they are?"

One short breath followed.

"Are they heading up to the surface? Is that where Dragonite means to confront them?" asked Loken, his mind racing as he thought on the maze of tunnels and numerous chambers riddling this mountain fortress.

Myron exhaled two short breaths in response.

"They must journey deeper into the earth," determined Celia. "Is that where they go?"

One quick breath was Myron's response.

"If the Princess and her comrades succeeded in avoiding all the traps Dragonite had set out, then they must have made it to the chamber where the Sorcerer houses the dreamstone," determined Loken. "Do you believe this is where Dragonite was in a rush to go to? He hopes to intercept them?"

Myron gave a short, sharp breath to make sure the Fairy and Sprite understood his answer as he forced his eyes to finally open.

"Progress!" Loken's hand slapped his thigh in delight as he watched this mortal's eyes slowly open, only to squeeze shut from the glare of the torch's light overhead. "We have movement!"

"No offense, my dear, but unless this mortal has learned to walk by the sheer strength of his eyelids, this is hardly progress," countered Celia, releasing a disheartened sigh.

"He still has his wits about him and he will regain his strength in time," assured Loken, rubbing his hands together in gleeful anticipation. "This is promising!"

"True," Celia nodded in agreement. "However, progress and the promise of rescue for Princess Rose and the others will not come soon enough at this rate, if Dragonite does indeed know they are here and he advances to confront them."

With eyes barely open, Myron slowly raised his head off the ground only to have it flop down again as a pathetic groan croaked from his throat.

Loken hovered before the slits of Myron's half-closed eyes.

"He is in no condition to walk, let alone fight to gain his friends' freedom," noted Celia.

"I know."

"So all is lost..." lamented Celia.

"I have a plan."

"Do tell."

"It is true this knight does not have the legs to walk on at this very moment, but you, my love, possess the magic to transport the three of us from this place," answered Loken, "while I have the power to dupe the Sorcerer."

Celia's eyes opened wide in surprise. Knowing the old Loken as well as she did, the Fairy knew what was on this Sprite's mind. She glanced at Loken, and then at Myron, as she said with a wry smile: "I sense a grand scheme is afoot; duplicity as it's best."

"Double the duplicity," vowed Loken, winking at Celia as he gazed at the knight. "Let's get to work."

"What is up with you?" groaned Tag, one hand smacking his forehead in frustration as the dreamstone dangled from the other. "Why are you always getting caught?"

"Why do *you* never do a better job of protecting *me!*" snapped Rose. She leaned away from the black crystal jabbing the side of her neck.

"And why are you two always bickering like two old, married folks every time I see you together?" Dragonite snorted as he stepped forth from the shadows. Bracing the Princess against his body, he used her as a human shield.

"We are *not* married!" Tag and Rose snapped simultaneously at the Sorcerer's snide comment.

"Well, you could have fooled me!" Dragonite's wiry brows furrowed as he scowled in disdain. "I swear there is something going on the way you two carry on!"

"Never mind that!" growled Tag. He cautiously unsheathed his sword. "Let the Princess go! Do so now!"

"Or what?" Dragonite grunted in mock concern as he pressed the dark, jagged crystal to Rose's throat.

"Or I'll drop the dreamstone!" Tag held the magic crystal over the churning lava. "You'll never get your hands on it, ever!"

"Come now, you insolent knave! Are you stupid? You are so bloody predictable!"

"I am?" Tag's hand wielding the bead of crystal drooped upon hearing this insult.

"Of course I knew you'd make that asinine threat."

"It is *not* a threat!" In defiance, Tag shook the necklace in his trembling hand for the Sorcerer to see. "I will destroy it so none will abuse its powers again!"

"You say that now, but if you drop the dreamstone; the Princess dies! You dare attack me; she dies! Your idiotic friends try to stop me; she dies! Need I say more?"

"And if you harm her; I will destroy the dreamstone *and* my friends and I will track you down. You will be nothing more than common prey to be hunted and slaughtered!"

"Say... where are your cohorts in crime?" Dragonite's beady eyes glanced about his ruined throne room, searching for the Dream Merchant and the Elf Lord. "Where did they go?"

"We were forced to go our separate ways!" answered Tag. His eyes remained fixed on Dragonite, but within the scope of his peripheral vision, he spied upon Silas Agincor and Rainus Silverthorn. They remained hidden behind the boulder of crystal; their shadowy figures now obscured by a multitude of impact fractures that clouded the centre of the once flawless sphere of quartz.

"Where did they skulk off to? I demand to know!"

"They are on their way to rescue our friend, Cankles Mayron," lied Tag, praying that Rose would do nothing to betray Silas and Rainus' position.

"Then they are on a fool's errand! If they do not die on their way to the prison where I held the fool of an idiot, they will run a treacherous gauntlet only to discover your friend is already dead."

"You lie!" snapped Rose, struggling against Dragonite's grip. "You are a liar!"

"I said it before, I will say it again! I am omnipotent! I am powerful! However, a liar? A pathetic, lowly liar? I think not! Your words confound and wound me, Princess."

"I wish my words had the power to just kill you!" hissed Rose. Her struggle came to an abrupt end as the obsidian crystal threatened to puncture the delicate skin on her throat.

"Control that flippant little tongue of yours or it will be your end, Princess. What I said was true. That thin rake of a man you call your friend met his demise not but a few hours ago, if that."

"Cankles is not dead!" insisted Tag. "You *are* a liar!"

"Bloody hell! Stop it with this petty name-calling! That stick of a man keeled over; dropped dead in his prison cell this very day."

"You murdered him?" gasped Rose, shrinking away from the keen edge of the Sorcerer's crystal.

"I wish! As best as I could tell, methinks that fool probably starved to death in spite of my best efforts to keep him well-fed."

"You fed him well?" questioned Tag, his words tainted with doubt as he hoisted his sword in threat.

"Fine! So I lied about that, but I did feed him when I remembered to do so."

"You fiend! You foul, nasty toad!" rebuked Rose. "No, I take that back! You are the pus-filled, festering wart on the backside of a foul, nasty toad!"

"Sticks and stones may break my bones, but I will most certainly kill you!" snarled Dragonite, yanking back on a fistful of hair to pull taut the chords of her neck.

"*Owww!* Not my beautiful hair!" cried Rose, as she winced in pain.

"Shut it, Princess! Just know that your friends' attempt to rescue Cankles Mayron will be all for naught. Unless they have use for a gangly, old corpse, I assure you, the fool is very much dead."

"If what you say is true, it shall only fuel our desire to see you captured and brought to justice, once and for all," snapped Tag.

"You and your cohorts have failed to capture me before. You will only fail again! And in the end, I will be the one with the power to dispense justice as I see fit! Now give me the dreamstone or the girl gets it!"

Once again, Dragonite thrust the black crystal to her throat.

"If I give you the dreamstone, then we are all doomed," reasoned Tag. "So, yeah! You might as well give it to her."

"*What?*" gasped Rose, her eyes wide in dismay.

"Say again," grunted Dragonite, his brows knitted together in a frown of confusion.

"You heard me! It is no great loss to me if you do away with that spoiled little snip of a princess. The world as we know it is in peril because of her and her selfish sense of entitlement."

"How dare you?" Rose sputtered in rage, struggling against the Sorcerer's hold so she may throttle her former jester. "You know I'm trying to set things right!"

"You speak in jest!" snorted Dragonite, ignoring his prisoner's rant. "It is your duty to keep Princess Rose safe from harm. Have you forgotten your fealty to King William? You owe it to him to abide by your knightly duties."

"I assure you, he *is* speaking in jest!" rebuked the Princess, as she glared in contempt at Tag.

"Yes, I do have a duty to King William, but what he does not know will not hurt him. If I destroy the dreamstone and you happen to do away with the Princess in retaliation, I will tell him the world is safe once more but sadly, his daughter was the casualty of this quest. I am sure he will grieve her loss, but he does have a kingdom that will be spared your wrath if this magic crystal is kept from your hands."

"If this madman kills me, so help me, Tagius Oliver Yairet, I will wring your scrawny neck with my own hands!" declared Rose. Her face was flushed with anger; her rage preventing her from seeing how illogical this threat was.

Dragonite's eyes narrowed in suspicion as he scrutinized Tag. Was this knight-in-the-making merely bluffing to trick him? Or did he speak the truth? After all, it would be no great loss to do away with this whiny, demanding, wretched girl and still get the deed done. And with no witnesses other than this boy to speak the truth, if he were inclined to do so, King William would be none the wiser to what really happened to his daughter if Tag allowed her to die.

"You mean to deceive me!"

"Yes," agreed Rose. "Tag really does not want you to harm even a single strand of hair on my lovely head."

"Hush, Princess! I was speaking to the Sorcerer!"

"Damn you, Tag! I will not be hushed!"

Rose's words were abruptly stifled as Dragonite slapped a filthy hand over her mouth. "Quiet! The rapscallion is speaking to me!"

"As I was saying: I have nothing to lose and much to gain, plus I'll be free of her nagging, hen-pecking ways," explained Tag, waving the dreamstone over the churning lava. "Hear me when I say I do not dupe you with a false threat. Besides, you are Parru St. Mime Dragonite. You are too clever for me. You'd be able to see through a simple act of duplicity."

"You are absolutely right," agreed the Sorcerer.

"So, if I were to destroy the dreamstone..." Tag hoisted it over the molten lava.

"*Stop!*" shouted Dragonite. "I suppose you did raise a valid point and I cannot say I blame you for wanting to be free of this royal wench! She would drive even me insane with all her whining and complaining."

"There you go then, Master Sorcerer! I have everything to gain, even at the expense of *losing* the Princess." Tag ignored Rose's squeals of protest, muted by her captor's hand still clamped firmly over her mouth.

"Very true!" acknowledged the Sorcerer. "However, if you have no concern for her life, I am sure the same cannot be said for yours!"

Dragonite turned his obsidian crystal away from the Princess' throat on to Tag. He inched closer, still bracing Rose against his body as a shield in case the boy turned his sword on him.

"If you kill me, then I shall fall into the lava. The dreamstone will be lost to you," reminded Tag, shuffling closer to the ledge. "Then what will you have accomplished?"

"Accomplished?" Dragonite grunted as he sneered at the mortal. "I will be free of you. I'd be free of this wretched excuse of a princess, that's for sure. In the big scheme of things, it is true! I'd no longer have access to the dreamstone, but I would no longer need to contend with the likes of you two morons!"

"But what about the dreamstone?" asked Tag. "Is this not the reason you sent that conniving little Pooka to secure it? To undermine our efforts to reclaim it?"

"I admit my desire for the magic crystal is great, but what good is it to me if the Princess is dead, unable to divulge the secret of how to utilize its power? If she is to die, it will be by the edge of *your* sword," disclosed Dragonite, as he crept closer to Tag.

"So you want *me* to kill her?"

"As you said: what do you have to lose if she were to meet her demise? It is apparent you have no qualms about it, if I were to dispense with the Princess. However, I hardly think you have the stomach to commit such a heinous deed with your own hands. Just as I believe you lack the courage to sacrifice your life just to prevent me from acquiring the dreamstone."

"I swear! I *will* jump! I'll take this crystal with me!" The heels of Tag's boots hovered dangerously over the burning chasm. If he shifted his weight even slightly, he'd lose his balance, plunging into the lava. "The dreamstone will meet its doom, just as I will."

"If you do that, then the Princess will follow! You will both be dead and I will have to find another way to ensnare the Dream Merchant to acquire a new magic crystal. He is already so close to me, bumbling about in my fortress with that fool Elf Lord. But, as I am feeling merciful at this moment, I am prepared to let you walk away from here, if you do the wise thing. Hand that dreamstone to me!"

Rose gasped in horror. Tag balanced precariously on the ledge. He wobbled to and fro, bumping against a pillar that prevented him from toppling over. Tears welled in her eyes as she spied the resolve on his face as he accepted his fate.

Tag nodded at her, offering a small, consoling smile as he whispered, "Forgive me, Princess..."

With these words, he fell.

17

Doomed if You Do. Doomed if You Don't.

Tag's eyes squeezed shut. His breath escaped in a loud gasp as he surrendered to his fate. His skin shrank, pulling taut on the flesh as the patina of sweat evaporated instantly, the raging heat swelling from the lava below engulfing him as he toppled over the edge.

In a fit of rage and panic, Rose bit down with a primeval ferocity she never knew she had. Her teeth sank into the fleshy pad where Dragonite's thumb joined his hand. The Sorcerer bellowed in agony, releasing her to shake off the pain. Before she could dash to Tag's rescue, Rainus bolted out from behind the boulder. His Elven rope whipped out from his hands, the loop snaring Tag about his body before he could disappear from sight. With a powerful heave, Rainus yanked the boy from the brink.

Tag landed with a hard '*thud*' onto the floor. The dreamstone was still clenched in his balled fist, but his sword hit the ground. The impact sent it clattering across the floor, coming to a stop at Rose's feet.

Snatching up the weapon, she spun about to confront the Sorcerer. Rose yelped in surprise as Dragonite's staff swung about, bashing the sword from her grip.

With a resounding crash, it slammed down onto the quartz floor, rattling as it skidded away until it came to rest against the scattered debris near the boulder of doom.

Before she could back away, Dragonite seized her. His bony hand wrapped around her throat as he growled in malice, "You royal brat! I will be your end!"

With a violent shove, he pushed her to the ground next to Tag as the boy struggled to remove the Elven rope from around his body. He caught her as she stumbled, falling to the floor to land in his arms.

Rainus roared as he unsheathed his sword. His bold dash to challenge the Sorcerer was short-lived as Dragonite turned the glowing black crystal mounted atop his staff on the Elf. It swelled with ominous light; a powerful energy waiting to be unleashed.

"Think again, Silverthorn! If you care not for your own life and safety, then surely you care about these two lowly mortals you regard as friends." The Sorcerer turned his weapon on to Tag and Rose.

Rainus froze. His sword drooped in one hand as the other came up in surrender.

"I thought as much!" Dragonite snorted in disdain. "You are even more predictable than the boy!"

"Predictable?" scoffed Tag, raising the Princess onto her feet as he stood up to defy the Sorcerer. "You had no idea I was willing to sacrifice my life for her, did you?"

Rose suddenly smiled. Squeezing his hand in hers, she squealed in delight, "Hey, you did do just that!"

"That was why I said the Elf is more predictable," admitted Dragonite, as he used the tip of his staff to direct Rainus to join his comrades. "Who would have thought there would still be that kind of honour or courage in a measly young whelp of a mortal?"

"No disrespect to the young sir, but I am an Elf, so inherently, I have more honour and greater courage. Hence, I am willing to strike up a deal with you, Sorcerer."

"Say again!" Dragonite sneered in contempt as he scrutinized the Elf Lord.

"Release them! You can take me as your prisoner." Rainus bowed his head in humility and surrender to pacify their captor.

The sneer on Dragonite's face, punctuated by the thin, drawn lips that turned down at the corners of his mouth into a bitter, seemingly permanent scowl, began to dissolve. His cracked lips began to quiver in mirth as he battled the urge to smile in mock ridicule upon hearing the Elf's gallant offer. His entire body began to tremble, and then convulse, as he burst into a fit of laughter.

"What now?" asked Rainus. He stared in confusion at his nemesis as he backed away, taking his place next to his friends. "What did I say? I said nothing humorous."

"Oh, yes you did! You may have more honour and courage than the boy, but what is for certain is you are even more of an idiot than he is," chortled Dragonite, struggling to compose himself to adopt a threatening persona more suitable for the occasion.

"I protest! No offense, Master Yairet, but I am not!" snorted Rainus, indignation flaring in his voice.

"Yes, you are! Why would I take your life in place of theirs'? You have no value to me!"

"I am the Lord of the Woodland Glade, the esteemed leader of the Elves inhabiting this realm! I do not mean to boast and I certainly do not mean to belittle present company, but surely that holds more weight than a young knight-in-training and a princess from one average-sized kingdom of mortals?"

"Perhaps if I were to hold you for ransom, but this is not about garnering material wealth. This is about *power:* all consuming, unadulterated, malevolent power!" snarled Dragonite, the staff trembling in his grip as the black crystal glowed, shining brighter with his rage. "I want the girl *and* the dreamstone!"

Rose snatched the magic crystal from Tag's hand, but before she could wish them away to safety, she shrieked in fright.

A ball of energy exploded forth, striking Rainus down. The Elf was slammed hard to the ground, writhing in pain as tiny blue bolts of lightning danced over his body.

Tag wrapped his arms around the Princess. He held on tight, preventing her from rushing to Rainus' aid should the energy surging through his body incapacitate her, too.

"If you do not wish for the boy to meet the same agonizing fate as the Elf, you best come to me with the dreamstone in your hands, Princess Rose." The Sorcerer aimed the obsidian crystal at Tag's heart, motioning for the boy to kneel in submission.

"Don't do it, Princess!" warned Tag, dropping to his knees as he raised his hands in surrender.

"I must," argued Rose, as she took a cautious step toward the Sorcerer. "I cannot have you sacrifice your life again! Instead, if I go with this madman, then you will be free to hunt him down. You will hunt him down and you will rescue me. I know you will."

"Your faith in this young knave is truly touching, but oh-so misplaced, you fool," grunted Dragonite, as a gnarled index finger flexed, motioning her to come hither. "Just know that you are doing a good deed by sparing his life, for the moment."

"Stop, Princess!" ordered Tag. "Don't listen to him! He'll kill me anyway!"

"Stop with that incessant chatter!" snapped Dragonite. The black crystal aimed at the boy began to glow, burning brighter with the Sorcerer's growing ire.

Rose stepped quickly, standing before her enemy. With that dreaded obsidian now pointed at her chest, to temper his anger, she opened her hand. The Princess presented the dreamstone to Dragonite. "Here! It is yours for the taking."

"Yes, it is! However, that bauble is useless to me unless you first tell me how it works."

"Have you already tried?" Rose frowned in curiosity as she stared at the dust-covered, innocuous-looking bead of crystal sitting in the palm of her dirt-smudged hand.

"Of course, I tried! It is either broken or it will only work for you. Why else would I go through all the bother of luring you here to my fortress in the first place? So, which is it, Princess? Is it broken or has the wily Silas Aginor placed an enchantment on the dreamstone so it will work only for you?"

"There is a very good chance it was broken while in the hands of your nasty Poodu – "

"My nasty *what?*"

"Pooka! She means to say Pooka," explained Tag, as he rolled his eyes in frustration.

"I see," grunted Dragonite.

"Yes, I was speaking of that nasty shape-shifting minion of yours, but it is true what you say. The Dream Merchant made it so, under the proper circumstances, the crystal works only for me." Her words were spoken with utmost certainty as she deliberately failed to disclose the true workings of the dreamstone.

"Prove it! Prove the magic crystal is still indeed magic; that it will only grant wishes to its appointed bearer!"

Rose glanced over her shoulder. Rainus lay immobilized by Dragonite's power while Tag knelt near to him, hands raised in defeat. He shook his head, dissuading Rose from complying with the Sorcerer's demand.

"Do not look to the boy for answers! If you mean to spare their lives, then show me that the dreamstone works. Prove it to be so!"

Rose stared at Tag, only to have Dragonite snarl in response. Without hesitation, he removed the sinister, black crystal pointed at her chest, turning it on the boy.

She screamed as Tag toppled over onto Rainus' twitching form. Though the power unleashed was nowhere near as great as the first one that struck the Elf down, the boy still writhed in agony as tiny bolts of blue lightning danced over his convulsing body. In close contact to the Elf, the residual power transferred to Rainus, now slowing his chances of recovering even more.

"No!" shrieked Rose.

Before she could dash away to aid Tag, Dragonite seized her by the wrist, squeezing it hard so her hand was forced open to reveal the dreamstone. Thrusting the black crystal to her throat, he growled with malice. The obsidian crowning this staff failed to flare with light to match the intensity of his rage, having been discharged in rapid succession before given the opportunity to recharge its powers fully.

"No! Harm them no more!" pleaded Rose, thrusting the dream-stone into the Sorcerer's angry face. "Here! It is yours! Just leave them be!"

"You heard her!" Silas Agincor growled as he emerged from behind the great boulder, the crystal crowning his staff glowed with intense, white light. "Release them all, Princess Rose included."

Dragonite glared at his archrival, sneering in contempt. "I should have known you were skulking about! And it is so like you to make an appearance only when your hand is forced."

"My hand was *not* forced! I was being prudent and calculating, waiting for the most opportune moment to confront you."

"You waited until I incapacitate two of your cohorts? So you'd have the backing of only this useless, fool of a princess to aid you in overpowering me? It is either a clever ploy or your mind has become addled with age," scoffed Dragonite. He snorted in mock laughter as he thrust the black crystal to Rose's throat, the jagged edge of this chunk of obsidian pressed against her throat. "Methinks it was the combined act of a true coward and the lack of a well-planned strategy that has failed you yet again, my old friend!"

"A well-planned strategy, indeed, you fool!" acknowledged the Dream Merchant as he cautiously advanced, his magic orb crowning his staff burning brightly as a visual threat. "I waited until you had discharged that evil crystal twice to effectively deplete its already wanting powers. If you attempt to harm the Princess with another blast of your magic, she will feel nothing more than a tickle of energy, enough perhaps to solicit a giggle, if that."

Dragonite unleashed a disgruntled huff as he glared at his nemesis. "*You* are the fool! Why do you think the razor-sharp edge of this crystal now rests against her throat? With just a flick of my wrist, it will easily slice through such delicate flesh. She will bleed out before you can come to her aid."

"Stay where you are, Master Wizard! I have no desire to have my life drained from me," whimpered Rose, as she spied him from the corner of her eye as he crept closer.

"Trust me, Princess," assured Silas, his staff at the ready. "I know what I am doing."

"Trust you? *YOU?* The girl is a twit, but she is not that stupid! She trusted you before and now look at the grief you and this blasted dreamstone caused her! Trust! Bah! You sly, old weasel of a Wizard, she trusted you before and now her life hangs in the balance because of you!"

"If you hurt her, I swear I will kill you!" vowed Silas, levelling the glowing orb of his staff toward Dragonite's chest.

"Of course you will! Just keep in mind that in the time it will take for your powers to strike me down, it will be too late for the Princess. As I said, all it will take is just a flick of my wrist."

Rose winced. Just flinching under his cruel taunt was enough for the sharp edge of the black crystal to lance her skin. A thin line of crimson blood seeping from this cut spoke of the true danger the obsidian posed.

"That was her own doing," insisted Dragonite. Shuffling the Princess about so she shielded him, he positioned his body just so, that now, she was in the direct line of fire if Silas unleashed his magic. "But do not test me, for I have no qualms of doing away with this wretched girl!"

"Then what? Who will show you how to use the dreamstone if you kill Princess Rose?"

The corners of Dragonite's drooping lips sneered into a demented smile as he hissed: *"You will."*

"Then why do you not kill her now? Be done with her than to prolong her torment?" questioned Silas, refusing to lower his staff.

"Please don't encourage him," begged Rose, as she attempted to lean away from the black crystal pressing lightly against her throat.

Ignoring the Princess' pathetic plea to spare her life, Dragonite growled at Silas, "There is no doubt you can share in all the secrets of the magic crystal and then some, however, this miserable excuse for a human being would be far more cooperative with a little proper *persuasion.* You, on the other hand, will only reveal how to unlock its powers after a great deal of coercing on my part."

"So you have grown too old to inflict torture," taunted the Wizard.

"No, as much as I would revel in the process, I have grown much too impatient to waste my time torturing you to cooperate with me."

"Hmph!" grunted Silas, nodding in agreement. "I suppose you do have a point."

"Of course I do!"

"But if you kill the Princess now, then where will you hide? When she falls to the ground, unable to stand any longer, you will be completely exposed – utterly vulnerable. I will smite you where you stand! And I hardly believe you are in the position, nor do you possess the powers, to subdue me now."

Dragonite stared at his flawed crystal, and then shrugged with indifference. Glancing over his bony shoulder, he grunted, "True, but they certainly can."

From out of the deep shadows, Dragonite's army poured from the entranceway flanking each side of the crystal throne. Shoulder to shoulder, one hundred mimes armed with spears and pikes formed a semi-circle behind the Sorcerer. Rather than a motley, disorderly group on the scramble, these mimes performed like a disciplined fighting unit. With timed precision, they fell into place, perfectly spaced with weapons poised in their hands, waiting for Dragonite's order to attack the intruders.

"What say you now, Agincor?" A smug grin cracked Dragonite's face as his brows bobbed up and down in ridicule. "You can strike me down, but my loyal followers are ready to retaliate. They will launch an assault that will see you *and* your comrades cut down."

"Oh my! I did not see this coming," gulped Silas.

"And now, even with my *'flawed'* crystal, I am mightier than you! So who will smite whom, Agincor? I get the sense I am now smitier than you are."

"*Smitier?* There is no such word," corrected Rose, her perfect brows crinkling into a frown. "Even I know that."

"Fetch off, Princess, I just invented it. It is a word of my own making, therefore, it *is* a word, a perfect one suitable for this occasion."

"But *smitier?* Come now!" mocked Rose. "Surely you can do better than that!"

"Silence! Or do you wish to die where you stand? For I am feeling mighty smitie as this moment!"

"Calm down! She meant no harm," urged Silas. Each time he raised his staff to take aim at Dragonite the mimes did the same, hoisting their spears not just at him, but at the Princess, Tag and Rainus, too, both still paralyzed by the Sorcerer's powers.

"Well, I do!" Dragonite growled, his weapon trembling in his hands. "She is making it so easy for me to want to just dispense with her now."

"I'll be quiet!" promised Rose, pinching her lips between her index finger and thumb so no offending words could leak out of her mouth to further raise his ire.

"Good! You shall speak when you are spoken to, or so help me, I will skewer you on this staff! As for you, Agincor, you will surrender now or you will have the blood of three not-so-innocent victims on your hands."

"So now what?" asked Silas. The glow of his orb waned as he rested against his staff as though it was nothing more than a harmless walking stick.

"You will put down your weapon! Join your cohorts over there," instructed Dragonite, using his head to motion the Wizard to move to where Tag and Rainus struggled to get their muscles to cooperate. "If you try anything funny, you will be no better off than those fools!"

"Funny? I am not known for being humorous," noted Silas, as he rested his staff on the floor before joining his friends.

"You know what I mean!" grunted Dragonite. He scowled in annoyance as the Wizard slowly raised his hands in surrender. Watching in silence, he waited for Silas to commiserate in misery with his downed comrades as the mimes moved in closer to lend their support.

"Yes, yes!" grumbled Silas. He heaved a disgruntled sigh as he knelt by Tag, helping him to sit up, only to have the boy topple over onto Rainus again.

"Now, let us get down to business, Princess," said Dragonite, his eyes narrowing as he stared in contempt at her. "Let me begin with a stern warning: If you trick me and disappear with the dreamstone, you will give me no choice but to kill your friends the very moment you vanish."

"I understand," gulped Rose, as she nodded in acknowledgement. "And if this dreamstone is indeed broken?"

"Then it is useless to me. I will have no choice but to let you and your cohorts free."

"Truly?" Rose gasped, renewed hope burning brightly in her eyes. "You would do that?"

"No! Now, I was being the funny one," smirked Dragonite. He delighted in watching this look of eager expectation being extinguished by his cruel words.

"But what will you do to us if this magic crystal is magic no more?" questioned the Princess.

"Need you even ask?" Dragonite slowly slid his index finger across his throat as a visual threat of what was to come if she failed to make the crystal work.

"Now, do not waste any more of my precious time! Prove to me the dreamstone still works."

"That is ill advised, Princess," warned Silas, shaking his head at Rose.

"Doomed if you do. Doomed if you don't," chortled the Sorcerer, the tip of his obsidian crystal tapping Rose under her chin to make sure he had her complete and undivided attention. "So shut it, Agincor, you dolt! Let the girl focus on the task at hand or her doom will only come sooner, no thanks to you. And yours will surely follow!"

"Fine! I'll do it!" cried Rose. "What do you want me to wish for?

Gold, silver and jewels? More than can fill this chamber?"

"Yes! Forget the silver, though. I prefer gold. Wait... No!"

"No?" repeated the Princess, frowning in bewilderment.

"You mean to trick me! If you wished for that, I have a sneaking suspicion you will do something drastic; like have me crushed beneath the weight of this treasure as it floods my throne room."

"Oh... that would have worked! Alas, I am not clever enough to devise such a sly plan to overpower you, unless Tag or the Wizard planted such an idea in my head."

Dragonite rubbed his chin in pensive thought. With a nod, he agreed, "You are right, Princess. You are not that clever."

"Suppose I start small? Perhaps a nice size treasure chest filled with gold and precious stones?"

"Is this a trick?" asked Dragonite, his eyes narrowing in suspicion.

"I found this dreamstone to be somewhat fickle. It is best to work up to a truly grand wish, especially as it has laid dormant since it was last in my possession."

"If you deceive me, I will kill you."

"I know! I know! This threat is getting old, Sorcerer, but what can I say? It is the very nature of the magic imbued unto the dreamstone. The Wizard was less than generous when he 'gifted' it to me, no doubt to teach me a lesson about greed. That cursed thing is like a stubborn, old horse."

"How so, Princess?"

"The dreamstone is like a petulant nag because you must persuade the temperamental beast to walk, then cajole it to canter before it is willing to break into a full gallop to reveal its true might."

"Well, knowing you and knowing how Agincor's feeble mind works, I am not surprised."

"So will you allow me to demonstrate?" asked Rose, holding forth the dreamstone for the Sorcerer to consider. "I will start with three wishes, the next grander than the last to prime this crystal for some truly astounding wishes to become reality. Will you allow me to do so?"

"Only if I dictate what these wishes are," agreed Dragonite, nodding in approval as he motioned for Rose to proceed.

"Very well. So, shall I begin with a treasure chest burgeoning with riches, one that will be the envy of every king in this realm?"

"No harm in that. Make it so!"

Rose clasped the dreamstone in her hand. Holding it close to her heart, her eyes squeezed shut so she could focus on this task.

With the image of a wooden chest gilded in gold taking form in her mind, her eyes snapped open as Dragonite growled: "Say the magic words, speak the enchantment to make this wish come true."

"Do you mind? You cannot just interrupt me while in the midst of conjuring up a wish!"

"You should have said so," grunted the Sorcerer. "But while you are here in the present, tell me the spell needed to conjure up whatever I can dream of."

"There are no magic words, at least, not as you would think."

"No hocus-pocus? No dibbly dobbly doop?" questioned Dragonite, his wiry brows twisting into a frown of confusion. "Surely there are words to be employed to unleash the crystal's magic?"

"There are words, but to say them aloud so others will be privy to this enchantment is a foolish thing to do," lied Rose, as she attempted to buy more time. "These special words must be repeated in my head or spoken in barely a whisper so none will hear. They must be said three times with each action to unlock its powers."

"What actions? This is unheard of!" disputed Dragonite.

"I thought so too, but the Dream Merchant deliberately made it difficult for me to utilize this magic crystal. Apparently, the old coot, no disrespect to the Wizard, felt it only right that I'd be made to 'work' to make my wishes come true. Can you imagine that? Me, a princess, being made to work!"

"As you should! You are a spoiled, little oik after all. You have never known a single day of hard work in your privileged life, so yes, it makes perfect sense." The Sorcerer nodded his head in approval to the Wizard. "Good job, Agincor! I tip my hat to you for making this snip of girl work for once in her spoiled existence."

Silas nodded, offering a forced smile in response. "In light of the Princess' wanting nature, I felt it was only prudent and in her best interest to do so."

"Then go to it, Princess Rose. Let us see if what you say is true. Make that chest of riches appear before me."

"Very well! Just allow me to do what I must without interruption or I shall lose track of what I must do and how often I must chant the words to unleash the dreamstone's powers."

Dragonite stepped back, his staff poised in his hands lest she trick him.

Rubbing her hands together, Rose drew a deep breath. Exhaling slowly, her lips moved, mouthing some gibberish of a chant she pretended to recite in her head as she began her performance.

With her arms folded like chicken wings, she mouthed some indiscernible words while hopping first on her right, and then her left foot. Doing this three times, she expanded on her routine. Like a great, flightless bird attempting to take to the air, she leapt. With arms flapping, she jumped here and there, each movement repeated three times before ending this display with a grand flourish of a twirl. Just when Dragonite thought she was done, Rose started shimmying, leaning back and forth to emphasize her movements. All the while, she kept mouthing pretend words of a chant. Finally, she ran around in circles like a girl gone mad as she whooped like a Trumpeter Swan choking on a dried crust of bread.

This performance came to an abrupt stop as she clapped her hands over her head three times, shouting "Deliver it now! Grant it now!" Her hands opened with fingers splayed wide, shaking to add to this grand finale.

In a brilliant flash, a wooden chest spilling over with shiny gold coins and dazzling, flawless diamond, emerald and ruby gemstones scattered at Dragonite's feet.

The Sorcerer's mouth fell open; hanging agape in astonishment to see the Princess' bizarre performance did indeed result in this treasure trove of riches.

"Amazing!" gasped Dragonite. Dropping to his knees, he dipped his filthy hands into the chest. The solid gold coins tinkled like music to his ears as they poured through his fingers.

"See! I told you it works if you start small," said Rose, in her best I-told-you-so voice.

"So you did," acknowledged Dragonite. With his guard down as he admired his ill-gotten bootie, his mimes remained alert for once. The point of every spear and pike remained fixed on the Princess and her comrades, in case she attempted to wish them away from this subterranean lair.

"How about another wish? One slightly grander than this to get the dreamstone better primed to handle the greatest of all your wishes."

Like an arthritic old man, Dragonite used his staff to upright himself, his hunched back standing a little straighter as he considered her words.

"For once, I agree with you, Princess."

"How about that crystal throne? I can wish for it to be gilded in gold and studded with some of these lovely jewels?" offered Rose, pointing to the exquisite seat against the far wall.

"Oooh! That would be magnificent!" Dragonite nodded in approval. "But wait! I like these lovely, loose gems the way they are. Instead, conjure up more rubies and pearls, too, this time. And not just any pearls, I want those rare *black* pearls and I want them to be the size of my eyeballs!"

"Amethyst, sapphire and emerald gemstones, too, while I'm at it?" asked the Princess, hoping to appease her captor.

"No, a gaudy display in a rainbow of colours will only make my throne look obscenely decadent, and not in a flattering way. Pearls and rubies will be more than adequate for that look of understated elegance I desire. It will speak of my refined taste."

"Pearls and rubies on a gilded throne, coming right up."

Closing her eyes, Rose repeated her performance as she muttered a phony chant to make this wish come true. Before she had a chance to envision the throne in all its glittering glory, she gasped in surprise, her eyes snapping open as the Sorcerer shouted, "Stop! Wait! I have come up with a better wish."

"Better than a dazzling throne encrusted with precious jewels? What can be better than that?"

"I was overcome by my excitement. I am a pragmatic man, so I must let common sense prevail. I must be sensible about this whole business of wishing for whatever I can dream of!"

"You have a better idea?"

"What I have in mind is practical for me, but should not tax the dreamstone too much as it gets primed to grant me the greatest wish ever!"

"Go on then, what is this next wish you desire?" inquired Rose.

"Why do you even ask?" muttered Silas, his hand slapping his forehead in frustration. The threat the Princess was unwittingly heading down a path from which there would be no return loomed large before the Wizard and his comrades.

"Shut it, Agincor!" snapped Dragonite. "When I am done, you will face my wrath! I may even subject you to sitting through a great performance by my best mimes, first!"

"Heaven forbid!" groaned Silas, shaking his head in dread.

"Go on then," said Rose, hands raised in submission to pacify the agitated Sorcerer. "Focus, before the dreamstone's powers begin to wane. Now quickly! What is your next command?"

The Sorcerer's eyes rolled skyward, as though searching through his mind for the most appropriate wish that would best serve him. After a moment of ponderance, he made it known.

"What would be truly grand is if my motley looking crew of mimes were attired in such a way they will strike fear in all at first glance, when they march into battle."

"You would like your men to be real soldiers instead of mimes?" questioned Rose.

"No! I have no desire to surround myself with an army of ordinary men. These mimes are true artists. I merely lack the means to make them *look* the part I wish for them to portray. I would like these mimes to not just act the part of soldiers that you can see they have been perfecting, I want the full package: helmets, greaves, gauntlets, mail vests, surcoats emblazoned with my heraldic symbol! You get my meaning?"

"Good gracious! I never knew you had a heraldic symbol," responded Rose.

"I do now! It is a black dragon against a blue... no! A red, yes! That's it! My heraldic symbol is a fearsome black dragon against a blood red background. That would make for a fearsome sight on any battlefield!"

"Are you sure?" asked the Princess.

"Positive! Why? Are you saying it cannot be done? This dream-stone lacks the power to outfit my mimes in soldierly apparel?"

"I assure you, it can be done, but dressing your mimes? I still think the bedazzled throne is a much better idea."

"I do not care what you think!" Pointing at his newly acquired wealth in the brimming treasure chest, Dragonite snorted, "I now have the means to hire all the best seamstresses in this realm, but I want my men outfitted *now!* They must look the part, if we are to move on with my plans of world domination."

"As you wish," conceded Rose, nodding in obedience. "I will make it so."

For the second time, Rose closed her eyes. As she cleared her mind, she envisioned each of Dragonite's mimely minions decked out in full battle regalia. With great zeal, the Princess mouthed the words of gibberish as she performed her less-than-breathtaking routine.

In a grand flourish, Rose clapped her hands over her head and shouted: "Deliver it now! Grant it now!"

Some mimes issued a silent scream of surprise as their tattered cloaks, ragged trousers and well-worn vests were replaced with fine vests of steel mesh, its hooded cowl flattening their matted tangle of hair as it bore the weight of a metal helmet adorned with horns designed to intimidate. Worn over the mail vests, the mimes were dressed in crimson surcoats, each boldly emblazoned with the design of a dragon stitched in black silk threads. Fitted with a doubled boiled leather vambrace on each forearm and steel enforced leather greaves protecting their shins, the mimes looked every bit the soldiers they pretended to be.

Dragonite's beady eyes seemed to bulge from his head as he admired his newly attired army.

"Excellent! Absolutely brilliant!" praised the Sorcerer, as he scrutinized his minions. "Now they will be fit for battle."

"I am glad you are so pleased!" said Rose. "Perhaps the next wish should be a trained dragon you can ride into battle? I can have a beast saddled and waiting for you on the outside of your fortress as it would be much too big to travel through your labyrinth of tunnels to make its way to the surface."

"Don't help him!" groaned Tag. Wavering to and fro, he leaned against an equally wobbly Rainus, as Silas tried to steady them on their feet.

"Too late!" snapped Dragonite, as he turned his black crystal on Rose. "I have a wish, Princess, but it will not be a trained dragon."

"What will it be, Sorcerer?" asked Rose, staring at the obsidian that began to glow with menacing light.

"I wish… no, I command you! Yes, I command you to fuse the powers of the Dream Merchant's magical orb to mine!" Dragonite thrust both his staff and Silas' before Rose's face. "I want you to make one powerful weapon that will invoke awe in all those to witness its might."

"Why not just invoke fear?" asked Rose, stalling for time in case, by some miracle, Rainus' band of Elves survived their dragon encounter to come to her rescue.

"Fear is good, but fear that has the added leverage of awe promises to make me all the more memorable to those who dare confront me," reasoned Dragonite. He then snarled at her, "And why am I justifying this to you? You are at my mercy. You will do my bidding! Now, make it so!"

Rose glanced over to Silas, hoping he would come up with a convincing reason to dissuade the Sorcerer from wanting this wish to come true.

"Go on, Princess," urged the Wizard. "In all your wisdom and discretion, grant the fool his wish."

Dragonite began to chortle, snorting loudly as he mocked Silas' words. "I would kill you now if you were not the source of such mirth! *You* are the fool to think this mortal girl has any wisdom in her empty, little head! Nor does she know the meaning of the word, discretion."

Rose drew a deep breath, gathering her resolve and whatever dignity she had left. "Hush! I need silence to make this complex wish come true. Allow me to concentrate."

"You heard her!" snapped Dragonite, angrily waving his staff at his followers. "Silence! The girl needs silence."

The mimes frowned in confusion, rows of shoulders shrugging in bewilderment as they mouthed words of protest to this order.

"Go on! Transfer the powers of Agincor's orb to mine," demanded the Sorcerer. He held forth a staff in each hand for Rose to observe, but not touch, lest she attempted to seize it as a weapon.

Silas shook his head in woe as Rose assured him, "Worry not, Wizard, I know what to do."

"Then do so quickly! My patience wears thin," snapped Dragonite, eager to be the recipient of this magical boost to his obsidian crystal. "And remember, if you trick me, if you should deplete the powers of my orb instead, my minions will be the ones to deal death to you."

Rose nodded in understanding. Closing her eyes, she focused on the task at hand. Drawing a deep, cleansing breath, she struggled to control her mind as it raced in panic.

As she slowly exhaled, she envisioned this transfer of power from the clear orb to the black crystal, but Dragonite's biting comment that she lacked wisdom and knew nothing of discretion gnawed at the back of her mind. So, too, that if she tricked him, nullifying the powers of the obsidian crystal, his mimes would eagerly make short work of her. A clever compromise was in order and the Princess could only pray it was going to work.

Mouthing the words of the phony enchantment she concocted, Rose performed the same ritual as before, doing so with great enthusiasm to lend credibility to the magic. This routine was punctuated by the grand flourish of her hands and her shout: "Deliver it now! Grant it now!"

Rose then stopped, bowing in submission to her captor.

"Is it done? Has my staff been quickened? Made more powerful now that it has been graced with the Wizard's magic?" asked Dragonite, his eyes gleaming with anticipation as his brows furrowed in curiosity.

Rose merely nodded once in response.

"Excellent! Now I am well on my way to having my powers restored to their full capacity," exclaimed the Sorcerer. He carelessly tossed aside the Wizard's useless staff to better admire his newly empowered weapon. "But first, I must test its might!"

"Yes," agreed Rose, pointing to the far end of the throne room. "I am confident it can easily destroy one of those great pillars."

"That is hardly a test," grunted Dragonite, his eyes glancing about for a more worthy target.

Gripped firmly in his hands, the obsidian crystal mounted on the staff started to tremble. The ember of light deep within began to swell, glowing with intensity. Thrusting it on high toward the ceiling, all in the throne room dropped to the floor as the chamber shook violently. A great surge of energy blasted forward as a single beam of cold, blue light exploded through the ceiling. The powerful energy punched a hole clear through tunnels and chambers directly overhead. It disintegrated earth, rocks and boulders, only stopping when it tore through the very top of Crystal Mountain.

"Bloody hell, Princess! What have you done?" cried Tag, as he and his comrades shrank back in fear.

18
Do it or Die!

"Brilliant! Absolutely brilliant! Nothing like a bit of natural light to brighten up my lair," marvelled the Sorcerer, slapping his bony thigh in delight. His eyes squinted as he stared up into the piercing blue shining on high. "An opening to allow the light of the sky to enter; a roof for the sun, so to speak!"

"See! I did as you requested," stated Rose. "Was that not a spectacular show of power? What more can you ask for?"

"Plenty!" grunted the Sorcerer. He hefted his empowered staff as the black crystal crackled with residual energy.

"Bloody hell, Princess, stop it!" ordered Tag. He staggered to his feet only to fall over again as his quaking legs gave out. "Stop helping that madman!"

"Silence!" Dragonite snapped, turning his newly imbued weapon on the boy. "If you wish to live, at least for a little while longer, you *will* be silent!"

"Leave him be!" pleaded Rose. "I will do what you want. Just ask it of me."

"Indeed, you will! I have one final wish I desire, one that is even grander than the last and then I will ask for no more!" exclaimed Dragonite, his eyes gleaming with anticipation of what was yet to come.

"Bad idea…" moaned Tag, as Silas helped him to sit upright, propping him up next to the equally unsteady Elf.

"What is it?" Rose dared to ask.

"I want you to gift the powers of that dreamstone to me!"

"What do you mean, gift it to you?"

"Make it so I can wish for whatever I please, whenever it pleases me, without the need of going through you to make all my nefarious dreams come true."

"But if you no longer need to turn to me for wishes, then I would be deemed expendable."

"Exactly!" grunted Dragonite, his eyes gleaming with malice as a sly smile cracked his weathered face.

"I see…" gulped Rose, as she considered this request.

"You will do it or die!"

"Let me get this straight. You mean to wish for the powers to be transferred to you as the new bearer of the dreamstone?"

"Yes! So it will work for me and me alone."

"I suppose it can be done, especially as this magic crystal has now been primed. It is ready to conjure up even the wildest of your wild dreams."

"*Suppose?* There will be no supposing! You will make it so, Princess!"

"Of course." She bowed her head in submission.

"Princess Rose, stop! You cannot –" The Wizard's sentence was cut short as Dragonite threatened him with his crystal. The black obsidian glistened like polished glass as the light within glowed with menacing intent.

"You will steady that tongue of yours, Agincor, or I shall take great pleasure in doing that for you! Is that what you want?"

Silas raised his hands in surrender, releasing his hold on his comrades. Rainus and Tag flopped onto their backs, struggling to regain their balance, at least enough to sit upright unassisted.

"No need to get testy!" scolded Rose, shaking an admonishing finger at the Sorcerer. "You are putting me off. I must concentrate if you want this dream to become a reality."

"It would be my single, greatest wish! So get to it, Princess. No more interruptions," promised Dragonite. He lowered his staff as the newly outfitted mimes held steady, looking and acting every bit the part of a disciplined army waiting for their order to attack.

Rose nodded in approval as she made another demand, "And tell your idiot mimes to stop pointing all those weapons in our direction. I cannot focus on such a stupendous wish under constant threat of danger. It is very disconcerting, to say the least!"

"I am no fool!" The Sorcerer growled in resentment. "If we let down our collective guard, then that is when you and your friends will take counter measures to attack me."

"Are you mental?" snorted Rose. Her tone was incredulous as her eyes rolled in frustration. She pointed to the Wizard. Tag and Rainus clung to him as they wavered to and fro from the shock of the power that coursed through them. "Look at the boy and the Elf! They are so wobbly they can barely stand. And that old gaffer? *Ple-ease!* You made me render his staff powerless! Or did you somehow addle your brain so you have no recollection of this?"

"No, I have not!"

"Well then, what do you think he will do to you, unarmed as such? The Wizard might throw a rock at you, but his aim is not so good, I can tell you that!"

Dragonite glared at Rose, a visceral growl rumbling forth through clenched teeth to punctuate his ever-growing disdain.

"Well?" The toe of her shoe tapped impatiently as her hands rested on her hips. "What say you, Sorcerer?"

Snorting in disgust, Dragonite snapped, "Fine! Stand down, my mimely minions, at ease!

The Princess nodded in approval as the tip of every pike and spear pointed to the ceiling, rather than at her and her comrades. She closed her eyes as she prepared to make the dreamstone conjure up a wish that will never be. Drawing a deep, cleansing breath, Rose pretended to clear her mind. Instead of picturing this terrible transfer of power to Dragonite, she imagined him attempting to copy her routine to make his wishes come true. She nibbled on her lower lip in a bid to stymie her urge to giggle as she envisioned the evil Sorcerer dressed in a less-than-flattering outfit.

In her mind's eye, Dragonite frolicked about as the skirt of his ball gown billowed around him. The delicate lace sleeves fluttered as he twirled, allowing for maximum flounciness. Hopping and swirling with the grace of a hobbled horse, he struggled to maintain his balance. The silk brocade shoes his bony feet were agonizingly wedged into pinched his gnarled toes. Spinning to show off this fancy gown, the heel of his shoe rolled over an errant pebble.

As if in slow motion, Dragonite's feet flew out from beneath him. His gleeful face abruptly contorted with an expression of horror as he hit the ground, face first. Skidding across the polished quartz floor, his smooshed visage squealed like a sweaty hand being forcefully dragged across a squeaky-clean windowpane.

Like an embarrassed cat that had lost its footing, electing to groom himself to divert attention from this mishap, the Sorcerer sprung up onto his feet as if nothing had happened. He nonchalantly smoothed back the stringy strands of thin, oil-clotted hair, taking care to properly reposition the dainty little tiara adorning his head.

"Well, go on!" urged Dragonite, his fingers snapping before the Princess' face to break this trance. "I haven't got all day."

This unflattering image dissipated from her mind as Rose proceeded to re-enact her feigned wishing ritual. Although her personal quota of three wishes for the day had been spent, with as much enthusiasm as she could muster, she hopped, spun and muttered the make-believe chant. With a grand flourish, Rose did the deed, clapping her hands thrice overhead as she shouted: "Deliver it now! Grant it now!"

Rose obediently bowed her head to the Sorcerer. "It is done! You are now the bearer of this powerful dreamstone."

Greedily snatching the magic crystal from Rose's hand, Dragonite's gnarled fingers squeezed around this bead as his eyes narrowed in suspicion. "If this is so, then why do I still feel the same? I feel no different!"

"Why would you? I felt the same as I always did when the Dream Merchant first bestowed me with the magic crystal. The power is within the dreamstone; it is not within you! You are merely the one to manipulate this magical bauble."

"Truly?" Dragonite's wiry brows furrowed in suspicion.

"I should not even dignify it with an answer, but would I lie to you?" responded Rose.

"I would not be surprised," grumbled Dragonite.

"Look here! Call me frivolous, call me flippant, but do not mistake me for being foolhardy! Why would I raise your ire when you threaten us with the promise of death? You now possess the power to control that cursed thing. To cross you at this point will be a fatal mistake."

Dragonite blinked hard as he gazed at the dreamstone in his clutches, and then at the Princess, searching her face for signs of deceit.

"YES!" shouted the Sorcerer. His eyes gleamed with cruel malice. His clenched fist pumped the air as the dizzying sensation of unadulterated power threatened to cause his overblown ego to explode. It permeated every fibre of his being with a grandiose sense of self and his omnipotent might, now that he had the means to restore his powers to its fullest, and then some.

Like a spry youth, Dragonite jumped into the air, his heels clicking together in glee as he shouted: "Mine! It is all mine!"

The Sorcerer frolicked like a skittish colt in a lush meadow on a beautiful spring morning. In the most undignified manner, he skipped about in this spontaneous victory dance with the magic crystal now in his grasp while his minions unleashed a silent 'hip-hip-hooray', waving their weapons on high in jubilant celebration.

While they were caught up in the throes of merriment, Rose took advantage of this moment. She used her foot to discreetly snag Silas' staff, dragging it to within her grasp. Snatching up the Wizard's weapon, she dashed to his side. Throwing Tag's arm over her shoulder to offer him support, she and Silas struggled to maneuver Rainus and the boy to safety behind the great boulder.

In spite of all the frivolity, one astute mime tugged on Dragonite's robe, urgently seeking his attention.

"What?" snapped Dragonite, yanking free of his grasp. "What do you want?"

The mime used the tip of his pike to point at the crystal boulder. Behind it, the Princess and her comrades hid, hoping to find safety and enough time to utilize Silas' magic orb to transport themselves away from this nightmare.

Dragonite growled in rage, spying on Rainus and Tag as they leaned against the giant crystal sphere to remain upright so they can grasp the Wizard's orb as it swelled with light.

Before Silas could utter the spell to deliver them from this chamber, the Sorcerer shrieked. With every intention of pulverizing his foes into oblivion with the same intensity of the powers required to blast the hole all the way to the surface of this crystal mountain, Dragonite unleashed his wrath.

The obsidian crystal surged with energy. This bolt of blue light crackled, rumbling like the roll of thunder as it struck the boulder they hid behind. Instead of deflecting off the sphere's smooth surface or penetrating through it to strike them down, the now-cloudy boulder seemed to subdue this surge of energy, its invisible powers radiating outwards. It was enough to forcefully throw Rainus and Tag.

This was *not* the cataclysmic annihilation Dragonite had anticipated. The Princess and her cohorts were to be vaporized along with the boulder, leaving only a wisp of ash in their passing, if that. Instead, this chunk of obsidian was now no more powerful than it was before. The Princess had tricked him and this only served to fuel his rage.

The force of this power rattled Tag and Rainus to the bones, throwing them hard against Rose and Silas to bowl them over. As all four hit the ground, the impact sent Silas' staff clattering across the floor, far from his reach. As the mimes closed their ranks to advance, one of the men kicked the Dream Merchant's staff away, sending it skidding off to the far corner of the throne room. The only thing that prevented it from falling into the lava to be lost forever was the scattered debris that served to slow its course. Silas' staff came to a stop against a chunk of the fallen ceiling so it now rested, balanced precariously at the edge of the floor.

Above the sounds of this frenetic energy, Rose heard Dragonite screaming orders at his army of mimes, "Seize them! Stop them before they escape!"

Rose pushed the dazed Tag off her body. Opening her eyes, she found the points of many spears and pikes encircling them. The mimes eagerly awaited their orders to skewer these interlopers.

Before she could stand, the small army parted, making way for their leader. Those not moving quickly enough for Dragonite's liking were unceremoniously shoved aside. He stormed forward, seizing Rose by a fistful of hair.

As she squealed in pain, Silas Agincor reached out to break the Sorcerer's hold. Instead, Dragonite kicked his hand away as several mimes turned their weapons on the Wizard, thrusting the tips of their pikes to his throat and chest.

"Do not hurt him!" pleaded Rose. "Do not hurt my friends!"

Dragonite growled in response. His bony fingers knotted around a fistful of her golden hair. Instinctively, her hands slapped down over his. Clamping it firmly against the crown of her head, it helped to minimize the tearing and pain as he yanked Rose onto her feet. Pushing the Princess, he steered her away from her comrades.

"You fool!" snarled Dragonite, shaking his head in disgust as he forced Rose to look him in the eyes. "Your friends will be the death of you yet!"

"My friends are my salvation!"

"You stupid girl! You would not be in this dreadful predicament if it were not for them. If they were strangers, mere acquaintances even, you would not have thought twice about using the dreamstone to wish yourself away from here, leaving them behind to suffer my wrath. Now, it is too late! You will die with those pathetic fools!"

"They are *not* pathetic! I am the one who is pathetic for involving them in my mistake to begin with."

"It is a pity that some of the greatest lessons are learned too late in one's life," smirked Dragonite, dangling the dreamstone before her to mock the Princess. "And now, you have one more lesson; one you will share with me!"

"What more do you want? I did as you asked!"

"You lied to me! You promised to imbue my crystal with the powers of Agincor's orb. But now, I know it lacks the same power it required to blast that hole through my mountain fortress!"

"So I misunderstood! I did as you demanded, but you were the one who failed to make it clear you wanted this transfer of power to your black crystal to be permanent."

"You wretched girl! Of course, I'd want it to be permanent! Since you are incapable of granting my wishes as I see fit, then I must do so myself. Now, tell me, and tell me true! What are the special words to incite the magic crystal to make all my dreams come true?"

"I will tell you, but you must not repeat them aloud, lest one of your minions decide they would like nothing more than to steal away with the dreamstone for their own devices."

"They dare not even think it, mind you, it is better to take no chances where this dreamstone is concerned," agreed Dragonite. Releasing his grip on Rose's hair, he growled, "So tell me, Princess. What are these words? Tell me true or I shall use a pair of dull, rusty shears to cut that lying tongue from your mouth."

Rose leaned toward his tattered left ear as she whispered, "The chant you must say is this: *Wish a wish that's not a fish! Jig a jig fit for a pig! Jump high, duck low; as of now, make it so!*"

Dragonite's sour face screwed up into a frown. It was tainted by an equal measure of bewilderment and anger as he mentally debated whether this mortal girl was telling the truth.

"And remember, you must say this three times, no more, no less!" instructed Rose, speaking with utmost sincerity. "You must repeat it only in your head or whisper it so none can hear to decipher these words. Then you must shout out: Deliver it now! Grant it now!"

"Well, given how ridiculous these words are, it is a bloody good thing this chant is not meant to be heard by others!"

"And do not forget, you must undertake the same routine I had performed. You must do so with the greatest zeal and with true intention, if you wish to make your wishes come true."

Dragonite's eyes narrowed in suspicion at he scrutinized Rose, searching for a hint of a lie.

"So you say!"

"I do! It worked for me. There is no reason it will not do the same for you, if you had been paying attention to what I was doing and repeat it just as I did."

"So, I will not look like a complete fool?" questioned the Sorcerer, scratching his head in pensive thought.

"No more so than usual! I mean to say, no more so than I did," promised Rose, nodding in approval as she invited Dragonite to make his wish. "The shedding of one's pride is the price to be paid for making a dream come true."

"If you mean to make a fool out of me – "

"I know! I know! You will kill me," grumbled Rose, rolling her eyes in frustration and disdain.

"You *and* your friends," corrected the Sorcerer. "In fact, I should make an example of you for messing up on that last wish!"

"Well, excuse me! You were the one who failed to be specific with your instructions. Other than that, look at the level of devastation you were granted, albeit short-lived."

"Short-lived, indeed! Perhaps I should dispense with your royal hiney for talking so much! Look at you yakking away! If it is not to annoy and chew my ears off, it is merely a ploy to buy yourself more time to dupe me again!"

"Oh, no! At this moment, I am completely dupeless, no dupe-de-doo for you, not at all," insisted Rose. She blinked innocently as she crossed her fingers behind her back.

"Now you mean to drive me mad with ridiculous words you are making up!"

"Hey! If you can invent words and say they are so because you are an evil Sorcerer, then I can, too! I would have more licence to do so, being a genuine princess and all, so there you go!"

"Shut it!" snarled Dragonite, tearing at his hair in utter frustration. "I will smite you where you stand."

"If you do, then what will happen if I had indeed tricked you this time? I'd be rather useless to you if you do away with me now."

"You have been a royal pain in my bony arse, hence, I should just kill you! Be done with it," sputtered the Sorcerer, the staff trembling in his hand. "However, as great as this desire is, and as tempting as you make it seem, it would not be prudent. First, I will make sure I am now the true bearer of this stone, and *then* I will kill you, and your friends, one by one and in no particular order."

"If you must, I recommend starting with the one you most detest," suggested Rose, glancing over at Silas Agincor.

"You are fast becoming even more detestable, a close second to that cunning Wizard, at this very moment. But enough! Enough with this incessant jibber jabber or I shall wish for you to be as mute as my mimes."

"Well, whatever you wish for, you better do so quickly before the dreamstone's power begins to wane once more," suggested Rose.

"How right you are! So shut that cake hole! Let me focus on testing this crystal's powers for myself."

"By all means! Go to it," invited Rose, taking a cautious step back. "As you think on what your wish shall be, repeat the chant I told you three times for each move of the routine meant to conjure up the magic."

Without further ado, the Sorcerer stepped forward as his mimes cleared a semi-circle around him, large enough for Dragonite to undertake this performance without hindrance or disruption.

Drawing in a deep breath as he had seen the Princess do, he exhaled loudly as he decided on his dream wish: to have his powers completely restored; to be mightier than all the Wizards in this realm combined.

Dragonite's arms folded like bony chicken wings, each hand tucking into an armpit as he mouthed the magical words Rose had whispered to him. Hopping first on his right, and then his left foot, he undertook this performance with utmost zeal. Doing this three times, he extended his arms like a great, ungainly, flightless bird attempting to take to the air. With arms flapping, he jumped here and there, each move repeated three times before ending this routine with a grand flourish of a twirl, his black cloak billowing around him like a small, ebony whirlwind.

Just when the mimes thought the Sorcerer was done, they were forced to stymie their laughter as Dragonite started shimmying, leaning back and forth to shake and shimmy as provocatively as the Princess did. All the while, he kept mouthing words of the phony magical chant. Finally, he pranced about in circles like a demented soul as he whooped as loudly as the Princess did.

This performance came to a show-stopping finish as he clapped his hands over his head three times, shouting "Deliver it now! Grant it now!" His bony hands opened with gnarled fingers splayed wide, shaking to add to this big finish like he was one of his performing mimes.

The mimely minions closest to him to witness firsthand this bizarre performance pursed their lips, adverting their eyes, lest they burst out in a fit of laughter, thereby inciting the Sorcerer's wrath.

"Behold! Witness the glory of all my infinite powers!" announced Dragonite.

Rose backed away as the Sorcerer levelled the black crystal toward the great boulder that concealed her friends. The trio dropped to the ground as the chunk of obsidian crackled with energy, and then flared. A rush of power surged forth to strike the massive globe. Instead of disintegrating and annihilating those concealed behind it, the crystal boulder merely moaned and heaved, shuddering as it cracked. Riven in two, the halves fell apart to reveal those hiding on the other side.

"What the bloody hell was that?" snarled Dragonite. With bony chest heaving and nostrils flaring, his eyes flew wide open in rage. Rose gasped in pain, reeling as the Sorcerer's hand lashed out, the back of his clenched fist striking her cheek.

"Princess!" cried out Tag, struggling to his feet only to fall again. He cursed himself for failing her.

Rose raised a hand in warning, showing Tag she was fine. She pretended she was unfazed even as the warm trickle of blood rolled down from the cut inflicted by Dragonite's thorny knuckle. The

Sorcerer towered over her, his mouth frothing mad as he bellowed, "You wretched fool! You lied to me! My wish was not granted. I am no more powerful than I was before!"

"I do not know what you speak of! Your powers cleaved that massive boulder in two! It did not have the power to do that the last time."

"You must take me for an idiot! My crystal is as it was. It is as wanting as ever; needing to rest before unleashing what power it has."

"You saw it with your own eyes! We all did! We all witnessed your might, destroying the great sphere!" argued Rose, attempting to pacify the Sorcerer while Silas seized his comrades by the shoulder of their raiment. He attempted to drag Tag and Rainus away, now that the great barrier was no more, offering nothing in the way of protection.

"I am no imbecile! That sphere was already damaged from its great fall into my throne room. It was further marred by the first blast of power I had unleashed on it. It merely gave way, splintering into two like a scratched pane of glass breaking with stress."

"I beg to differ, Sorcerer! Go on! Test its might. Bring down that pillar, " urged Rose, pointing to the column of quartz at the far end of the throne room. She was confident one more discharge would render the obsidian crystal completely inert. "See what damage it can truly do."

Dragonite's eyes narrowed. He glared at the Princess. His teeth gnashed, then ground together in frustration, his body trembling with anger.

"I am on to you and your tricks! I know what you attempt to do! You have been in the company of the Dream Merchant for too long! His sense of cunning has rubbed off on you."

"Cunning? I am nothing but a foolish twit of a princess, remember?" sniffed Rose. She shrank back on the floor, her arm coming up to block his blow.

Instead, Dragonite retracted his trembling fist, using his staff to stand tall before her.

"You have tested my patience for the last time! Your insolence will be your end." Dragonite scowled in anger as he waved the closest mime to step forward. "Disarm her!"

The large man stared down at the girl, shrugging in confusion to his master after failing to spy a sword or dagger on her person, a weapon worthy of confiscating.

"You idiot! Her sling! Take her damned sling before she pelts you to death!"

The mime nodded in understanding. He snatched the leather sling that hung from the sash of her dress.

"Her ammunition, too," ordered Dragonite, as the mimes parted to clear a path to his crystal throne.

The mime's hand latched onto the suede pouch that was tied to her sash. He could feel the six steel balls clattering together as he wrapped his hand around this ammunition bag to tug it free.

Rather than submit, in a final act of defiance, the Princess resisted. She hung on tightly as the mime pulled, attempting to wrench it away from her tenacious grasp.

"Let go! You have the sling, these balls are useless without it," argued Rose. She dug her heels in as she held on with all her might.

Even as the mime raised his hand to strike her face, Rose refused to submit.

"It is not worth it, Princess Rose, go on now," encouraged Tag, giving her a discreet nod of his head. "Give it to him! Let him have it."

She promptly untied the pouch, freeing it from her sash. "Fine! You can have it, alright."

Rose tore it open. Flinging its contents before her, the steel balls spilled out. To the surprise of the mimes, many more metal bearings followed. This supply was magically replenished as quickly as she emptied it. The sound was deafening at the steel spheres clattered against the quartz floor, scattering between her and Dragonite and his army.

As the mime lunged forward to seize the magic pouch, he issued a silent scream as his feet flew out from beneath him. With a jarring *'thud'*, he crashed to the ground, the steel balls beneath his body painfully pressing against flesh and bone as he landed on the unforgiving floor. He flailed about like a helpless turtle trapped on its back as Rose continued pouring out the contents of the pouch on and around him, scattering the steel balls far and wide.

"You bloody fool! Get that blasted thing before she buries you alive beneath a mountain of steel!" shouted the Sorcerer.

The more frantic the mime's attempt to stand, the more futile it became. He slipped and tripped about, arms flapping like a clumsy bird struggling to fly as he fought to find a solid patch of ground that wasn't rolling beneath his feet.

With a final lunge, he seized the pouch from Rose's hands, albeit accidentally when he was actually trying to grab her arm to regain his footing. His victory dance was short-lived as he stumbled, arms and legs flying in all directions. His fellow mimes watched in horror as their comrade rolled to the edge of the floor, landing with a sickening *'splat'* into the flowing lava, taking the enchanted pouch with him. The red-hot ooze filled his mouth, stifling his agonized scream as the molten lava swallowed him up.

"What are you waiting for? Seize them!" demanded Dragonite. Using the end of his staff, he smacked the man nearest to him to break his horrified trance. He waved his army forward, commanding the mimes to take Rose and her comrades as his prisoners.

The uniform ranks suddenly broke formation as the front line of mimes charged forward, only to fly through the air. Painful moans escaped their lips as they landed flat on their backs. The many steel balls rolling against the smooth quartz floor made for a footing as stable as walking with greased soles across slippery ice. Arms and legs were flailing everywhere as mimes fell in the most dramatic manner as only mimes could. They toppled against their comrades that pressed forward behind them, unaware of the danger presented by the rolling steel balls scattered across the floor.

In anger and frustration, Dragonite bellowed in rage. Slamming the tip of his crystal to the quartz flooring, there was just enough energy left to crack the white and black squares of floor tiles, creating a raised path straight to the Princess. She watched in stunned silence as the obstacle of steel balls rolled away to either side, giving the Sorcerer a clear route.

Dragonite charged toward her, screaming in rage. Drawing back with both hands on the staff to swing with all his might, the razor-sharp edge of the obsidian swung about to slash her throat.

19

Revenge

Before the dark crystal could touch her, Rose felt the Sorcerer's killing intention, that unmistakable, rampant fury swelling from his black heart. It surged forth like a powerful tidal wave waiting to cut her down as surely as the deadly edge of this obsidian.

Rose's eyes squeezed shut, her breath catching in her throat.

Tag's anguished cry echoed in her ears. He struggled against his useless body, fighting to come to her rescue, but going nowhere.

The only thing to fill her mind was the overwhelming sense she had failed her friends for the last time. Her life of privilege and her indulgent, but cursed sense of entitlement had drawn them into this terrible quest, and now, it had come to a tragic end because of her.

Instead of falling back to escape the sweeping glance of the razor-sharp crystal, Rose thrust her chin up high, exposing her slender neck to welcome a hasty death.

She gasped in surprise, tumbling to the floor as she was pushed from harm's way. The sharp, biting *'clank'* of metal striking staff forced her eyes to snap open.

"*YOU!*" snarled the Sorcerer. "You are dead!"

"Wishful thinking," grunted Myron. The tip of his sword batted away Dragonite's staff as he maneuvered about, standing between the Princess and the Sorcerer.

"I saw you with mine own eyes! You were dead - deader than dead!" With staff poised in his hands, Dragonite scrutinized this apparition come to life, momentarily stunned by this spectre that had dropped down through the gaping hole created by the fallen boulder.

"I *am* alive and this madness stops now!" With the air of a truly gallant knight, Myron challenged the Sorcerer, his old sword gripped firmly in his hands as he held his ground.

"Cankles! You *are* alive!" declared Rose. Scrambling onto her feet, she was never so glad to see the man she usually ridiculed. "You've come to our rescue!"

"The name is Myron – Sir Myron Kendall! But feel free to call me Myron the Magnificent!" He struck a dashing pose for her to admire while the Sorcerer struggled to compose himself for another attack.

"Say again!" gasped Rose.

Ducking beneath the swing of the staff meant to strike her rescuer down, she inched her way toward the relative safety of her comrades.

The mimes watched in amazement, grateful the Sorcerer boldly gave the order to stand down. Dragonite was determined to face this foe on his own with a mighty swipe of the staff. Myron merely stepped back, angling away as the tip of his sword redirected the weapon. The keen edge of the black crystal glanced by dangerously close, narrowly missing his midriff.

With Rose's help, Tag stood up on his feet. As the Elf was too unstable, he snagged Silas' arm instead, struggling to regain his balance as he stared at the man he had always known as Cankles Mayron.

"Sir Myron Kendall? M-my father's first officer?" sputtered Tag, shaking his head in doubt. "Impossible! He died years ago!"

"Cankles Mayron is dead, but I am very much alive," explained the knight, easily swatting away the tip of Dragonite's staff as it swung about in an attempt to strike him again.

"How can that be?" asked Rose, baffled by this claim.

He looked like their gangly friend, but this man certainly did not behave like the village idiot she had come to know and love for his peaceful ways and grandiose, but altruistic ideals.

"There must be some kind of enchantment involved, perhaps some dark magic," decided the Dream Merchant, watching this man's calculated moves governed by his unwavering confidence.

"No time to explain," grunted Myron, as he parried a blow.

"You won't have a chance," snarled the Sorcerer.

Lunging at Dragonite's bony body, Myron managed to pierce his foe's billowy robe as he twirled about, spinning away from the tip of the sword.

Moving with speed, the Sorcerer brought down the end of his staff to cleave his enemy's head.

Myron angled to one side, his sword swinging up and away. The tip of the blade clipped the wooden toggle holding Dragonite's cloak in place. It continued onward, grazing the end of his nose.

"A little more and you would have had two noses!" mocked Myron, admiring his handiwork as the blood flowed freely down the Sorcerer's snarling face.

"You dare draw blood? *My blood?*" raged Dragonite. The staff trembled in his grip as an ember of light ignited in the obsidian once more.

Before Myron could offer a cheeky response, the Sorcerer attacked with a vengeance, swinging his weapon like a madman. As quickly as he swung the end of his staff at the knight, Dragonite spun it about. The edge of the black crystal met its mark. Cutting Myron from the right hip, it ripped upward, slicing through his raiment to slash his chest. The powerful momentum followed through, bashing him soundly under the chin. The impact of the blow sent the knight flying onto the rubble-strewn floor, knocking him out cold.

Before Myron's unarmed comrades could dash to his aid, the Sorcerer rushed in, the black crystal at the ready to slash his throat. Dragonite's grip tightened, preparing to deliver the killing blow, but under a swell of light, Myron vanished! The tiny Pooka suddenly appeared in the mortal's place.

All gasped, stunned by this abrupt transformation as recognition set in.

"Traitor! You conniving, shape-shifting miscreant of a traitor!" cursed Dragonite. He trembled in fury, staring in disbelief at his former minion. "How dare you betray me? Now you will pay for your insolence!"

As the Sorcerer's boot slammed down to stomp the life out of the Pooka, the real Myron Kendall appeared in a flash of golden light. By his side was the Queen of the Tooth Fairies. His shoulder rammed Dragonite, sending him sprawling into the arms of his mimes.

"Quickly! Save Loken while you can!" ordered Myron, as he snatched up his sword the Sprite had dropped during the assault. "I'll take it from here."

"Can you handle it?" asked Pancecelia. She scrutinized this mortal for signs that he was of sound body and complete presence of mind, at least enough to meet this enemy head-on with half a chance of surviving this confrontation.

"I am more than capable now," Myron answered as his steely gaze fixed onto the Sorcerer, "and more than ready!"

"What the bloody hell…" Dragonite stared at the downed Pooka and the Fairy by his side, and then at the mortal standing defiantly before him. "What is the meaning of this?"

"Yes, what the devil is going on here?" asked Silas, as Tag and Rainus shook their heads in confusion while Rose stood there, her mouth agape in stunned bewilderment.

Glancing down at Loken, Pancecelia knew by the blood seeping from the gash inflicted upon him, this Sprite was in a bad way. She gazed over to Rose and the others; theirs eyes gleaming with hope of salvation from this dire predicament.

"I am sorry! I can vanish with only one at a time..." explained Pance, her eyes filled with concern as she clasped Loken's limp hand.

"No! You can't possibly be thinking of saving him!" exclaimed Rose, gasping with disbelief.

"He is evil! He aids the Sorcerer! How can you possibly side with him!" reasoned Tag, trying to understand why the Fairy would choose to spare the Pooka's life.

"Forgive me, but there is no time to explain. I shall be back when I can."

Holding onto Loken, Pancecelia closed her eyes, waving her wand overhead. In a brilliant flash of light, the two disappeared, leaving only a glittering shower of Fairy dust and the group's crushed hopes of rescue.

"We're doomed!" gulped Tag, his knees buckling beneath him.

"Not if I can help it!" vowed Myron, standing tall and proud before his foe.

Without hesitation, he confronted the Sorcerer. With the old, cracked shield strapped and braced to his left forearm, he gripped his sword with purpose. It was like a trusted, old friend that had served him well in previous battles. There was an air of confidence about this man his comrades had never seen before.

Tag's eyes opened wide in amazement. He suddenly recognized the shield trimmed with brass that was now tarnished by a green patina of age. Even with the steel boss heavily dented and the red paint, now faded, along with the gold leaf embellishments that had flaked away where the shield was cracked, there was no mistaking this once was owned by a captain. And with absolute certainty, he knew it once belonged to Captain Oliver Yairet. Tag gasped in surprise as he declared to Rainus, "My father's shield... That was once my father's shield!"

"Never mind the shield! What is going on?" asked Rose. "If this is the *real* Cankles Mayron, he is useless with the sword. He will get himself killed!"

"He remembers," determined Rainus, his eyes searching about through the rubble for his sword. "He finally remembers!"

"There's not much that Cankles usually remembers! What do you speak of?" asked Rose, as confused as ever.

"*He* is Sir Myron Kendall," revealed Rainus.

"Why is this name familiar to me?" wondered Rose. She stared in disbelief at the poise and confidence exuded by this man she only knew as the Village Idiot of Cadboll; a humble wisp of a man known for his honesty and simple truths, but never for his courage or skill with the sword.

"He was the former first officer to your father's army," answered the Elf, speaking with utmost certainty.

"Marvellous!" Silas nodded in approval now that rescue was close at hand. "We can use the help of a gallant knight."

"He better be the knight you claim him to be!" prayed Rose. "For he is our *only* hope!"

Dragonite stood before his former prisoner. With staff gripped firmly in his hands, he taunted the mortal, "So, you have finally regained your memory! You remember the chivalrous knight you once were, the one that so willingly sacrificed his life for king and country."

"That, I do! And I will do it again."

"It is a pity you remember nothing else."

"I remember plenty, including *everything* you ever did to me," growled Myron, as he squared off against his nemesis.

"Perhaps, but you now lack the skills nor do you possess the might to wield that sword as you did before, as the great knight you once were!" Dragonite cautiously circled around the mortal. "I failed to break your spirit before, but this time, I will most certainly kill your body!"

Just as the mimes rushed in to attack, Dragonite snarled at them, "Back off! This one is mine! I mean to kill him this time! I will gut him, mount his head on a pike, then feed his scrawny corpse to the dragons while his friends watch."

Eager to obey this order than to deal with this feisty man with the eyes that burned with deadly intent, the mimes gladly backed away. Even with their limited knowledge of true warfare, these men sensed this lethal blade seemed to sing for blood as the former knight twirled the sword in his hand with the expertise of a seasoned warrior. They regrouped to create a semi-circle, an arena for this battle to the death to unfold.

With perfect timing and impeccable footwork, Myron skillfully parried each blow. His muscles recalled all the years of training that had been dormant, but remained thoroughly ingrained, in both body and mind.

The more this mortal successfully repelled the attack, the more enraged the Sorcerer became. Dragonite wildly slashed, hacking and lunging at his adversary.

"Die! Just die, why don't you!" bellowed the Sorcerer. Threads of saliva spewing from his frothing mouth mingled with the blood trailing from his sliced nose as his staff failed to connect with each blow he dealt.

Just as Dragonite's frantic swings began to wane in strength, as though smacking the old shield like he was wearily flogging a stubborn mule that refused to yield to him, with flawless timing, Myron attacked. Driven with purpose, he countered, each strike deliberate and powerful.

The sun's light glaring through the great hole danced, shimmering across the silvery blade of his sword, as though this weapon was heralding the Sorcerer's demise. Motes of dust floating through this beam of light swirled in the wake of Myron's blade as it sliced through the air to slash Dragonite across his left cheek.

With adrenaline coursing through his veins, the Sorcerer ignored the stinging pain. The hot blood poured from this new wound, adding to the one inflicted on his nose. Dragonite issued a visceral growl, the light in the black crystal growing brighter with his rage. Just as he charged at Myron, levelling the chunk of obsidian to unleash a blast of energy at the mortal's chest, the knight did something quite unexpected. Instead of backing down, Myron met the Sorcerer head-on.

Before Dragonite could unleash his magic, the mortal swung about, bashing the Sorcerer with his shield. The blow sent Dragonite reeling, crashing into his army of mimes as the stray discharge of energy struck down the men on the front line. Those avoiding the debilitating force issued a silent scream of fright, dropping to the ground to dodge the errant magic.

Refusing to admit defeat, the Sorcerer attacked. With staff hoisted on high, he charged again.

Before Myron's sword could parry this blow, Dragonite screamed in surprise as fate conspired against him. A single, steel ball underfoot sent the Sorcerer flying up and over, landing hard on his bony back.

As Silas and his comrades cheered, the mimes that remained standing glanced over at Dragonite, sprawled on the ground and immobilized in agonizing pain. The Sorcerer was now at the mercy of Myron Kendall. Rather than coming to their master's aid or surrendering in defeat, they had no second thoughts as they beat a hasty retreat. Scattering like cockroaches exposed to the blinding light of day, they fled from the throne room, escaping than to be made to face the wrath of the prisoner they had treated so poorly.

Pressing the edge of the shield to the Sorcerer's throat, Myron stepped on the staff, pinning Dragonite's hand to the floor. He stared down are his nemesis. "Your crystal's powers have been all but spent.

Do you surrender, Sorcerer?"

"I went through hell for this," sputtered Dragonite. He opened his other hand to reveal the dreamstone he clung to throughout the battle. Balling his hand into an angry fist, he pounded against the shield in defiance and anger. "I would rather die than to surrender to you!"

"Then you will die another day, for it shall not be by my hands that you will meet your end. Now give me the dreamstone."

Dragonite's lips curled in malice as he growled like a trapped and wounded animal.

"Return the magic crystal to the Princess and I will take you as my prisoner. Master Agincor and the brotherhood of Wizards will be the ones to decide your fate and to dispense your punishment. Now, on your feet, Sorcerer!"

Dragonite was slow to rise. Like a doddering old man, he used his staff like a walking stick to help him stand. He glared at the knight as he hissed, "You want to kill me. I know you do. It is the only way you will take this dreamstone from me!"

"For all you have done, you *do* deserve to die, but I am a man of honour. I will *not* be the one to kill you.

"Come now! You want revenge." Dragonite dared him to commit the dark deed. "Go on, kill me. Do it!"

Instead, Myron lowered his sword, extending his hand to hoist the Sorcerer onto his feet. "I choose to forgive you."

"You are weak. Only the weak forgive!"

"The capacity to forgive is an attribute of the strong," countered Myron.

"Coward! You had your chance, and yet, you are too weak to seek revenge when it is within your grasp. This is the ultimate show of weakness!"

"This *is* my revenge. To lead a better life, unhampered by vengeance, to rise above and not be poisoned by your actions! To be a better person than you will ever be; *that* is the ultimate revenge. To find happiness, love and friendship; something you will never know, is the choice I make. And I am *not* like you! I choose not to take your life, no matter how vile or worthless you truly are."

"Then you are a bigger fool than I believed possible!"

Just as the knight spied a flash of light in the black obsidian, Dragonite lunged, thrusting the jagged crystal to his chest. Before Myron could raise his shield to deflect the weapon, the Sorcerer reeled, suddenly lurching forward. His eyes were wide open in shock, the tip of a sword protruding from his midriff. A stifled gasp escaped Dragonite's lips. His trembling hand clutched at this wound, the blood drenching the dreamstone. His grip tightened on his staff as he struggled to remain upright.

Myron looked on in surprise as his foe dropped to his knees. Tag appeared from behind the Sorcerer, his sword sheathed in blood.

"You're right! You'll not be the one to kill the Sorcerer," agreed Tag, as he nodded at Myron. "And I certainly wasn't about to let that fiend kill you."

Just as the Sorcerer fell onto his side, Myron and Tag squinted from the glare as Dragonite's black crystal swelled with light. In a flash, the Sorcerer vanished, leaving only a thin wisp of black smoke that dissipated, swirling through the muggy air.

Rose ran up to her rescuer, embracing him in a grateful hug.

"Cankles, Crinkles, Mayron, Moron! I don't care what your real name is! I'm just so glad you are alive!" cried Rose, throwing her arms around him.

"What happened? Where did the Sorcerer go?" asked Tag, glancing about for signs of his presence.

"No doubt, your actions and Dragonite's vile heart worked in tandem to see to his demise," determined Silas, as he turned to retrieve his staff that was abandoned by the fleeing mimes.

"You think?" asked Rainus, slow to upright himself as he picked up his sword from amongst the rubble.

"I hope," answered Silas, polishing the dust from the orb mounted atop his staff. "If it was not a lethal wound inflicted on him, then the most we can hope for is that it will be a long time before he dare show his face again."

"But what about the dreamstone? It disappeared along with the madman," reminded Tag.

"Who cares about what happened to that wretched soul and the cursed dreamstone?" said Rose, as Myron hugged her and Tag. "As long as the evil toad is gone, that's all I care about! And I sense that if the Sorcerer even survived Tag's blade, he will waste an eternity reciting a useless chant and performing an equally useless jig trying to get the dreamstone to work."

"Well, all I can say is I am grateful you are safe," sighed Myron, giving his friends a warm smile as he sighed with relief.

"Are you truly my father's first officer?" asked Tag, staring with unmistakable wonder into Myron's familiar eyes. It was the only feature he now recognized that remained unchanged in all these years.

"Yes," answered the knight, his hand playfully ruffling Tag's head of hair like he used to when this young man was a small boy. "And I was as proud to be Captain Yairet's friend as I was to be appointed his first officer."

"So, we are all good? We are all safe?" asked Silas.

"It would appear so," answered Myron.

The Wizard leaned against his staff as he watched Rainus take a moment to heal the gash on Rose's cheek that was inflicted by Dragonite. With a light touch and the whispering of Elvish words, Rainus set his healing magic to work on this mortal.

"So now what?" asked Rose.

"We return to Fleetwood," answered Tag, wiping off his father's old sword before sheathing the blade in its scabbard. "It's as simple as that."

"I suppose there is no need to rush home. I've lost track of the days, but I have no doubt my sixteenth birthday gala has come and gone by now.

"Well, happy birthday, Princess Rose," bade the Wizard, as he nodded his head in respect. "If you wish, I can conjure up another dreamstone as a gift to mark this auspicious occasion."

Rose's eyes grew wide in dread as she addressed the Dream Merchant in no uncertain terms. "Thank you, but no! I am done with wishing. I now know the difference between want and need."

"You do?" responded Silas, his brows knitting into a frown as he searched her eyes for the truth.

"Absolutely," stated Rose, her hand over her heart in solemn promise. She smiled at Tag as he nodded in approval. "I have all that I need and all I could ever wish for. I want for naught."

"Very well!" Silas bowed his head in understanding

"Darn!" cursed Tag, snapping his fingers in disappointment.

"You had a wish?" asked Rose, surprised by his words.

"Just one," admitted Tag, his shoulders rolling in a shrug. "Had I been granted a wish, I would have wished for the skills and knowledge of a full-fledged knight, as I've fallen well behind in my formal training regimen. Now I must rush to catch up with the others of my age."

Myron smiled in empathy as he gave Tag a consoling pat on the back. "Young sir, it is not about how fast you go. It is all about how far you get, for in the end, the true satisfaction of reaching your final destination is determined by the journey to get there."

"That sounds wise, in a preachy sort of way," mused Tag, as he thought on this grand adventure he had endured and survived with his comrades.

"I never thought of your father as the preachy type," said Myron, offering Tag a knowing smile.

"My father said that to you?"

"Yes, in my youth when I wanted nothing more than to become a knight in good standing and complained about how long it would take to attain my goal, your father spoke these words of wisdom that I now share with you."

Tag drew a deep breath as he considered Myron's words.

"You know your father's advice is true."

"Yes," acknowledged Tag. He graciously accepted the cracked shield Myron passed on to him. "My father was as wise with his words as he was noble in his conduct."

"Say, what of the Pooka? Was that truly Pancecelia Feldspar in his company?" questioned Rainus. He was as baffled by the Queen of the Tooth Fairies' abrupt appearance, and then departure, spiriting away the wounded Sprite.

"That was indeed Pance," admitted Myron. "And the shape-shifting Sprite was not what he appeared to be."

"You mean he was someone else?" asked Rose, bewildered by his comment.

"No, I mean to say, Loken was not evil. He was not the villain we all believed him to be."

"What?" gasped Tag, scratching his head in thought. "I'm sorry, but that wicked little being was far from good."

"He was bad, very bad," added Rose.

"All I will say for now is that there are times when good men are forced to do bad things," responded Myron, giving the Princess a knowing wink of his eye. "Loken was a victim of circumstances beyond his control. He was only doing what he could to save his ladylove."

"Pancecelia Feldspar?" asked Rose, her eyes wide in surprise.

"Yes. No doubt she tends to his wounds as we speak, and all will be well."

"How romantic!" sighed the Princess, hands clasping together in delight. "They will be off to find their happily ever after."

"Come now, my lady! This so-called *happily ever after* only happens in the tales of make-believe," teased Rainus, smiling at the Princess and her hopeful words.

"Instead, they shall live as happily as possible as they return to the Fairy's Vale to undo the damage Sparks Firestar had done," said Myron. "If the fates conspire, then the happiness they desire will be long lasting."

"Hey! There they are!" a familiar voice boomed and echoed through the throne room. "Lord Silverthorn, you live!"

Rainus glanced up to see his captain, Halen Ironwood and his small band of warriors peering down through the opening blasted through the mountain of crystal to the outside world. Halen and his comrades tossed down their lines of Elven rope, nimbly climbing down to land lightly upon the floor to greet their lord and leader.

"I thought you were killed by that monstrous dragon!" marvelled Rainus, greeting his friend with a brotherly hug.

"We are Elves! It would take more than a cantankerous old reptile to do us in," declared Halen, nodding in salutation to the Wizard and the mortals in his company. "In fact, when that beast tried to kill me, I convinced it to do otherwise. We wrangled and tamed the dragon, enough so it could be handled."

"Amazing!" praised Rainus, nodding in approval.

"Yes, we flew over here on that very creature when we saw the powerful magic that pierced through this great mountain," added Denatheen, clasping Tag's wrist in greeting. The Elf glanced over at the Princess, and then the great hole they used to hasten their arrival to the throne room, "Does that opening have something to do with you and the magic crystal, my lady?"

"Oh, no! As much as I would like to take credit for this reunion and that great hole that brought you here, it was not my doing," responded Rose. "In fact, no more magic! No more wishes for me! I am done with that cursed but miraculous dreamstone."

"Say what you will, my lady," said Denatheen, giving her a wink of his eye, "but it is nothing short of a miracle that we are here now and find you, your friends and our Lord Silverthorn safe and sound."

"Yes, and wonders happen around us everyday, if you know what to look for," said Rose, smiling in agreement.

"Well, this is a miracle if I ever saw one," said Tag, hugging Rose and Myron.

"That the quest is over?" questioned Rose.

"Yes! That, and you did not get us killed in the process!" teased Tag.

"That is a miracle unto itself!" declared Myron, giving his young friend a jovial slap on his back.

"So this is it?" Rose unleashed a wistful sigh. "This is the end? The quest is over and our adventure is done."

Myron and Tag exchanged glances, and then smiled as they gazed upon Rose.

"Who can say, Princess?" responded Tag, his shoulders rolling in a shrug as he patted the hilt of his trusty sword. "I suppose we'll have to wait and see.

"Well, I am done with all the misadventures that comes with the dreamstone and granting wishes," announced the Wizard.

"Then what do you plan to do with your life?" questioned Tag.

"Perhaps I will write about these events in a cautionary tale. Change the names and places so there will be no backlash in doing so should the characters' namesakes protest about the contents of these stories."

"And what will you call these stories, Master Agincor?" queried Rose.

"I do quite like the sounds of *The Dream Merchant Saga*," disclosed Silas, giving his silvery whiskers a thoughtful tug as he pondered this new venture.

Rose, Tag, and Myron exchanged bemused glances, and then they burst out in a fit of laughter.

"No offense, Wizard, but that is the dumbest thing I have ever heard of... The Dream Merchant Saga!" giggled the Princess.

"Careful, my lady," cautioned Silas. "Be mindful of what you say or I shall write you into my stories, and then smite you, at least in character."

Rose's brows arched up in surprise. "You speak in jest!"

The old Wizard gave her a sly smile. His eyes gleamed with mischief as he chuckled, "It could be just the thing to keep you on your best behaviour, Princess Rose."

The End?

YA Fantasy Series
(in reading order)

The Dream Merchant Saga: Book One,
The Magic Crystal

The Dream Merchant Saga: Book Two,
The Silver Sword

The Dream Merchant Saga: Book Three,
The Crack'd Shield

Adult Fantasy Series
(in reading order)

Imago Chronicles: Book One, A Warrior's Tale
Imago Chronicles: Book Two, Tales from the West
Imago Chronicles: Book Three, Tales from the East
Imago Chronicles: Book Four, The Tears of God
Imago Chronicles: Book Five, Destiny's End
Imago Chronicles: Book Six, The Spell Binder
Imago Chronicles: Book Seven, The Broken Covenant
Imago Prophecy (Prequel to Imago Chronicles series)
Imago Legacy (Sequel to Imago Prophecy)

About the Author

L.T. Suzuki is a fantasy novelist, script-writer
and a senior instructor of the martial arts system,
Bujinkan Budo Taijutsu;
incorporating six traditional samurai schools
and three schools of ninjutsu.

Please check out L.T. Suzuki's official website at:
www.newmobileme.com/imagochronicles9